CU00926172

The Necronomicon

Selected Stories and Essays Concerning
the Blasphemous Tome of the Mad Arab

Chaosium Fiction

CALL OF CTHULHU® FICTION

The Necronomicon

Selected Stories and Essays Concerning
the Blasphemous Tome of the Mad Arab

STEFFAN B. ALETTI
MARTIN D. BROWN
JOHN BRUNNER
LIN CARTER
FRED CHAPPELL
HENRY DOCKWEILLER
FRANK BELKNAP LONG
H. P. LOVECRAFT
ROBERT A. W. LOWNDES
FRED L. PELTON
FREDERICK POHL
ROBERT SILVERBERG
D. R. SMITH
DAVID ST. ALBANS
RICHARD L. TIERNEY
MANLY WADE WELLMAN
ROBERT M. PRICE

Selected and Edited by ROBERT M. PRICE
Cover Artwork by HARRY FASSL
Chapter Decorations by EARL GEIER

A Chaosium Book
1996

The *Necronomicon* is published by Chaosium, Inc.

This book is ocpyrighted as a whole by Chaosium, Inc. ©1996; all rights reserved.

"The Figure in the Flying Carpet" ©1996 by Robert M. Price for this volume. "The Terrible Parchment" ©1937 by The Popular Fiction Company for *Weird Tales*, August 1937; appears here by permission of Frances Wellman. "Dr. Xander's Cottage" by Martin D. Brown; first appeared in *Scorpio*, March 1941. "The Mantle of Graag" by Frederick Pohl, Harry Dockweiller, and Robert A. W. Lowndes; first appeared in *The Unique Magazine*, October 1941. "Settler's Wall" ©1988 by Robert A. W. Lowndes for *Crypt of Cthulhu* #62, Candlemas 1989. "The Howler in the Dark" ©1984 by Richard L. Tierney for *Crypt of Cthulhu* #24, Lammas 1984; appears here by permission of the author. "Demons of Cthulhu" ©1959, 1987 by Agberg, Ltd.; first published under the pseudonym of Charles D. Hammer; appears here by permission of the author, Robert Silverberg. "The Castle in the Window" ©1966 by Health Knowledge, Inc., for *The Magazine of Horror* #22; appears here by permission of the author, Steffan B. Aletti. "Concerning the Forthcoming Inexpensive Paperback Translation of the Necronomicon of Abdul Alhazred" ©1992 by John Brunner; reprinted by permission of John Hawkins & Associates, Inc. "The Adder" ©1989 by *Deathrealm* for *Deathrealm* #9, 1989; appears here by permission of the author, Fred Chappell. "Preface to the *Al-Azif*" ©1973 by Owlswick Press; appears here by permission of the author, L. Sprague deCamp. "The *Necronomicon*: The Dee Translation" ©1989 by Cryptic Publications for *Crypt of Cthulhu* #70, Candlemas 1990; appears here by permission of Robert M. Price, agent for the estate of Lin Carter. *The Sussex Manuscript* ©1989 by John T. Pelton for *Crypt of Cthulhu* #63, Eastertide 1989; appears here by permission of Edward Paul Berglund, representative of the author's literary estate. "The Life of the Master", including accompanying illustrations, by David Pudelwitts, ©1984 The Strange Company for *Etchings & Odysseys* #5; appeared under the pseudonym David St. Albans. "Why Abdul Al Hazred Went Mad" ©1950 by THE NEKROMANTIKON for *The Nekromantikon, Amateur Magazine of Weird and Fantasy*, volume 1, number 3, Autumn 1950.

We invite any authors whom we have been unable to trace to contact us.

Cover art by Harry Fassl. Chapter decorations by Earl Geier. "The Life of the Master" illustrations by David Pudelwitts. Cover layout by Eric Vogt. Editing and interior layout by Janice Sellers. Editor-in-chief Lynn Willis. Proofreading by James Naureckas.

Similarities between characters in this book and persons living or dead are entirely coincidental.

The reproduction of material from within this book for the purposes of personal or corporate profit, by photographic, digital, or other electronic methods of storage and retrieval, is prohibited.

Please address questions and comments concerning this book, as well as requests for free notices of Chaosium publications, by mail to Chaosium, Inc., 950 56th Street, oakland, CA 94608-3136, U.S.A. Also visit our web site at :
http://www.sirius.com/~chaosium/chaosium.html.

2 3 4 5 6 7 8 9 10

Chaosium Publication 6012.

ISBN 0-56882-070-4

Printed in Canada.

CONTENTS

The Figure in the Flying Carpet

by Robert M. Price

The name *Necronomicon* (νεκρος, corpse; νομος, law; ικον, image = An Image [or Picture] of the Law of the Dead) occurred to me in the course of a dream, though the etymology is perfectly sound.
—H. P. Lovecraft, letter to Harry O. Fischer, February 1937

Do you not know, brethren—for I am speaking to those who know the law— that the law is binding on a person only during his life?
—Romans 7:1

What can one say about the fabulous *Necronomicon* that has not already been said? Much in every way! Because nothing has been said. The title is a word that points with a spectre's empty sleeve to the nothing to which it refers. In that it is like all words, like all texts. The Book that is said to be the anti-Book, the book that brings oblivion and madness in the name of a knowledge that is knowledge of the Nothing, and thus no knowledge at all, is, ironically, the paradigm case of all books, the most bookish of books, the most textual of texts. For, as Jacques Derrida, a modern reincarnation of the Apostle Alhazred, says, we have witnessed not only the "death of the author" (Roland Barthes' phrase, i.e., the utter negation of authorial intent by the simple autonomous existence of the text once written), but the "death of the book" as well. In fact, it might be more helpful to render the meaning of the Greek word Νεκρονομικον not as "the book of the dead", as has been suggested, but rather as "the death of the book." Because, as Derrida says, the death of the book signals the birth of the *text*. The difference between the two amounts to the imaginary closure, the supposed self-sufficiency, of a "book" versus the boundless, blinderless, illimitable ocean of text.

Since all texts refer to one another, presuppose one another, are in dialogue with one another, shed new light on one another, this fact of intertextuality connects and embraces all texts, all books and utterances, as part of the infinite field of signifiers to which we assign arbitrary meanings by placing the boundaries just so. By imposing our limiting conditions (Shankara called them *upadhis*) upon the All of the text, the Abyss of meaning upon which every text, like every individual *atman*, opens, we divide off a text like a momentary froth of sea foam cast up by a wave, immediately to join with it again. The universal megatext is analogous if not identical with the implicit repertoire of language (*langue*) as opposed to actual, concrete utilizations, actualizations of it in individual speech-acts (*parole*); thus it is susceptible of any meaning, any interpretation, just like the alphabet which can be kabbalistically recombined to yield an infinite number of words. This is because, again like the alphabet, language has in itself no meaning at all! It could mean everything and anything because it means nothing. As Uddalaka said to his son Svetaketu in the *Chandogya Upanishad*, "*Neti, neti!*" The truth is neither this nor that. It is the Void, the Plenitude of emptiness. And so it is with the infinite ocean of the megatext, the intertext. Why?

Because there is no objective "meaning center" about which speech and language and texts rotate. As Nietzsche, the Mad Aryan, said, God is dead! Truth is dead! The earth has become unchained from its sun and now wanders freely through chartless gulfs of cosmic infinitude. All coordinates, all longitudes and latitudes are henceforth meaningless. Truth is in the eye of the beholder. Thus it is fiction. In terms of language and texts, this means that (as Ferdinand de Saussure reckoned it) all language is meaningful not referentially but differentially. The meaning of words derives not from their pointing to some object signified by the word. That is out of the question, simply because of the imprecision of language, the "ideal type" character of definitions which real things never quite match. Words refer only to other words, gaining their meaning from their similarities to and differences from each other. Every word, as traditionally understood, promises meaning. It says to us, "Just a moment, and I'll point you to your destination." But it never does. It leads us on a wild goose chase. It is a bullet fired against the impenetrable dome ceiling of language, which it can never escape. It can only ricochet.

There is nothing outside language, no meaning underlying or overlying the curving wall of words. Nor *could* there be anything beyond. The curvature of the linguistic firmament is like the curvature of the universe as envisioned by some physicists; it is not like the hull of a ship, but just describes the pattern of motion on the rim. There is water beyond the hull, but there is nothing beyond the arc of possible motion. And there is no Transcendental Signified to which words, symbols, signifiers point. They only point to one another, like annoying flunkies in the Motor Vehicle Department: You stand in line for hours, waiting to get to the window, where your questions will all be answered. Only they're not. Instead, as you know, Marge Simpson's sister directs you to a different mile-long line. Her other sister, at the head of that one, will in turn send you to a third, or back to the first. It's like a dictionary which defines a word in terms of something else you have to know first, but you don't, so you keep your finger in the page and look up the other term, only to find that it is defined in terms of the word you were looking up to begin with! Meaning continually eludes you, like a will-o'-the-wisp, leading you on, but like the Frost Giant's Daughter or the White Sybil, ever the same distance beyond you. That endless deferring is what Derrida calls *Différance*. Meaning will never appear. As so often, the destination is not a place at the end of the road, but the road itself, because the road in this case is a circle. You must come to love the road and live as a pilgrim. You will never arrive at the Truth, as if language were merely some gift wrapping you had tediously to figure out how to undo to get to the goodies inside. The rainbow is far more beautiful than any pot of gold that might ostensibly lie at the end of it—and doesn't.

Let me tell you how the *Necronomicon* is a prime example of textuality. First, its very name is a jumble of signifiers onto which order must be imposed by the reader who seeks to *find* what is not readily apparent: the meaning. It is very significant that Lovecraft himself received the title in a dream. He knew the title was "Necronomicon", but not what it meant. He had to get out the lexicon and try to dope out the meaning, admitting that his was an educated guess, nothing more, as if the title were exterior to himself, as if it had not originated with his own cleverness. This is exactly right: It *hadn't*! He got the name in a *dream*! It came from the creative depth of the subconscious or unconscious mind and was presented full blown to Lovecraft, all in one piece. He approached it as an artifact, just as the scholars in his stories do when confronted by a relic of ancient extrahuman cultures.

In trying to translate Νεκρονομικον into English ("the Image of the Law of the Dead"), he was doing pretty much what the ancient oracles of the gods did. They interpreted the glossolalic speech of the gods. This is what Apollo's oracle at Delphi did. This is what happened in Corinth when someone would "speak in tongues", as if to speak "mysteries in the Spirit" and have them "interpreted" by one with the prophetic gift of interpreting glossolalia (1 Corinthians 12 and 14). The idea was not to translate as if from another earthly language, but to render intelligible "the tongues of angels", the word of God. It required interpretation in the same manner that a dream does, not because it is an unknown language, but because it is no language at all. The whole point is that the divine truth is not something linguistically possible for human beings. "As the heavens are higher than the earth, so are my ways higher than your ways, and my thoughts than your thoughts" (Isaiah 55:9). But there would then seem to be an unbridgeable gap between the two. The "word" of God is no word at all, because God is self-aware Gnosis, thought thinking itself; how can it have occasion to communicate? Why should it need to send thoughts across the flimsy rope bridge of ambiguous words? To say something is the word of God is to say it is no word at all, just as when we say, "God only knows!" we mean *no one* knows.

There can be no word if it is from God. And if it is a word, it cannot be from God. It is of a different order altogether. In other words, the interpreter of glossolalia is playacting, using human words to pretend to convey the inexpressible, the ineffable. Recently a channeler in my area spoke to a crowd under the pretense of being an ancient Tibetan monk with plenty of trivial opinions to share. The "Channeled Entity" spoke with a bogus Asian accent. But "he" spoke in *English*! Look, if it's really old Lopside Rumpus himself, why the hell doesn't he just speak Tibetan? Or if he's going to speak the language of the channeler and her hearers, why not just speak in plain English without the Fu Manchu accent? Because the accent is a theatrical sham, tricking you, lending the Tibetan act a sense of verisimilitude as long as you don't examine it too closely. That's the pretense of human speech when it tries to speak what 2 Corinthians 12:4 calls αρρατα ρηματα, "unutterable utterances." It's so transparent a pose as to be simply symbolic of some imagined Truth *beyond language*. Such a truth must be non-linguistic, not an answer analogous to the blank you'd like to fill with it.

When Lovecraft ("Image of the Law of the Dead"), George Wetzel ("Book of the Names of the Dead"), Manly Bannister ("Book of the Laws of the Dead"), Colin Wilson ("Book of Dead Names"), S. T. Joshi ("Book Concerning the Dead"), and Pierre de Caprona ("Knower of the Laws of Death") all try to dope out "*the* meaning of" the title *Necronomicon*, they are doing just what the interpreter of glossolalia does, treating an anti-meaningful, non-signifying jumble of text as if it were a puzzle with a coded message waiting for some enterprising scholar to hit on and reveal it, like Henry Armitage trying to decode Wilbur Whateley's diary. But there *is* no meaning in that line of self-referring signifiers. Like the poem according to New Critical doctrine, the word "Necronomicon" should not *mean* but simply *be*. Like the book *Vastarien*, which is not *about* a thing but *is* that thing.

Which of these scholars has correctly read the word? None. All have *mis*read it, as Paul de Man would say, since there can only be "misreadings", guesses at the meaning, as if the "true" meaning resided somewhere in the text, like Cthulhu in R'lyeh, like the inverted small print at the bottom of the puzzle page. But it doesn't. That God is dead. Remember, the world has become unchained from its sun and continually plunges. Language does not orbit a Logos-center (a word-center, meaning-center), does not point like sun rays in reverse, to a Transcendental Signifier. There is only the crazily hilarious Chaos Sultan Azathoth whose random thrashings give each frail cosmos its eternal law. The chaos of interpretations of the very word "Necronomicon" illustrates this point as well as any word could.

Other good examples would include the early Christian slogan *Maranatha*, which is Aramaic for either "Our Lord comes!" or an invocation, "O Lord, come!" Either way the phrase anticipates the Parousia of the

Logos, the Advent, the Presence of the Word of God (see Revelation 19:11-13), the Second Coming of Christ. The very ambiguity of the word (indicative or imperative?), depending how you divide the syllables (just like "Necronomicon"), proves that this long-anticipated Parousia, the Presence of the Word of God in simple truth, the ripping away of the veil of ambiguous language so we may know as we are known, face to face—will never occur. Meaning is always at arm's length ahead of us, and we will never catch up. Language is a maze, a labyrinth, scarcely the straight and narrow path. The Messiah who is to come can never arrive, by definition. He comes from the future and is always on the point of arriving but for that very reason can never actually arrive! The Christ who appears is by definition a usurper of the prophetic promise, an impostor, an Antichrist. The only meaning there can be for us is that glimmer of light at the end of the tunnel. It helps us navigate, though we will never reach it!

The same chain of associations appears with the Buddhist title the Tathagatha, the Thus-Come-One. We know it's an epithet of the Buddha, the Enlightened One, but what does it mean? It sounds like it means that with the Buddha, the true meaning, the Transcendental Signified has at last come present. But what is that Noble Truth? Alas, we don't know what the word means!

Witness the oblivious irony of the Protestant fundamentalists: They think they have every question's answer in an infallible Book—the meaning of which their exegetes continuously debate! What good is an infallible book if you don't know what it *means*? And that's the way all books are, all texts, which is why there can never be an *authoritative* book. Because the *author's* intention, the *authorial* meaning, the ostensibly *author*itative meaning, can never control the reading of the text. Since all texts merely pass through the medium of the writer from the unconscious megatext, for the author's meaning to be the only or "real" meaning would be as absurd as for Lovecraft to maintain (which he didn't) that his particular guess-definition of "Necronomicon" must be the right one since, after all, he was the one who had the dream!

Martin Luther, the inventor of fundamentalist biblicism and literalism, wanted to canonize authorial intention (assuming it could be recovered!), the straightforward "plain sense of the text" as the controlling, "official" meaning, because he wanted to cut the ground from under the Catholic Church. Catholics had long resorted to figurative and allegorical exegesis to conjure up a scriptural warrant for their gratuitous dogmas. What Luther hated about such creative, figural interpretation was that it was *uncontrollable*. You couldn't bind anyone to the letter of the law if readers of the text could employ it like a Tarot card or a Rorschach blot to catalyze new meanings of their own. "There were double meanings in the *Necronomicon* of the

mad Arab Abdul Alhazred which the initiates might read as they chose."
Note the Protestant anxiety of certain Lovecraft scholars who fume over
"heretical" readings of the sacred texts of HPL and seek to enforce an orthodoxy of interpretation based on Lovecraft's own philosophy.

It is not only the ambiguity of the title that makes the *Necronomicon* a
paradigm case of indeterminate textuality. There is the technique of the
mise-en-abyme, the receding picture within a picture device, the endless
reflections of facing mirrors. It is a Chinese box technique, where an opened
door reveals only another door, and another and another, ad infinitum. This
means an endless deferral of meaning, the replacement of each stripped-
away veil with another identical to it. When the Prisoner rips the mask from
the face of Number One, he finds—another mask! And finally his own face!
What you thought was a window was a mirror. The response from the darkness is only an echo of your own question. Lovecraft uses the *Necronomicon* in
just this way time and again.

First, note the many instances in many of the stories, such as *At the
Mountains of Madness* and "The Haunter of the Dark", where we discover that
the forbidden and abhorrent *Necronomicon*, that book sought out by the
Faustian seeker for its promise of revealing all secrets, speaks only in mad-
deningly reticent ambiguities. To spare his readers the worst of it, Alhazred
has "mercifully cloaked" this or that awful truth or "nervously hinted" of this
or that. He protests too much that certain horrors have not in fact occurred,
leaving mysterious and terrible inferences to be drawn. Why is this ostensible
revelation so cryptical? It is supposed to be the answer key, not the puzzle
book! Once you actually have a look at it, you find that Alhazred was on your
side looking in, not on the other side looking out. In all such Lovecraft tales,
the locus of terrible revelation and final truth shifts to the alien Entities who
turn out to be the real referents of Alhazred's misty meandering. All right,
Wilmarth, now, thanks to the lobsters from Yuggoth, you find the loathsome
truth cloaked under the myth of Azathoth. But what is it? Why won't you
tell us? Simply because there is nothing to see! It has been deferred yet again!

Dostoyevsky explained the mechanism perfectly in the parable of the
Grand Inquisitor: Mystery, miracle, and authority are the three shells in the
game that keep the mob stupefied and obedient. They will have to resort to
faith if they are to accept some truth they cannot understand. If something
like the oxymoronic doctrine of the Trinity were held up for rational scrutiny, it would not long survive, and neither would the passive attitudes of the
flock. Once invited to exercise critical scrutiny, it will be too late to exercise
blind faith ever again. A new habit will have been formed. So one must keep
them mystified and happy not to question. The submissive faith into which
Lovecraft wants to hoodwink the reader is what Coleridge called "poetic
faith", or the "temporary willing suspension of disbelief", without which

any story falls flat and becomes laughable. This is why Lovecraft, like Dostoyevsky's Grand Inquisitor, employs all the wiles of "priestcraft" to construct a hoax to deceive the reader. Rationalists said the priests had pretty much cooked up the Bible to keep the masses docile, and that it was a tissue of superstitions and scare stories. In the same way, Lovecraft advised writers of weird fiction to use all the ingenuity and attention to detail that a genuine hoax would require. This priest(Love)craft gulls the reader into (poetic) faith by hiding the promised Holy behind the veil of mystification.

He did not want readers believing in the *Necronomicon* once the story was ended, but he did his work too well. Many wrote him asking if the volume really existed. What was his secret? Lovecraft supplied a lot of convincing but bogus bibliographical detail, but he never opened the bag and showed what was inside. There could never be anything inside that could justify all the hype! This is why, once he actually allows a glimpse inside the *Necronomicon*, it is only the vestibule, the "antechamber of hell", and not hell itself. The real truth lies cloaked by the veil mercifully cast over the subject by the author. And we are not going to get to see that. Because there is nothing to see! Better to keep 'em guessing.

Lucius Apuleius, author of the second-century A.D. novel *The Metamorphosis, or The Golden Ass*, uses the same device, only he is about halfway between Lovecraft and the Inquisitor. That is, he describes some tantalizing aspects of a secret initiation he had undergone in the Isis religion, but he has to fall silent at a particular point, being sworn not to divulge the deep secrets of the cult to outsiders. Enough is revealed to set the mouth of our fertile imagination to watering. We can imagine (or, better, *almost* imagine) vague revelations that would far surpass the real thing if we were allowed to see it. Scholars suspect that the basket containing the holy of holies—was empty! Just like the Ark of the Covenant when René Belloq (in *Raiders of the Lost Ark*) opens it and finds nothing inside. And that's as it must be. The *seen* is ever only the evocative trace of the potent *un*seen, which itself is no Transcendental Signified, but only a powerful symbol pointing to other symbols in a dizzying display of ricochet fire.

Talbot Mundy did a superb job conveying the mysterium profundis of his Theosophical faith in his novels like *Old Ugly Face*, *The Thunder Dragon Gate*, *The Devil's Guard*, and *Om, the Secret of Ahbor Valley*. He hinted, he implied, he revealed the potent trace. He even invented his own "ancient" scripture, corresponding to Lovecraft's *Necronomicon*—*The Book of the Sayings of Tsiang Samdup*—of which, like HPL, he furnished occasional evocative/equivocal glimpses, and all to great effect. It all fell flat and sounded preposterous once he removed the veil in his puerile and didactic nonfiction book *I Say Sunrise*. Hey! Pay no attention to the man behind the curtain! Apuleius understood better than Mundy, which is why in the very midst of a revelation of the secrets of the cult, Apuleius draws the curtain again! Similarly, in 2 Corinthians 12, Paul is letting the reader in on the story of a secret revelation he had some fourteen years before (a novelistic touch to lend an air of mysterious antiquity to the revelation). Paul was mystically taken up to the third heaven, to the very throne of Christ, and there he heard mysteries that man may not utter. So he doesn't utter them! He's drawn you far enough along to make you think you've gotten a glimpse of the hidden truth, but it's the old game of bait and switch. You come away without any revealed secrets, but with an enhanced respect for the guy who did get an earful. "Mystery" —> "miracle" —> "authority."

This is why, once Lovecraft allows us, like Henry Armitage, to read the *Necronomicon* over his shoulder, he again conceals the revelation at the very moment he seems to be revealing it. No, Alhazred didn't give it to us straight; he was scarcely in a better position than we are. He had only hints.

Another way of reproducing the original secrecy in the very midst of the ostensible revelation of the mystery is to have Alhazred himself allude to a *still more ancient* source of information that he holds in the same awed regard as we hold his own tome. In the *Necronomicon* passage drafted by E. Hoffmann Price and revised by HPL in "Through the Gates of the Silver Key", we are surprised to hear Alhazred say that, not himself, but both 'Umr-at-Tawil and the ancient *Book of Thoth* are where you have to go if you want the real scoop. Lin Carter followed a hint left by Lovecraft to the effect that the opening section of the *Necronomicon* was an account of Alhazred's early sorcerous escapades. Carter told these stories in his own *Necronomicon* as cautionary tales. In other words, the "master" of blasphemy and sorcery himself shuddered at the horrors he related. It was for Yakthoob and others like him, whose arcane knowledge dwarfed Alhazred's own, to protect the deeper secrets, the elder blasphemies. Again, as soon as we open the book, the perspective shifts. We thought the page of the *Necronomicon* would be a window like that in Lovecraft's sonnet "The Window", revealing suppressed secrets, but it turns out to be a mirror reflecting our own frightened ignorance. We are like Antonius Block in Bergman's masterpiece *The Seventh Seal*, when he says to the Grim Reaper, "[Soon] you will divulge your secrets." The Reaper, like Alhazred, retorts, "I have no secrets. ... I have nothing to tell."

Lovecraft once replied to a letter from young fans James Blish and William Miller, Jr., who urged him to write the *Necronomicon*, as if it already existed and only lacked being transcribed, like the Mother of the Book, the heavenly prototype of the Qur'an from which the angel Gabriel dictated only fragments to the Prophet Muhammad as he had need of them. Really, Blish and Miller were little different from those credulous fans who asked Lovecraft if the *Necronomicon* really existed and where they could secure a copy. Like those, Blish and Miller seemed to imagine there was already such a book, full blown, but in Lovecraft's imagination. Just put pen to paper! Get it down so we may dare to read of the mind-blasting horrors to which you have alluded! Just as Lovecraft had to disabuse the literalists among his fans, confessing that the book was purely imaginary, he had to make Blish see that not only was the *Necronomicon* imaginary in nature, but that not even Lovecraft himself could really imagine it. The *Necronomicon* is but the trace, the empty track left by the unseen horror. It does not contain that horror but contains its absence, which is the only mode of its presence, because the imaginary, fictive Transcendental Signified, the Awful Truth that is hinted there, is the opposite of anything words could say. It is the Word of God, the Wholly Other, which can never be spoken or heard, a tree falling in an empty universe bereft of any ears to hear. The imagined and implied horrors of the *Necronomicon* are the faint echo, perhaps more felt than heard, of a distant explosion you did not actually hear. You discover that there was an earthquake only later, once you are knocked off balance by the *after*shocks.

So Lovecraft leveled with Blish and Miller, telling them that he himself, HPL, could never write a tome that would come near to justifying all the shuddersome references he had made to it. Best leave it to the imagination. "One can never *produce* anything even a tenth as terrible and impressive as one can awesomely *hint* about. If anyone were to try to *write* the *Necronomicon*, it would disappoint all those who have shuddered at cryptic references to it" (letter to Blish and Miller). "I might, though, issue an *abridged Necronomicon* - containing such parts as are considered at least reasonably safe for the perusal of mankind" (letter to Robert E. Howard, May 7, 1932), "the less terrible chapters, which ordinary human beings may read without danger of laying themselves to siege by the Shapes from the Abyss of Azathoth" (to Blish and Miller). Again, that *deferring*! The closer we get to it, the more it recedes, again and again. If Lovecraft actually supplied us with the book, he would have at the same time *scissored out the very parts we wanted to read!* As if Jerry Falwell handed over your subscriber copy of *Playboy*, having cut out all the naked babes! What's left? Do you really want to waste time reading those moronic party jokes?

Like the Christ, the Antichrist is a figure always coming, never arriving. The horror is that of anticipatory dread of the impending doom which, when it does come, is always less dreadful than what we imagined before the fact. Blish certainly learned this lesson, as witness his own later tale "More Light." Blish actually provides the text of the mind-blasting play *The King in Yellow*, but he stops before the dreaded climax. He withholds the revelation at the very moment he seems to be disclosing it.

The technique by which the concealment of the mystery is repeated in the very scene of revelation is itself paradigmatic, then, of the deferring character of language itself. In the same fashion, we can find in the fear-rhetoric of Lovecraft's tales a precise allegory of reading for the function of this bait-and-switch technique of apparent but always deferred revelations. I am thinking of the oft-repeated anxiety of the Lovecraftian narrator that the revelation of the secret of R'lyeh or of the Crinoid Old Ones or of the Outer Ones must be at all costs prevented because "such knowledge is not good for man." It would shatter our comfortable world view and we would have to face our true perilous position in the cosmos. The narrator wishes to spare his contemporaries that. So he says he will take the secret to the grave with him—just as soon as he finishes this account of that very same secret for posterity to read. This is another contradiction pregnant with rhetorical meaning. Its purpose is to make you see yourself in the role of the delver. As the narrator—e.g., Francis Wayland Thurston in "The Call of Cthulhu"—gradually recounts how he gradually connected all the dots, you are reliving that process with him, so you may be brought to the same shuddering conclusion. It is another mise-en-abyme effect, this time with the miniature scene within the page projecting itself *outward*, reflecting itself, magnified, onto the reader.

Beyond this, this theme of knowledge so terrible as to shatter our world view, which is nonetheless never really revealed to the reader, reflects a structural feature of narrative itself, as Tzvetan Todorov points out in his analysis of "The Figure in the Carpet" by Henry James ("The Secret of Narrative", in Todorov, *The Poetics of Prose*). A reader of a famous author meets his hero, who tells him to reread his stories again with a view to isolating an underlying theme that runs through all of them like the design in a carpet, itself unnoticed but integral to the artistic effect of the carpet as a whole. He never finds it. Todorov says this is because a certain unsaid element in any story can only perform its function as long as it remains implicit. If for a moment attention is drawn to it and it is named, it no longer functions (which is why so much literary analysis, by laying bare the hidden anatomy of the effective story, ruins the story). It is a matter of the "blindness and insight" dialectic of Paul de Man, whereby we are enabled to see some things in a text precisely by our inability to see others. Ironically, if we became aware of these latter right off the bat, we would be walking before we had learned to crawl, and we would do neither very well.

The hidden blasphemies of the *Necronomicon* are the figure in Alhazred's flying carpet. That figure is the undisclosed part of the text Lovecraft himself would have "omitted", the truths at which Alhazred only dares hint in the text and which he credits to sources older and more mysterious than his own book. If these horrors were to become known, were to be baldly presented to the reader, the effect of the stories would be shattered, since the tension and wonders of suspense would have been dispelled by an inevitable anticlimax. The horrors of the *Necronomicon* chill us precisely by *not* being revealed. They can only be present and effective in their mode of absence.

We can look at Medusa's visage only in a blurred mirror, or the story will, for the reader, be turned to lifeless stone.

**

A concluding word about the contents of this collection. Individual story notes will explain most of what you need to know. I would just like to explain how the conception of the *Necronomicon* as a symbol of ancient arcana has dictated our selection of material. It is obvious that the subtext of the "forbidden book" story, the invisible, real-life hook that draws us in, is the challenge of delving among old book shops for a long-desired rare book. When a Lovecraft devotee sees the word *Necronomicon* in a tale where someone is trying to get access to it or turns it up on a shelf in an abandoned building, what such a reader sees is *The Outsider and Others*. Stories like Robert Bloch's "The Shambler from the Stars" or Robert E. Howard's "The Thing on the Roof" are cut from the same cloth as the rumors one hears among Lovecraft fans of so-and-so once stumbling upon a discarded copy of *The Outsider* for a buck in a garage sale. The real-world counterpart to the Lovecraftian delver after forbidden secrets is not the pathetic believer in one or another of the Necronomical pseudipigrapha (on these, see the examples in the present book), but the avid collector combing every second-hand book shop and dealer's table in search of the last stray volume he needs to complete his collection. Accordingly, the stories in this volume are mostly scarce items which most readers will have either never heard of or at least never laid eyes on. Most are from the pulp era, a few from more recent fanzines or magazines.

Mythos collectors are notoriously eager to read and catalog any tale which makes any use, however modest, of the various Lovecraftian grimoire titles, divine names, or place names. The use may be purely marginal, a light touch of associational shading. Such references merely garnish a story that ought to be effective for other, more substantial reasons of plot, characterization, philosophical vision, etc. While Lovecraft fans are delighted to discover such marginal references to Cthulhuvian lore in the fine print of a story, editors and anthologists are more concerned about using stories that are strong in their own right. Thus several old tales whose chief interest for us lies in their slight Mythos references have not remained readily available or have even been forgotten by editors who have different priorities. Lucky for you, the Cycle Horror Series has an editor who is a completist fanatic just like you! I am joining you in the ghoulish buffet that stretches wide before you in these pages.

Robert M. Price
Hour of the Ominous Shuffling
Behind the Thrice-Barred Door
July 5, 1995

When, in 1971, the late, great Wellman looked back on this story for its reappearance in the landmark Lovecraft fan publication *HPL*, he reflected on what he had had in mind when he wrote it over thirty years earlier. (It appeared in the August 1937 issue of *Weird Tales*.) Here is what he said: "It's set in the apartment we had back during the 30s on East 24th Street, NYC—comfortable though not showy. The couple here might well be myself and my wife, whose name is not Gwen. The Kline mentioned was the late Otis Adelbert Kline, a good friend of mine, a writer and an Orientalist. Clark Ashton Smith and Robert Bloch are themselves. Father O'Neal was an old family friend in another part of the country. The 1930s were grim, with the Depression in full cry and Adolf Hitler making unpleasant noises; but Kline and Smith and that great editor Farnsworth Wright were alive and vigorous, and you could buy *WT* for a quarter if you had a quarter."

The Terrible Parchment

by Manly Wade Wellman

(To the memory of H. P. Lovecraft, with all admiration)

"Here's your *Weird Tales*," smiled my wife, entering the apartment.

"Thanks, Gwen," I said, rising and taking the magazine she held out. "But surely it's not the first of the month."

"Not for two days yet," Gwen assured me. "But just as I came to the front door, a funny old man bobbed up with an armful of magazines— advance copies, I guess. He stuck a copy of *W.T.* right under my nose. I gave him a quarter and—oop!"

I had opened the magazine and a page fluttered to the floor. We both stooped for it, both seized it, and we both let go.

Gwen gasped and I whistled. For that fallen page had a clammy, wet feel to it. Dank is the word, I think. Still stooping, we grimaced at each other. Then I conquered my momentary disgust, picked up the page, and held it to the light of my desk lamp.

"It's not paper," Gwen said at once.

No more it was, and what could it be doing in *Weird Tales*? Though it looked weird enough. It was a rectangle of tawny, limp parchment, grained on the upper side with scales, like the skin of some unfamiliar reptile. I turned it over. The other surface was smoother, with pore-like markings and lines of faint, rusty scribbling.

"Arabic," I pronounced. "Let's phone for Kline to come over. He reads the stuff."

"There's a Greek word," Gwen said. Her pink-tipped finger touched the string of capitals at the upper edge:

NEKPONOMIKON

"*Necronomicon*," she spelled out. "P would be *rho* in Greek. Sounds woogey."

"That's the name of H. P. Lovecraft's book," I told her.

"Book? Oh, yes, he's always mentioning it in his stories."

"And lots of *W.T.* authors—Clark Ashton Smith and Robert Bloch and so on—have put it into their stories," I added.

"But Lovecraft imagined the thing, didn't he?"

I laid the parchment on the desk, for my fingers still rebelled at its strange dankness. "Lovecraft describes it as the work of a mad Arab wizard, Abdul Alhazred, and it's supposed to contain secrets of powerful evils that existed before the modern world. It's become legendary."

Gwen stared at it, but did not touch it. "Is it some sort of Valentine or April Fool's joke, stuck in to thrill the subscribers? If so, it's cleverly made. Looks a million years old."

We pored over the rusty scrawl of Arabic, our heads close together. If it was a fake, there was every appearance of dimmed old age about the ink.

"Kline must have a look at it," I said again. "He may know what it's doing in *Weird Tales*."

Gwen studied the last line of characters.

"That part isn't faked," she said suddenly. She paused a moment, translating in her mind. "It says, 'Chant out the spell and give me life again.'" She straightened. "Let's play some cribbage."

We both felt relief as we turned away. Light as had been our talk, we had been daunted by a sense of prodding mystery. I got out the board and the cards and we began to play on the dining table.

Ten minutes later, I turned suddenly, as if a noise had come to my mind's ear. The parchment was no longer on the desk.

"It's blown off on the floor," said Gwen.

I rose and picked it up. It felt even more unpleasant than before, and this time it seemed to wriggle in my hand. Perhaps a draft had stirred it. Dropping it back on the desk, I weighted it with an ash tray and went back to the game.

Gwen beat me soundly, adding to her household money thereby. I taunted her with suggestions of a girlhood misspent at gaming-tables, then turned idly toward the desk. I swore, or so Gwen insists, and jumped over to seize it.

"This is getting ridiculous," said Gwen, fumbling nervously with the cards.

I studied the thing again. "You said the last line was in Latin," I remarked.

"It *is* in Latin."

"No, in English." I read it aloud. "Chant out the spell and give me life again." And the next to the last line was in English, too, I realized. It also was written with fresh ink, in a bold hand:

> Many minds and many wishes give substance to the
> worship of Cthulhu.

Gwen looked over my shoulder. "You're right, dear, 'Many minds and ...'—what does Cthulhu mean? Anything to do with the chthonian gods— the underground rulers the Greeks served?"

"I shouldn't be surprised," I said, and it sounded even drier than I had intended. "Cthulhu's a name that Lovecraft and Smith and the others used in their yarns. A god of old time, and a rank bad one at that."

Gwen shuddered, and turned the shudder into a toss of her shoulders. "Maybe the many minds and wishes gave substance to this page of the *Necronomicon*."

"Nonsense, the *Necronomicon*'s only Lovecraft's imagination."

"Didn't you say it had become a legend?" she reminded, utterly serious. "What's the next step after that?"

"What you suggest," I said, trying to be gaily scornful, "is that so many people have thought and talked about it that they've actually given it substance."

"Something like that," she admitted. Then, more brightly: "Oh, it'll turn out to be a joke or something else anticlimactic."

"Right," I agreed. "After all, we're not living in a weird tale."

"If we were, that would explain things." She warmed to the idea. "It was turning deliberately into language we could read. When we hesitated over the Latin—"

"It accommodatingly turned into English," I finished.

"There are more things in heaven and earth, Horatio, than are dreamed of in your philosophy."

"Trite but true. Still, my name's not Horatio, and it's bedtime. Let's not dream any philosophies that'll turn into nightmares." Once more I picked up that clammy parchment. "I'm putting this under stoppage."

Opening the dictionary on the stand beside my desk, I laid the parchment inside and closed the heavy book on it. "There it stays until we get Kline here tomorrow. And now to bed."

To bed we went, but not to sleep. Gwen squirmed and muttered, and I was weary in every portion of my body except the eyelids. We got up once for sandwiches and milk, and again for aspirin. A third time we lay down and I, at least, dozed off.

I started awake to the pressure of Gwen's fingers on my shoulder. Then I heard what she had heard, a faint, stealthy rustle.

I reached for the light chord above the bed. The room sprang into radiance, and through the open door I could see the living room. I sat up in bed, staring.

Something hung down from between the leaves of the dictionary by the desk, something that moved. Something that would be rectangular if laid flat, but which now seemed to flow from its narrow prison like a trickle of fluid filth.

"It's going to come here for us," breathed Gwen, almost inaudibly.

The parchment worked free and dropped to the floor with a fleshy slap, as though it had soft weight. It began to move across the rug toward the bedroom door. Toward us.

Perhaps I might describe painstakingly how it looked as it moved, how it humped up in the middle and laid its corners to the floor like feet. But how can I convey the horrid nastiness of it, how visualize for you the sense of wicked power that it gave off in waves almost palpable? You might get an idea by draping a sheet of brown paper over a creeping turtle ... no, that sounds ludicrous. There was nothing funny in the way that parchment moved, not an atom of humor.

Gwen crouched, all doubled up and panicky, against the headboard. Her helpless terror nerved me. Somehow, I got out and stood on the floor. I must have looked unheroic with my rumpled hair and my blue pajamas and my bare feet, but I was ready to fight.

Fight what? And how?

It came hunching over the door sill like a very flat and loathly worm. I saw the writing on it, not rusty-faint but black and heavy. Snatching a water glass from the bedside table, I hurled it. The foul thing crumpled suddenly sidewise. The glass splintered on the floor where it had been. The parchment came humping, creeping toward my bare toes.

"Smash it," wailed Gwen. She must have been ready to faint.

Against a chair leaned her little parasol, with a silken tassel at its handle and a ferrule of imitation amber. I seized it and made a stab at the invader. The point thrust the center of it against the floor, pinning it there for a moment. Then I saw in what manner it had changed.

At the top NEKPONOMIKON still stood in aged ink, but the Arabic writing was transformed into English, large and gold and black as jet. Stooping to pin it, I read at a glance the first line.

A thousand times since I have yearned to speak that line aloud, to write it down, to do something to ease my mind of it. But I must not, now or ever.

Who shaped so dreadful a thought? Abdul Alhazred is a figment of Lovecraft's imagination. And Lovecraft is human; he could never have dreamed those words that lie on my mind like links of a red-hot iron chain. And they were but the start of the writing. What could it have been like in full?

I dare not surmise. But suddenly I knew this for truth, as I tried to crush the parchment beneath the inadequate parasol—the formless evil of centuries had taken form. An author had fancied the book; others had given it being by their own mental images. The legend had become a fearsome peg on which terror, creeping over the borderland from its forbidden realm, could hang itself, grow tangible, solid, potent.

"Gwen," I called, "hide your eyes. Don't look. Don't read."

"What?" Her pale face moved close as she leaned across the bed.

"Don't read!" I yelled at her.

The parchment squirmed from under the tip of the parasol. It reached my foot, it was climbing my leg.

Would it scale my body, drape itself upon my face, force its unspeakable message into my mind? Because then I'd have to speak.

The burden would be too great. My lips would open to ease the torture. "Chant out the spell ..." and the world would be crushed under the fearsome feet of Cthulhu and his brother-horrors. What sins and woes would run loose? And it would be I, I who spoke the words to release them.

Dizzy and faint, I ripped the thing from my leg. It clung, as though with tendrils or suckers, but I dragged it free and dashed it into a metal waste basket, among crumpled bits of paper. It tried to flop out again. I snatched my cigarette lighter from the bedside table. It worked; it burst into flames and I flung it into the basket.

The mass of paper kindled into fire and smoke. Up from it rose a faint, throbbing squeak, to be felt rather than heard, like a far-off voice of a bat. Deeper into the little furnace I jabbed the outcast messenger of destruction. It crinkled and thrashed in the flames, but it did not burn.

Gwen was jabbering into the telephone.

"Father O'Neal!" she cried. "Come quick, with holy water."

Then she hung up and turned to me. "He'll be here in two minutes." Her voice quavered. "But what if the holy water doesn't work?"

It did work. At the first spatter, the parchment and its gospel of wickedness vanished in a fluff of ashes. I pray my thankfulness for that, every day I live. But what if the holy water hadn't worked?

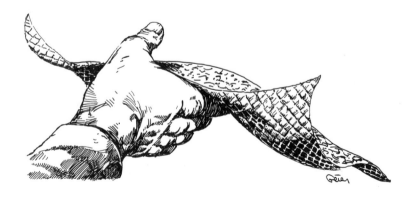

This too-brief tale returns to fresh air from the moldering pages of the almost unknown fan magazine *Scorpio*, March 1941. It took the investigative and archaeological skills of Edward P. Berglund (editor of *The Disciples of Cthulhu*) to unearth a copy when all other avenues had dead-ended.

The *Necronomicon* passage alluded to in this story must be the one cited in "Through the Gates of the Silver Key" by E. Hoffmann Price and H. P. Lovecraft. Or, depending on what Martin Brown thought it meant, possibly he has in mind the *Necronomicon* text from "The Festival."

One wonders if the name "Xander" is as symbolic as that of the artist Pickman, whose counterpart he appears to be. If "Pickman" brings to mind a pack of jackals picking clean the bones of a juicy morsel of carrion, "Xander" might be intended as a combination of "X" for the unknown and *ander*, German for "other", or alien.

Dr. Xander's Cottage

by Martin D. Brown

"Is he out of sight yet?"

"No," I whispered, "and keep down, you dope. He certainly walks slow." It was true. Dr. Xander *did* walk slowly. He was not an old man, but he shambled along as if he had some deformity—something not quite right, and obscurely sinister.

"Is he gone yet?" Parker queried again.

"Yes." The stooped figure had disappeared around the far-away bend in the road. Parker and I both straightened up. "Darn," he said, picking up his camera, "I'm sure stiff."

I was stiff too. Lying in the grass, watching a little house out in the middle of nowhere, isn't a reporter's idea of a good time. But a story is a story, and the public must have its sensations.

For the little village of Elwood had suddenly sprung into the spotlight, with the revelation that for years its inhabitants had been mysteriously disappearing. It was as if a creeping, deadly plague were at work. People vanished, and were never heard of again. The local authorities seemed to be powerless. My newspaper had sent me to investigate.

My investigations had finally centered around the stooped and mysterious figure of Dr. Xander. He was an object of terror in the little rural village, but no person dared to make a move against him. Folks shrank away as he passed them on his infrequent visits to town and no one could be coaxed or bribed to go near his little cottage after dark. Parker and I could find no definite reasons for this fear—just the vague rumors, dark whispers of rustics about that which they cannot understand.

So Parker and I had staked out near the place, and waited until the shunned figure set out for town. And now, approaching closer to the house, we smelled—or rather felt—something peculiar in the air.

"I don't like this," Parker muttered.

I didn't like it either. For some reason the shadows seemed to cling closer than they should around the porch, and the vegetation was too lush and thriving. I felt a cold chill as I went cautiously up the steps and tried the door.

It was ajar. Apparently Dr. Xander relied on the current fear of his dwelling to keep the curious away.

Inside, the strange odor—it was an odor—was stronger. I looked about, using my flashlight, though it was bright day outside. The room was bare, but it gave off a feeling of having been in use recently.

There seemed to be vague marks of diagrams on the floor and on the walls, and at one end of the room seemed to be marks, as if some heavy object had been removed. The place reminded me of the headquarters of a devil-cult that I had investigated some years before, and with this in mind I shot the light about, and noticed what seemed to be a bowl of some sort lying in a corner. Before I could investigate it, there was a noise somewhere in the house.

My pistol leaped into my hand. It was not the Doctor returning, for the noise came from before us rather than behind. Thinking that perhaps some of the disappeared villagers were being held prisoner in this old house, I gripped the cold steel of the gun and opened the door.

The room was empty, and we crept in. It seemed to be a laboratory or an operating room, with chemical equipment and tables scattered everywhere. In the far wall was another door, from behind which the noises came.

I strode forward, shot the heavy bolts on the door, and opened it. Parker was right behind me. What we saw, in the one brief instant before I slammed the door shut and fled from the cottage, nearly robbed us of our sanity.

Never, till my dying day, will I be able to erase the sight that met us. For the room was filled with monsters—ghastly caricatures of the human form. Whether human or animal I can not say. They seemed to be gray, hairless, deformed—and the stench that welled from the room was overpowering. Worst of all was the *sound*—a wet, bestial *slopping* as the things moved.

We ran madly back to the village, roused the authorities, and returned—to find the cottage in flames. A passerby told of having seen Dr. Xander enter shortly after we had fled.

The house was completely destroyed, though later we found some traces of what seemed to be caves under the foundation. At my frantic insistence these were dynamited and closed, despite those who wished to explore them in search of the missing villagers.

"Dr. Xander must have been operating on the kidnaped people, and making them into those things," said Parker, as the sound of explosives rang in our ears. I shook my head.

"I've read the *Necronomicon*," I told him. "Those—*things*—live in caves, and in tunnels under graveyards. And they live on—well, we won't talk of that. I never really believed they existed. But you saw them. They'd probably sacrificed the villagers to their obscene gods."

"But—was Dr. Xander a party to all this?"
"Not a part—no. He—was *one* of them."

It's amazing how the patina of antiquity makes things once-despised gain a palpable sense of venerable classicism. Crumbling old fantasy fanzines from the first wave of post-Lovecraft fandom (especially *The Acolyte*) have taken on great interest as the vestiges of the "sub-apostolic" generation. Many Lovecraftians are almost as avidly interested in the lives and works of all the Lovecraft Circle writers as they are in the work of the Old Gent himself. Then the aura of holiness spreads by contagion to the fanzines and fan fiction of those days. The idea is, I guess, "shake the hand that shook the hand that shook the hand."

At any rate, there is something increasingly fascinating about the amateur fiction of those pioneer Lovecraft fans, Duane Rimel, Kenneth Sterling, Richard Searight, and others. "The Mantle of Graag" is one of those tales. The story first appeared with the byline "Paul Dennis LaVond", a collective pseudonym (a house name?) for three young and aspiring writers: Frederik Pohl, Harry Dockweiller, and Robert A. W. Lowndes. The tale appeared in *The Unique Magazine* (how's *that* for an example of Derrida's paradox of iteration?), October 1941.

The Mantle of Graag

by Frederick Pohl, Henry Dockweiller, and Robert A. W. Lowndes

"Not exactly the Hartley you expected to see, eh?"

I gasped, staggered back; the thing I saw struck me like a swift blow to the solar plexus; I reeled for breath while something crawled and crawled up and down my neck. Then a myriad of voices shrilled inside my brain: *It can't be! It can't be!*

He—it—stood before me, trying to smile. It reached out with claw-like hands in the old gesture I had known; then the hands fell away. The shrunken lips writhed and the voice came to me as from a distance. I was dreaming—it must be a nightmare!

"Come in, Harvey." I followed the thing that had been Frank Hartley into the hallway I knew so well, down to the quiet, luxurious room at one end of the apartment. Unchanged, quaintly carved furniture lay before me with its wealth of barbaric wrappings: Oriental rugs, tapestries, and exotic bric-a-brac. Over the fireplace, the full-length painting of Hartley, executed years back by an artist acquaintance.

The mummy sank into Hartley's favorite chair, extended to me the familiar box of tobacco, a weird composition of blends mixed with incense, a concoction which effectively curtailed consumption save for a few choice friends who shared the mixer's exotic tastes. I struggled for composure, bluing the air with scented smoke.

"Remember Roche, Harvey? Roche, Klarner, and Paulsen?"

"Yes," I muttered. "Of course. I've read enough of Roche and Klarner's opi, seen Paulsen's splendid drawings. Always intended to correspond with them but never got around to it. You recall I asked you several times for their addresses. Where are they now?"

"Dead," he croaked. "All dead. Paulsen went first, then Klarner. Roche got tired of waiting for ... them ... and took poison. He always was more practical than the rest of us. If I were less of a fool ...."

Silence. Then: "But you will want to know what happened .... It all began when Hank invited Roche, Paulsen, and myself up to his hunting lodge in Maine for an extended weekend. Paulsen had just gotten his divorce and wanted something to take his mind off personal troubles; Roche was well enough ahead of the editors to take it easy for a while, and I decided I could do with a change. So we packed, climbed aboard Klarner's one-lung vintage of '20, and motored it to Maine. En route, Hank told us about the place he'd picked up for a ridiculously low figure. Nicely secluded, not more than a quar-ter-mile from the main highway—a glorified snake-track through the woods, in other words—and a fairly traversible path running in. It was not far from a reasonably large, secluded lake and there were several excellent beaches there replete with that special quality of white sand you find only in Maine."

"I was in Maine just about that time," I interrupted. "Had no idea you were about. But go on …."

"Well, it turned out that Hank had obtained the place but had never spent any time there. Just been around once or twice to see if all was in livable shape, then closed it up. So he was as unprepared as any of us for what happened. It's hard to describe. If I were writing one of my own weird tales, it would be sim-ple. But this was different. No tangible signs of anything, of any kind. No wind howling, or the like. But something in that place got under our skin the very first night, and we couldn't shake it off. We didn't see, hear, or smell anything. No odd dreams. But it grew on us, grew so that we began looking around the corners, tapping the walls for hidden panels and the like. Hank said he wished Lovecraft could have spent some time there; *he* could have made a real descrip-tion of the place, made his readers feel just as we felt, and work up to a terrif-ic climax to boot. After the fourth night, we were just about to admit that it had us whipped. We felt damned sheepish feeling this way about nothing when we all spent most of our existence conjuring horrors on paper. But you can't fight nerves that won't lie still. The fifth night we had something of a storm; lightning struck the chimney and tumbled a load of bricks down into the fire-place. It was when we were clearing out the mess the next morning that we found the book." His voice stopped. For a moment he sat staring into empty space. His skeletal frame twitched convulsively. "Strange," he whispered. "I can feel *them*, but there is no pain. No more pain. But I can feel … *them*."

"What is it, Frank?"

He shuddered. "Wait … where was I? … oh, yes, the book. It was a very ordinary-looking thing. Quite old yellowed pages, old print; complete-ly in Latin. The former owner had scribbled a lot of notes in the flyleaves, partly translation, partly comments. Sometimes there were large question marks in reference to certain paragraphs, notations referring to certain pages in other books … the *Necronomicon* and *Song of Yste* principally. The trouble was that none of us read Latin very well, but from what we could make out it was definitely a book on the old lore-things that Roche, Klarner, and I paraphrase in our stories. Oh, don't mistake me; it's not all Lovecraft's invention, you know. He changed a few names, and added his own details. But the sources are genuine enough.

"We found a real treasure in a few closely written pages stuck near the back. They were by the nameless builder of this lodge, the owner of the book. There was reference to a grisly thing he had done some twenty years before—"

"Wait!" I cried. "This lake of which you speak: Was it shaped roughly like a hand with five inlets to correspond to fingers? Was there a huge rock on the beach a short distance from a large cave? Were you some fifteen miles or so from a dilapidated little village popularly known as the hamlet of the dog?"

"Yes," he answered. "How did you know?"

"I've been there, too," I replied. "I've been all around that district, seen the lodge, explored the cave, and talked with an old fellow they call the Captain. He tells a story of what happened there twenty years back."

"Then you know of the treasure … of Graag?"

"Graag? That was the name of the man … the wizard who built the lodge. It must have been his book you found. But I never heard of any treasure—"

"The reference was in those written pages we found stuck in the book. There was a ritual to be performed. We really didn't believe a treasure would be found buried in the cave, but we thought there might be something of interest there. Some base for a few horror tales. Roche talked us into going through with the ritual. We learned the signs and made the marks prescribed. Then we went out and dug in the spot mentioned by Graag. Nothing was found after a half-hour and we were just about to strike out for the lodge when Paulsen's spade struck something metallic. He became very much disturbed at this, wanted to get away, but Roche insisted we unearth whatever it was. Paulsen became increasingly nervous … he had read much more of the book than we … and began to mutter about something he called the *Other*, the thing that Graag had called for his sorceries. But we smiled at this and Roche forced the chest open with his pick." Hartley's lips trembled.

"It … it was a worm, a large white worm in the chest lying on silken padding. When Klarner touched it, the thing crumbled away into dust. We were puzzled, but Paulsen was beside himself with terror. He muttered things about the scourge of the white worm, and the mantle of Graag. It was dark there, just enough light came from our hand-lamps to see what we were doing.

"Suddenly Paulsen screamed out something and pointed behind us, toward the cave's mouth. We looked; saw nothing. Paulsen went off his head at this and began to babble about a fourth figure and rave about the mantle of Graag until Klarner quieted him with an uppercut. We carried him back and left the place the following morning. Paulsen never recovered from the shock of what he thought he saw, died after about two weeks in delirium. Then one night I got a call from Klarner. The man was positively gibbering with terror; I couldn't make out what he said. Something again about the mantle of Graag. Next day a special delivery package came for me. It was the book. And with it, a long letter from Klarner. After I read that letter, I burned both it and the book. Never saw Klarner alive again; I'm glad of that.

"The letter told everything … about the *Other*, what must be done when the sorcerer is about to die and the *Other* must be allowed to return.

It tells of the rituals of burial of the worm, and the protective curse of the sorcerer over the earthly remains of the *Other*, that curse that is known as the mantle of the sorcerer. And it told further of what happens to all who violate the remains, what happens to all who are present whether or not they take part in it."

His voice raised in pitch. "The worm! The worm! The mantle of Graag fell on all of us. On Paulsen, but he died from the sheer insane terror before *they* found him. On Klarner: He knew what the mantle of Graag means. On Roche: He took poison before *they* could reach him ... and on me. *They* have found me, too."

He rose quickly. "Harvey," he whispered, "get out. Get out quick before you see! It has come; *they* have made a place for *it*. Get out while you're still sane, and goodbye, Harvey; you won't see me again!"

He seized me, pushed me roughly into the hall. "Goodbye, Harvey, now leave quickly!"

Something of the terror he felt flowed into my soul. I did not wait to inquire further. As my hand fell on the doorknob, I half turned, looked back. I wish to God I hadn't! I did not read the newspapers the next day, but I know they couldn't describe *how* Hartley was found. They dared not tell the truth. I knew because I saw .... Later I verified his story—his words about the *Other*, about the casting of the mantle, and the doom awaiting all present when the tomb of the *Other* is violated.

You see, Paulsen was not mad when he screamed about a fourth figure, standing apart from the others, at the mouth of the cave that night.

I was that figure.

One of the too-few Mythos tales by Doc Lowndes involves the *Al-Azif*. More importantly, it involves the odd premise of a strange wall which resists every attempt to cross over it or circumvent it. The connection between this bizarre phenomenon (a good premise for a *Twilight Zone* episode) and the abhorred volume of the mad Arab is not arbitrary, as if the *Necronomicon* must be called in for every type of paranormal phenomenon (like Superman forever being pestered by that nuisance Jimmy Olsen—"Why did I ever give him that damn signal watch in the first place?"). No, there is an important and effective symbol here, namely that the impassable wall stands for the boundary between the familiar cosmos we know and the unspeakable horrors lying in wait beyond the rim of our sane world. When the *Necronomicon* is invoked to figure out how to cross over that wall, we have as potent a symbol as that of the *Necronomicon* itself—a fantastic world that is unsealed when the covers of a book are opened. The cover board of this book (like any book) is the door to eldritch dimensions. "I had the book that told the hidden way across the void and through the space-hung screens that hold the undimensioned worlds at bay, and keep lost aeons to their own demesnes." But that's any book, isn't it?

Robert Lowndes is known most widely for his editing of *The Magazine of Horror* in the early sixties, a mostly reprint digest which made many classics of the pulps available again, bridging the gap between the early Arkham House and Gnome Press collections and the paperback revival of pulp fiction. Lowndes also discovered new and gifted writers in the old tradition, as well as penning a small canon of tales himself. Another, "The Abyss", is available in the anthology *Tales of the Lovecraft Mythos* (Fedogan & Bremer,1992). His macabre poetry, the two series of "Annals of Arkya", deserves to be reprinted, along with the "Fungi from Yuggoth", "Dreams of Yith", and others in the *Innsmouth Jewelry* collection long ago planned by Lin Carter. Lowndes certainly did not shirk his duty in creating his own Mythos book, the *Song of Yste*, references to which you will find here and there in this book and other volumes in Chaosium's Cthulhu Cycle Book series.

"Settler's Wall" appeared first as "The Long Wall" in *Stirring Science Stories*, March 1942, under the pseudonym Wilfred Owen Morley. A revised version appeared in *Starling Mystery Stories* #10, Fall 1968. The present version appeared originally in *Crypt of Cthulhu* #62, Candlemas 1989.

Settler's Wall

By Robert A. W. Lowndes

While I am not the most tidy of persons when it comes to some of my effects—books and records are in order, but every time I open a drawer of my desk, I groan and vow to put things in shape next week—I do like to see things worked out thoroughly, and that is why I have been reluctant to tell this story, even in the guise of fiction. I was not there at the finale, nor was anyone else; no living person actually saw what happened; the only evidence is some photographs, and while the camera may not lie, some first-class liars are very adept at working with cameras.

It happened in 1934, when my cousin, Frank, was spending a summer at the CCC camp at Flagstaff, Maine. The Great Depression may have passed its nadir by then, but it was far from over, and I had been fortunate enough to get into a publishing venture with a high school acquaintance, Will Richards. If it did not make us rich, at least it kept us ahead of the Big Bad Wolf; our *Advertiser* covered the Stamford-Norwalk area, and we had reached the point where we would have to decide whether to expand further or see if we could settle down comfortably in our present slot. The immediate decision was to take a brief vacation and let the question ferment in our subconscious for a time. And why not, Will asked, drive up to Maine, see Frank, and get a look at what the CCC was doing up there, and then roam a bit before heading back?

Why not indeed? We did it, transporting a fair number of Frank's colleagues back toward their camps or toward their homes, depending upon whether they were going on leave or returning, and found the 178th Company at Flagstaff to be a very good deal for a young fellow who was willing to do an honest day's work, and conform to a reasonable amount of discipline. It wasn't army-degree discipline, but nonetheless, the reserve army and navy officers who commanded the camps could make life uncomfortable for the fellow who tried to buck the system, or just wouldn't make the effort to fit in. The already-delinquent youth (I don't recall whether that term was used then) didn't last; he went out with a DD (Dishonorable Discharge) rather soon. But I could see that there were many, who might have crossed the line into delinquency otherwise, for whom this was exactly the opportunity they so urgently needed; and they were taking it.

There were no provisions at the camp itself for overnight visitors, but we found accommodations near the village of Flagstaff, and the coolness of

early morning found us on the way to Skowhegan. Just where we had
planned to go after reaching the town, I no longer recall—Will said something about acquaintances up there—nor does it matter, because we did not
reach Skowhegan that day. In 1934 road signs throughout New England
existed, of course, but they were sparse compared to 1968; and while I have
not been back to Maine, I wouldn't be astonished to find that area considerably changed.

Mrs. Wing gave us directions, which amounted to looking for some
sort of barn "down the rud a mite", where we should keep to the right, and
then another landmark a mile beyond that, where we would make a turn,
etc. Frank had warned us about the local conceptions of distance, and there
were various of his associates in camp who averred that the standard of a
mite in Maine was the distance that a healthy and startled pony could run
before it dropped; everything, everything mind you, was "down the rud a
mite." And we'd be on dirt roads for quite a time.

Eventually, we came to a sign (predicted) and later on we came to a
branching in the road, which had been left a surprise to us. Exactly one car
had passed us, and we had passed all of three habitations—very decent looking farmhouses. July in Maine, Frank said, makes you forget things like the
fact that when he arrived in camp near the end of April, there were still four-
foot snowbanks to be seen.

Although we were on vacation, and we weren't really going anywhere,
I was beginning to get the feeling that we ought to stop at the next house
and see if we could get our bearings. I rolled down the side window, knocked
my pipe speculatively against the frame, chipping off still more of the faded
blue paint, and wondered aloud if we had made the correct turn.

Will Richards looked at his wristwatch. "Obviously, Clyde, we didn't.
By now we'd be on some sort of improved road, and close to Skow if not
there." He sidled the car to a stop. "Let's rest awhile, rouse out the maps,
and take our bearings after a sandwich or two."

There wasn't a breath of air stirring as we emerged onto the tufty grass,
and the clouds in the sky seemed to have been painted there. It was a dry
heat, though, and the only real discomfort was the cramps one got from driving along dirt roads in a vintage 1927 Ford. The tea in the thermos bottle
was cool enough, and Mrs. Wing's sandwiches both tasty and moist enough.

Will picked up a pebble and threw it across the road, where it bounced
off the high wall on the left side. "That's quite a thing, isn't it?"

Right then, I had the oddest feeling. I had seen this wall and yet not
really noticed it, even though it extended as far as we could see in either
direction. There were no markings on it visible from across the road, and
when we got around to examining it close up, we found none still. Our
guess that it was ten feet high turned out to be correct; there it rose, dull,

gray, and well weathered. Within the range of our vision, there was not a single distinguishing sign; at no point did grass eclipse it, or vines, or trees. In fact, the grass ended just about a foot away from it, in as straight a line as one could imagine, and the well packed earth between the end of the grass and the wall itself was perfectly clean. Not a leaf—well, of course; there were no trees anywhere near—not a pebble. The one Will had thrown must have bounced back into the grass; I hadn't thought he'd thrown it that hard. We stood first to the left and then to the right; the wall ran parallel to the road, straighter than the road, and we could not see the end of it in either direction.

"It must be miles long," Will said softly, then, as if wondering why he had dropped his voice so, he cleared his throat to pick it up again. "Did you notice when we hit it?"

I shook my head. "Wait," I said. "It was right after we went over that bump in the road. Or was it a hole? Anyway, I felt a jolt, and I'm sure the wall began just a little beyond that."

"You know, something like this ought to be marked on the map. Or at least there ought to be some sort of sign saying, 'You are now two miles from the famous Long Wall,' or something like that. And you'd think that Mrs. Wing or Frank or someone would have mentioned it."

I looked out over the open meadow to the right of the road, which eventually ran into wooded hills near the horizon. There was no sign of human habitation or occupancy visible. In the distance, I could see birds in the sky, but around us there had been no signs of life at all: not an ant, not a spider, not a fly, not a yellowjacket, not a beetle, not a snake.

"And who built it and why?" Will was going on. "A ten-foot-high wall this length just doesn't get built ten-twenty miles from nowhere, for no reason at all. You know, it doesn't really look as if there's been anyone living around here for an awful long time. I guess maybe the land was cleared once, since it isn't all forest now—or maybe there were natural meadows here to begin with. Have to ask a naturalist about that some time but I suppose it has a lot to do with the way the soil quality can shift here and there. I'll bet we're miles from the nearest house of any kind."

I was listening, but not only to Will. "Have you noticed how quiet it's been since we came upon this wall?" I walked right up to it—we'd been standing at a respectful distance—and scrutinized it the way a sleuth is supposed to examine evidence, magnifying glass or no magnifying glass. "You know, it looks as if it's made of one piece. I don't see a sign of separate stones; this is not stucco or concrete—and it can't be metal."

Will joined me and laid his hand upon the surface. "Feels like stone, all right. But it ought to be a little hotter .... Clyde, put your palm on it like this."

"Well—it's about 12:30. What say we take a little walk before going on. Half hour's exercise."

I am not a devotee of exercise for its own sake, but I'll walk twenty miles with a minimum of complaint—well, three—if there's a good reason for it. My curiosity was aroused almost to the point where it matched my ever-present desire to see the new issue of my favorite science fiction magazines, even if it meant a hike to a nearby town—usually Darien. (Up to very recently that had often been a necessity, when subscriptions ran out and I didn't have the renewal price; gas couldn't be wasted just so I could pick up a new issue the day it appeared on the stands.) I said to Will, "Look, you start down that way and I'll go this way; I want to walk around this thing. We'll meet after awhile."

Will looked at me in silence, since that was the first indication he'd ever had that I was willing to indulge in any sort of physical exertion that wasn't positively necessary. "It may be longer than you think. A lot longer."

"Well, then let's walk in different directions for fifteen minutes. At 12:45 we stop, turn and see if the other is in sight, then head back toward the car."

So I started briskly (briskly for me, anyway) down the road whistling between my teeth. Why was this wall ten feet high? How had it been made? Nothing about it changed in any way as I strode along; it still looked and felt like stone, and there were still no breaks or joins anywhere in it, no cavities, no irregularities, and nothing growing near enough to it to touch in any way.

And what was behind it? I could see nothing but the sky above. What about the upkeep? How had it been kept so clear? I examined the line of grass that ended a foot from the wall and was sure that it was not kept that way by a gardener; there were no signs of cutting; no, it grew that way. Soil differences again? Soil differences following a perfectly straight line, parallel to a perfectly straight wall? Then why hadn't the road been made straight?

And why hadn't we been bothered by insects during lunch time? Mrs. Wing's jelly sandwiches certainly should have roused up the yellowjackets. At least one grasshopper should have come into sight, not to mention butterflies; and the grass was the sort of grass where one found daddy-long-legs, and flies. ... I shook my head, lit up the last cigarette in the pack I was carrying (I'm omnivorous when it comes to tobacco), and crumpled up the empty package, tossing it against the base of the wall. A moment later, I went back to look at it; the crumpled package was in the grass, not lying on the bare strip.

I continued and then saw something up ahead, on the other side of the road. A few minutes later, it was identifiable as a parked car. Someone had been driving not too far ahead of us, obviously, and had also stopped, very possibly to examine this wall, I thought. A second thought told me that the conclusion was unwarranted, requiring the party ahead also be a tourist; it might just as easily be a native of the district to whom the wall was a commonplace. If that were the case, then perhaps we could get some information. I looked at my watch. 12:45; I turned and peered carefully behind me, but Will wasn't in sight. Well, it would do no harm to go a bit farther and see who was there up ahead.

Up to this point, there had been peculiarities, things that made one wonder, things which you would tell someone to elicit a whistle or a smile of disbelief at your attempt at a tall tale; but all of them, anomalous as they might be, were of the sort of piece which one could look back upon years later with a sort of pleasure. You would feel that there must be, there certainly was, some sort of entirely natural explanation, even if it included some rather bizarre human behavior and motivation. There was nothing thus far that really threatened anyone, omitting the type of nervous wreck who feels threatened by just about anything unusual.

It was at this point, I say, that the wall ceased to be strange, unusual, amusing, fantastic, etc., and became shocking.

For the car up ahead was our own 1927 Ford, with badly chipped blue paint, parked over by the side just as we had left it. When I turned around, to look behind me, there was Will Richards coming up, with an equally amazed expression on his face.

"Where did you come from?" I asked, then paused as I realized that we were speaking simultaneously.

He had walked for fifteen minutes in the direction opposite to my course; had stopped at 12:45, turned, seen nothing, started back, still seeing nothing between him and the car—then, suddenly, I was there.

I tried to say something about this being a two-pipe problem, but my heart wasn't it in. Nonetheless, I knew I had to rest, and a little tobacco would offer tranquilization, since we had no other sort handy. We were torn between the desire to get into the car and drive away at top speed, and the feeling that we had to know more. I have often wondered if it would have been worse had we driven away, if we wouldn't have been virtually compelled to return. Well, there's no answering that, but somehow I've never been able to feel that it would have been *better* had we taken a different course.

What we did, of course, after a rest period, was to try again; only this time, we walked together, in the same direction, the one I had taken which left the car behind us. We started out at exactly 1:15, and it was 1:24 when we passed the crumpled cigarette package. We looked at it, then continued, our eyes shifting from the wall to the road up ahead; the stillness, the absence of insect life was beginning to become a positive irritation.

"Watch closely, now," Will said. "If it's going to happen again, it should happen very soon. What's the time?"

"1:26," I said. We did not increase our pace, and Will let me set it; I kept as closely as I could to the stride I had used before, suppressing the urge to go faster with an effort. I kept my eyes fixed on the road ahead, on the right side of the road. There was nothing visible except the road itself, nothing but the meadow to the right, the wall to the left ... nothing ... nothing— There!

"Time!" gasped Will. "What's the time?" He seemed to have forgotten that his own watch ran better than mine.

"1:33 exactly," I said, my eyes reluctantly moving from the dark speck over to the right of the road ahead of us. We both knew what it was. We were right.

2

To say that there were more Wings around this part of the country than there are Smiths in the Manhattan telephone directory is to exaggerate, but not to give a false impression, really. The one at whose house we found accommodations for the night was named Thad, and he was a distant relative of the one we had spent last night with. The missus was away for a spell, he said, but he could handle things. I didn't see much physical resemblance, but he was like his relative in old-fashioned courtesy and friendliness. His comment upon the fact that we looked as if we'd had a rough time was put in just the right manner which indicated he'd listen with interest and sympathy if we wanted to talk, but not take offense if we didn't.

So after a hearty New England supper, we accepted his invitation to sit awhile on the porch, where the insect life was by no means lacking. Both Will and I wanted to talk so badly, we barely noticed.

I'm not going to try to reproduce anyone's enunciation of the local dialect. Not only does it make for tiresome reading after a sentence or two, it's like marking in a music score which the composer hesitates to put in for fear it will be exaggerated, finally does, and then finds that his fears are generally realized. I tried to do it, anyway, and had to throw some pages away because it just isn't right. "You" comes out "ye"; "catch," "ketch"; "your," "yer"; "now," "naow," etc.—but reading it back aloud, relying on memory as well as I could, I realized that I hadn't gotten it right. Let it pass. That should give you a general idea.

Thad Wing eased us into the subject by telling us some of the local gossip, pungent and bawdy quite a bit of it, and after a while, we started to talk about the wall, at which point he asked how it was we didn't see the sign indicating that that was a private road at the turnoff, which should have brought us on to the asphalt road to Skowhegan. I told him that there wasn't any such sign; we'd both been looking for a landmark (we actually found it after we got back onto the right road, Wing's place being the first we came to thereafter) and certainly would have seen it had it been there. He allowed that it might have been blown away last week, when there was a very high wind. Will continued up to the point where we'd found our car there by the side of the road ahead of us.

Wing struck a match on his shine and applied it to the oversize bowl of his corncob. "What did you do when you found you couldn't walk *around* the wall, Mr. Richards?"

Will looked at me, then took a swallow of the hard cider with which we had been provided.

"Well," I started out, "the next thing we did was to see if we could find out what was on the other side. We walked back into the field over by the side of the wall until we could see beyond it."

"And what did you see, Mr. Cantrell?"

I sighed. "Nothing. That is, nothing unusual. There was apparently just an open field, running into wooded hills, like the side we were standing on ... I guess we would have turned around and gone back then if something hadn't happened."

"I slipped and went down to my knees," Will said. "I'd stepped on a little colored rubber ball. The red of it was faded, but there was a definite design on it that we could see pretty clearly. I picked it up and threw it over the wall. I watched it—Clyde did, too—and it just barely cleared the wall, but we both saw it go over. It should have fallen just a little bit on the other side. There wasn't much bounce left in it—I don't think it would have bounced hardly at all.

"But when we got back to the car, my eye caught something in the grass across the road. I went over to it and picked it up. It was a rubber ball, and I'd swear it was *the same ball we had just seen drop over that wall.*"

"The markings were the same," I said. "Of course, Mr. Wing, there are lots of little rubber balls made with similar markings. But Will and I had both walked along this wall and even if the colors were faded, I just don't see how we could have missed noticing it there. The grass wasn't high enough to conceal it. It was just a little ahead of our car, on the grass in front of the wall—I couldn't have missed seeing it before. ... I couldn't."

"And I was looking at the wall all the time we were walking back to the car," Will added. "If someone on the other side had tossed it back, I'd have seen it coming over ... but that was just the start. I picked the ball up again and threw it over, high. You saw me do that, didn't you Clyde?"

I nodded. "And there was no wind. It couldn't have blown back," I said.

"No ... the air was perfectly still ... well, I threw it over as I said, and turned around—and *there was the ball on the grass just a little beyond the car.*" He paused and we both looked at Wing, expecting some sort of reaction of disbelief. But he nodded and rocked a little in his chair.

"Settler's Wall is very unsettling," he said. "We're used to it, but it bothers people coming from outside. That's why the major's father put that sign up, back around the time Cleveland was running for reelection. Missed, he did—but made it next time. Oh, the sign's been replaced a few times, but we've tried to keep it there. Gets knocked down every once in a while, and this will be the second time it's just blown away. Next time I see the major, I'll have to tell him."

Will was deep in thought. "Settler," he said. "Major Settler. Now where have I heard that name before?"

"Well ... he was a major before your time, Mr. Richards, and hasn't done anything to get himself in the papers since the scrap we had in Cuba when Teddy Roosevelt got things going." Wing rubbed the grizzle on his chin which passed for a beard. "Unless maybe you went to college a few years ago and came across his nephew then. Reckon you'd have had to, because Dave's name wasn't Settler."

"Wasn't ...?"

"Dave got himself drowned in a lake a spell back. Darn shame, too." Wing broke off in a way that suggested there was something more he could tell if he had a mind to.

"There was a Dave Fenner, who was a fraternity brother of mine at Columbia, in 1930 and 1931," Will said. "One of the reasons why I decided to come up to Maine was that I hoped to look him up."

I sat there staring. It's amazing how you can know people, even work with them in close quarters for months, sometimes years, and not know them. Will had never mentioned going to Columbia, not even going to college for that matter. Something of what was going through my head must have penetrated to him, for he grinned rather lopsidedly at me.

"Yes, Clyde, I'm a certified Bachelor of Arts, graduated *summa cum laude* from Columbia in 1931. I'm a real Latin scholar—or I would have been. Can you think of any other specialty more useless in these times? I was a fool not to switch in 1930 to something more practical—that's why I don't like to talk about college. But I did want to see if Dave was around. He'd concentrated on Latin, too, before he transferred to Columbia. I forget where he'd gone before. He didn't talk much about it, but he learned a lot of obscure Latin there."

"I've heard it mentioned," Wing said. "Housatonic? No—that's in Connecticut and a river, not a school. Something like that. It was around

Massachusetts Bay, not too far from Marblehead. ... but I've dragged you away from what you were telling about the wall. Did you try anything else?"

"Yes, I picked up the ball and was going to throw it over again with all my strength, but Clyde stopped me. We took a paper plate we had in the trunk and wrote our names on it. Then we skimmed it over the wall, and it sailed over as neatly as you could ask. Then we turned around and started looking for it behind us ... I'd say it took ten seconds to locate it."

Thad Wing poured himself another glass of hard (actually illegal) cider and offered us refills from the jug; we did not refuse. "Most folks give up by that point," he said, "but I got a feeling that you two didn't. You look and talk as if you'd tried something else and got a still worse shock. Am I right?"

"You sure are!" I said. "Will was determined to try to climb over the wall. He worked for the telephone company for a while as a linesman, and we had special climbing shoes in the car—figured we might tackle a mountain hereabouts—and plenty of rope. So I tied the rope around his waist, then gave him a hand up the wall, and grabbed hold of the rope so that he could climb down the other side, if he didn't want to jump, and give him a start when he wanted to come back.

"He got up to the top—there's enough room to stand there—and stood like a statue for a minute or so. Then he turned around, and his face was whiter than I ever saw it before. He didn't say anything, just nodded and started climbing down the other side while I let the rope out, keeping it taut. Then ... the rope seemed to slip out of my hands ... and ...."

"And you found that he'd come down on the same side of the wall you were on, only you didn't see him coming," finished Wing. He nodded to Will. "And you, Mr. Richards, I reckon I know what gave you such a turn when you got on top of the wall and looked over to what was beyond it. You saw the same thing you saw on this side. You saw your car on the far side of the road, and I'll bet you saw Mr. Cantrell here looking up at you. You see, it's all been tried before—but the fact of the matter is that *you can't walk around Settler's Wall and you can't go over it*. If you want my opinion—and the major holds to it likewise—there's only one side to that wall, the side you're on."

"But that's impossible!" I protested. "There's no such thing as a wall with only one side."

Wing chuckled. "That's the sort of thing us farmers are supposed to say when we see a giraffe. I'll tell you what I can about the wall. It's been called Settler's Wall as long as anyone can remember, because it's on Settler property. But none of them built it.

"There's been Wings and Settlers here for a long time, and that property had belonged to the major's family since before the War of the Rebellion. Whether a Settler or a Wing was in these parts first doesn't make much difference, I guess. But nobody seems to have seen it much before

1840, or maybe the late 1830's, when they first started to clear the land in these parts.

"My father told me, and it's been passed down for quite a while now, 'There's a lot of things which may seem peculiar, but so long as they aren't hurting you any, or hurting anybody else, don't you bother about them. Leave them alone.' And that's the way it's been around here; that's the way we look at the wall, just about all of us. Settler's Wall has never harmed anybody, but a few folk have hurt themselves getting all het up about it."

"What happened to them?" I asked.

"The wall itself didn't do a thing to them," Wing said. "It just stayed there and paid no attention to them. But they couldn't let well enough alone—they just had to know all about it. A couple of them have gotten themselves brain fever and died of it. And Jim Garlan—he was the son of old Ben—but no use going into that—well, that was around the '80's, and he'd gone to university in England and Germany; he was determined to solve the secret of the wall." Wing took another deep swallow of hard cider, then stuffed his pipe again.

"What happened to him?"

"Went mad. Didn't talk so that anyone else could make out any sense from it, not even the fancy doctors and professors who came here. It was a funny kind of Latin they said he was talking, and a couple of the professors were pretty sure that he was quoting from some book, though it wasn't a book any of them had ever read. I think one of them had an inkling, but he wouldn't say anything—I got all this from my grandfather—except that Jim must have gotten access to a book in the British Museum that people weren't supposed to see. But that's all he would say, though my grandfather was sure he knew a lot more, except that the best thing to do about the wall was just to leave it alone. I'm sure Dave was more interested in it than was good for him.

"Tell you what, you being an old fraternity brother of his, I reckon the major would like to meet you. If you have time, we could go over there tomorrow, and I think the major would let you look at Dave's notebooks. None of us can read parts of them, because they're in Latin, too, and the only person around here who knows any Latin says that it's too danged corrupt Latin." Thad Wing puffed away at his pipe, and I didn't feel like breaking the silence then.

"And if you want my opinion—because that's all it is, I don't know— I think the reason why Dave left that college in Massachusetts and shifted to New York was because he found out too much and had the sense to stop before he went off his head like Jim Garlan. They had old books locked up at that college, too, and what we could read of Dave's notebooks says that he got to see some of them. Well, the major and I, we both calculated a bit, and we figure that the books Dave was reading in corrupt Latin in 1926 and 1927 were the same books that Jim Garlan found in London. They were real old books, copied out by hand ... Dave used to correspond with a writer who lived in Rhode Island, and he'd get long letters from him every now and then. But when he came back from that place, he was a different person. He burned all the correspondence and I think he might have burned the notebooks, too, except perhaps he figured that no one could read them, and there were some things in them—personal things—that he didn't want to lose. Maybe he'd have copied those out and burned the rest if he'd lived. I don't know. One of those things where you have to say that just nobody knows, that's all."

Will turned to me. "What do you say, Clyde? Had enough of it or can you take a little more? Shall we go to see Major Settler?"

3

I have often felt irritated, in reading weird fiction, when the author has taken the trouble to tell me that something is shocking—particularly when he has taken the trouble to present his material clearly—and now on looking back over this manuscript, I see that I have done the same thing myself. Perhaps I've been wrong and misjudged some of my favorite writers, for I see now one use of this term which strikes me as entirely legitimate. That is why I have left that passage just as I first wrote it. I do not mean that *you* ought to find the matter referred to as shocking, or again that you never would unless I gave you the cue; what I was talking about was the effect that the experience of trying to walk around Settler's Wall had upon Will Richards and me.

It was more than upsetting; it had a profound effect not only on our ability to think and reason with what I like to consider our normal ability. We were in something very much like a hypnotic situation, or at least like being under the spell of a first-class stage magician who induces you to look where he wants you to look and thus be completely taken in by his illusions and deceptions. That was part of it; the astute reader has long since thought of something which just did not occur to either of us until the next morning.

Of course it was only a partial release, for it did not begin to explain everything; but it seemed like a major victory to me, when I awoke finally at the sound of the Wing contingent of roosters who, having done their essential duty earlier, were now rehearsing for the next morning. A thought hit my mind as daylight struck my opened eyes.

Will had preceded me to the bathroom. I looked at him carefully, wondering if it had occurred to him, too. I didn't think it had; he just didn't look as if it had. So I yawned and said to him, "Hey, why don't we just try to get up on the wall from behind? Go around the back way?"

He dropped his razor, which was as much applause as I could ask for. I marched triumphantly down the hall to the bathroom and left him there, thinking that I'd better mark the date on the calendar, since I'd forgotten the last time I'd beaten him to the mental punch.

It was a fine day, and I enjoyed it heartily for all of ten or maybe fifteen minutes, until we went down to the breakfast table, met the neighbor who had come in to help, and, after a bit of desultory conversation, I mentioned my idea. Thad Wing looked thoughtful and a little sympathetic, then murmured, "It's been tried."

He chewed on his ham for a moment then added, "Jim Garlan was the last to keep on trying and trying, and that was when he began to go queer. There's woods there, not too much different from the woods you see on the other side. What happened was, every time Jim would work his way out of the woods, on to a meadow, he'd find himself on the other side of the wall, across the road. You don't have to take my word for it, Mr. Cantrell. No law here against seeing for yourself."

The flavor went out of Mrs. Sully's fine Maine breakfast at that point. I knew that the last thing in the world I wanted was to go through that experience myself.

"What I don't understand—along with other things," Will said, "is why we've never heard about the wall before."

"Well ...." Wing paused for a moment. "Don't want to sound offensive. Don't mean any offense neither, but most folks around here just mind their own business. Course it's no fault of yours that the sign was down; I'm sure you wouldn't have taken that road if you'd seen it. But the fact is that since the sign has been up hardly anyone except the major and his family have used the road, and folks just sort of generally agreed not to talk about the wall since Jim Garlan went crazy. Most people around here have never seen it or heard of it. And those of us who have leave it alone and it leaves us alone."

Wing started to talk about something else, I guess to assure us that he didn't mean anything personal and that we hadn't stepped on his toes in any way. After breakfast, we got into his buckboard and rode over to the Settlers'. Just like that, no telephoning, though Wing had a wind-up telephone in his kitchen—a three-party line affair. He sort of appreciated our adventure, he said, because he hadn't seen the major for a spell, and this gave him a good reason to drop in.

Later we learned that this period of "a spell" was over two years. Settler and Wing had had a little disagreement and stopped talking to each other, each of them willing to be friends again if the other would just make the first move. So something good came out of our discovery of the wall after all.

Unless you have rubber bones, I do not recommend the buckboard as a desirable means of travel over unimproved roads. It did, however, help to take the edge off the feeling of dull horror that had crept back over me. I was somewhere in between the feeling of wanting to crawl into a cave and go to sleep, hoping to awaken in a different world, where something like Settler's Wall really couldn't exist, and a morbid fascination which kept me wanting to see this thing through, though to what end I couldn't imagine.

Major Horace Wingate Settler, U.S. Army (ret.) looked the part to perfection. Take the build of Theodore Roosevelt, but remove the glasses; something of the stoical quietness of Calvin Coolidge—who *could* talk when he had a mind to—but pour in more warmth; a touch of the friendly but firm sincerity of Eisenhower, in situations where his command of self expression has not been shot away; and you have our initial impressions.

He greeted Thad Wing as if he hadn't seen him for a week or so, and they talked a bit after we'd been welcomed and made comfortable upon the porch. After awhile, Wing gave a concise report upon how we'd happened to come across the wall, and our experiences, mentioning that Will had been a classmate of Dave's at Columbia.

The major thawed visibly at that. "Seem to recall Dave mentioning some fraternity brother named Will. Well, if you can read what he wrote in his notebooks, we'd sure like to find out. About the wall, we all reckon. Not mine. I never built it and neither did anyone else. That wall was here when we first came here, and folks around swore at the time they knew nothing about it. You can't find any mention of it, even in Indian legends. It was just there, somewhere around 1840."

I didn't feel like arguing, and neither did Will, I could see. It was obvious to both of us that the major and his forbears had solved the problem of the wall in their own way; they ignored it. The only thing they'd talk about was the unpleasant results of getting too curious.

"Nope, it never hurt anyone who didn't get too close to it, and didn't try to pry too far," the major went on. "Never did anyone a lick of good, either. But you're welcome to look it over in any way you want to except one. Damnation, you can tear it down and cart it away if you can figure out how to do that, so long as you don't do any damage to the rest of the property or make me liable for anything."

"What's the one thing that's ruled out, sir?" I asked.

"Trying to dig under it. That was what drove Jim Garlan crazy, and a couple others before him got brain fever and died." He got up showing little traces of age. "Set now, and I'll bring you Dave's notebook. Reckon Thad would like to hear what you can make out of it. No hurt if it's all Chinese to you—nobody else has been able to make much sense out of it."

"You mean," I asked, "that no one has been able to translate anything in it at all?"

"Nope, some have got words and sentences all right. But what they got didn't leave us any better off than before."

He was back a few moments later, during which time Wing told us that the major's cousin's family lived here and took care of the place. We might see them later if the visit took that long. I got the impression that, so long as we behaved ourselves and were of interest, we could stay for days, as Wing's paying guests. When the others had nothing else important to do, they'd visit with us; when they did, we were on our own. The younger ones had daily tasks, but Wing and the major worked when they felt like it—which was more often than not.

Dave had attended a college in Massachusetts before coming to Columbia. Will had thought he started college late, but we found out now that he'd had a breakdown at "that place" and was out for a year or so before continuing. The college to which he had gone at first wasn't named, though I suspected that Wing really did recall the name. But the custom here was to refer to it, if one positively had to mention it at all, only as "that place." The major had closed the iron door upon it.

Settler reappeared now with a medium-sized copybook under his arm. "Never did think much of that place," he started out, "but Dave wanted to do research in Italy and other countries. Had the notion from reading about da Vinci that some of those other old writers came across some useful military ideas that got overlooked, because they were so obscure in the way they wrote things down. He'd need a real foundation in medieval Latin and maybe earlier and figured that place was the only school in the East which had the facilities for him. So I had to allow that it might be worth taking the risk."

He filled up his pipe and lit it carefully. "Wasn't a pacifist, but I could see that he wouldn't make a good soldier for an army career. Heart wasn't in it. He'd do his duty if the war broke out again, but otherwise, no. Sort of disappointed me at first, but then I started thinking. Had lots of time to think after my wife died. That's why those Germans came so close to beating the world. They did research. They worked out new ideas. Can't win a war with old ideas that everybody knows about, no matter how many men you have. May not be long before the Japanese or the Russians, or even the Germans again, come up with new ideas and make another try. We have to keep ahead of them." He puffed on his pipe. "Education plus imagination. That's what the army needs up at the top. I didn't have the education. Just had notions and didn't have the sense to keep them to myself. Found myself retired ... but figured if Dave learned something important, and we could get someone with a West Point background interested enough, we'd be doing the country a real service."

In the next half hour, while I tried to restrain my impatience, we learned that the League of Nations was on a par with the league of mice which solemnly decided that the way to security was putting a bell on the cat, and that disarmament was the next thing to treason. There were other countries who signed pacts and continued to rearm secretly, etc., and if we didn't have some new ideas to match them when they were ready to move, etc. Letting the Japanese take over Manchuria should have shown any intelligent person how worthless the League was, and with the kind of government we had now, it was just as well we were out of it, etc. I tried not to glance too often at the notebook in the major's lap, and even to make some intelligent remarks when Wing moved the conversation into the North's state of unpreparedness when anyone could see that the South was going to secede and there would be war.

Eventually, the notebook was in Will's hands, and he was puzzling over the first paragraph in Latin. Finally, he looked up. "It's a quotation," he said, "from a book that Dave identifies only as 'AA'—must be one of the rare ones at ... that place. I think I can make out what it says." He cleared his throat, and read slowly.

"'There is that which is not of the malignancy of those which serve the elder ones, yet scholars say that it has somewhat of a passive alliance with them. It is in space and yet not in space, in time yet not in time, and many and manifold are the prodigies that attend it. It moves not after it comes, nor does it harm any who pay it no heed. Yet cruel is the compulsion it has upon those who come near, and fearful the magic it enacts upon them, that they become locked in its spell which leads to madness. Seek not to go around nor over, lest you be captured, and dig not in there toward that which lies beneath. The spells of'—I can't make this out—'avail not, nor does any demon impart knowledge of it. It comes in the time of'—well, something; I cannot grasp the reference—'and goes when the time is departed.'"

The major let his breath out. "Dang it, that's better than anyone else has been able to do. And you learned that much Latin at Columbia?" The major swore to himself for a moment. "Then Dave never had to go to that place at all!"

Will shook his head. "I've read some other things, sir, which gave me an idea of what to look for—particularly when you said that Dave had been studying at—"

"It's about the wall, all right, wouldn't you say so, Thad?" Wing nodded vigorously. "Of course we were pretty sure it was. But this ties things together. There's been others like it in the past, and this is a sort of warning to leave them alone. Only, it says that once you've started to pry, you find you just can't let it alone—not easily, anyway."

"Like it had captured you and was studying you," Wing said. "You know what those initials 'AA' stand for?"

Will nodded. "I think so. It's a very old book dealing with magic and spells and very strange lore. And it fits in with some pretty awful things that are supposed to have happened. It ties in with that correspondence Dave had with—the man in Rhode Island. He's written some things as fiction but he knows a lot about this book and—that place. I'd have to study the rest of the Latin a long time to get any more, though. This first was a little easy for me, but I could see from skimming over the next passage that it's beyond me. You have to know a fair amount of what is being talked about to make any sense of this sort of Latin."

"Then I guess Dave did get his foundation there," the major agreed. "Would have gone to Italy last year, if. ...." He was silent, and we didn't break the brown study into which he fell for a while. "You can borrow that notebook for as long as you need it," he said. "And if you want to look at the wall a bit more, that's all right with me, so long as you don't dig. Even that author says you shouldn't dig—I'm sure he's talking about the wall. Must be others like it—or there were others like it back whenever it was he wrote. Middle Ages, I guess."

"Older than that," Will said. "This book is a translation from the Arabic."

The major whistled. "Arabic, eh? That goes way back. Those old boys had one helluva civilization when we were still in a pretty barbaric state."

"There's one thing I'd like to try," Will said slowly. "I had another fraternity brother who lives around this area. He was an aviation enthusiast and had a plane of his own the last I heard from him. Taught me a little flying and parachute jumping. I'd like to see if I can come down behind the wall in a parachute."

"Now that would be interesting," allowed Thad Wing.

And the upshot of it all was that Will made a long distance call and managed to contact Max Bentley. There seemed to be no end of new things I was learning about my partner on this trip. It was not exactly news to me that Will was interested in flying and had done a little while he was knocking around after graduating from college. But he'd never mentioned parachute jumping. The plans were that I'd stay on with Wing while Will drove over to make arrangements with Max. Will was going to try to come down behind the wall via parachute. Both Wing and the major were impressed, and I reaped some of the benefit of our advanced status; I was invited to join them fishing the next morning.

I had thought I knew a little about fishing. Wing and the major had a fine morning, and I suppose they chuckled for years afterward about my part of it. If you don't mind, we will shift scenes here and cut directly to that afternoon, when Wing, the major, and I gathered in the meadow to await Will's arrival with Max in Bentley's autogyro. He'd phoned to let us know when they'd arrive, and what he wanted me to do.

Will looked a little pale when he climbed out, but recovered enough to introduce Max around. We learned the reason for his distress quickly enough. The wall could not be seen from the plane at all. Looking down, they saw a symmetrical layout of wooded hill, large meadow flat enough for a plane to land, and the road.

"It's about as easy to explain as what we've come up against so far," Will said. "And you saw how low we were when we were going right over the road. I took some pictures ... did you bring the flags, Clyde?"

I nodded, and set them up in a twenty-foot triangle. "As soon as you spot them with the binoculars, you get into position and jump," I told him. "We'll all see whether or not you come down behind the wall."

Thad Wing knocked out his pipe and spat, and the major kept a poker face, but it was pretty clear to me what they were both thinking. I was tempted to ask them if anyone had tried this before, but I just couldn't. If it had been tried before and hadn't worked, I didn't want to know that yet. The one thing I could be sure of was that if it had been tried before, the failure had been no more harmful than trying to walk around the wall or climb over it. We took some pictures of the wall from where we stood.

We watched the autogyro ease up gradually. There was no wind, so it shouldn't be too difficult, Will had said, to make the jump right. If he failed the first time, he could try again.

We all had glasses, and the three of us fixed them on Max's plane. There! There went Will, twisting and tumbling; he was a black speck for a moment, then the white of the parachute mushroomed out and the abruptness of the fall stopped.

It seemed agonizingly slow, but after a while it was clear to us that he would land behind the wall. There could be no doubt about it. If he couldn't get over it to us, then Max could make a landing on the same side and fly him out. I cut loose with a cheer when I saw that drifting shape float down on the other side of Settler's Wall, out of sight, but I cheered alone. Wing and the major had interested expressions on their faces; they waited for a moment or two, then, as if on command, turned around.

So did I. I saw why I had cheered alone. Will Richards, parachute and all, was behind us.

The major stood there like a statue for a moment, and then he said one word: "Dynamite." He said it without raising his voice, or using any particular inflection, unlike his usual way of talking. But I knew at that moment that he really did have feelings about the wall after all. He hated it.

Max Bentley was upset. He, too, was sure that Will had come down on the other side, and this was a lot different from just hearing a fantastic story. I was glad that I hadn't asked my question earlier. When Bentley joined us, and Will had struggled out of the harness, the parachute was folded, etc., I put it to the major. He nodded. "He's the third," he said. "A friend of Dave's tried twice. No one's been able to get to the other side of that wall at all."

"So you're going to blow it up?" asked Bentley.

Thad Wing shook his head. "Nope, just try to blow a hole *through* it."

It was clear that Wing and the major knew a great deal more about the wall than they had let on. My feeling was that the attempt would show that you couldn't penetrate the surface at all, but the drill that I held seemed to go in easily enough when Bentley struck it with the hammer. Wing prepared the dynamite and set the fuses, three sticks in holes as close together as feasible. The major lit the fuses, then we let him lead us to the proper distance. I felt a momentary sense of relief that working with dynamite was not among Will's irritating list of accomplishments and experiences.

The explosion sounded impressive to me, but Thad Wing shook his head. "Not quite right. Didn't sound quite right when the drills were going in, either."

Well, it looked promising enough. There was a good-size section blown out, leaving a deep cavity. Fragments of stone—substance—were on all sides; we dragged out several large chunks and threw them aside. The wall now had a definite mark upon it, a hole of particularly deep-looking darkness. But no daylight. We had knocked a hole into the wall, but not through it. Will walked over to the autogyro and came back with a flashlight which he poked into the cavity.

"It goes down," he said. "It goes way down."

We got some rope and Will tied it around his waist, as if he were going to be let down into a well. Somehow, the idea seemed acceptable, just as we found ourselves accepting everything about Settler's Wall, bit by bit, even while something inside us was screaming. Bentley and I held on to the rope; three tugs would be the signal to haul Will back.

We saw him go in, saw the momentary gleam of the flashlight, and watched the rope play out. It seemed like hours, but could not have been more than a few minutes at the most, when the tugs came. We all started pulling until Will came into sight. He was very pale, but managed to keep a poker face to match Settler's. "There's no way through the wall, either, Major."

None of the photographs taken from the plane came out, and we never so much as thought of taking some fragments with us.

4

The next day, we said goodbye to Major Settler and Thad Wing, with thanks for their hospitality and cooperation, and Will promised to return the notebooks. He spoke a little more quietly than before, but apparently he had slept all right. I hadn't; I'm not used to sleeping with a light on. Taking it all in all, I wonder if he hasn't recovered better than I have. It is true that he always carries a flashlight with him, won't go into a dark room without turning it on first, won't switch it off until another light is on, and won't turn off the last light in a room under any circumstances. He nearly died a year or so later when there was a power failure, no electricity for nearly forty-eight hours, and we had to rely on candles and oil lamps. The batteries in his flashlight ran out, and I'll never forget the gasp he gave as he saw the light give its warning flicker. He pressed it into my hands, whispered, "Clyde, turn it off and light the lamp," then clapped both hands to his eyes and faced the wall.

Now and then he talks in his sleep about a hole which keeps going down and down, and he's dropped his flashlight, which goes out. But the light from the flashlight isn't off. It's still there, drifting away gradually like smoke. He has this dream every so often, and apparently it is always the same, but he never talks about it when he wakes up. I've never mentioned it to him, and I don't want to ask him any questions. I've tried not to write this story for thirty years ....

He worked on Dave Fenner's notebooks that autumn, but wouldn't discuss them—not yet, was the way he put it. He was waiting for something. He wouldn't tell me what it was. I tried to decipher some of the Latin quotations, but could make nothing of them except that there was something about magic and something about monsters—or maybe it was something monstrous. We had photographs of the wall, showing how it looked before and after the dynamite experiment. A few months later, Will returned the notebooks to Major Settler with a letter of thanks, saying that they contained a great deal of ancient lore, valuable to a scholar, and very likely of use to someone who wanted to research old Latin manuscripts—especially ones in corrupt Latin—but nothing further that really related to the wall. I didn't accuse him of lying, but I can't help but feel that he was.

5

Early in March 1936, a letter came from Thad Wing, with a photograph enclosed. Wing had not only included his car, with the 1936 license plates clearly visible, but had followed our lead with the photographs we took before dynamiting; we had written our names and the dates on the back. The major and a couple of others endorsed the picture he sent.

It showed the wall, and there were still traces of the hole in it. Traces. Most of it was filled in. The accompanying letter avowed that neither Major Settler, Wing himself, or anyone else had made any moves toward repairing the wall. All the fragments had disappeared.

You can see now why I've been reluctant to tell this story, as interesting as some of the aspects of it are. Settler's Wall was not of stone, or any other substance we're familiar with, though it seemed to me to be more nearly like stone than anything else. There was some sort of phenomenon connected with it, as a result of which one could neither go around it or over it, nor through it—in fact, it seemed that there just wasn't any other side at all. I've heard of mobius strips, of course, but it couldn't have been a mobius strip.

Then came the hurricane of 1938. I was in Brooklyn that night and, oddly enough, there was no indication where I was that the storm was anything really unusual. The wind was considerable, and there was a lot of rain. But it wasn't until the next day that I found out how serious it had been.

When I got back to work, a week or so later, Will was away, and a letter from Maine arrived before he returned. I didn't open it, but I felt sure that there was news of the wall in it.

There was. The letter included another authenticated photograph of a long trench beside the road we had traveled. The wall was gone. Some people in the area, Thad Wing wrote, believed there had been a slight earthquake, but seismologists did not agree with them.

That is the end of my story, except for what Will said when he looked at the photograph.

"Of course," he whispered, "of course. 'In space yet not in space ....' It swam away."

Richard L. Tierney has the rare ability to weave together a tapestry of what might at first seem incompatible threads. His Simon of Gitta tales (soon to appear in this series as *The Scroll of Thoth and Other Tales of Simon of Gitta*) and novels like *The Winds of Zarr*, the Red Sonja series (with David C. Smith), *House of the Toad*, and *Lords of Pain* manage marvelously to combine elements of Robert E. Howard's Hyborian Age, Lovecraft's Cthulhu Mythos, Clark Ashton Smith's decadent mysticism, plus bits and pieces of C. B. de Mille, George Lucas, and the Bible. You can see who taught Simon his tricks! In this early and entertaining tale, Tierney combines a formula Mythos tale with a theme from various campy fright flicks, grotesquely horrific in the same way some of the tabloids' headlines are. I'm thinking of classics like *They Saved Hitler's Brain*, *The Brain That Wouldn't Die*, *Re-Animator*, *The Man with Two Brains*, *Frankenhooker*, etc.

Those with long memories may recall the original appearance of this story in *Crypt of Cthulhu*. It appeared there minus a few lines of text which are restored here. The use made of the *Necronomicon* here reminds us that even for Lovecraft the Book of the Arab need not always denote the looming of the Cthulhu Mythos and its cosmic Entities. Alhazred had plenty of nasty secrets to share. Note, too, how, as in many or most stories in which the blasphemous text appears, its chief role is to take the part of the chorus in the ancient Greek tragedy, interpreting the action much in the fashion of a movie voice-over, a TV laugh track, or even the musical score of a movie.

"The Howler in the Dark" was written back in 1957, but first appeared in *Crypt of Cthulhu* #24 (vol. 3, no. 8, Lammas 1984).

The Howler in the Dark

by Richard L. Tierney

I.

I rving Hamilton pulled the collar of his topcoat closely about his throat as a gust of icy wind lashed his face with tiny snow crystals. Far below he could hear the thunder of the waves dashing in wind-lashed fury against the base of the cliff. Carefully he followed in the footsteps of his companion, keeping close behind him and occasionally glancing out over the storm-tossed sea. He wished the narrow footpath was not so near the edge of the precipice and that it did not wind so obscurely among the jagged boulders and protruding rock formations.

As they topped a rise, Hamilton's companion stopped and pointed away toward the next jagged ridge of the clifftop. Hamilton thrilled as he saw the irregular outlines of an old castle silhouetted against the gray northern sky.

"There it is," said his guide. "Duncaster Abbey—or what's left of it."

Hamilton eyed the dark pile with careful interest. Much of the ancient edifice had crumbled into ruin, and only one dark tower now protruded intact above the ragged battlements to stand, like a symbol of mystery, against the lowering sky. The entire structure seemed almost part of the cliff—a pinnacled outcropping balanced high and precariously above the roaring sea. To the east, wooded hills rolled away to form a panorama of wild beauty—frozen, snow-clad and desolate.

"How delightfully Gothic," exclaimed Hamilton. "And you say, Clyde, that it's supposed to be haunted?"

Clyde Mayfield, turning his back on the chilling wind, answered his friend with a gesture of derogatory amusement.

"Not haunted," he laughed, "just inhabited. The townspeople like to dramatize this place."

"I can see why! It's so picturesque and colorful ...."

"Not so very colorful today, I'm afraid," said Mayfield, shivering. "We should have picked a better day to come out."

"I suppose we'd better start back, then—though I *would* like a closer look. Perhaps we can come back another day when it's not so cold."

They threaded their way carefully back along the wind-swept footpath and, ten minutes later, after reaching the road and Mayfield's parked car, were speeding back to the town of Duncaster.

"Sorry I coaxed you into bringing me out here on a day like this," said Hamilton, "but I didn't realize the weather would be so nasty."

"Quite all right—I wanted to show you the place sometime during your visit, and Sunday's the only day I can leave the pharmacy for long. Besides, I find the walk and the view invigorating."

Hamilton settled back contentedly and watched the countryside flow past. There was something strange and awesome about these desolate hills—something about the way the black, gnarled oaks clung to their craggy, snow-covered flanks that suggested fleeting visions of olden times. He turned once more to Mayfield.

"Why do the townspeople dislike the castle so much?"

Mayfield laughed. "They don't—they love it. You'll learn to take what they say with a grain of salt if you stay here awhile. That castle is Duncaster's only claim to fame, and it's kept the gossips hereabouts entertained for centuries, ever since it was finally abandoned around 1700—"

"But I thought you mentioned that it was inhabited," protested Hamilton.

"Ah! so I did. This year two fellows have been living there. Come to think of it, they're Americans—fellow-countrymen of yours. Since you're so interested in the place, perhaps you could strike up an acquaintance with them and get them to show you around."

Hamilton, an architect by trade and possessing a passionate interest in antiquarian architecture, leaned forward eagerly and asked: "Do you think they would?"

"I don't see why not. Still ...." Mayfield pursed his lips thoughtfully. "It's hard to say. I've seen them only the few times they've come to my pharmacy. They're not at all talkative. I think they're engaged in some kind of scientific research."

"A ruined castle seems a strange place to conduct research."

"Maybe they want privacy."

Hamilton laughed. "You're too unimaginative! Don't you see what we have here? Two mysterious strangers living in the remains of an ancient castle, procuring strange chemicals from the local pharmacist for some nameless purpose—ha! All we need is a distressed damsel in a white nightgown and we have all the elements for a first-rate Gothic horror story."

"Now you're beginning to sound like the townspeople—"

"Aha!" cried Hamilton triumphantly.

"Furthermore," Mayfield continued, "the men have never ordered any 'strange' chemicals from me—merely a variety of common pharmaceutical and medical supplies."

"Simply no imagination," grinned Hamilton.

Mayfield shrugged. "Maybe not, but imagination nets me no profits. I don't care if they're building Frankenstein monsters if it keeps them as good customers of mine as they have been."

Now, as the car topped a rise in the road, the lights of the village of Duncaster hove into view, softly brilliant beneath the mantle of dusk creeping out from the westward hills. Those lights, gaily colored, amid the quaint decorations in the house windows, reminded the pair that Christmas was only a week away, and their conversation turned involuntarily to brighter things.

As Hamilton shared a cheerful Sunday dinner with Mayfield and his family, the topic of the afternoon's discussion was far from his mind. Later, however, as he retired to the Mayfields' comfortable guest room and lay listening to the winter wind before drifting off to sleep, he could not help but recall his visit to the old castle by the sea—that bleak, age-haunted pile of masonry standing black and wind-swept above the angry, pounding sea—and wondered about the two strange men who chose to live there in such lonely isolation.

II.

When Hamilton woke next morning it was late; Mayfield had already left for the pharmacy. Accordingly, after partaking of a breakfast Mrs. Mayfield had accommodatingly kept warm for him, he set out on a solitary jaunt through the streets of Duncaster.

The sky was clear and blue. A crisp wintriness sparked the air. Hamilton breathed deeply, enjoying the quaint atmosphere of the old village and watching the townspeople bustling about in their preparations for Christmas. Though he had been here only a week, many of the people hailed him by name as they passed him on the street, and he began to feel a sense of easiness and belonging steal over him.

Entering a small bookshop which he had begun to frequent almost daily, he closed the oaken door with its diamond-paned windows and stamped the snow from his boots.

"And how be you today, Mr. Hamilton?" asked old Mr. Scott, the white-mustached proprietor, his blue eyes twinkling from behind his thick, square spectacles.

"As chipper as you look to me, Eric—or so I hope," said Hamilton. "I'm wondering if you can show me any books recording the history of this region."

"I think so." Eric Scott fumbled around on his bookshelves and presently withdrew a dark, worn volume. He thumbed through it rapidly, peering intently at the yellowed pages.

"Here it is," he said finally, pointing to a chapter heading. "This covers it all from Roman times to the nineteenth century. Please handle it gently, Mr. Hamilton—that book is over one hundred and fifty years old."

"I certainly will. May I read it here?"

"Of course. Use the table by the window. It's a pleasure for me to see a man of your age enjoying the old things that so many have forgotten how to enjoy."

Hamilton sat down and opened the old book. He felt again the comfortable sense of belonging. It was a privilege, he knew, even to be allowed in old Eric Scott's bookshop, let alone to be free to browse amid his fascinating, antiquated tomes. Scott's stock was entirely of rare, old items and all his business was done by mail-order, so that profane hands never touched a book without a prior reimbursement sizable enough to indicate that the book would receive shelf space in a loving home. Only Mayfield's assurance, plus Hamilton's obvious enthusiasm toward ancient architecture and all writings pertaining thereto, had relaxed the old man's guard and finally endeared the American to him.

Hamilton soon lost himself in the old book. The chapter he was reading dealt with the history of Duncaster and the larger, nearby community of Burntshire. Presently he was gratified to find a fairly lengthy description of Duncaster Abbey. The castle, it seemed, was far older than Duncaster itself. The conquering Romans had found ancient rings of stones there and, after abolishing the pagan rites which the natives had practiced, had built a fine, colonnaded temple of their own—which was, in turn, destroyed centuries later by bands of Vikings who for a time overran northern England.

It was during the twelfth century that the Norman-French Baron Hugo de Taran returned from the Crusades and built the first castle on the site that was later to be Duncaster Abbey. Baron de Taran ruled his serfs with no more than the usual harshness of the time, but was reputed to practice non-Christian rites which generated a great deal of gossip and repugnance—rites which, it was said, included even human sacrifice. Baron de Taran's Frankish mother was of the "d'Erlettes of Averoigne", a lineage and a region both long associated with sorcerous practices; moreover, it was said that the Baron, during his campaigns against the Paynim in the Holy Land, had acquired for spoil certain ancient documents written by the magi of Arabia and Egypt. However, Church rule was weak on the frontiers of what passed for civilization in those Dark Ages, and the heads of Baron de Taran's accusers were soon skewered on pikes to dry in the sun.

The descendants of Hugo de Taran, according to legend, used their position of lordship to carry on the blasphemous tradition their sire had begun. Some even claimed the ancient Roman and Celtic rites had been revived. Lights and sounds were seen and heard about the castle on certain nights of the year, while people who mysteriously vanished on those same nights were never seen again.

These sinister activities began to decline during the fourteenth century as Catholicism became ever stronger in England. By the 1660's, perhaps because of the iron rule of the Calvinistic Church of Scotland, the activities had ceased altogether. But then, in 1690, when the problem of witchcraft was also being confronted in the American colonies, the village of Duncaster was smitten with a strange terror which might have been a plague. The cause of the widespread deaths, however, was unanimously believed to be connected with the last members of the declining de Taran line, and the Church of Scotland was called upon to take action. There followed the witch-burnings of 1690, which apparently ended the reign of the hated lords who had ruled for so long with such superstition-inspiring terrorism.

The clergymen chronicling these events were vague, and only hinted at the things which were dragged to light from the towers and dungeons of the ancient castle. Signs of paganistic ritual were abundant, and there were remains of bloodstained altars inscribed with primal symbols of forgotten meaning. Of the volumes of accursed elder lore alleged to have been collected down the centuries by the wicked barons, not a trace could be found, and it was assumed they had been carefully secreted in some inaccessible nether crypt. On these grounds, the Church ordered that the entire castle be burned, so that the frightful knowledge of the de Tarans might never be brought to light and spread abroad.

Though the castle was not destroyed utterly, its charred remains lay abandoned for over a century. Then an attempt was made by the Anglican Church to use the edifice, and it was partly rebuilt and given the name of "Duncaster Abbey." For some reason, however, the building was used as a monastery for only a few months, after which it was abandoned once more. This time it lay vacant until the present day—or, rather, Hamilton reflected as he finished reading the account, until the two Americans had established themselves in it nearly a year ago.

"Did you find what you wanted?" asked the old bookseller as Hamilton closed and laid aside the aged volume.

Hamilton nodded. "Fascinating! What do you know about the two men now living in the castle? I'm hoping to get their permission to look it over."

Eric Scott brushed back his thinning hair thoughtfully, and Hamilton sensed a slight uneasiness in the expression of his watery blue eyes.

"Those two are an odd pair," he said. "I'm not sure I'd care to know them better. Just my own impression, of course—but you'll find most people hereabouts will say the same."

"Why?" said Hamilton.

"It's nothing anyone can lay a solid finger on—but let me tell you something ...."

The old man launched himself into an account of what he knew and what local gossip had to say about the strangers, and Hamilton leaned forward on his elbows and listened attentively.

It was during the previous February that the strangers had first appeared in Duncaster, residing in old Mrs. Knapp's rooming house near the sea-road and having nothing to do with the townsfolk. Here they lived for more than a month, making occasional trips to the city of Burntshire or out to the deserted castle by the sea. Their brief appearances on the streets of Duncaster, sporting their brown beards, wide-brimmed hats, and long, dark overcoats, soon earned them the reputation of ludicrous, albeit somewhat sinister, eccentrics.

Old Mrs. Knapp talked a great deal about the pair, and about the many crates of electrical apparatus, glassware, and books which they had lugged from their station wagon to the upstairs rooms they had rented. The men gave their names as Pitts and Taggart, though for some reason Mrs. Knapp preferred to think these were not their true appellations. Indeed, the landlady, gossip that she was, took a certain pride in her mysterious tenants and no doubt often exaggerated their peculiarities. Their main trait, however— outstanding in such a small community—was their extreme taciturn reticence. Their accent proclaimed them Americans, but other than this bit of information nothing factual could be deduced.

Next to old Mrs. Knapp, however, Eric Scott himself was probably the foremost authority on the men. They had actually written to him shortly before their arrival, professing an interest in certain rare old books, and had subsequently visited him several times in his musty old bookshop. Scott had been vaguely disturbed at some of the titles they had mentioned, for he had heard terrible things of the blasphemous *Necronomicon* of the mad Arab Abdul Alhazred, and he associated monstrous legends of evil with certain odd names inscribed on the yellowed papyri of the fragmentary *Book of Thoth-Ammon*. He was somehow glad that he was almost entirely unable to aid the strangers in their quest, and hoped they would not be inclined to seek further for the information they desired.

Besides Eric Scott's old bookshop, the strangers also began to frequent Mayfield's Pharmacy and Howell's Medical Supply store. Occasionally they would drive over to Burntshire to make use of the library there and, as the gossip soon had it, to request from the librarians anything pertaining to the ruins of Duncaster Abbey.

Then, during March, the strangers journeyed to London and apparently made some transaction with those who owned the castle, for on their return to Duncaster they immediately began to transport all their belongings to the ancient edifice. After finally completing their change of residence, Pitts and Taggart had paid off old Mrs. Knapp, thus breaking all ties with the world. Many of the townsfolk had been shocked at all this, for to the religiously orthodox the castle was symbolic of supernatural evil from time immemorial.

For several months the two continued to dwell in their strange abode, virtually cut off from the outside world, for the nearest road was more than half a mile from the castle. Infrequently they would pick their way over the old footpath along the ragged sea cliffs and drive into town to purchase large quantities of food and other supplies. Finally they sold their station wagon to a man in Burntshire, retired to the castle, and vanished into utter seclusion. The town gossips, of course, speculated wildly but futilely on the activities of the two Americans.

Toward summer, however, events took a darker and more sinister turn with the disappearance of little Tommy McCallister, who vanished mysteriously one afternoon while playing with several friends near the bluffs by the sea. According to the other children, Tommy, who was known as a rather aggressive youth, boasted that he was not afraid to approach the forbidding castle and attempt to spy on its two mysterious inhabitants. Against the advice of his companions, the lad had set out to prove good his boast, charging the rest to wait for his return. They had seen Tommy walk off toward the northern horizon and vanish into the dark woods which surrounded the castle on its three landward sides; though they waited for nearly three hours, the boy did not return. At last, seeing that dusk was near, the youngsters turned reluctantly homeward.

At first the children said nothing to their elders about Tommy, for their parents had sternly warned them not to play near the sea; but next day, when the frantic McCallisters began to inquire about their missing boy, the youngsters finally broke down and confessed what had happened. Immediately a search party set out to scour the wooded hills near the sea. Yet, though the searchers persisted throughout the day and part of the night, they found no trace of the missing child.

The townspeople, however, were not totally surprised at this failure, for many had already begun to hint sullenly that the boy had met with foul play. It was Constable Dunlap, the town's single law-enforcement officer, who suggested this possibility most strongly, pointing out that the boy had been last seen actually approaching the old castle with the intention of spying on its inhabitants. Was it not possible that these reclusive eccentrics might be madmen who would not hesitate to inflict harm on any they considered trespassers?

On hearing Constable Dunlap's opinions, the villagers immediately accepted them as fact and displayed a great deal of emotional indignation.

They loudly demanded that Dunlap go forth and arrest the pair—though none volunteered to accompany him—and the very next morning the constable set out to question the dwellers in Duncaster Abbey.

He did not return. When it was learned that the constable had vanished as mysteriously as Tommy McCallister, a great furor ensued. Officials in Burntshire were informed, and the sheriff and several of his local constabulary were sent immediately to check up on the inhabitants of the castle. This they did, but the results of their investigations fell far short of satisfying the citizens of Duncaster.

According to the sheriff, the two Americans had received him and his men openly and even hospitably. They were very accommodating, offering no resistance to a search of the premises and answering all questions with seeming frankness while expressing a desire to help in any way they could. The sheriff was not convinced of their sincerity, of course, but search as they might, his men could find not the slightest trace of anything even remotely suspicious. Judging by the furnishings and books about the castle, the Americans were merely a pair of scholarly bachelors engaged in antiquarian pursuits. After several hours the sheriff and his men left, annoyed at having no evidence on which to base an arrest.

It appeared, however, that the townspeople might have been wrong about Pitts and Taggart; for the very next day, when a group of fishermen found the body of Tommy McCallister washed up on the seashore just south of Duncaster, there were no indications whatsoever that the boy had met death by violence. The autopsy performed by the mortician in Burntshire revealed no indications of murder, and it was officially assumed that the thirteen-year-old boy had fallen from the cliff into the sea while returning from the castle by way of the narrow footpath.

Constable Dunlap's fate, however, was more perplexing. No trace of him was ever found. For many weeks the sheriff continued his investigations, several times requestioning Pitts and Taggart and searching their Gothic residence for some clue. Each visit was met by the same lack of either resistance or evidence, and the sheriff was at last reluctantly compelled to admit—officially, at least—that the curious pair probably had nothing to do with the disappearances. Probably Constable Dunlap had fallen into one of the fairly numerous pits or crevices which were known to be a hazard in the hilly woodlands along that seacoast.

The case was brought to a final close early in the fall by the sheriff's untimely death, and the official who replaced him filed the report of the affair and soon forgot about it. Having no personal interest in the case, the new sheriff was content to regard it as largely a sensationalistic uproar. The people of Duncaster, however, held to their opinions and continued to regard the castle and its inhabitants with distaste. Dark speculation continued to flit from mouth to mouth—whispers not only of possible murder, but of wilder things like torture, witchcraft and human sacrifice. There were even those who maintained that the old sheriff's death might not have been as simple as it seemed—that Dr. Bannister's diagnosis of some "strange, epileptic-like seizure" may have been only a cover-up for his own ignorance. Certainly there had been something disturbing about the way the sheriff had screamed out in the night just before he was found dead in his room, his eyes fixed wide as if in horror—but then, all this was idle gossip by rustics whose only traditions were handed down from superstitious peasants of the Dark Ages.

Twice more the strangers visited Duncaster, hiking to town on foot, but now they were regarded with revulsion rather than amused curiosity. Only a few local tradesmen, whose shops they patronized lavishly, would look upon the pair with anything less than aversion. Both times they visited the old bookshop of Eric Scott, purchasing various old volumes of ancient religious and Rosicrucian lore. Scott remembered that these books dwelt largely on subjects such as hypnotism, astral projection, and hidden powers of the mind, and that the men had referred to older and darker texts dealing with half-forgotten secrets that had barely managed to struggle down the ages from times of unguessed antiquity. What these men sought to achieve through the acquisition of such long-suppressed knowledge, Scott did not like to guess.

For the rest of the autumn, Pitts and Taggart were seen no more except by a few early fishermen who, from the distant vantage of their boats, claimed to have noticed the pair combing the beach beneath their crag-perched castle, gathering objects washed up by the Atlantic tides. However, the citizens of Duncaster did not forget, and the gossips whispered of dim lights and wild cries which had issued from the castle on the night of All Hallows Eve; while thereafter, some claimed, one could hear an eerie, mournful howling if one stood in certain places at the base of the castle-crowned precipice. Few ventured to prove these things for themselves, however, most preferring to accept the testimony of the local story-tellers. And so it was that, after nearly an entire year, the mystery of the dark strangers of Duncaster Abbey was as baffling—perhaps even more baffling—than it had been on the day of their arrival.

III.

At first Hamilton did not realize that Eric Scott had finished speaking; the old man's story had held him enthralled. Feeling vaguely uneasy, he tried to bring his mind to focus on the present.

"That's quite a story," he said. "Just what do *you* believe about the Americans?"

Scott shrugged. "I'm not ready to believe everything I hear, Mr. Hamilton, but at the same time I'll not go out of my way to scoff at everything that seems strange. It's my opinion that those men are up to something they shouldn't be. I know too much about the books they've sought to doubt that."

Hamilton's uneasiness increased. There were many points in common between Scott's story and the account he had read of the de Taran line of olden days—mysterious disappearances, forbidden books of dark lore, hints of witchcraft and fearful rites practiced within the castle's black precincts .... He rose from his chair and, thanking the old bookseller, set out rather hurriedly into the open air of the street. Somehow he was glad to leave the bookshop with its dry atmosphere of age and stuffiness, glad to feel the winter wind blowing cold against his face.

Later, however, as he chatted with Mayfield at the pharmacy, he found himself actually chuckling over the odd notions of the aged bookseller.

"Yes, old Scott is quite a storyteller," said Mayfield. "He's full of odd notions—especially when it comes to the subject of Duncaster Abbey."

"He certainly has excited my curiosity," grinned Hamilton. "I simply can't leave without seeing that old castle now—and meeting its inhabitants!"

Mayfield glanced at his watch. "Look, I'll be busy for the rest of the afternoon, so why don't you take my car and drive out there yourself? The weather is fairly decent now, and you know the way."

"You mean it? You're sure you won't be needing the car?"

"Not at all." Mayfield handed over his car keys. "Just be back in time for supper or my wife will throw fits. There's an extra tire under the back seat if you should need it. Good luck!"

A few moments later Hamilton was motoring rapidly out of Duncaster, enjoying the wild beauty of the wooded hills and feeling a bit uneasy about driving upon the left side of the road. During the solitude of the drive his mind returned to the things he had read and heard in the quaint old bookshop, and he pondered again over the odd coincidences between the past and the present. Probably Scott and the rest of the townspeople, knowing the legends concerning the bygone de Taran line, had projected similar characteristics on the two strangers now residing in the Abbey.

At length Hamilton pulled over to a short turnoff and parked the car. Doubtless this was where the Americans used to park their vehicle, also. As he stepped out, he could hear the pounding of the nearby surf. It was but a short walk to the footpath along the cliff edge, and thence to the ridge from which the castle could be seen.

The place seemed less foreboding under blue sky and sunlight, but the wind still blew in from the sea with considerable gustiness, causing angry waves to crash loudly upon the rocks below. Carefully Hamilton picked his way along the footpath, remembering suddenly that the young McCallister boy must have fallen from the ledge somewhere nearby. The thought was not pleasant, and he found himself wondering again about the fate of Constable Dunlap and the odd things people had hinted concerning the sheriff's death.

Presently, the path turned away from the cliff and entered the thick grove surrounding the castle. Hamilton lost sight of the building as he picked his way among the dark boles of gnarled oaks whose branches twisted weirdly above him. His uneasiness grew as he realized how completely isolated the castle was. Yet, at the same time, he was enjoying his adventure, anticipating what his friends back home would say when he told them of the old "haunted castle" he had visited in England.

Emerging from the wood, Hamilton saw that the castle was quite near, looming above him on its rocky crag with imposing grandeur, its ruined battlements dark against the sky. He stopped to gaze at it for a moment, wishing he had thought to bring a camera; and, as he looked, he heard a strange, drawn-out wail that seemed to emerge from the base of the cliff. It was obviously, he decided, a trick of the wind as it howled among the jagged rock spires of the cliffside—and yet, it seemed at times so like the cry of a person in anguish, as though someone were actually trapped in some dark crevice or cavern within the rock, that Hamilton could easily see how the imaginations of the locals had conjured up voices from nowhere.

He climbed the remaining distance up the footpath and picked his way among the tumbled, frost-covered blocks of the shattered walls. The path ended at a door of solid oak set in a massive wall. Overcoming a momentary hesitation, Hamilton raised the heavy iron knocker and let it fall noisily against the door.

Several times Hamilton knocked, but no one answered. Perhaps, he thought, the inhabitants were ignoring would-be visitors. He had about decided to leave when he heard a clanking as of heavy bolts being shot back, and the next instant the door swung open on grating hinges.

Hamilton glanced quickly over the figure that stood in the doorway, wondering what to say for an opening. The man confronting him was slightly shorter than himself, slender, and sporting a trim brown goatee and mustache which merged together. He wore a dark coat, of a type fashionable in the early nineteenth century; it hung about his form like raven wings. His alert brown eyes gazed suspiciously at Hamilton from behind dark-rimmed spectacles.

"Sorry to trouble you," began Hamilton, "but I'm interested in the construction of this castle, and was hoping you might allow me to examine it more closely. You see, I'm an architect by trade and an antiquarian at heart—"

The man suddenly grinned and his eyes lost their suspicious glare. "Ah, of course—an antiquarian! There aren't many of us left, I fear. Do come in." Hamilton, pleased at being accepted so readily, stepped quickly inside. His host immediately closed and bolted the door once more.

"I hope you don't mind my intrusion," said Hamilton, "but I fear my curiosity concerning ancient architecture is often more than good manners can hold in check—"

"Please don't apologize. I sympathize with your interest—which is one of the reasons I chose to live here, Mister ...?"

"Hamilton. Irving Hamilton."

"Mr. Hamilton. And I am John Taggart." The man wrung his guest's hand, then motioned him to follow. They walked through several vaulted stone corridors, which Hamilton admired with great interest, and presently entered a large room sparsely but comfortably furnished with articles of nineteenth-century manufacture. Two plush easy chairs and a large mahogany table occupied the center of the room, the table being littered with books, papers, and a few glass containers of assorted sizes and shapes. Heavy, thick drapes flanked the single arched window of the chamber, hanging limply from the ceiling to the stone floor, while on either side of this narrow casement rested massive bookcases, their many shelves filled with books both ancient and modern.

"Our living room and library," said Taggart. "The table is rather cluttered, but we weren't expecting company." He began somewhat hurriedly to clear the table of its volumes and papers, placing them in various niches in the bookcases. "I judge by your accent that you're a New Englander."

"That's right. And judging by *your* speech, I'd say you're originally from the upper Midwest."

"You are perceptive," said Taggart briefly. "But, come—I'll show you around the castle. It isn't often I meet anyone with interests similar to my own, and it does me good to know there are still those who find joy in the antiquated things of the world."

So saying, Taggart conducted Hamilton through several halls and chambers on the main floor, then gradually worked upward to higher suites of rooms. Hamilton became deeply absorbed in everything around him and in his host's comments on the history of this aged Gothic structure. He reveled in the imagined glories of ages past, and speculated a bit uneasily about those who had dwelt in the castle so many centuries ago. Taggart was quite attentive to his questions and insisted on accompanying him as a guide; the man obviously took a certain pride in his strange home, and commented with great knowledge on every detail of the antiquated architecture about them. Almost it seemed that he was conducting a guided tour over which he had been many times before.

At length, after ascending a long, narrow stairway of worn stone, they emerged onto a small circular area beneath the open sky. Here the wind blustered cold and strong, but Hamilton forgot the chill as he gazed over the massive battlements of the tower and beheld the landscape of dark, wooded hills stretching away on all sides, save to the west where the gray sea roared in, all flecked with whitecaps, to crash on the coast below.

"It was from this tower," said Taggart, "that the Taran barons used to survey their broad domains."

"Ah! you know of the Tarans?"

"Of course. Why should we not—we who now occupy their ancient home? They were men of great power and vision, and their history is worthy of study. They might have ruled all England if they had not been too eager to show their hand—"

Taggart stopped speaking—rather abruptly, Hamilton thought.

"De Taran is a very unusual name," said Hamilton. "I've never run across it before."

"It is indeed. As a matter of fact, it was not the original name of the founder of the line at all. Taran is the name of one of the oldest gods to be worshiped in Europe, a god of lightning and thunder. When Caesar's legions first marched into Gaul they found the inhabitants offering up human sacrifices to this god, and certain records far more ancient than the Roman chronicles indicate that his origins go far back indeed. Christianity suppressed the worship of Taran, of course, but Baron Hugo later took up a furtive devotion to him for reasons of his own, at which time his enemies all died off rather suddenly. His power grew swiftly after that, till finally, after amassing great wealth in the Crusades, he openly styled himself Baron de Taran, removed himself from public eyes, and built this stronghold here in the north of England. Since then, they say, the enemies of the Taran line have had a tendency to die off early in life. Ridiculous, of course, but fascinating legendry nevertheless, as I'm sure you'll agree."

"I'd heard they were greatly feared—"

Hamilton abruptly ceased speaking as a low, moaning howl drifted up the shaft of the tower—a wild, despairing, windy cry like the sound he had heard near the cliff base. Taggart, however, acted as though he had heard nothing, and Hamilton wondered uneasily if the sound might have been due merely to the wind howling amid the shattered walls and battlements.

"I'm afraid there's little more to show you," said Taggart. "Come on— let's get out of this cold wind." Then, as they made their way down the tower stairs once more, he added: "I hope you have enjoyed your visit as much as I've enjoyed having you come."

"I've enjoyed this immensely, thank you; but have you really shown me everything? If I'm not being overly demanding, I'd very much like to see the wine-cellars and dungeons as well—"

"I would willingly show them to you if it were possible," said Taggart, "but, unfortunately, the cellars of the castle lie beneath the ruined portion and were filled with rubble at the time of the destruction. They are quite inaccessible."

At this point they had arrived at the ground floor and had just re-entered the spacious, sparsely furnished library when, suddenly, Hamilton heard again that faint, wailing howl of despair. This time it was clearer, and he could hardly doubt that it was the anguished cry of some living thing in dire torment. Before he could speculate further, however, a third man strode rapidly into the room and stopped abruptly upon seeing them. He was tall and lean, his pale face clean-shaven and scowling. He was dressed in the same manner as Taggart. Hamilton realized that the man must be Pitts.

The newcomer's blue eyes glared with unconcealed hostility at Hamilton. "Who is this?" he demanded of Taggart.

"A guest in our house." Taggart's voice was even yet emphatic. "This is Mr. Hamilton, an architect from Massachusetts, who is very interested in our ancient abode. Mr. Hamilton," he continued, "this is Mr. Jeremy Pitts, my friend and fellow scholar."

Pitts nodded slightly to Hamilton, then turned to Taggart. "Come quickly," he muttered, then turned abruptly and strode out of the room, his dark cloak stirring the dust into whorls behind him.

"Excuse me," said Taggart, waving Hamilton to a chair. "I have some matters to attend to briefly. I'll only be a few minutes."

So saying, he strode rapidly away into the corridor, leaving Hamilton alone and puzzled. A moment later Hamilton thought he heard the strange howling once more, but it ceased abruptly following a heavy, grating sound as though a huge stone were being moved across the floor. After this, the castle grew utterly silent.

Some time passed, but Taggart did not return. As Hamilton waited he felt more and more uneasy. His memory of the strange howling, and the present atmosphere of silent gloom, were working upon him oppressively. He found himself impatient to be gone, yet a part of him insisted that he should not leave without thanking his host. Accordingly, he selected a book from the shelves and settled back in an easy chair, intending to read until Taggart's return.

The book was a large, black volume entitled *The Complete Works of Edgar Allan Poe*. Its leaves fell easily and naturally open to a certain page, as though it had been opened at that page frequently, and Hamilton noticed several lines heavily underlined in dark pencil. The lines read:

> A wrong is unredressed when retribution overtakes its
> redresser. It is equally unredressed when the avenger fails
> to make himself felt as such to him who has done the wrong.

The lines were from Poe's story "The Cask of Amontillado"—a tale of morbid and terrible revenge. Hamilton felt his spirits darken subtly, and he no longer wished to read. Laying the book aside, he began to pace restlessly about the room; as he did so, he noticed on the table an aged tome of ponderous dimensions. Its yellowed pages were held open by a heavy paperweight; when out of mild curiosity he happened to glance at its title, Hamilton was slightly shocked to find that it was the mysterious *Necronomicon* which old Eric Scott had spoken of so hesitantly.

His curiosity aroused, Hamilton examined the book more closely. It was painstakingly hand-printed in archaic English by a certain Dr. Dee, evidently the translator rather than the author. Between the pages of this book several loose papers were thrust; some were ancient and brittle parchments covered with mystifying lines of Egyptian hieroglyphics and hieratic symbols, as well as glyphs of languages Hamilton could not identify; the rest, apparently the translations, were written in English on modern typing paper. Hamilton glanced over these translations briefly, but did not read them; certain names which he glimpsed, such as "Taaran, God of Evil" and "Nyarlathotep, the Crawling Chaos", were vaguely disturbing.

The great book itself was obviously written during a time when the world was rife with the wildest sort of superstition, for the single page Hamilton glimpsed was probably but a sample of the fantastic ideas contained within the entire volume.

> There are Ways (read the text) in which the Mind of a
> Man is like unto an Eye, in that it can be used as a Lens
> to focus the Powers that exist in the Spaces between the
> Worlds. Indeed, the Mind of any Man can be used, when
> severed from the confining ties of the Flesh and put into
> a state of Trance, as a Weapon of great Power. To the
> Sorcerer who brings such a Mind under his Control,
> nothing is impossible, for he will be able to see into the
> farthest Lands of the World by means of that Mind's Eye,
> and shall be able to inflict upon his Enemies a Vengeance
> of such Type as will leave no slightest Mark, but shall
> cause them to expire with Fear and great Terrors.

Before Hamilton could read further he heard once more the loud, grating sound, and hurriedly replaced the ancient book as he had found it. For some reason he was unwilling to have his host find him looking at the volume. He seated himself once more, and a moment later Taggart entered the

room, apologizing for having left so suddenly but stating that it could not
be helped. He did not explain the cause of his departure, however, and
Hamilton, after exchanging a few final civilities with him, took his leave.
As he walked back along the windswept path by the sea, he was
strangely troubled. Taggart, it was true, had shown him every courtesy, but
his feeling that there was some concealed mystery had only increased. For
one thing, Taggart had said there were no rooms left intact beneath the castle, yet, now that Hamilton thought of it, those weird howling sounds had
seemed to come from below—or rather, had somehow carried with them a
sense of *depth* ....

And what, he wondered, could be the cause of the sound itself? The
more he tried to recall it, the less likely it seemed that it could have been
caused by the wind or any other inanimate agency. There had been a suggestion of agony and frustration in the sound, faint as it had been, and
Hamilton grew angry at the thought of some hapless animal undergoing
strange, painful experiments in some dark chamber beneath the castle. Was
this why Taggart had been so hastily summoned—to aid in some such morbid experiment? Or was there an even darker reason? Certainly those
ancient books he had glimpsed, though ridiculous and harmless in themselves, were not the sort of books to be taken seriously by rational men.
Could the castle-dwellers be madmen who were performing magical rituals
of sacrifice for secret purposes?

As Hamilton drove back to Duncaster, mulling over his impressions, he
had to admit to himself that there was nothing on which he could put his
finger. It troubled him that there were so many points of coincidence
between the activities of the Americans and the accounts of the ancient de
Tarans. He no longer cared for the flavor of mystery which had at first
seemed so colorful to him, nor did he like the thought of those old books he
had seen, with their hints of vengeance and strange powers. The afternoon
had given him pleasure enough, but it had also left an unsavory aftertaste
with him.

IV.

"You've far too great an imagination," said Mayfield as he and Hamilton left
the supper table to retire to the den. "You say you were received very hospitably. What was it you didn't like about the men?"

Hamilton settled comfortably into a plush lounging chair as Mayfield
poured the brandy. "I'm not sure, really. Maybe it was just old Eric Scott's
gossip that set my mind going. I must admit the world seems more prosaic
now, here in your cozy den—thank you." He accepted the glass of brandy

from Mayfield, then added thoughtfully: "It's just that there's such an intense air of mystery about it all—"

"Well, forget it." Mayfield handed over a copy of the London *Times* and pointed to an article. "This should interest you, considering your taste for mystery. Have you heard of the 'screaming deaths?'"

"No. I'd sworn off newspapers at the start of this vacation."

"Ah, but you devoured the account of the Loch Ness Monster last week readily enough! You'll like this, too, I'm sure."

Hamilton sighed and began to scan the article. It seemed that several Americans visiting England had, in the last month or so, been afflicted with a strange disease which the newspapers, with typical sensationalism, referred to as the "screaming death." Although only a half-dozen people or so had so far succumbed to the disease, the strange nature of these cases had caused considerable comment. Indeed, the term "disease" had been applied only for lack of a better term. Doctors had referred to the deaths as "seizures", while psychiatrists had called them "suicidal epilepsy" and other ridiculous names, but none seemed able to point to any rational cause for the attacks. In fact, the police had gone so far as to consider them possibly an ingenious form of murder, though they were at a loss for explaining the *modus operandi*.

Specifically, the cases were alike in that the disease always struck suddenly and at night, usually in the early hours of the morning. It was as swift as it was deadly, giving no symptoms or forewarning whatsoever. The victims were invariably seized with great pain a few minutes before their deaths, as was evident by their wild and terrible cries in the night, often waking people in neighboring houses. This agony was also doubtless responsible for the hideous, contorted expressions found on the faces of the deceased, the victims invariably being dead before anyone could arrive on the scene. In every case their rooms were in chaotic disorder, suggesting that their deaths had been accompanied by violent physical spasms.

Those who advocated the murder theory pointed to this last fact as evidence of a struggle, while they also drew attention to the fact that each victim came from *the same city in the midwestern United States*. Apparently, during the last month or two, each had decided—independently and rather impulsively—to vacation in England, despite the adverse weather conditions there during the winter season. Moreover, each had held a job in the fields of law practice or legal administration; one had been a petty judge, another a former police chief, while the rest had been either policemen or lawyers. Thus some sort of pattern seemed apparent, but one which pointed in no particular direction.

The murder theory was further weakened when autopsies revealed no marks of violence or evidence of poisoning in any of the deaths. Meanwhile doctors pointed out that the common origin of these unfortunate visitors was proof of *their* theory of strange disease or plague, and urged that American medics would do well to check out the possibility.

When Hamilton finished the article, his forehead was damp with sweat and his hands shook perceptibly. Mayfield, noticing his agitation, wondered if he felt ill, but this Hamilton denied hastily, saying that he was merely somewhat fatigued and that he wished to retire early. Accordingly, after bidding his host good night, he departed to the guest room.

Hamilton did not sleep that night, however. Too many coincidences kept turning up in his restless mind—coincidences that hinted at terrifying things beyond the threshold of sane reason.

All night he tossed and turned, trying to rationalize away his terrible imaginings. He could not. His mind held too many bits of information that fit together too well. What of the old sheriff who, according to Eric Scott, had died in a way so similar to the visitors from the American Midwest; had he perhaps died because he suspected too much? What of the fact that Taggart and Pitts were also Midwesterners, as was evident from their accent?

The conclusions these ideas suggested were ones Hamilton's modern mind could not accept, yet the more he tried to shut them out of his mind the more they disturbed him. Most disturbing of all, perhaps, was the memory of that passage he had scanned in the pages of the forbidden and terrible *Necronomicon*.

At the first crack of dawn following a sleepless night, Hamilton stole silently out into the streets of Duncaster and made his way to the old bookshop of Eric Scott; his breath turned to fog before him in the cold, still air.

Scott was already puttering around the shop and, at Hamilton's insistent rapping, the old man permitted him to enter. He seemed surprised at the early visit, but his surprise changed to grave concern as Hamilton hesitantly began to tell his story.

The gossips of Duncaster never learned what was said that day behind the closed doors of Scott's bookshop, though they knew that only a matter of great importance would have kept the mercenary old shopkeeper from answering his door or telephone. Probably it is just as well—things that tend to link unguessed realms of horror with the apparently commonplace world are often better left unsaid. It was guessed only that strange volumes were diligently perused, and that knowledge of a strange kind was doubtless gained and correlated with certain facts—but what this knowledge might have been, neither Scott nor Hamilton would ever say.

That evening Mayfield, on Hamilton's return, greeted his guest with curious questions. Hamilton, though polite, seemed strangely evasive. He was thoughtfully silent at supper that evening, and hardly spoke at all until Mayfield happened to mention a topic that quickly caught his attention.

"Remember the outlandish article I showed you last night?" he remarked. "The one about the so-called 'screaming deaths?'"

"Oh—yes, I recall it," replied Hamilton, who had thought of little else all day.

"Well, there was another story in this evening's paper—"

Hamilton felt a pang of dread. Yet his voice was deliberately steady as he asked: "You mean there have been more deaths?"

"Yes—five, to be exact. This time an entire family was wiped out; people by the name of Pearson or Parson—I don't remember exactly. But they were all from the same American city as the others. Isn't it the most puzzling thing you ever heard of? The local paper's full of it—they were staying at the Claibourne Inn at Burntshire, practically next door, you might say. If you and old Scott hadn't been so lost in the past all day, you'd have heard the whole town talking about it!"

Hamilton hoped his face showed none of his inward turmoil. He knew now that he and Eric Scott must soon take some sort of action. The law, he was certain, would never solve this mystery, nor would medical science ever find a cure. By some obscure twist of chance, Hamilton realized, the mad fiends of fate had chosen him and Scott to face alone the full import of the situation, and his soul seemed to shrink within him at the thought of the terrible responsibility that now rested upon his shoulders.

V.

The wind whistled dismally among the rocks as Hamilton and Scott struggled up the steep footpath by the sea. Their uneasiness grew as the castle brooded ever more darkly and closely above them, and Hamilton wondered whether anyone had ever before spent a Christmas vacation more strangely.

"What shall they think of our visit?" asked Scott nervously. "They're sure to suspect."

"Just try to act natural. Tell them you're interested in seeing some of their old books I told you about. If they do suspect, well ...." He fingered the handle of the compact Smith & Wesson revolver that nestled in his coat pocket—an item he stubbornly risked carrying on all his travels whatever the local regulations might be.

As they reached the top of the cliff, a faint noise like rough pounding reached their ears. Hamilton gripped his pistol and led the way forward among the tumbled stones of the ruins. When they came to the end of the path they saw, to their surprise, that the oaken door of the castle hung open. It swung back and forth on its rusty hinges, causing the pounding noise as the wind banged it to and fro in its stone casement. The pair looked at one another questioningly.

"Could they have fled?" said Scott.

"We'll soon know. Come on."

They entered the castle. Fine wisps of drifted snow lay along the stone corridor. Without pausing, they hurried on until they came to the great library-room. It was as empty and cold as the corridor. The long drapes by the window stirred slightly in the draft. Most of the books, Hamilton noticed, were gone from the shelves, but a few lay scattered about on the floor. Scott began to examine these with interest, and was quickly absorbed in them.

"Incredible!" he muttered as he glanced over a mildewed volume. "I thought this work had been lost a hundred years ago." And again, picking up another: "Surely the Church would not knowingly have suffered *this* one to exist—"

Suddenly a long, low-pitched howl echoed dimly through the castle. Hamilton started as he recognized it.

"Stay here, Eric," he said. "I'm going to find out what that is, once and for all."

"I'll go with you," said the old man, but Hamilton waved him back.

"You're unarmed, and I don't know what we're up against. If I haven't returned to this room within thirty minutes, don't hang around—go back to town and bring the police."

Scott nodded and turned back to the books. Hamilton set out into the corridor. He had not walked more than a dozen paces before he heard the howling once more. Turning into a branch passage, he continued on toward the origin of the sound, uncertain that he was going in the right direction, however, so faint and echoing had been the cry …

The passage was dim, and Hamilton produced a flashlight he had brought. As he flicked it on he heard the sound once more, this time louder and obviously ahead of him. Hurrying on, he reached the end of the passage and found it blocked by a massive stone door. This door was open about half a foot and looked like nothing but a huge slab cut from the wall. It would probably be undetectable when closed, Hamilton realized. He braced himself and tugged heavily at the door, and it came slowly open with a harsh, grating sound. A surge of dank air fouled his nostrils, and he glimpsed stone stairs leading down into an inky blackness.

So there *were* still underground regions of the castle, after all! Slowly Hamilton began to work his way down, careful not to slip on any loose stone or patch of moisture. He shivered slightly at the touch of the damp walls, and brushed away strands of clinging spider web with disgust.

The sound came again, welling up from the depths, and Hamilton stopped with a momentary pang of horror. There was now evident a distinctly *human* quality in the cry. Were the castle-dwellers actually engaged in the torture of some hapless fellow being? Holding his pistol ready, Hamilton continued on.

After many windings under vaulted archways, the stair ended in a large subterranean chamber. Against the walls of this room stood several stone tables littered with great quantities of chemicals, flasks, electrical apparatus, tools, and mildewed books. It suggested to Hamilton a combination of alchemist's laboratory and electrician's workshop. Much of the floor was scrawled with strange, smudged designs, and many half-melted candles stood upright. On one stone slab in the center of the room stood several empty wine bottles and two human skulls, and Hamilton noticed that the tops of these skulls were missing, having been cut off just above the eyes. On closer examination he was appalled to observe that the skulls had evidently been used as drinking vessels!

His speculations were cut short by the weird howl from the darkness, and he continued on across the great room and entered a narrow corridor on the far side. After only fifty feet or so he emerged into a still vaster space. This, he saw with surprise, was not man-made at all, being evidently a huge cavern hollowed within the rock by natural forces. A new sound came to his ears, and he realized it was the pounding of the sea. He knew now how he had first come to hear the howling from the outside; there must be hidden fissures in the cliffside leading to this cavern.

Swiftly he crossed the stone-flagged floor, heading for a black opening on the far side. It was an artificial tunnel, obviously cut into the rock long ago. As Hamilton entered, he detected for the first time a sound that seemed quite out of place in these dim, archaic recesses. It was a soft, throbbing, pumping sound of machinery.

He advanced slowly down the narrow tunnel, keeping his flashlight partially covered so that its light would not shine out far ahead of him. The throbbing grew louder, mingled now with a rhythmic, wheezing sound which he could not identify. He clutched his revolver more tightly.

Suddenly he became aware of a low mumbling that seemed to ripple softly along the slimy walls. Advancing cautiously, he saw that he was approaching an archway to a dark chamber at the tunnel's end. The mumbling resolved itself into muttered words, and as Hamilton caught their import, he froze in the grip of a strange horror.

"Holy Mary mother of God," muttered the voice, its tones conveying a hideous undercurrent of utter despair and madness; "pray for us sinners now and in the hour of our death Holy Mary mother of God pray for us sinners now and in the hour of our death Holy Mary mother of God pray for us ..."

As the voice repeated this phrase over and over, it grew steadily louder and shriller in pitch, until at last it lost all form and coherency and burst forth in a wailing, demonic howl of frustration and misery. Hamilton, feeling himself becoming unnerved, unveiled his flashlight and cried out:

"Who's there? Answer me!"

The voice grew silent, and only the sound of the throbbing machinery pulsed down the corridor.

"Who's there?" cried Hamilton again. "Come out of there—quickly! I've got a gun, and I'm not afraid to use it!"

A hollow laugh echoed from the dark chamber, and Hamilton felt his spine prickle strangely.

"Why should I fear death?" droned the voice. "I, to whom all in life is lost?!"

"What do you mean? Who are you?"

"Men once called me Dunlap," the voice murmured, "but now they would call me—horror!"

"Dunlap! Then—you're the constable who disappeared several months ago—!"

"I was; but if you have come to rescue me, you are too late."

"But you're still alive—" began Hamilton, taking a step toward the black archway. A terrible shriek of warning from the voice made him stop short, trembling.

"No! Do not enter here if you value your sanity!" it cried.

"What—what do you want me to do?" said Hamilton. "I want to help you. Where are Pitts and Taggart?"

"They are gone," wailed the voice. "They left me here alive. They condemned me to linger on in these vaults—damn them!—and bade me remember all those I had ever aided in sending to prison while I languished here in darkness. ..."

The voice became more rapid and shrill as it raved on, and Hamilton listened in growing horror. "I *was* right about the boy—it was they who captured little Tom McCallister, and killed him in some strange way when they found his mind was not developed enough for their hideous purpose. Ha! ha! ha! But mine was—and when I came for them, they were waiting—"

"What do you mean?" urged Hamilton, horrified at the rising madness in the voice. "What have they done to you?"

"They used me—ha! ha! They took me out to unformed spaces between the stars, and made me sign the black book of Azathoth, that my mind might be put to dark and terrible uses. Then they brought me down to this room and did terrible things ... terrible things ..."

To Hamilton it was obvious the man was utterly mad, but he could not help listening with spellbound horror as the voice raved on:

"Then they looked into my eyes, and I could see into far places. There were strange and vast powers surging invisibly about me, and they forced me to use those powers in horrible ways. First it was to summon, summon, summon—and then to kill! God forgive me! It was not so bad when they made me kill the fat police chief, or the lawyers, or that senile, bloat-faced old judge; but that last time, over in Burntshire—" The voice broke in a desperate sob, then went on: "Perhaps the man *had* used his wealth for corrupt and cruel purposes and deserved to die as he did, but when they had me first slay his wife and young daughters before his very eyes—God help me! My soul shall burn forever in Hell for what I've taken part in—but, Heaven be merciful to a sinner! *Can even Hell hold agonies worse than these?!*"

The voice had risen to a shriek and now dissolved into an anguished howl of despair. Getting a grip on himself, Hamilton strode forward, determined to give what aid he could to the demented sufferer, and shined his light into the room. The light revealed a wooden table and, beneath it, a complex tangle of wires, tubes and mechanical devices—obviously the source of the strange throbbings and wheezings. Upon the table was a single pallid object, vertically ovoid and set into an iron ring at its base. At first Hamilton's mind refused to recognize this object distinctly; but, as his light fell directly upon it and he could not avoid realizing what it was, all his courage vanished in an instant of electrifying terror.

"*Kill me!*" shrieked the voice madly. "*Kill me!*"

But Hamilton, his entire being shaken with horror, ran screaming and gibbering back down the dark tunnel and out into the vast cavern beyond. His wild yells reverberated in the awful blackness as he raced back the way he had come, stumbling blindly through the subterranean halls and rooms and up the dank, slimy stairway in a mad effort to escape those hideous black regions of utter horror. And all the while that terrible, mad howl of the voice rang in his ears, urging him on in his frantic flight from those nocturnal dungeons and the horror of what he had glimpsed therein ....

Hamilton remembered nothing of what followed during the next few moments; there are some experiences too utterly terror-charged for the human mind to retain. His next conscious sensation was that of the cold sea wind against his face, and the realization that he was following stumblingly behind Eric Scott along the snow-swept footpath.

"I had to burn them," Scott was saying. "The knowledge contained in those evil books should never have been written down. I hope you will understand—"

"I understand," muttered Hamilton. "God help me—I understand!"

"What was it you saw beneath the castle?" asked Scott, disturbed by his companion's shaken condition and odd pallor. "And what happened to Pitts and Taggart?"

"They are gone—don't ask me where. Perhaps they've hidden themselves amid the wild hills to the north, or have vanished to some far land, or—or somewhere else. Wherever they are, they've accomplished their terrible revenge, and I hope we'll see them no more.

"What did I see beneath the castle? I can never know for sure, for I got only a glimpse, and God knows how overwrought my mind was in that moment—but if my senses did not deceive me, then I must forever curse the weakness that kept me from doing that which was necessary and decent. The thing that was once Constable Dunlap should not have lived on in its condition, and was kept alive only by means unknown to medical science. No, Eric, the thing I glimpsed in that black, unholy chamber beneath the castle was not entirely a man; *it was only a living, breathing, hideously animated human head!*"

Here is a tale in which the *Necronomicon* is taken merely as an "Alhazred's Lamp" capable of conjuring up worldly goodies. It serves as a kind of allegory of reading, not for the story itself, but for other close relatives in the genre, like "Legacy in Crystal" by James Causey, "Black Bargain" by Robert Bloch, "The Man of Stone" by Lovecraft, and "I Know What You Need" by Stephen King. The authors of such stories are implicitly satirized by Robert Silverberg. They are represented in the role of the short-sighted kid who manages a feat beyond the ability of Wilbur Whateley, stealing the *Necronomicon* from Miskatonic's Rare Books Collection. His criminal ingenuity may have exceeded Wilbur's, but his vision of what to do with the book was myopic indeed. He only wanted a steak dinner and some strutting babes.

That's all some writers seem to want out of the books of the Mythos, making hackneyed use of them. But Silverberg has cast himself in the role of Vorys, the serious occultist from whom Marty diverts the stolen tome. He warns the stupid kid of the powers he's trifling with. Sure enough, Yog-Sothoth appears to punish this trifler. The *Necronomicon* is meant for far greater things. The key passage here is when Marty asks Narrathoth (= *Thoth*, the Messenger of the Gods and the *Narra*tor of their myths) who the Old Ones are and receives a catechism about the Cthulhu Mythos; he pretty much shrugs it off.

"Demons of Cthulhu" originally appeared, as by "Charles Hammer", in *Monster Parade*, March 1959.

Demons of Cthulhu

by Robert Silverberg

Some pathways are too dark; they should never be explored. Some dust-covered books should never again be opened. Certain slumbering gods, their dark powers shrouded by sleep, should never again be permitted to walk in the light. The price of boldness is death, hideous and lingering.

Marty wasn't looking for any trouble, at the start. Trouble came and found him. Marty was seventeen and worked in the library of Miskatonic University as a stock boy. He wore a white smock and wheeled books around from place to place, fetching them as the professors requested them, putting the books back on the shelves at the end of the day. Marty wasn't interested in books at all. He was interested in girls, and in sneaking drinks, and in basketball. But he got $42 a week from the University for taking care of its books, and that much was okay. The money came in handy when he wanted a new muffler for his souped-up modified 1938 Ford, or when he wanted to make a big splash with one of the town girls, or when he and some pals got together over a bottle of booze that somebody had bought with a phony ID card.

Marty liked money. Money could get you nice things. So Marty pricked up his ears and listened, one day near closing time in the library, when Mr. Vorys came over to him and said, "Listen, Marty, how would you like to make an easy ten bucks tonight?"

Marty's eyes widened. Mr. Vorys was a graduate student who worked in the library to help pay his university fees. He was a tall, stoop-shouldered young man of about twenty-six, with a hollow chest, thick glasses, and a dried-out, corpse-like look about him. His first name was Theophilius, but everybody called him just Mr. Vorys. He was Marty's immediate superior in this particular section of the library stacks.

"Ten bucks? How?"

"Come in here," Mr. Vorys said, beckoning Marty toward a quiet alcove where the encyclopedia sets were stored. "Sit down."

Marty sat down facing Mr. Vorys, wondering what this was all about. He knew it didn't look good for two library employees to be sitting down so close to the end of the day. If the library supervisor came along right now and looked into the alcove, there would be trouble.

But what the devil, Marty thought. Mr. Vorys was the superior. *He* would be blamed. Marty stared into Mr. Vorys' weak, watery, washed-out-blue eyes and said, "What's the proposition?"

Mr. Vorys licked his thin, pale lips. "First promise me this: In case you decide not to go along with me, you won't reveal a word of this conversation to anybody. Is that all right?"

Marty shrugged. "Sure. I'll keep mum."

"Good." Mr. Vorys steepled his fingers. "Briefly, here's the scheme. There's a certain book in the Special Collection of the library that I want to consult. I mean, I want to take it home and consult it. But you aren't allowed to take Special Collection books out of the library, of course. So I've obtained the key to the Special room. What I propose to do is go in there after closing hours, wrap up the book I want and tie it with twine, and lower it out the window. You'll be outside waiting. You pick up the book and go away. I'll meet you at the campus coffee shop in twenty minutes and give you your money. Well?"

Marty smiled. He knew all about the library's Special Collection. He had never actually been *in* the little room, but he knew it contained forbidden books. Marty understood the pitch. Mr. Vorys had a hankering to consult one of the forbidden books in the privacy of his own bachelor flat.

It didn't seem very risky. Vorys was eager, all right, if he was willing to pay an accomplice ten bucks. Maybe he wasn't just *borrowing* a book, Marty thought. Maybe he was heisting a rare one with the idea of selling it at a profit. A new thought glimmered in Marty's head. He winked conspiratorially at Mr. Vorys, who was waiting with great anxiety for Marty's answer.

"I'm with you," Marty said. "It's a deal."

At closing time that night, when the last scholar had left the library, when Marty had hung up his smock and punched his time-clock card and checked out, he went downstairs into the little garden that fronted the library. It was late autumn, and shadows wrapped the garden in a shroud of black. A cold wind whisked through the university grounds. Marty waited.

He looked up. The window of the Special Collection room was three stories above him, a small lead-inset window that opened outward. As Marty watched, the window opened. A hand appeared, holding a package wrapped in brown paper. A stout piece of twine had been tied around the parcel. With great care the hand extended the package out over the window ledge and began to lower it. Marty watched, checking to see that no one else was around. Inch by inch the package descended.

He waited until the package had touched the ground. Then he jerked three times on the twine and sliced through the cord with his pocketknife, as arranged. Immediately Mr. Vorys, upstairs in the Special Collection library, began to reel the dangling twine in.

Marty picked up the package. It was heavier than he had expected. The book inside the wrapping paper was about the general dimensions of a telephone directory, only thicker. Vorys had sure picked out a big one to grab, Marty thought. He figured the book weighed at least ten pounds, maybe more.

Thoughts with dollar-signs attached revolved pleasantly in Marty's head, as he trudged along the campus with the package innocently tucked under his arm. He reached the coffee shop where he was supposed to meet Vorys and give him the book, but he kept on going, out the main exit of the university and along the city streets toward his home.

There was no point in handing over the book for a measly ten bucks, Marty thought. Not at all. A book rare enough to be kept in the Special Collection might be worth fifty or even a hundred bucks. Instead of turning it over to Vorys, he would take it home and read it himself, and then one weekend he would take the train down to New York City. In New York there were lots of rare book dealers who would buy anything without asking questions about it. All Marty had to do was tell them he had found it in the attic of his house, and that would be that.

A pleasant glow illuminated Marty as he made his way home. Let Vorys squawk! He couldn't do much about it without admitting that he had stolen the book in the first place.

Marty lived in a big old house in downtown Arkham. He shared it with his aunt, his father's eldest sister—a woman of close to seventy years, who paid no attention to Marty except to provide meals for him, which was the way Marty liked it. His father had been an instructor at the University until six years ago. He and Marty's mother had been killed in an auto crash then. The house was full of his father's old books, but Marty never bothered much to go near them. Books didn't interest him much. But the Dean of the University had arranged for Marty to get a job at the library, out of friendship for Marty's father.

He trotted upstairs to his room, lugging the heavy book along. He closed the door and began to rip the brown paper away from the book. He wondered what the book was.

Hurriedly stripping away the wrapping, he laid the book bare. It was thickly bound in black leather that had begun to wrinkle and corrode. The title was stamped into its front cover in letters of gold: THE NECRO-NOMICON.

Marty frowned and lifted the heavy cover. The title page read:

THE NECRONOMICON OF ABDUL ALHAZRED

Translated from the Latin version of Olaus Wormius as printed in Spain in the seventeenth century.

Shrugging, Marty turned the thick, parchment-like page and found a heading on the next: *A Warning To Those Who Peruse This Book*. He skipped that and started to flip through the book.

It was very disappointing. There was a lot of gabble about witchcraft and Elder Gods, and some stuff in a language Marty had never seen before. Certain names kept popping up on many of the pages: Yog-Sothoth, Cthulhu, Nyarlathotep. Marty began to wonder just why Mr. Vorys had been so keen on getting it out of the Special Collection.

He kept skimming, in hopes that he would come across something interesting. But the whole book seemed to be about witchcraft and stuff like that. Hundreds and hundreds of pages rambled about the Elder Gods who sleep in other dimensions and who yearn to break through once again to this world. Marty was getting bored.

Then his eye fell on one particular passage near the middle of the book:

> ... lightest of all are the slumbers of Narrathoth, who may be wakened by the veriest novice in the art. Narrathoth lies drowsing beyond the Great Gate, hideous in form, servant to the sleeping Old Ones who wait for their day once more to dawn. But Narrathoth may be summoned from his blasphemous dreams and forced to serve. One who achieves control over him has access to the wealth of the world; but great care must be exercised, for fear of Narrathoth's wrath, for even he shares the might of the Old Ones, and pity be upon him who summons him and loses control.

> Narrathoth is called by simple incantations. The blood of a male cat is needed, and the undergarment of a woman and ...

Marty read with deepening interest. He had once seen a movie in which an old book such as this had given a formula for conjuring up a spirit, and the spirit had been forced to bring food and drink and gold. Maybe there *were* such things, Marty thought. Maybe that was why this book was kept under lock and key, and why Vorys was so anxious to get hold of it.

Just as he was getting really deep in what he was reading, there was a knock on the door—the timid double knock of his aunt. Hastily Marty shoved the big book under his pillow and dumped the wrapping paper into the wastebasket. He didn't want the old lady to ask embarrassing questions about the book.

"I'm coming," he grunted, and went to the door. His aunt stood there, frowning slightly.

"There's a gentleman here to see you, Marty. His name is Mr. Vorys and he says he's from the library. He looks upset. You haven't done anything wrong, have you?"

"Not that I know of," Marty said glibly. "Okay, tell him to come up."

Aunt Martha vanished and a moment or two later Mr. Vorys came bounding up the stairs and into Marty's room. He was panting and badly out of breath. He looked as if he had run all the way from the coffee shop.

"Well?" he demanded immediately. "Where is it? Where did you put it?"

Marty grinned. "Put what?"

"The book, the *book*!" Vorys whispered harshly.

"Book? Do I have a book of yours?"

Anger flared in Vorys' washed-out eyes. "I don't know what sort of game you're playing, young man," he said in a cold, waspish tone. "I waited for you for nearly an hour, and you didn't show up." He took a ten-dollar bill from his pocket and held it out toward Marty.

"Here," Vorys said. "Here's the money I promised you. Now give me the book."

"What if I don't?"

Vorys looked ready to explode. "What do you want with it, you young hooligan? It's a book of scholarly interest. It doesn't even have any pictures in it."

"I've decided to have a look at the book myself. Maybe it's worth more than ten bucks, Vorys. Why should I hand it over to you?"

"I'll notify the authorities!" Vorys blustered. "You won't get away with this! You—"

"You stole that book from the Special Collection," Marty reminded him. "I was only your accomplice. You start howling to the authorities and they'll throw you out of the University so fast you won't know what happened for a week. You can't touch me, Vorys. So scram."

The skinny scholar drew a deep breath, puffing up his skimpy chest. "I ask you for your own sake. That book is dangerous. There are things in it that aren't for your eyes—not for the eyes of anyone who isn't properly prepared. I implore you—"

"Scram!'

"You don't know what danger the book has!"

"I know I can get a good price for it in New York. Now, will you get out, or do I have to—"

Vorys got.

After he was gone, Marty pulled the book out of hiding. So it was dangerous, eh? Maybe some of the crazy formulas in it really worked, then.

That was why Vorys wanted it so badly. Maybe you could call up demons with it. It was worth a try, Marty decided.

Tonight was Tuesday, the night Aunt Martha's sewing circle met. After dinner Marty drove her over to Mrs. Jamieson's place, arranging to pick her up around half past ten. Then he returned home. He fetched *The Necronomicon* from its hiding place once again and opened it to page 638, where the instructions on summoning Narrathoth were printed.

It wasn't really very complicated. Six or seven ingredients were necessary, and the right sort of circle had to be drawn in chalk, and certain words pronounced. If what the book said could be believed, that was all that was needed to fetch old Narrathoth from his age of slumbers.

Quickly Marty gathered the ingredients. For the woman's underwear, he borrowed one of his aunt's slips. As for the blood of a male cat, that gave Marty a bit of trouble at first. He felt squeamish about it. There was a mangy old tomcat who prowled the back fence, making noise at night and keeping people up. He came running when Marty called. Marty told himself that the tomcat would never survive the cold Arkham winter anyway, and stuffed the beast into a pillowcase.

Taking the protesting animal upstairs, Marty slit its throat—it died with a single loud squawk—and sprinkled the blood as indicated. He lit the candles, arranged the chalk properly, put the necessary props in their place, and switched off the light in the room.

Squinting by candlelight to make out the words, Marty began to read the passage from *The Necronomicon* that would summon Narrathoth. After two minutes of pronouncing the incomprehensible syllables, Marty began to feel faintly foolish about the whole thing. It was stupid to believe in things like witchcraft and demons and Elder Gods. All this rigmarole was a waste of time.

But he felt a chill creeping through the room, and it was not altogether the coldness of Arkham autumn, but a different sort of coldness. He kept reading: *"Ph'nglui mglw'nath Cthulhu R'lyeh wgagh'nagl fhtagn. Iä! Shub-Niggurath! Narrathoth! Narrathoth! Narrathoth!"*

On the final repetition of *"Narrathoth!"* a bolt of lightning leaped across the sky and thunder sounded like doom's crack in the front yard. Marty smelled ozone in the house. Everything was very quiet.

A strange light was shimmering in the five-pointed star Marty had drawn on the floor of his room. The light was now red shot through with greens, now a vivid blue, and it wavered and swayed and slowly solidified into—into a thing that gibbered and moaned within the confines of its chalk prison, and which finally spoke in a deep bubbling voice that seemed to come from the bottom of the sea.

"Who is the rash one who disturbs Narrathoth's sleep?"

Marty gaped at the apparition in his room and stepped back a few feet. So it really worked! In a dry voice he recited the formula: "I have called you by your True Name, Old One, and I command you to do my bidding."

The thing in the pentagram howled and grimaced, but it bowed down to the words. Marty stared at it. It was bigger than a man, all white and loathsome, with a ghastly bulging head and a single three-lobed eye that burned with baleful fury. Scabrous scales covered its body, and the stench it gave off was that of life older than the pyramids, life as old as the stars. Marty trembled but kept control of himself. Narrathoth could not harm him so long as the chalk barrier remained intact.

"What is your bidding, you who have captured me?" Narrathoth asked sourly.

"Get me food and drink," Marty ordered. "A bottle of champagne, make it. And a thick steak, smothered in onions."

"I obey, foolish one."

Again the lightning, and the hideous thing vanished for an instant. When Narrathoth returned, a table had been set in the middle of the room. On plates of gold rested a meal beyond Marty's powers of imagination to describe. Champagne in ice buckets, succulent meats, sherbets, salads, and all else.

Marty's eyes gleamed. "Where does all this come from?" he asked.

Narrathoth replied, "Conjured from the fabric of space and time, stupid one. Foolish it is of you to use the mighty resources of Cthulhu and the Elder Ones for fleshly things and food, but if such is your wish, I obey."

"This food—it's safe to eat?"

"I am bound by the spell you cast to serve you and to keep you from harm," the creature murmured. "So long as you control me, I cannot harm you in any way."

Marty's mouth watered. "Let's have a few dancing girls, then. Just as entertainment before dinner. And—oh, better make sure that nobody interrupts me tonight." This was going to be good! Real good!

The dancing girls appeared—three of them who looked as if they had been plucked from a Minsky chorus line. They wore only necklaces round their waists, and they danced for half an hour while an unseen musician played weird Oriental music. Then Marty grew bored, clapped his hands, and they vanished.

It was nearly ten-fifteen when Marty finished his evening's enjoyment. In fifteen minutes he would cast Narrathoth back to the darkness and go down to Mrs. Jamieson's to pick up his aunt. But his heart beat exultantly. With Narrathoth at his command, the world was his! No wonder Vorys had been so desperate to have the book!

Marty ordered the creature to whisk away all signs of the feast. Then, replete, satisfied, Marty stretched out wearily on his bed and stared at the unutterably grisly thing in the middle of the room.

"Where did you come from?" Marty asked. "I mean, how is it I was able to call you?"

"I am one of the lurkers at the threshold of the universe," Narrathoth rumbled. "In aeons gone by mighty Cthulhu and his hordes from beyond the stars ruled this world and all others, and I was of the company of Cthulhu. Now we sleep in outer darkness, waiting for Cthulhu to wake and lead us back to the worlds we ruled."

Marty shuddered. "How about this book—The Necronomicon?"

"The mad Arab, Alhazred, divined many of our secrets and wrote them therein. Many men have opened the gate to Cthulhu and peered beyond. But few mortals have walked the reaches of antique and shadowy Khem and long have lived thereafter."

"What happens to them?"

"They die," the demon said malevolently. "They fail to control the powers they have unleashed. But I weary, boy. My time is not yet come to walk the human world again, and I long to return to the slumbers you have disturbed. Free me, so I may sleep once more."

But Marty would not free Narrathoth. He made the creature talk: of Yig, Father of Serpents, and of the monstrous nuclear chaos beyond angled space that The Necronomicon cloaked under the name of Azathoth. The creature told of dead Cthulhu sleeping in his palace at R'lyeh, and of the Outer Ones who waited for the day of their return to Earth. Marty's jaw sagged open in wonder. He understood only the merest fraction of the being's story, but even that fraction filled him with awe and terror.

But time had come to dismiss the demon for tonight, and return to the prosaic world of aunts and sewing circles. Marty rummaged through The Necronomicon for the spell that would send Narrathoth back to his slumbers until called once again. There was plenty of time to examine the book carefully and discover its riches.

He began to recite the spell. Strangely enough, Narrathoth did not fade as the words continued. Instead the Elder Demon grew brighter, larger, more repellent of appearance. Several times rumbling laughs escaped Narrathoth's fleshy, drooling lips. Marty felt terror racing inside himself. The smell of ozone became strong in the room. Narrathoth still remained imprisoned within the chalk star, but he was growing more frightening of aspect every moment.

Suddenly Marty heard footsteps on the stairs. The door burst open. Vorys came running in, his face white, his eyes nearly popping from his head.

"You idiot!" Vorys exclaimed. "What have you been doing?"

Marty growled, "Get out of here!"

"You've been casting spells, but you don't know what you're doing! God, you should see the sky over this house! Purple and swollen with the Thing hovering waiting for the gateway to open!"

"I'm reciting the spell that sends Narrathoth away," Marty said. He was angry that Vorys had dared to break in on him.

The scholar rushed across the room and peered at the page from which Marty was reading. "You teenage madman!" he exclaimed. "That's the wrong page! You're reading the Invocation of Yog-Sothoth—opening the gateway to the most blasphemous of—"

It was too late. A tremendous roar of laughter rose from Narrathoth.

There was the sudden sound of smashing glass. Marty whirled in horror and saw something long and blunt at the tip come writhing through the window of his attic room. It was green and barnacle-covered, and looked like the monstrous tentacle of a giant squid or octopus, with great suckers along its foul-smelling underside.

Falling to his knees, Vorys began to chant in a panicky monotone, as if to drive away the creature that Marty had accidentally summoned up. It was to no avail. The mighty tentacle, as thick through as a man's body, moved with deadly purpose, eradicating the chalk pentagram that restrained Narrathoth. The barriers removed, Narrathoth cried out in glee, bounded up, and vanished.

Still Vorys chanted, while Marty clung to the book and shivered in terror. Marty realized what had happened now; inadvertently turning to the wrong page, he had recited a spell that invoked one of the most malignant of all the Elder Gods—and now it had come to claim its revenge!

The ghastly tentacle groped through the room, reaching out for its summoner. Marty shrank back, cowering against the wall, but the tentacle sought him out; the dread suckers fastened themselves to his body

Slowly, it drew Marty out through the shattered glass of the window. Opening his eyes for a moment, Marty looked up to see a creature whose eyes were flaming beacons the size of dinner trays, whose loathsome beak loomed disgustingly above him ...

There was a single loud shriek, and that was all.

When Marty's aunt, tired of waiting for his arrival, gave up and accepted a lift back to her house, she found a strange sight awaiting her. The entire upper floor of her house had been caved in as by a mighty hand. Crouching in the splintered ruins of the upper story was Vorys, unharmed but utterly mad, clutching to his bosom a thick book bound in black leather and muttering incomprehensible things about the Whisperer in Darkness. Stunned neighbors, unable to credit the evidence of their eyes, whispered to each other that a vast thing with tentacles and blazing eyes had hovered that night on the gables of the dead boy's home, splitting the night with obscene laughter and greedily devouring the raw and bloody doll that once had been a human being.

Doc Lowndes, reanimator of *Weird Tales* fiction in what was otherwise something of a time of famine, paid a very few new authors a high compliment: He placed their tales among the classics of the pulp era which he reprinted in *The Magazine of Horror*. This meant, in effect, that Doc was retroactively canonizing people like Steffan B. Aletti into the pantheon. For a new writer it was like getting a chance to go back in time and join your favorite baseball team.

Doc wasn't the only one who thought Aletti deserved it. Reader feedback indicated a general acclaim for Aletti as the most promising discovery the magazine had made, "the best new writer following in the vein of Lovecraft. His images are sound, his narrative smooth" (Gene D'Orsogna). Yet after a mere four stories, all published in Doc Lowndes' magazines, Steffan Aletti seemed to be gone with the wind. He seemed to have gone down with the ship when the mags folded. He moved into writing and editing in other fields and has only recently reestablished contact with the fraternity of weird fictioneers. Look for a collaboration between Steffan Aletti and your editor to be called "The Horror in the Genizah."

"The Castle in the Window" appeared in *The Magazine of Horror* #22. One more note: You will find in this story a passage that pretty well sums up the *raison d'être* of the present anthology: "I was about to put the book down ... when my eyes struck the title of *Necronomicon*!"

The Castle in the Window

by Steffan B. Aletti

I

Of course, you understand, this narrative is absolutely true, and I don't expect you to believe a word of it. I will admit that several points of this business could be explained away by chance, or power of suggestion, but I am, though an artist, a pragmatist; and I assure you, it takes only the strongest of facts to convince me of the necessity of using the supernatural, witchcraft, or fourth dimension, as an explanation. So believe what you will; I have done justice to Colin Black, and to this whole business, by way of this report. And I shall go back to my painting.

It was an unusually pleasant winter day last March, when I decided on a walk to Soho to make the rounds of the little used-book shops that abound there. I had been copying some Turners at the British Museum and, as I was up on my work, I decided to spend the evening with a book.

I went into the first one on Quill Street, Dorian's by name; it was exceedingly dusty, an unpleasant little place with books stacked waist level in boxes and bins, and stored way above arm's reach in cases along the walls. I straightaway came upon a copy of Shaw plays, and settled for it. I was on my way to the register when I saw in the back of the store a selection of ragged-looking stuff in a large basket labeled "Old personal diaries, record books, etc."

Since first-hand evidence of the past has always fascinated me, and since my roommate, Colin Black, was, in every sense of the word, a true antiquarian, dabbler in past mystiques, and occultist, I wandered over to have a look.

Most of the volumes were falling apart, having been badly bound and written on cheap paper, yet one, bound in 3/4 buckram, caught my eye because of its fresh condition. I opened it and read: *Diary of Dr. Michael Gwynn, being a daily account of his researches.*

The "researches" business piqued my interest, and I began to thumb through the dusty thing rather absentmindedly; the first date recorded was September 17, 1806, and I was about to put the book down as being of too recent a date to interest the antiquarian in both me and my roommate, when my eyes struck the title of *Necronomicon*! Farther on, under October 15, I found mention of the *Song of Yste*! I knew the titles of these monstrous books only through my roommate's interest in them, and it was for that reason that I bought the diary; how ironic it is that I thought the thing cheap at a half crown.

I took it home that evening, and presented it with a flourish to my roommate; he was at once thankful and astounded, and immediately fell to reading it. At one point he got up, and, after rifling through his desk drawers for a time, came up with a map of England. He perused it, and, tracing his finger about the surface of the thing, nodded and exclaimed in triumph. I was about to ask what he was up to, when he raced back to his chair and resumed his reading. I heard no more from him other than his occasional puffs at his pipe, and gentle curses as it would go out.

At length I finished *Don Juan in Hell,* and decided to save *Mrs. Warren's Profession* for another time. I arose and was rummaging through the refrigerator for something to eat, when Colin came into the kitchen and stood, looking at me.

"Have you read this book?" he asked in a reasonably sepulchral tone, a manner which he reserved only for moments of the greatest import.

"No," I answered simply, while suspiciously eyeing a piece of cheese that had probably been residing at the back of the refrigerator since the previous spring.

"This is probably the greatest find of the century!" he continued.

"You don't say," I replied with an interest clearly second to my interest in the cheese, which was now residing between two pieces of bread and was about to be eaten. With that irreverent reply, he jerked me away from my cheese and dragged me to the book. He commanded me to read.

> January 7, 1807.
>
> Today I have achieved the impossible. I have baptized the glass while still molten and glowing, with the terrible rites of R'lyeh. The glass is cooling now.

> January 8, 1807.
>
> The glass is perfect. It is night now, and the glass is cold, yet it still glows. Tomorrow night I shall set it in its place, and I shall be lord of Time. It is alive, and I know it will work.

> January 9, 1807.
>
> I have done it. I am now looking out into the past. I see a castle over the moor I know to be empty. I see, within walking distance, a castle's turrets. Through the mist I can see its ramparts and promenades, its stonework and crenellations. I am fascinated; I cannot leave the window.

The following pages related how the doctor was powerless to move or leave the window. He at length grew ill and was forced by physicians (thinking he was not altogether sane—he refused to show anyone the window) to leave the house. He had the window boarded up in his absence, and, being obscure enough, evidently went somewhere and died, leaving no record there of what had happened to him. The diary breaks off in May of 1807, when he was taken from the house. It was apparently left around for a generation or two, and was then auctioned off to a collector. It had on its first page two booksellers' names stamped above Dorian's.

"That's all very interesting," I said putting the book down. "What do you propose to do about it?"

"Go to Cornwall this weekend, find the house, and see if the window is still there," he answered triumphantly.

I registered innumerable complaints and objections, all of them sound and containing impeccable logic. They did not, of course, prevent us from going.

II

I had managed to put off the adventure until early that spring. I did not want to go at all, especially since I did not expect to find anything, but Colin was not about to give me a moment's peace until I relented.

We arrived in the south of Cornwall in April; it was a pleasant, but rather dry, dusty day, much hotter than it tends to be in that vicinity. The little town of G—— was just the sort of rural place that one would expect: dismal, and with life conducted on a rather microscopic scale. The only place of interest was the surprisingly large library, devoted mainly to housing the collections of manuscripts from, and dealing with, the medieval castle and monastery of the vicinity, both of which were destroyed during the reign of Henry VIII, and of which no traces remain, other than a few capitals and gargoyles now in the British Museum.

After we settled at the hotel, I went about the surrounding countryside to sketch, and Colin headed for the local historical society to track down the late doctor. He later told me that he had found Dr. Gwynn's house, and that it was at present unoccupied! This depressed me no end, as I had rather expected to make a vacation out of this idiotic search and not be bothered by checking the walls of an old building for a magic window. As for the doctor, as I have stated, he never returned to G——, so I was forced to agree with Colin that, unless the house had undergone extensive alterations (an unlikely prospect, as the entire town looked shabby enough to have undergone no severe alterations since well before Gwynn's time), the window would still be there, probably imbedded in plaster.

The next morning we visited the house—now known as the Reynolds' house. Somehow Colin had convinced the owner to let us fiddle around with the place. I don't know whether he lied to the owner, or managed to fascinate the man with the diary, but either way, we were soon in the house. We moved the sheet-covered furniture into the center of each room and began, from the attic down, carefully to check each wall with a southern exposure.

I had rather expected to find the window in the attic—the whole affair sounded like attic doings to me—but apparently the doctor's laboratory was in what was now a bedroom. The window had been easy to find, as it had been plastered over very roughly, and was not flush with the rest of the wall; my artist's eye caught the quarter-inch difference immediately.

"You don't propose to break through the plaster, do you?" I asked, not imagining that the landlord had given Colin permission to pull the place apart. "You know that we can be arrested for damaging property."

Colin stood and looked at me. "That doctor, in this very room," he said, gesturing wildly about, "over a century and a half ago, discovered a means of seeing the past—maybe entering it! Do you think that a couple inches of plaster are too valuable to destroy? That can't stop us!"

"Well, it will stop me," I said calmly, and picked up my jacket, slinging it over my shoulder. Colin looked as if he were undecided between being hurt and being furious, so I added, "Besides, I want to get back to town to the library; they've got the old castle's chronicles there. After all, if Gwynn looked at them, maybe they looked at him and wrote it up. I'll see you at dinner." I quickly left before Colin could say anything.

The library's records were very full: hundreds of pages of Middle English blather—I'm not good at reading it, as I haven't had any practice since school, when I went through Chaucer and Gower. I could, however, find no mention of anything other than ordinary castle doings, with an occasional holiday for the burning of a sorcerer or witch. In general, castle life appears to have been a bore.

Colin did not come to dinner that evening, and, after waiting in the lobby until about nine o'clock, I decided I'd better wander up to the house to see if he had been arrested for damaging the place. It was a fine, crystal, moonless night, the sky so studded with stars as to almost give the impression of some sort of rolling celestial moor; the air had cleared, and was sweetly cool, with the smell of the spring earth perfuming its way into the brain. I was quite light-headed by the time I reached the path to the house, but my spring reveries were quite shattered when I spied Colin atop a huge ladder, virtually attacking the outside of the old house.

"Colin, you idiot!" I cried, "Get off that ladder and stop this nonsense. The owner will have your head." He did not look at me, but kept on wildly tearing off boards; he continued for about a minute, the boards making a ghastly ripping sound as he tore them off and threw them to the ground.

He finally turned to me, gesturing toward the now visible, black window. "I've found it, but this face is covered with black paint, too. I've already scraped the other side clean. Come up and help me with this side."

Reluctantly, I climbed up the none-too-steady ladder and began to help him scrape the window.

"Gently," he said, "the glass is quite thin; it wouldn't do to break it." His voice was almost metallic with nervousness, and his hand was unsteady. He was covered hair to shoes with dry plaster, and he looked for all the world like a ghost.

"It's damn lucky for you that this place is out of the town; if there were neighbors around they certainly would have called the police, and I can't say that it wouldn't have served you right." I was vexed, but nevertheless, the excitement of the moment had quite gotten through to me.

The window was quite small, about two feet wide by two and a half feet high, and was now completely clear. From the scraping process, I had perceived that its surface was bubbly and uneven, obviously not the work of the professional glass makers that abounded in Cornwall at the turn of the nineteenth century.

We climbed down the ladder, folded it, and let it rest on the ground by the old house, and dashed in and up the stairs. I hesitated at the threshold of the bedroom, very unsure of what I was to find. I still don't know which would have been worse—to find the window truly a window to the past, or find that the whole affair was the raving of a long dead, demented physician.

Colin, of course, sped into the room, and by the time I had entered it, was leaning on the sill and staring through the window. As I walked up to him, I was made uneasy by the radiance that seemed to be cast upon his face; the night being quite dark, the radiance must have been from the window, not through it.

"Come here; look," he said, very quietly. I walked over, and he made way for me to see. You may say it was power of suggestion, but I'm sure it wasn't. I swear to you that that window overlooked quite clearly a castle. It was not translucent, not a phantom likeness, but a true, solid building, stone for stone, step for step, a medieval castle. It was undoubtedly the castle of G——, unseen (except for those few days in 1807) by a human being since the sixteenth century. About the castle loomed a smoky silence that, mist-like, rolled over the gray stonework. It was exactly as the old doctor had described it; every detail, every crenellation and joint stood out in superb relief. Were it not for the rolling fog that lent animation to the scene, it would have looked more like a dull, muted, but very sharp focus color photograph.

"Well," I said, with no small amount of awe, "it looks as if Gwynn weren't mad after all." I backed away from the window and continued, "But now that we've got it, what do we do with it?"

"There must be a way to get through to them," Colin said quietly. "They are out there, separated from us only by a pane of glass." I was, I found to my surprise, trembling. I had never before faced anything so palpably unknown and bizarre. I was also confused; now that we had it, what *would* we do with it? A certain mystic—and not wholly pleasant—fascination for the window's view was already growing in me, and I felt that I could tear myself away from it only with the greatest of effort.

I finally pulled myself away from those mist-enshrouded turrets and walks and told Colin to do the same.

"Go to bed if you like," he replied sharply, "but I simply must figure it out. There must be a way through it!"

"If you should go over there, do you think they'll give you a hero's welcome?" I asked acidly. "I can't say that I'd care for being the twentieth century's representative to the Middle Ages. You'd have a lot of explaining to do. Think about that!" With that parting shot, I left the house and went back to the hotel.

The next morning I returned to find Colin still staring, unshaven and sloppy, through the window. The day was splendidly bright and sunny, yet the castle still appeared foggy and forbidding. Colin was clearly distracted, and I could see him repeating the doctor's descent into madness. I tried to pull him away from the window, but he pushed me back against the wall and told me to keep my hands off of him.

"I'm not going to move until I can figure out the secret of getting through it!" he shouted, and returned to the window. This time, he leaned heavily on it with his hands.

"Be careful!" I cried. "That window's too thin to lean on!" Barely before the words died on my lips, with the terrible cracking and tinkling sound of glass giving way, Colin fell through the window. For one split second, he balanced halfway over the sill, and then, screaming wildly, he disappeared, headfirst, from my view. I just stood there for a moment, completely paralyzed and cursing myself for the whole adventure. It was only one story down, but Colin did go headfirst, and he could have been badly hurt, either by the impact or the broken glass. It was only after these reflections that I realized that Colin's scream had sounded terribly drawn out, and that I hadn't heard him land.

Once again mobile, I rushed over to the window, where I was stunned to see, on the ground below, pieces of broken glass, but no Colin. I told myself that he had not been hurt and had run back into the house; a subsequent search proved that there was no one in the house. On the ground, below the window, were pieces of glass which, incidentally, were blackened and smoky, rather like the pieces of a burned-out light bulb; there was no mark or depression to suggest that anything but a few pieces of glass had fallen there. I had, and still have, no choice but to assume that Colin never hit the ground.

He is now listed as a missing person, and his whereabouts will, I imagine, never be found. However, shortly after that tragic morning, I did find a reference in the castle records that explains the mystery to my very reluctant satisfaction. (In giving it, I shall merely try to convey a light touch of the style, for a faithful transcription would be unreadable save to scholars of Middle English.)

> From some place unknown there hath been visited
> upon us a servant of Satan who did appear upon the
> fifth day of Spring in this year of Our Lord 1243. He
> did wear upon his back garb of an unknown variety,
> and his speech, though somewhat like unto our own,
> was of a cast and color most curious, so that none but
> clerks could comprehend much of his saying; and they
> did find it ill, for he prated of black arts and magickal
> doings, averring that he did arrive through a window
> that over-looketh our century from one nigh eight hun-
> dred years removed. Examination did prove that he was
> indeed a man, and he was taken under the protection of
> the Church in hope, however scant, of preserving his
> soul from hell. He did remain unyielding and our good
> bishop did finally declare him contumacious, a creature
> of Satan sent to practice most abominable sorcery and
> black art amongst us, and did release him to the secular
> arm, which did duly condemn him to the pyre. He did
> die unshriven and unrepentant, cursing all about him
> most foully. May God have mercy on his lost soul.

Who was it that said if the *Necronomicon* really existed it would by now have appeared in a paperback edition with an introduction by Lin Carter? I thought of that the day Lin and I sat in the back room of a magic paraphernalia shop in New York City, listening to the mad author of a paperback grimoire purporting to be the *Necronomicon* answer questions from a naive crowd of unwashed occultists who wanted to know, for instance, if you could use your scrying crystal to get a peek at the Old Ones. "I guess you could, but I wouldn't advise it!" Yuk yuk. Lin wrote his own *Necronomicon*, which now resides between the covers of this volume, itself an inexpensive paperback edition of the *Necronomicon*! Isn't it ironic?

John Brunner, though not a name one ordinarily thinks to associate with H. P. Lovecraft, was certainly one of the great old ones of science fiction and fantasy. His classic works include *Stand on Zanzibar*, *The Sheep Look Up*, *Catch a Falling Star*, *The Whole Man*, and many others. *Weird Tales* of Spring 1992 featured the story you are about to read, and it is definitely HPLish. I am always fascinated to see the result when a veteran writer who has never before evidenced an interest in the Lovecraft Mythos suddenly shows his colours out of space. You have to look fast; you may never see them again. Someone who's been viewing the game from the sidelines will likely have noticed things the rest of us, clashing on the field, have missed, and his perspective will be fresh. The present tale is a case in point.

(I don't want to spoil anything for you, so I suggest you stop right here, read the story, and then come back and we'll compare notes. Finished? All right, here goes ....) I see this tale as reshuffling major themes from "The Dunwich Horror." The setting of the story in the British Arkham and Dunwich almost sounds like a joke based on August Derleth's advice to the young Ramsey Campbell not to place his stories in the too-familiar towns of Lovecraftian New England, but to use equivalent English settings. What would Derleth have said had Campbell sent the stories back, still set in Arkham and Dunwich, but on the other side of the Atlantic?

Brunner's use of these locales has the effect of setting the story in an alternative universe, a parallel world. He signals us that he is going to tell one of the old stories a different way. Notice, if you will, that our protagonist is someone very much like Henry Armitage. Jasper Abraham Wharton (whose name almost sounds like a mix of "Whateley", "Armitage", and "Wilbraham", the region that inspired Lovecraft's Dunwich countryside) is an erudite librarian who suffers the stormy visitation of an uncouth ruffian from the sticks. This time the intruder is not Wilbur Whateley, local yokel, but Hiram Schultz, ugly American, whose coarse slang is fully as outlandish as Wilbur's backwoods accent. Like Wilbur, Schultz comes possessing his own copy of the *Necronomicon* but seeking a better one (though Schultz doesn't quite know that yet).

Like Armitage, Wharton undergoes a shock of "acute spiritual fear" as he reads the book of blasphemous revelation. Wilbur's hybrid monstrousness has been transferred to another character, much as Derleth used to do in his Dunwich-Innsmouth crossovers, namely the fishy Abner Marsh. As if due to affirmative action, a deep one has landed a teaching job smack dab in the middle of what Fritz Leiber and Brian Lumley had once made a bastion of fierce opposition to the Old Ones. Ironically, it is as if Wizard Whateley has taken Henry Armitage's job at Miskatonic U.! This play of musical chairs is a clear illustration of Greimas' idea of "actantial roles." Certain narrative functions, or "actants", must be present, but the characters who occupy those roles may be reshuffled at will. The result is pretty much the setting free of the shambling subtext Donald R. Burleson always maintained ("The Mythic Hero Archetype in 'The Dunwich Horror'", *Lovecraft Studies* #3) lies at the root of "The Dunwich Horror" —the Whateleys win after all!

Concerning the Forthcoming Inexpensive Paperback Translation of the *Necronomicon* of Abdul Alhazred

by John Brunner

I: The Peabody Legacy

My hand shakes, my spirits fail, as I attempt to set forth this record which is at once a catharsis of the terrors that besiege my broken mind, and—more significantly—a warning you will disregard at your peril.

It has been said, "None so blind as those who will not see." That at best is only half a truth. Still blinder are those who desire, without regard for consequences, to see what ought never to be seen!

What follows is an exact account of the circumstances which have led me to a noisome dungeon, under constant observation by alienists, brutally misused by simian thugs in white coats should I so much as refer to the hateful knowledge in my brain. I have committed no crime! On the contrary, I am a benefactor of humanity! But not even the consular representatives of my own country will aid me! Has the stock of once-Great Britain truly fallen so low that its citizens can be unlawfully confined in one of our former colonies without a whisper of diplomatic protest? It seems so, for the official who visited me the day after my arrest was scornful of my tale—though, of course, he may have been an impostor ....

I ramble. Small wonder after the fearful experiences I have endured! But let me with all my forces compose this narrative into logical order. One dare not look forward to long supremacy for logic in the world, now the denizens of primal chaos press upon us anew.

Be it known, then, that I bear the honourable name of Jasper Abraham Wharton; that I am fifty years of age; and that my tale for present purposes commences at the small town of Arkham, overlooking Marshwood Vale in the county of Dorset, England. There, in accordance with the bookish nature which I have been pleased to acknowledge since my childhood, I have for many years discharged the duties of a librarian. The stipend of such a post is small; my needs, however, have always been few, particularly since

I have never been a victim of those promptings of the flesh which drive the majority of men to marriage, or to even worse predicaments. I have appreciated far more highly the pleasures of the mind than those of the body; and, although the setting of a rural community may not *a priori* seem to afford any great variety of intellectual stimuli, it was my good fortune while still in my twenties to become acquainted with the then Lord of the Manor of Dunwich, a parish whose boundaries adjoin those of Arkham. I speak of Sir Adrian Peabody, Baronet, scion of a family long established in the Vale, and last of its direct line inasmuch as its more vital cadet branch had emigrated to the New World.

Sir Adrian was a recluse, not entirely from choice. At all events he was shunned in the vicinity. Gossip has never appealed to me; I could not however escape gathering that there had been some sort of scandal before I was born, the nature of which I did not inquire about. It made no difference to the fact that he befriended me despite the disparity in our ages, he being well advanced in years. Fortified by recollection of vicious rumours circulated long ago, the townsfolk would have it that he was senile. I never found him so. Labouring under the burden of a failing frame, admittedly, and resentful of the cataracts that rendered him three-quarters sightless, he yet retained a mind of great keenness behind the deceptive mask of his slack features. Indeed it is past a doubt that he remained in possession of his essential faculties, else he would not have been permitted by his legal advisors to amend his will, as he did some five or six years after our first meeting, to make me the inheritor of his compendious and *recherché* private library, amassed over five centuries by his ancestors.

A small legacy accompanied the bequest, which enabled me to finance an extension to my modest dwelling adjacent to the Arkham Public Library—I have always preferred, for personal reasons, to live as close as possible to the place of my employment—and equip it with suitable storage for the eight thousand, two hundred, and seven volumes Sir Adrian had left me. There was some outcry locally upon news of this provision being noised abroad, from two quarters: from the native farming folk (one would not do them injustice by terming them "the peasantry"), who had notoriously little love for the baronet and his predecessors; and likewise from newcomers to the area, city-dwellers lately become *nouveaux-riches*, who had tried and failed to cultivate their titled neighbour; who upon it being learned that Dunwich Great Hall would be put up for sale fell to squabbling over the estate and the lordship of the manor like cur-dogs over a bone; and who were (as I told a reporter from the *Arkham Gazette* on the only occasion of my granting a newspaper interview) solely interested in the library as an investment rather than a repository of knowledge ... a point which I regret to state was not repeated in print.

The reporter, I recall, demanded with quite insolent persistence whether I had pressurised—dreadful neologism!—Sir Adrian into making the codicil to his will. I denied the charge, but admitted that I had suggested the financial component, Sir Adrian not having been entirely aware of my straitened resources. What else could I have done, once it was plain he had set his heart on my receiving the library? To have sent it piecemeal to auction would have put me on all fours with those greedy strangers above-mentioned!

That clamour, fortunately, died away upon the destruction of Dunwich Great Hall a week or two later, the consequence of suspected arson. The tune of these invaders from the city altered immediately, and they conceded it was a stroke of luck that the books had not lain among the embers. (And incidentally, I may say, then proceeded to prove my point about their limited concern for the collection by never requesting the opportunity to consult a single one of its items!)

For my own part, at the time of the conflagration I wholly concurred in the opinion that the removal of the volumes had been beneficial. It was not until later that I realised how much better it would have been for the world had certain holograph texts, certain rare and curious tomes—not, according to the British Library, the Bodleian, the London Library, and other authorities, to be found elsewhere in the United Kingdom—been incinerated in the pyre ....

On the other hand, but for my acquaintance with them, all knowledge of their contents might now repose in the deformed cranium of that fiend in—dare one debase the phrase "human form?" No, never! *Sub-human* is the word! As are the diabolical machines to whose mindless circuits he proposes to commit ....

But I race ahead of my promised logical order.

II: The Visitor from America

Suffice it to say, then, that for two full decades after the demise of Sir Adrian I led a rewarding albeit solitary existence, much engaged in cataloguing my acquisitions, a task for which (as Sir Adrian had recognised with perceptiveness belying the charge that he was senile) I was ideally suited. I do not say so in any immodest sense, for it is a matter of simple fact that there was scarcely one script or language among that vast array of literature with which I could not claim some passing familiarity. Disdaining the company of my rude school-fellows, who regarded learning as inferior to barbaric pastimes such as football or stealing apples, from boyhood up I had explored the byways of philology. By ten I could make shift at the decipherment of Umbrian, Dorian, Sanskrit, and other commonplace tongues, and I had subsequently investigated—in addition to the Indo-European—the Semitic, the Ural-Altaic, the Sino-Mongolian, and (insofar as they have been committed to writing) the African linguistic families, not to mention those of the Pacific and its conterminous zones from Japan to New Zealand as well as countless shamefully inadequate transcriptions of aboriginal Australian dialects. I had appended a footnote or two to the literature, particularly in connection with the vexed matter of Basque radices.

It had, I confess, occurred to me that in the twilight of my days some meed of glory might befall me for having all by myself completed such a monumental undertaking. Vain dream! Obstacle after obstacle impeded me. It certainly was not my wish that the existence of the unique items in what I had now come to regard as my collection should be publicised, for an absolutely quiet life was imperative for success. I have ever been fond of orderliness; the greater world, the metropolis, the hurly and burly of travel, held no charms to tempt me; and while on occasion a fellow-enthusiast in my own speciality who happened to be touring in the area might presume upon my time to request assistance in unravelling some conundrum in bibliophilic lore—and while I never refused such counsel if it lay within my power—those who did visit me were for the most part sufficiently sensitive to my preferences to confine themselves thereafter to Her Majesty's Posts.

Yet, inevitably, there were certain lacunae in the wall of protective indifference which I contrived around me. For all my fervent pleadings, untrustworthy members of the staffs of the great libraries to which I must now and then have recourse, to confirm or refute hypotheses concerning the provenance of a binding-material, the characteristics of a scribe, or the regional frequency of a turn of phrase, abused my confidence and repeated the content of my inquiry to a third party. Time and again I was pestered by requests, bribes, and even barely-veiled threats from what I had previously imagined to be respectable academic bodies whose directors had got wind of the Peabody Bequest and demanded that it be ceded to them!

Horrors! To set these priceless tomes at the beck and call of every long-haired, unwashed, half-literate student on his or her way to a degree in some fashionable but nonsensical subject! I not only learned of the existence of such persons as I describe from the newspapers I daily perused at the public library (arriving early for the purpose so that no one should be deprived of their use during opening hours); during university vacations I actually saw some of them on our premises ... though fortunately I never had to deal with them personally, since I had grown accustomed to concentrating on administrative matters and left encounters with the subscribers to my assistant Mrs. Craven, widow of a former schoolteacher in Dunwich. Despite this small mercy my salaried employment seemed daily to grow more onerous as an ever-greater proportion of *hoi polloi* were accorded that superficial veneer of education which nowadays serves as an *Ersatz* for the real thing. In order to escape I devoted every instant I could spare to my correspondence (which was extensive) and my catalogue.

But escape was to be forbidden me.

On a certain morning in the spring of the present year—I recall it must have been a Monday, since I was engaged in making up the weekly account of books overdue for return—Mrs. Craven informed me that an American was at my door, a certain Hiram Schultz, claiming to be a doctor of letters and engaged as a lecturer at a university with a peculiar name. I heard it (as one might expect, he had not the courtesy to send in a visiting-card) as "Mixed Atomic", the very epitome of that misguided and futile bias toward the sciences which has been the bane of true scholarship for the past century. "Doctor of Letters!" What a sham!

I demanded the ostensible purpose of his call, and Mrs. Craven advised me that he was engaged in analysing the verbal content of incunabula and other rare works by means of computers.

"Computers!" I exploded. My outburst, born of conviction that they are anathema to honest scholars and those who trust in them lack souls, was louder than I intended—so loud, it reached the ears of the stranger. He, with the insensitivity typical of American so-called academics, interpreted it as due to excitement rather than fury.

At any rate that is the only excuse I can conceive for his ill-mannered intrusion, a second later, into my private office, beaming all over his bovine features and exclaiming, "That's right, sir! The greatest breakthrough in the attribution of—"

He broke off, doubtless on seeing how my expression contradicted his erroneous assumption, and stood abashed. Since he was, however, a very tall young man, his single stride had taken him halfway from the door to my desk. The rateable value of a community like ours being small, naturally the Arkham council has only an exiguous fund from which to provide premises for its public servants. Finding himself adjacent to the chair which Mrs. Craven used when discussing administrative matters, he proceeded to sit down, stare me in the eye as though we were old friends, and pour out a garbled, parasyntactical, and barely more than half-comprehensible explanation for his discourtesy.

"Well, sorry to crash in on you like this, Dr. Wharton—-hey, sorry! It's *Mister* Wharton, isn't it? Just that I thought, reading your bits in like the *Journal of Philology* and the *Annals of Biblophily* and all like that, no one could be that good without he had at least three pee-aitch-dees, heh-heh." (I transcribe his barely articulate utterances with such precision simply because every word ate into my memory with the fierceness of acid.) "But you see when I cottoned on to this link between our little thinkshop in Arkham,

Mass., plus this great deal we have going with all those like old forgotten em-esses we turned up, I don't mean *we* but this crazy chief of mine Dr. Abner Marsh, you should meet him, you really should, you'd get on like a house on fire—like Dunwich Hall, heh-heh ...!'"

It might occur to the reader at this point to pose a question I have some reluctance about answering; I must, however, oblige myself to forestall puzzlement, and state candidly that among the reasons I prefer a life of seclusion is that I have been since infancy afflicted with a stammer. Confrontation with even an old acquaintance may trigger it, and when it comes to a boisterous and unwelcome stranger my difficulties are redoubled. Additionally I am perhaps not the most prepossessing of men, and living in a small community with little society I have never taken great pains over my dress or appearance. One may readily deduce from that another reason why my preference is for contact by letter; persons given to making hasty judgements based on superficial impressions could so easily form a wrong impression of me as an individual.

Nonetheless I was on the verge of being able to tell him to leave my office at once and write for an appointment, which after such rudeness I would be disinclined to grant, when something in the midst of his chaotic outpourings caught my attention.

He had spoken, with casual familiarity, of the *Necronomicon* of Abdul Alhazred!

III: An Appalling Discovery

It was like a thunderbolt! I had believed the manuscript copy in Latin, in a crabbed late-medieval chancery hand, which I had discovered—although not perused, its decipherment clearly being a long and quite likely unrewarding task—in Sir Adrian's collection, to be the only one extant. The British Library, the Bibliothèque Nationale, and every other authority I had consulted had assured me that nothing was on record concerning that text, apart from veiled unhelpful references in other works of a slightly later period, uniformly suspected of being the products of disordered minds.

So great was my astonishment, it deprived me of speech completely, to the alarm of Mrs. Craven, who turned as if to offer assistance even though she knew how I detested any reference to my disability. Scowling at her, I fought my disobedient tongue towards a newly-framed denunciation: not now of this brash intruder, but of those supposedly dedicated to the same cause as myself, those scholars unworthy of the name who must, I presume, have let word of my letters loose along that channel of communication known as "the grapevine"—a graphic image enough, though why such an innocent plant deserves to be tarred with so foul a brush I have never established.

Then, as more facts emerged from Schultz's gabbling, I realised with a still more violent shock that my initial conclusion had been mistaken. It was not the fault of those I had confided in that this disgusting person had broached the secret of my prized volume.

There was another copy in existence!

Worse yet! No mere translation like mine, *but in the original Arabic!*

How often had I planned, given enough time in this vale of tears following completion of the catalogue which was my major task—albeit not yet half accomplished after twenty years—to redact and publish for the first time ever the most select items in my possession: this one whose name Schultz was bandying about, those others by von Junzt and d'Erlette which, judging by their titles, might constitute a valuable accretion to the corpus of accounts of medieval demonolatry ...!

Trembling with rage and frustration, disappointed beyond measure, I was told how it was that he had heard about my—no, not "my", only "the"—*Necronomicon*. Shorn of its trans-Atlantic jargon and sub-literate verbal frills, his story ran as follows.

The peculiarly-named college where Schultz worked (it transpired he had accepted his post on a temporary basis, in the hope of moving on, once he had accumulated a morsel of renown by publishing a few papers, to some more august centre of learning) was located in the equally oddly-named state of Massachusetts, and indeed in a town which was the namesake of my own birthplace, another Arkham. Eager, by his own admission, not to remain any longer than necessary in such a "one-horse burg", he set about determining what if anything in those fields of study touching on his own other members of the faculty were engaged upon.

He decided almost at once that Professor Abner Marsh, already mentioned, was the likeliest candidate for international fame, so he "thought he might as well take a ride on the guy's coat-tails." He set out to cultivate him. For reasons he did not elucidate this proved a difficult chore, but in the end his efforts were crowned with success.

Marsh, termed "crazy" in an almost affectionate tone—which puzzled me—was apparently a respected though not greatly liked individual, of outstanding intellect but little given to companionship. (I recognised an echo of myself in the description, discounting it however in case it was as I suspected founded on pointless sympathy.) Despite whatever handicaps they were that Schultz was hinting at, he had nonetheless stumbled on an academic treasure trove. During the demolition of an old house—situated, remarkably but not astonishingly, in a nearby town named after the village which had so long been the seat of the Peabody line, another Dunwich— certain books had been found behind a roughly-plastered wall. Mouldy, damaged by time in addition to frequent earlier use, they were brought to the college by the workman who disinterred them in the hope some reward might be forthcoming. The Dean had been inclined to dismiss them as worthless; Professor Marsh, by contrast, on being asked to evaluate them, realised they were rare and potentially valuable. (I stifled my normal reactions at this point. I have always loathed people who paste financial labels on pure scholarship—but I realise now, only too clearly, how ingrained that attitude must be among Americans!)

The workman was fobbed off with a tip, and Marsh wished to confide in someone how clever he had been. The lot fell to Schultz, and he now recounted to me with equal glee that the main prize was ... the *Necronomicon*. Having only some fifteen volumes on his hands, Marsh proposed to edit and issue them, and would do so long before I had even finished listing the eight thousand-odd that I was saddled with! My gorge rose; my mouth tasted of bile.

In order to lay a veneer of colourable scholarship over his slapdash work, Marsh wished to investigate the connection between the Dunwich of the Old World and that of the New. Being unable to travel—Schultz intimated that he was in constant need of some sort of medical attention—he invoked the aid of his younger colleague, who consented in exchange for the right to publish computer analyses of the texts. Heaven help us! As though a machine could read and appreciate a book!

Arriving in Dorset, learning of the Peabody Bequest, he had no other thought than to "barge in" and offer—this took my breath away with its sheer gall!—a thousand dollars for the opportunity to "glance over" my collection. Moreover he assured me his colleague would willingly buy the lot for a to-be-negotiated sum, because "it would provide thesis material for our kids for years!"

That was the absolute limit. Rage lent me fluent speech for once, and in no uncertain terms I told him what I thought of him and his professor. When I finished he did no more than shrug and rise.

"Too bad," he said. "I did think you might help out with translating. There aren't many as well-equipped as you are for the job. Even proof-reading, come to that."

"You're actually going to publish them?" I whispered.

"Sure! Original and English on facing pages. Thanks to the computers you hate so much, we can keep the costs right down. A few years ago we'd have had to charge two hundred bucks a copy, but now we can do it for a fraction of that. We can design any type-face we like, you know, and using a laser printer and an OCR ..."

He went on talking, but I could no longer hear. I was envisaging defeat: hundreds, maybe thousands of reprints of what had been unique books, cheaply bound in card or even paper covers—no leather, no gilt tooling, no—

On the point of leaving, he sensed my lack of attention.

"Mr. Wharton!"

I recovered, a little.

"If you change your mind"—he commandeered a pen from my desk, and a sheet of paper, writing rapidly—"this is where I'll be for the next few days. Get in touch, hm?"

I accepted the address with nerveless fingers, and he was gone.

I fought my anger for long minutes before recovering a semblance of normality. I tried to resume my work. I failed. At last I was compelled to abandon the attempt. Telling Mrs. Craven that I needed a breath of air, I adjourned homeward—more exactly, slipped by a private route into the library extension of my home. There I at once sought out the *Necronomicon* and clutched it to me, foolishly seeking assurance that it was indeed still here, had not been purloined so that Marsh might boast of owning both the original and the translation. I had not thus far made any attempt to read it, beyond a preliminary inspection to ascertain the general run of its contents. I knew it was ascribed to an otherwise unknown Arab writer, that some pages had been defaced with a poor-quality ink through which the original text might with great effort be deciphered—and of one thing more I was abruptly certain.

I was not going to let Marsh cheat me of my right to edit and issue a translation first!

On reflection, perhaps I had been over-ambitious in my plan to catalogue the entire collection before publishing any of the individual items. More to the point, I could thank Schultz for a useful new idea. Why should I toil day in, day out, behind the scenes of the Arkham library, when—without actually *selling* the book, which I would have regarded as a betrayal of Sir Adrian's trust—I might request financial support from a publisher in order to translate and annotate it?

My course of action became clear at once. I had gathered the distinct impression from Schultz that American so-called "scholarship" was organised like an office job; one put in a certain number of hours per week, and the rest of the time ignored one's proper duty. Given that, once free of my quotidian grind, I could call the rest of every day my own apart from time wasted on eating and sleeping, a dedicated person like myself could not fail to beat Marsh into print, if not with preliminary announcements (his, Schultz had stated, were already *en route* to the appropriate quarters), then at least with the actual text. That would be a blow struck for genuine devotion to learning!

If only he had the translation, and I the original …!

But there it was.

My decision made, I acted on it instantly. I instructed Mrs. Craven not to bother me except in emergencies, selected those dictionaries I foresaw as being most useful and disposed them handily by my chair, and after locking my house-door and barring my windows to prevent interruption (owing to my problem with unpremeditated conversation I had never installed a telephone, so I was safe from that devilish form of distraction), with tremulous hands I opened the precious volume and applied myself doggedly to the elucidation of its mysteries.

Within at most an hour, as my practised brain gained the measure of the obscured and abbreviated writing, I made the acquaintance of the Elder Gods.

IV: The Time of Torment

No reference to those Beings was to be found in the preface, a passage clearly not belonging to the original work but an addition by the translator—composed, what is more, prior to the inception of this main undertaking. As I mentioned above, I had read portions before but with scant attention. Now I had to concentrate, for on the second page the text grew more turgid as the anonymous writer explained how he had been told of the importance of this book, how he had sought far and wide for a copy from which a version in Latin might be derived, how having achieved his goal he was settling down "early in the morning of St. Priscus's Day in the year of Our Lord MCDXXXII" to his long-delayed task, trusting to Divine Providence to guide him where meanings were obscure—and, I may say, doing little to assist his readers to avoid the same problem, for he displayed all those irritating habits common to scribes of his generation, employing cryptic abridgements, running his i's, u's, m's, n's and even o's into shark-tooth jags where sometimes only a bar above a doubled letter offered guidance to the intended word, plus such other tricks of the trade as sometime deducting a numeral from the larger following it, sometimes presenting the larger first and adding the lesser behind. I pictured him as an old man, or maybe sick; at all events impatient, uncertain whether he would survive to his last page. (I noted that down for possible use in my commentary.)

In his preface he also explained the supposed authorship of the original—stating, with unexpected awareness of bibliographic niceties, that an Islamic invocation had been pasted into the front of his Arabic copy, warning that Alhazred had gone insane, so that the book would have been burned as diabolical has not its author been renowned for his early poems, of great delicacy and beauty, "wherefore it seemed amiss to the Moor that Satan be fancied to have claimed such a sweet singer." This enabled me, after delving into the *Encyclopaedia of Moslem History*, to date his lost Arabic

MS to a period of half a century between two outbreaks of intolerance and book-burning.

That remark was, by the by, accurate. It was not Satan who claimed the "sweet singer"—whoever or whatever did so ....

But there would be time later to deal with the trimmings. My eyes raced over the last paragraph of the preface ("Ignoring the unbelievers' invocation to their false Lord and praying for their early gathering into the fold of the True and Triune God, I commit my mind and purpose to the will of heaven, *In Nomine* ..." and so forth), and as I turned the page I made my first contact with that fearful, that abominable, that loathsomely obsessional history which tells of unspeakable horrors beside which the foulness of modern war, torture, concentration camps, and whatever else anyone may care to name pales into insignificance. It was like being shown the interior of a madman's mind.

At first I did not realise what was happening to me. I mistook my almost hypnotic fascination with the subject for simple concentration, born of my determination to complete an English rendering ahead of Marsh. Little by little, though, I came to understand. Feverish, I stared at an obscure word and tried to deny to myself what I knew it must mean; I fought to distract my attention by searching for it in a dictionary where I knew it could not be found, hoping that afterward I might laugh at my own intensity, but in vain. Hour after hour leaked away. It grew dark, and I strove to prevent my hand from switching on the light that would enable me to continue—and failed, and saw those implacable lines stretching on for page after hateful page .... My eyes sought to roll upward in their sockets, to fasten on some object other than the book, and were no more successful than had been my hand in avoiding the lamp; at last my very brain felt as though it were curling up inside my skull to hide from the external world, and I lapsed into exhausted slumber across my table.

Even in sleep there was no surcease. Down the haunted corridors of memory they stalked me: sinister Nyarlathotep who had perambulated the temples of Egypt in a rictus of scorn for those bastard reconstructions of ancient deities whose forms surrounded his passage; revolting Cthulhu who bided his time in a sunken city so monstrous it alone was a fit frame for his appalling shape ....

I woke moaning, and it was only midnight, and the lamp still shone, and I was afraid to go on sleeping. My glance fell on the page where I had broken off my reading, and a half-grasped phrase concerning one 'Astur (or Hastur, or "Xastur" as the scribe had here set down, employing by a *lapsus calami* the harsh aspirate of the Greek letter *chi* as the nearest counterpart to the Arabic sound) lured my terrified mind back to those scenes of fear and desolation where he had reigned ... I could not stop. I read on, guessing *here* and failing despite my best efforts not to understand *there* ....

When I had, absolutely had, to close my sore eyes again, although dawn was painting the window red, I happened to glance at the remaining thickness of the book.

I had read barely a tenth of it!

Those nightmares! Within the day they had escaped from the zone of sleep which now I suspected I would never again dare to enter without some drug to blot my consciousness entirely out, and were assembling in the shadowed corners of the room to mock me in my waking state. I turned leaves randomly, noticing by chance that next beyond the folio I held open there was a page partly obliterated by that ink I have already referred to—and deluded myself for an instant with the hope that that might prove a barrier, break the train of thought I was embarked on—and found my hope hollow, for the context and the strong dark strokes of the original writing which showed through the futile overscores indicated what the meaning was, what it must be.

Haggard, worn-out, bleary-eyed, head ringing, belly rumbling (in all the time I was riveted to the book I believe I ingested a little water and a spoonful of sugar that I did not taste), I followed the tale to its end. I learned of the tremendous conflict between the forces that reigned before man; I realised that our species had arisen on the planet when it was already the abandoned battleground of a struggle between more-than-titanic opponents, whose psychic forces were drawn from the stars, and in particular from the evil (or delightful? I was too confused by then to draw a merely human distinction between the two) Hyades—where by a lake called Hali pitiful creatures, vulnerable as men, scuttled to hide from grasping tentacles—shattered the very boundaries of being, confounded the progress of evolution, diverted high intelligence into brute forms as soft as slime, grafted features both batrachian and saurian onto bodies that walked as upright as do we ....

Some sort of portal, it appeared, had been barricaded between Earth and its sky. Barricaded only; it was still where it had been, and what closed it was capable of being eroded. Certain chinks had been created, by the application of those psychical forces which (as I now learned against my will) are stronger than the forces powering the stars, those that we poor fools of men believe to be the ultimate and seek to mimic with our puny H-bombs. Given that proper ceremonies were enacted (being an Arab, the author had not compared them to keys, but the translator had thought to do so), those chinks might be held open. Whereat what lay beyond would re-emerge.

There was mention also of a still more ancient power, that strove to counteract such work. But I could not imagine anything capable of overcoming Yog-Sothoth, and Shub-Niggurath, and ....

Bright sunshine gleamed outside. It drove away the dreadful visions haunting me. Resolution hardened in my mind. If an archaic Latin translation could so affect myself, inoculated by long study against ancient superstitions, what might a version rendered directly from Arabic to English (and with the help of machinery, what's more!) not do to an ignorant and untrained mind? At any cost, Schultz and his professor must be prevented from fulfilling their intent. I could foresee horrors: mass insanity, an epidemic of suicide, worst of all a cult arising dedicated to the recall of the Elder Gods! We are, heaven knows, capable of all and any foolishness!

Rising, I caught sight of myself in a mirror. I was haggard and pale almost beyond recognition. With immense effort I forced myself to wash and shave and change my shirt, before returning to the library, if not to my duties there. Fortunately Mrs. Craven was alone. At the sight of me she nearly dropped the books she was disposing on that anomaly, the over-size shelf. (I always detested that. It disturbs the tidy order of—but never mind.)

"Mr. Wharton, you look ill!" she cried.

I admitted that I wasn't feeling myself, and added, "In fact I think it's time I took some leave."

Setting down the books, approaching with a look of sympathy, she said, "Haven't I told you before, and often? It can't be healthy for you never to take a holiday. Even at Christmas and New Year you never go away anywhere, do you?"

My excuses were obvious at once. I said dishonestly, "I should have listened to you before. Could you manage without me for a week or two?"

"Yes, of course!"—huffily.

"Very well, then. Where's that piece of paper Dr. Schultz wrote his address on?"

"You're not thinking of going to America?" she breathed.

"That's exactly what I am thinking of."

"To look at those books he was talking about? Oh, dear! That'll be as bad as staying home! It won't be any sort of rest, will it?"

"It'll be a change," I retorted. (With Mrs. Craven I seldom stammered, we having worked together for so long.) "And they say a change is as good as a rest. Where's that bit of paper?"

"Where you left it, on your desk."

So, with determination, I employed the detestable telephone, and caught Schultz in his hotel. After many false starts, avoiding words I knew to be tricky, I conveyed to him my change of mind.

"That's great!" he exclaimed, sounding as though he meant it. "We'll cover your expenses, naturally. How soon can you come over?"

"Well, I suppose I'll have to get a passport, and a visa as well, I believe, but I don't imagine that will take too long."

"Spring vacation doesn't end for another two weeks. If you can come over say a couple of days after the start of the new semester, that'll be fine. And by the way!"

"Yes?"

"I'm sorry about that joke I made, the one about Dunwich Hall. I didn't realise you'd been so close to the old guy. But you and old Marsh will get on swimmingly, I promise."

So he'd been making inquiries about me! Why?

I controlled my voice with surprising ease. I said only, "Will you arrange for me to receive a formal invitation, including some assurance of reimbursement I can show my bank?"

"I'll get it faxed over right away," he promised.

"Excuse me—what did you say?"

It took a while to make him believe our library had no such facilities. He shrugged off the problems and suggested air express instead. I settled for that, and he rang off, leaving me in a state of total disbelief at what I had committed myself to—and more than a little scared.

But, I consoled myself, it was for a greater good.

V: A World of Abominations

I had been wrong to assume that a passport and visa could be obtained with promptitude. Bureaucracy delayed their issue for a good five weeks, during which time I was frequently incapable of discharging my regular duties. Luckily the arrival of summer entailed as usual a down-turn in demand for books while people turned to more sybaritic pastimes—among them "sunbathing", a custom dedicated in my view to the sole purpose of making normal human skin resemble the hue of a boiled lobster.

Not that, this year, I saw any of its victims. I spent every moment of spare time poring over more of my books.

Was that delay in issuance of my passport perhaps a blessing in disguise after all? Certain it is that, had I been able to depart at once, though I would have done my utmost to dissuade Schultz and Marsh from their appalling scheme, I would not so completely have comprehended the menace that looms over us. I would still have been mercifully ignorant of the full range of abominations haunting the world: the creatures that assail the island of Ponape, after which the inhabitants pattern grotesque masks that reflect a mere fraction of their originals' repulsiveness; or those beings, partly

human, partly of the race of toads, that live among and interbreed with isolated littoral communities, giving rise every so often to children possessed of
powers passing the human, totally repugnant; or what may emerge at certain phases of the year from deep lost canyons underneath the sea, to claim
unwitting sacrifice of man or beast ....

Compared to some of those I had first encountered, though, these later
horrors seemed almost benign. When they came to me in dreams I bade them
welcome, hoping they might distract me from Shub-Niggurath and Cthulhu.

Yet those ghastly monsters loomed ever shapeless in the distance,
loomed like the aura of a rumoured plague ....

Over the yet further agonies inflicted on me once my passport and visa did
at last arrive, I shall pass lightly. Let me no more than animadvert upon the
aeons that I spent among folk more devoid of hope than even I, trapped in
the uncertainty of an anteroom to Hell, awaiting with sad countenance and
weary limbs the call that would release them from one captivity to another;
the succeeding prison-close confinement that I feared would never end, or if
it did would terminate in tragedy; the strange unwholesome food, the dark
and bitter drink that were the common lot of all us pitiable souls—surely
such torments could only be hatched amid the primal source of evil in whose
nature I and I alone in modern times had been vouchsafed a glimpse!

Yet how could these sheep-like apologies for people be so dumbly
unaware of the truth? Regardless of which way I looked, I detected symptoms of what I now recognised to be the archaic infection of humankind
with non-humanity. That woman moving her neck sinuously, like a serpent;
that fat child, broad-mouthed, slack-lipped, engulfing food like any frog or
toad; that pot-bellied man shamelessly stripped to a singlet, marked with
suggestive tattoos in blue and red that writhed with every movement of his
biceps ...!

In semi-darkness images of corruption danced before my eyes, a parade
of seventy times seven deadly sins. I tried to drowse, if not to sleep, but had
no surcease. Time stretched elastically, making each hour seem like two.

I wished I could pray, but knowing what I did I had dismissed all
notions of a kindly god, and was afraid to make appeal to any other sort.

Or ashamed.

Then, at last, at what should have been five in the afternoon but, so
declared our bright-faced jailers, was actually midday, the plane touched
down at Logan Airport, Boston, USA.

So altered was my case that when Schultz spotted me amid a seething
throng, reunited with my luggage but at a loss which way to turn, I positively welcomed him and even shook his hand.

"You look like death warmed over!" he exclaimed. "You must have had a Hell of a trip! Come on! My car is just across the way!"

I raised no objection, not even when he took my arm, not even when he started to address me as Jasper. I let him guide me to and into his car— small and cramped, unlike those that I (even I!) had seen portrayed by films, if not the television which I do not own—and drive me away to a destination that might as well have been in the middle of a jungle. It had crossed my mind to look up the New World Arkham in a gazetteer, but none of the atlases in the public library included it. Nor Dunwich, come to that. At least I had located Massachusetts, and knew I was already in it.

So, I assumed, the ride would be a short one. I had not bargained for the sheer size of this young country.

My impulse to respond politely to Schultz's garrulity fell foul first of a recurrence of my stammer, then of the overwhelming urgency of my mission, which I wished to complete with all possible dispatch, having already developed an extreme distaste for America. My impediment, however, prevented me from interrupting the tour-guide lecture he delivered as we followed a series of identical concrete roads aswarm and astink with such traffic as I had never seen (and in which I once more detected the force of evil at work). Before he finally broached the subject that had lured me here I had fallen prey to exhaustion, so that instead of impressing on him the need to abandon his and Marsh's project I yawned and yawned, and yawned again, in vast embarrassment.

"Sorry, Jasper!" he cried. "You go ahead and get some shuteye! I guess you must be pretty badly jetlagged!"

Miraculously, as though the images that had been haunting me had proved incapable of crossing the Atlantic, lulled by the susurrus of the engine and the wheels I fell into a dreamless sleep.

From which, all too soon, I was aroused. Yet it was as though I was continuing to sleep, despite my open eyes, my coherent answers to such questions as were put to me, my ability to register what room I'd been assigned to in the guest accommodations of the university whose name I'd first misheard as "Mixed Atomic." I even glimpsed some rather handsome buildings dating at a guess from the late eighteenth century. (My accommodation was not in any of them, alas, but in an ugly modern abortion of concrete and glass.)

Moving like a somnambulist, I declined refreshment and the offer of an "evening" meal, and contrived to indicate how much I needed rest. Schultz took his leave with a final promise that penetrated the veil of my fatigue.

"I'll pick you up at seven, okay? We can breakfast before going to the lab."

Lab? My sluggish mind interpreted: *laboratory*. But what could one of those ghastly places have to do with the study of ancient manuscripts ...?

Oh, yes: that was the sort of place where they kept computers.

"There'll be plenty of time to show off what we're doing before you meet old Marsh. He never turns up much before nine. See you in the morning—pleasant dreams!"

I almost screamed at him. How pleasant did he think the dreams could be of someone acquainted with Tsathoggua?

Still, I had slept relaxedly in the car; perhaps with an ocean between me and the revolting *Necronomicon* I might look forward to more blessed rest. I tumbled into bed with a degree of hope.

Blasted once more. As though a tentacle of thought had stretched immaterially from a place beyond our universe into my brain, when I awoke at three o'clock their time, a lazy eight by British, it was to hear a soundless sniggering voice: "Ah, but all you have is a translation. Here they have the Arabic original."

I slept no more, and when Schultz called for me I was as haggard as I'd been the day before.

VI: My Worst Fears Confirmed

A few nearly familiar items among what I was offered for breakfast—cereal, offensively sweet and drenched with "milk" that tasted as though it emanated from a factory and not a cow; coffee, dilute and lacking in aroma—restored a fraction of my spirits, though I was completely unable to match Schultz's effusive morning *bonhomie*. I had bravely swallowed the last mouthful before he summoned me to his laboratory.

Apprehensive of imminent dyspepsia, I perforce obeyed.

Conceivably, had I not been exposed to awareness of the horrors that underlie the most idyllic scenes on Earth, I might have approved the surroundings in which I found myself, for—unlike my preconceived impression of American towns and universities—there was some sense of history, of continuity, about this Arkham, petty though a memorial boasting of events in 1812 might appear beside the timber frames of Dunwich Great Hall, erected in the fourteenth century ... ah, but I'd seen those shrouded in ash, then sold for kindling-wood—"One with Nineveh and Tyre!"

Indeed the taste of ashes filled my mouth as we entered Schultz's laboratory, where two swarthy young men and an olive-skinned young woman (I guessed them to be Egyptians or Syrians) were busying themselves about luminous screens and humming cabinets. Here was a room from which all sense of the past had been excluded so completely that even the stench of its air made one feel queasy. This place was consecrated to the false gods of tomorrow—those of hope and progress, those of enterprise and understanding. How could anyone aware of Shub-Niggurath and Cthulhu, Yog-

Sothoth and Tsathoggua, look on such empty dreams and be convinced? Sooner or later, inevitably, it would be the fate of places like this to be trampled into dust. What hollow aspirations, what sins of self-delusion, did they stand for!

Schultz immediately lapsed into jargon I found incomprehensible. His talk of "flops" and "mips" sounded like puerile gibberish. In vain I searched the screens, that displayed letters as well as numbers, for plain honest English. I found nothing but nonsensical abbreviations and ungrammatical incomplete sentences:

> PROCESSING JOB #216—SEARCH
> UNSUCCESSFUL ALLOT PRIORITY↵
> @p:X*vocab\sort—STALLED DUE UNDEFINED
> PARAMETER <<limit+>>...↵

As someone spotted the last and, appearing to understand what it implied, pressed a key that started the machine working again, I found my voice and forced out, "But what exactly is it you are *doing?*"

As so often when I at last utter a question after being frustrated by my stammer, the words emerged shrilly, in a near-screech. All those present turned to stare at me—Schultz, discourteous as ever, had not troubled to make introductions—exchanged glances and shrugs, and went back to what passed for their work.

Schultz said after a moment, "Ah, that's right. You don't even have a fax at your library, so I guess you don't have computers, either."

His pitying tone made me feel like some kind of naked Kaffir, which I presume was the intention. Before I could bridle at the offence, though, he was talking again.

Slowly and more comprehensibly, thank goodness—though what he told me was the reverse of reassuring.

"These kids here are native-born Arabic speakers. I set them to producing a rough translation—"

My heart sank. I blurted, "*What of?*"

"You mean I didn't tell you? I'm sure I did, back in Britain!" He stared at me blankly.

"Not ...," I ventured faintly

"Sure! The *Necronomicon*, what else? You were the only guy I ran across who even seemed to know what I was talking about, so .... Sorry anyway. But since we seem to have absolutely the only copy in the world—and since it is referred to in a good few other texts—it struck the prof and me as the obvious place to start. And on the basis of the rough draft ...."

I lost the next couple of sentences, overwhelmed by the realisation that he was still unaware of the existence of my copy in Latin. When I heard clearly again, he was saying, "Hey, Sayeed! Mind if I suspend the run on

Two? Dr. Wharton here—excuse me, Jasper!—*Mr.* Wharton wants to see how the text is being processed."

"Sure, go ahead," said Sayeed, who was about twenty-five and handsome with a dark pencil moustache. At that age he was plainly the oldest of the three. The girl looked as if she might still be in her teens. What in the world could these *children* bring to the decipherment of so precious a bibliographic treasure?

I forced myself to go on listening.

Pressing keys, Schultz (he had told me to call him Hiram when he started addressing me as Jasper, but I was disinclined to comply) continued in the patient tone of one addressing a dullard.

"First, of course, we catalogued all the words in order of frequency of appearance. See?"

A vocabulary list sprang to the screen, Arabic on the right, on the left known and tentative equivalents. The first few score were so commonplace I asked why they were included.

"Oh, the incidence of use of conjunctions, common verbs, and adjectives—that can help determine whether it's the work of a single author or whether it's been added to by other hands …. I'll skip this, and show you the list of words that don't appear anywhere else—no, hold that. You should see the anomalous frequencies first. Look how often the word 'horror' shows up, and 'evil', and 'monster!'"

He turned his head and grinned, displaying massive white teeth.

"No wonder they said the old guy was nuts!"

"But…"

The word emerged late, as a whisper. He had already dismissed that list in favour of another. I shook in my shoes as I saw, in a dozen variant spellings, Cthulhu, Hastur, Shub-Niggurath, Tsathoggua, Yog-Sothoth …!

Why are these people not aware of what they've stumbled on? Is it that their machines still insulate them? If so, what will happen when they find themselves reading a text superior to mine?

"These appear to be names," he went on didactically. "None of them are Arabic." (I wanted to correct him: he should have said "is"—but again it was too late.) "What we need to establish now is what language they were borrowed from. That's what Fatima is doing."

Overhearing her name, the girl turned and smiled. She was pretty in a dark-complexioned way, and it horrified me to think that someone so young and innocent had been assigned to delve into such arcane and dreadful matters. In that moment I could have strangled Schultz … but most of all I needed to sit down with him and his professor and reason with them, tell them why they absolutely must give up this perilous notion of making a cheap translation freely available to the public!

So I calmed myself as best I could. I even said, "Go on."

"Fascinating, isn't it?" he crowed. "So ... ah, yeah. Fatima is running comparisons of the possible roots of these here names, using a data-base containing first of all the languages known to have donated a word or words to medieval Arabic."

I found my voice at last. I said, "I bet she hasn't made a single match."

Schultz straightened, beaming at me. "I *knew* it was a good idea to bring you over!" he declared. "Here you haven't been in the lab half an hour, and you have that much insight into the problem! You're right! We drew a blank with all the non-Arabic languages of North Africa and the Middle East, barring a few possible resemblances in Coptic."

He paused meaningfully. More or less against my will, I said, "Surely those are more likely to be borrowings from the same common source."

"*Pree*-cisely the conclusion we already came to!" he said in delight. Glancing at his watch, he added, "The prof ought to be here soon. I look forward to seeing his face when I tell him what you just said. We need insights like yours to get this show really on the road."

Unscrambling his *argot* as best I could, I hazarded, "Am I to assume so far you haven't translated the whole work?"

"Hell, no!"—with a rueful shrug. "We have a credible rendering of maybe a quarter, but a lot of that is still pretty tentative. That's why I appealed to you. Want to see how far we've got?"

I drew a deep breath. Did I ...? Though my palms were sweating and my heart was pounding, scholarly curiosity overcame my terror and I gave a nod.

Up on the screen came a complexly-annotated version of the first page. For an instant my heart leapt; I thought this was a completely different work, perhaps a forgery—but no. Subconsciously I'd been expecting to see what I had so often read and re-read, the introduction in my own copy. Instead, here was the Islamic invocation the translator had mentioned, in virtually the identical form. A horrifying thought: could these people be in possession of the actual copy he had worked from?

If so ...

Here "Satan" was rendered as "Shaitan", but that was the sole difference apart from phrasing. I began to shiver.

Over his shoulder Schultz said, "Be interesting to find some of Alhazred's juvenilia, hm? I've got Gamal looking into that"—with a jerk of his thumb at the so-far nameless third student. "No luck so far, but we live in hope."

My gorge rose. I tasted bile. The resources these—these *charlatans* disposed of, while I was compelled to eke money from my food-budget in order to buy stamped return envelopes for distant libraries!

The display changed again. In utter despair I read familiar meanings in unfamiliar form. My Latin version was, it seemed, at best fair. Its unknown author had missed subtleties and overtones in the original, so vivid even in this cold and passionless context that my skin crawled. When Schultz asked if I had seen enough I waved impatiently: go on, go on!

At last the screen blanked, and standing up, stretching his long arms—they struck me suddenly as ape-like, and my nape prickled—he said, "That's as far as we've got. How does it grab you?"

I stared at him in disbelief.

"How can it not grab *you?*" I countered, borrowing his crude but graphic phrase. "Have you actually read this?"

"Sure! Lost count of how many times!"

"And you're not affected? You're not worried"—here at last I came to the purpose of my visit, so different from what he was blithely assuming—"about making this available in a cheap paperback?"

"Why should we be?"—dropping his arms again. "It is kind of esoteric, granted, but with the right promotion it might attract a cult following, sell maybe a hundred thousand, cover a good slice of our costs. Provided, of course, it takes off among the New Age people. The Dean wasn't too sold on the deal at first, but since Professor Marsh ran a snow-job past him he's gung-ho for the idea. Speak of the devil—! Prof! You're early! Eager to meet this bright spark from Britain? I told you he'd turn up trumps, and he's already second-guessed us on at least two points!"

I turned very slowly to see whom he was addressing, and the moment I set eyes on Abner Marsh, I *knew*.

Knew why these people were untouched by the horrifying truths Alhazred had expressed.

Knew why they were so eager to mass-market them.

Knew why they wanted to trap me, the only person in the world who could have given them the lie direct ....

For this—this *thing* that lumbered into the laboratory was clad in scales! Stumping along, it slobbered from its loose-lipped mouth. Between crusted eyelids its evil gaze met mine. It offered what was not a human hand disguised in a cotton glove, its other hidden in the pocket of the jacket that it wore. Its voice was less than human, too: instead, a croak!

Yes, in that instant all was clear. I had had access to books these idiots did not—books which would have let them at any rate suspect the reason for this frightful plan to loose the Elder Gods upon the world. They did not know about the masks of Ponape—about the dwellers in the ocean deeps—about the doom upon the Tso-Tso of Tibet—most of all about the unholy liaisons between human and inhuman that had taken place here in this very state of Massachusetts since the arrival of the first settlers from Europe!

Here, plainly recognisable save to those whom it had duped, was just such a hybrid monster as would serve the purpose of the Elder Gods. Under its sway Schultz and his companions were engaged in opening not one path for their return but thousands, soon as a horde of pitiable fools laid hands upon their version of the *Necronomicon*! Most would fail in the enactment of its ceremonies, but here and there a gifted mind, perverted to the paths of evil, must of a certainty succeed ...!

The doom that came to Sarnath would be as nothing to the horrors so vast a breach in our defensive barricade might let loose on the world!

I had to act! For the sake of humankind, of life on Earth, I had to act!

Casting around for a weapon, I found none—not a stick, not a paperknife, nothing. At least, though, I could smash and strangle with bare hands! I know nothing of computers, but it seemed plausible that if I slammed down all the keys on all the keyboards randomly that might disrupt their evil task. I did so, trusting that I could distract them while I poised to launch myself at the weakly-seeming entity who posed as Marsh. I flailed to right and left, heard cries of anger first, then gratifying terror, knew I had achieved the first part of my plan, and rushed at Marsh. Talon-curved, my hands approached his throat—

Something hard and heavy struck my nape, just below the occiput. I had not even time to cry aloud before I fell.

VII: The Triumph of Evil

"None so blind as those who will not see?" It's worse than that! None are so deaf as those who will not listen! They've spun me endless lies concerning Abner Marsh—used words like "ichthyosis" expecting them to baffle me. Me, who read fluently in Ancient Greek at ten? It implies skin growing scaly, like a fish's. I know that!

When I ask them *why* a human being grows a scaly skin, they cannot answer. I tell them why, and they refuse to listen! The same when I ask why a biped should have eyes with crusted lids, a flattened nose, a wide slack mouth, stump legs and hands so deformed they must hide in gloves!

I know! I can tell them! I have told them, over and over! Such is the power of the hybrid servants of the Elder Gods, their ears are closed alike against my pleading and my reasoned arguments.

I wrote to Mrs. Craven, who did not reply. No doubt they destroy my letters. I wrote to others, people who once respected me for my scholarship though I had never met them, and likewise had no answer, not a single one. I already told you how useless were my country's diplomatic representatives ....

I can feel a throbbing underground, that makes my prison tremble. My jailers attribute it to subway trains, but I sense it to be the working of a giant press, turning out copies by the countless thousands of the *Necronomicon*. Now I am no longer there to protect it, sooner or later Marsh and his victims will trace my Latin version and use it (better than computers!) to verify their text. Its translator, after all, was closer in time to Alhazred ....

All I can do, after so much struggle, is sit here and wait.

I pray occasionally to Nyarlathotep. At least he wears a quasi-human guise ....

Sometimes, especially at night, I hear faint words, not in any of the languages I've studied. Yet, thanks to my reading in the Peabody bequest, I find I can make sense of certain phrases, and the sound of them strikes chill into my marrow. I hear eldritch voices moaning:

"Llllll-nglui, nnnn-lagl, fhtagn-ngah, ai Yog-Sothoth!"

"I know what it means! Yog-Sothoth is the Lurker at the Threshold! When fools breach the barrier He will be first to pass! But what I want to ask is a question none will answer:

Why me? Why me and no one else?

"Nyarlathotep, who bearest at least the guise of humankind: wilt Thou not answer—?"

What a waste of breath! For this, above all, Alhazred taught about the Elder Gods:

They do not care, and that explains the universe.

Fred Chappell is the author of *Dagon*, one of the most horrific of Mythos tales because it recalls the secret that the rest of us have forgotten, that Lovecraftian horrors are in large measure allegorical transfigurations of worldly horrors we dare not acknowledge. His Cthulhuvian works are few and far between, as scarce as the overt Lovecraftian references in *Dagon*. Thus when he pens a new one, it is sure to be well worth going to some trouble to seek it out. His remarkable tale "Weird Tales" can be found in *The Year's Best Horror Stories: Series XIII*, 1985. Here is another, which appeared first in Mark Rainey's wonderful magazine *Deathrealm* #9, 1989.

In some of the tales in this collection the *Necronomicon* is fairly tangential. It may serve mainly as a lamp of darkness, lending some atmosphere to the story in which it appears. In others it serves as a Greek chorus, interpreting the action for the reader at certain crucial points when no character knows enough to explain it. In Chappell's "The Adder", as in Wellman's "The Terrible Parchment", the *Necronomicon* has become almost a character in its own right, an antagonist. Here is where the conceptuality of structuralist A. J. Greimas comes in handy. Greimas speaks of "actants" and "actanial roles" integral to a narrative. An actant is a narrative role or function that may correspond to a character, or two or more characters may divide the same function (say, of villain) between them. Or a single character may play more than one actanial role at different points in the same narrative (as when, in the play *Godspell*, the same character plays first the "donor" role and then the "betrayer/false friend" role, whereas in the Gospels, these two roles are played by two different characters, John the Baptist and Judas Iscariot). In "The Adder" the *Necronomicon* is no mere prop, but occupies an actanial role. To adopt Seymour Chatman's distinction, it is no longer part of an "event" (something which befalls characters) but of an "action" (something initiated by a character).

What is the fiendish role of the *Necronomicon*? It is the incarnation of Dissemination, that rampant force of file corruption, that runaway virus of Dionysian free play and meaning-variation that is always already rampaging through all texts simply by virtue of their being texts. Any use of language is a stone of *parole* (a distinct speech act) dropped into the sea of *langue* (the implicit text of *arche*-writing presupposed by all speaking or writing), and waves will be unleashed that cannot be controlled. It is a calling up of that which cannot be put down. Dissemination is like the invisible letter scattered throughout the body of the Torah-text, as posited by Kabbalistic scribes, which would one day become visible to play havoc with what we had thought was the plain sense of the text, any text.

Finally, what has the adder to do with the fly? (You'll see what I mean.) The fly that escapes to spread abroad a poison of text-chaos, letter-mutation, is again Dissemination. It cannot be found and swatted, leaving an ointment of meaning free of it. The *Al-Azif* is Dissemination, the uncorked demon that can never be gotten back into the bottle; it is the fly, because *al-azif* means "the buzzing", a fact Lovecraft derived from the *Arabian Nights*. This association, in turn, derives from the fact that ancient, pre-Islamic *kahin* (fortune-tellers, mad poets) used to receive their revelations in the form of the insect-like chitterings of the desert *jinn* who whispered secrets into their ears. And you know the notorious ambiguity (dissemination of meaning) of oracles.

The Adder

by Fred Chappell

My Uncle Alvin reminds the startled stranger of a large happy bunny. He is pleasantly rotund, and with silver blond hair that makes him look a full decade younger than his sixty years. His skin has a scrubbed pink shine that the pale complexions of English curates sometimes acquire, and he has a way of wrinkling his nose that one irresistibly associates with—well, I've already named rabbits. He is a kindly, humorous, and often a mildly mischievous fellow.

My admiration of Uncle Alvin has had a large measure of influence upon my life. His easygoing manner has seemed to me a sensible way to get along in the world. His occupation is interesting and leisurely, though it's unlikely he'll ever gain great wealth by it. I can support this latter supposition by my own experience; I followed my uncle into the antiquarian book trade and I am not—please let me assure you—a rich man.

We don't compete with one another, however. Uncle Alvin lives in Columbia, South Carolina, and runs his mail order business from his home. The bulk of my trade is also mail order, but I run it from a shopfront in Durham, North Carolina. My shop sells used paperbacks, mostly to Duke University students; in the back I package and mail out rare and curious books of history, the occult, and fantasy, along with some occasional odd science fiction. Uncle Alvin specializes in Civil War history, which in South Carolina almost guarantees a living income, however modest.

Anyone in the trade is likely to happen upon any sort of book, whether it belongs to his specialty or not. When Uncle Alvin called one Saturday morning to say that he had come into possession of a volume that he wanted me to see, I surmised that it was more in my line than his, and that he thought I might be interested in making a purchase.

"What sort of book is it?" I asked.

"Very rare indeed—if it's genuine. And still rather valuable if it's only a forgery."

"What's the title?"

"Oh, I can't tell you that on the telephone," he said.

"You can't tell me the title? It must be something extraordinary."

"Caution never hurts. Anyway, you can see it for yourself. I'll be by your place with it on Monday morning. If that's all right with you."

"Say, that's grand," I said. "You'll stay overnight, of course. Helen will be thrilled to see you."

"No," he said, "I'm driving through to Washington. I'll stop off on the way. Because I don't want to keep this book in the car any longer than I have to."

"We'll have lunch, at least," I said. "Do you still crave lasagne?"

"Day and night," he replied.

"Then it's settled," I said and we chatted a little longer before ringing off.

******

Monday morning he entered my shop—called Alternate Histories—carrying a battered metal cashbox, and I knew the book was inside it. We sounded the usual pleasantries that friendly kinfolk make with one another, though ours may have been more genuinely felt than many. But he was anxious to get to the business he had in mind. He set the cashbox on top of a stack of used magazines on the counter and said, "Well, this is it."

"All right," I said, "I'm ready. Open her up."

"First, let me tell you a little bit about what I think we have here," he said. "Because when you see it you're going to be disappointed. Its appearance is not prepossessing."

"All right."

"In the first place, it's in Arabic. It's handwritten in a little diary in ordinary badly faded ink and it's incomplete. Since I don't read Arabic, I don't know what's missing. I only know that it's too short to be the full version. This copy came to me from the widow of a classics professor at the University of South Carolina, an Egyptologist who disappeared on a field excursion some thirty years ago. His wife kept his library all this time, hoping for his return. Then, last year, she offered up the whole lot. That's how I happen to be in possession of this copy of *Al-Azif*."

"I never heard of it," I said, trying not to show the minor disappointment I felt.

"It's the work of a medieval poet thought to have been insane," Uncle Alvin said, "but there is debate as to how crazy he actually was. His name was Abdul Alhazred and he lived in Yemen. Shortly after composing *Al-Azif* he met a violent and grisly death—which is all we know about it because even the eyewitnesses dispute the manner of his dying."

"Abdul Alhazred. Isn't that—?"

"Yes, indeed," he said. "The word is more recognizable under the title of its Greek translation. The *Necronomicon*. And the most widely known text—if any of them can really be said to be widely known—is the thir-

teenth century Latin translation of Olaus Wormius. It has always been surmised that the original Arabic text perished long ago, since every powerful
government and respected religious organization has tried to destroy the
work in all its forms. And they have largely succeeded in doing so."

"But how do you know what it is, if you don't read Arabic?"

"I have a friend," he said proudly. "Dr. Abu-Saba. I asked him to look
at it and to give me a general idea of the contents. When I handed it to him
and he translated the title, I stopped him short. Better not go on with *that*.
You know the reputation of the *Necronomicon*."

"I do indeed," I said, "and I don't care to know what's in it in any detail.
In fact, I'm not really overjoyed at finding myself in such close company."

"Oh, we should be safe enough. As long as we keep our mouths closed
so that certain unsavory groups of cultists don't hear that we've got it."

"If you're offering it to me for sale—" I began.

"No, no," he said hastily. "I'm trying to arrange to deposit it in the
Library of Congress. That's why I'm going to Washington. I wouldn't put
my favorite nephew in jeopardy—or not for long, anyway. All I would like
is for you to keep it for a week while I'm negotiating. I'm asking as a personal favor."

I considered. "I'll be happy to keep it for you," I said. "To tell the truth,
I'm more concerned about the security of the book than about my own safety. I can take care of myself. But the book is a dangerous article, and an
extremely valuable one."

"Like an atomic weapon," Uncle Alvin said. "Too dangerous too keep
and too dangerous to dispose of. But the Library of Congress will know what
to do. This can't be the first time they've encountered this problem."

"You think they already have a *Necronomicon*?"

"I'd bet money," he said cheerfully, "except that I wouldn't know how
to collect. You don't expect them to list it in the catalog, do you?"

"They'd deny possession, of course."

"But there's a good chance they won't have an Arabic version. Only
one is known to have reached America and it was thought to have been
destroyed in San Francisco around the turn of the century. This volume is
probably a copy of that version."

"So what do I do with it?" I asked.

"Put it in a safe place. In your lockbox at the bank."

"I don't have one of those," I said. "I have a little old dinky safe in my
office in the back, but if anyone came to find it, that's the first place
they'd look."

"Do you have a cellar in this shop?"

"Not that I'd trust the book to. Why don't we take a hint from Edgar
Allan Poe?"

He frowned a moment, then brightened. "A purloined letter, you mean?"

"Sure. I've got all sorts of books scattered about in cardboard boxes. I haven't sorted them yet to shelve. It would take weeks for someone to hunt it out even if he knew it was here."

"It might work," Uncle Alvin said, wrinkling his nose and rubbing his pink ear with a brisk forefinger. "But there's a problem."

"What's that?"

"You may wish to disregard it because of its legendary nature. I wouldn't. In the case of *Al-Azif*, it's best to take every precaution."

"All right," I said. "What's the legend?"

"Among certain bookmen, the *Necronomicon* is sometimes known as *The Adder*. Because first it poisons, then it devours."

I gave him a look that I intended to mean: not another one of your little jokes, Uncle Alvin. "You don't really expect me to believe that we've got a book here that eats people."

"Oh no." He shook his head. "It only eats its own kind."

"I don't understand."

"Just make sure," he said, "that when you place it in a box with other books, none of them is important."

"I get it," I said. "Damaged cheap editions. To draw attention away from its true value."

He gave me a long mild stare, then nodded placidly. "Something like that," he replied at last.

"Okay," I agreed, "I'll do exactly that. Now let's have a look at this ominous rarity. I've heard about the *Necronomicon* ever since I became interested in books. I'm all a-flutter."

"I'm afraid you're going to be disappointed," Uncle Alvin said. "Some copies of this forbidden text are quite remarkable, but this one—" He twitched his nose again and rubbed it with the palm of his hand.

"Now don't be a naughty tease, Uncle Alvin," I said.

He unlocked the metal box and took out a small parcel wrapped in brown paper. He peeled away the paper to reveal a rather thin octavo diary with a worn morocco cover that had faded from what would have been a striking red to a pale brick color, almost pinkish. Noticing the expression on my face, he said, "See? I told you it would be a disappointment."

"No, not at all," I said, but my tone was so obviously subdued that he handed it to me to examine without my asking.

There was little to see. The pinkish worn binding felt smooth. The spine was hubbed and stamped Diary in gold, but the gold too had almost worn away. I opened it at random and looked at incomprehensible Arabic script so badly faded that it was impossible to say what color the ink had been. Black or purple or maybe even dark green—but now all the colors had become a pale uniform gray. I leafed through almost to the end but found nothing in the least remarkable.

"Well, I do hope this is the genuine article," I said. "Are you sure your friend, Dr. Hoodoo—"

"Abu-Saba," said Uncle Alvin primly. "Dr. Fuad Abu-Saba. His knowledge of the native tongue is impeccable, his integrity unassailable."

"Okay, if you say so," I said. "But what we have here doesn't look like much."

"I'm not trying to sell it. Its nondescript appearance is in our favor. The more undistinguished it looks, the safer we are."

"That makes sense," I admitted, handing it back to him.

He glanced at me shrewdly as he returned it to the cashbox, obviously thinking that I was merely humoring him—as to a certain extent I was. "Robert," he said sternly, "you're my favorite nephew, one of my most favorite persons. I want you to follow my instructions seriously. I want you to take the strongest precautions and keep on your guard. This is a dangerous passage for both of us."

I sobered. "All right, Uncle Alvin. You know best."

He wrapped the volume in the brown paper and restored it to the scarred box and carried it with him as we repaired to Tony's Ristorante Venezia to indulge copiously in lasagne and a full-bodied Chianti. After lunch he dropped me back at Alternate Histories and, taking *Al-Azif* out of the metal box, gave it over to my safekeeping with a single word of admonition. "Remember," he said.

"Don't worry," I said. "I remember."

******

In the shop I examined the book in a more leisurely and comprehensive fashion. It hadn't changed; it was only one more dusty faded stained diary like thousands of others and its sole distinction to the unlearned eye was that it was in handwritten Arabic script. A mysterious gang of sinister thieves would have to know a great deal about it merely in order to know what to search for.

I decided not to trust it to a jumble of books in a maze of cardboard boxes. I took it into my little backroom office, shoved some valueless books out of the way, and laid it flat on a lower shelf of a ramshackle bookcase there that was cluttered with every sort of pamphlet, odd periodical, and assorted volume from broken sets of Maupassant, Balzac, and William McFee. I turned it so that the gilt edge faced outward and the word "Diary" was hidden. Then I deliberated for a minute or two about what to stack on top of it.

I thought of Uncle Alvin's warning that no important books were to be placed with *Al-Azif* and I determined to heed it. What's the point in having a favorite uncle, wise and experienced in his trade, if you don't listen to him? Besides that, the dark reputation of the book was an urgent warning in itself.

I picked up an ordinary and utterly undistinguished copy of Milton's poems. Herndon House, New York, 1924. No introduction and a few sketchy notes by an anonymous editor, notes no doubt reduced from a solid scholarly edition. It was a warped copy and showed significant water damage. I opened to the beginning of *Paradise Lost* and read the first twenty-six lines, then searched to find my favorite Miltonic sonnet, number XIX, "On His Blindness."

> When I consider how my light is spent
> Ere half my days, in this dark world and wide,
> And that one Talent which is death to hide,
> Lodg'd with me useless, though my Soul more bent
> To serve therewith my Maker, and present
> My true account, lest he returning chide ...

Well, you know how it goes.

It's a poem of which I never tire, one of those poems which has faithfully befriended me in periods happy and unhappy since the years of my majority. Milton's customary stately music is there, and a heartfelt personal outcry not often to be found in his work. Then there comes the sternly contented resolution of the final lines. Milton requires, of course, no recommendation from me, and his sonnet no encomium. I only desire to make it clear that this poet is important to me and the sonnet on his blindness particularly dear.

But not every copy, or every edition, of Milton is important. I have personal copies of fully annotated and beautifully illustrated editions. The one I held in my hand was only a cheap mass edition, designed in all probability to be sold at railway bookstalls. I placed it on top of the Arabic treasure and then piled over both books a stack of papers from my desk which is always overflowing with such papers: catalogues, booklists, sale announcements, and invoices. Of this latter item especially there is an eternal surplus.

Then I forgot about it.

No, I didn't.

I didn't in the least forget that I almost certainly had in my possession *Al-Azif*, one of the rarest documents in bibliographic annals, one of the enduring titles of history and legend. And one of the deadliest. We don't need to rehearse the discomfiting and unsanitary demises alleged of so many former owners of the book. They all came to bad ends, and messy ones. Uncle Alvin had the right idea, getting the volume into the hands of those prepared to care for it. My mission was merely a holding action—to keep it safe for a week. That being so, I resolved not to go near it, not even to look at it until my uncle returned the following Saturday.

I was able to keep to my resolution until Tuesday, the day after I'd made it.

******

The manuscript in its diary format had changed when I looked. I noticed right away that the morocco covers had lost their pinkish cast and taken on a bright red. The stamped word Diary shone more brightly too and when I opened the volume and leafed through it, I saw that the pages had whitened, losing most of the signs of age, and that the inked script stood forth more boldly. It was now possible to discern, in fact, that the writing actually was clothed in different colors of ink: black, emerald green, royal purple, Persian rose.

The *Necronomicon*, in whatever version, is a remarkable book. All the world knows something of its reputation, and I might have been more surprised if my encounter with it had been uneventful than if something unusual transpired. Its history is too long, and a knowledgeable scholar does not respond to mysterious happenings in the presence of the book by smiting his breast and exclaiming, "Can such things be?"

But a change in the physical makeup of the book itself was something I had not expected and could not account for. Not knowing yet what to think, I replaced it just as it had been, beneath the random papers and the copy of Milton, and went on with my ordinary tasks.

There was, however, no denying the fact of the changes. My senses did not belie me. Each time I examined it on Tuesday and Wednesday—I must have picked it up a dozen times all told—our *Al-Azif* had grown stronger.

Stronger. As silly as that word seems in this context, it is still accurate. The script was becoming more vivid, the pages gleamed like fresh snowbanks, the staunch morocco covers glowed blood-red.

It took me too long to understand that this manuscript had found something to feed upon. It had discovered a form of nourishment which caused it to thrive and grow stout. I am embarrassed to admit that more hours elapsed before I guessed the source of the volume's food—which had to be the copy of Milton's poems I had placed on top of it.

Quickly then I snatched up the Milton and began to examine it for changes. At first I could discover no anomalies. The print seemed perhaps a little grayer, but it had already been rather faded. Perhaps too the pages were more brittle and musty than I'd thought—but, after all, it was a cheap book some sixty-odd years old. When I turned to the opening of *Paradise Lost*, all seemed well enough; the great organ tones were as resonant as ever:

> Of Man's First Disobedience, and the Fruit
> Of that Forbidden Tree, whose mortal taste
> Brought Death into the World, and all our woe ...

And I thought, *Well, I needn't have worried. This poetry is immune to the ravages of time and of all circumstance.*

So it was in anticipation of a fleeting pleasure that I turned idly to glance at sonnet XIX:

> When I consider how my loot is spent
> On Happy Daze, a fifth of darling wine ...

The familiar opening of the sonnet had lost much of its savor; I was missing something of that intimate stateliness I was accustomed to. I set down my pallid reaction to tiredness and excited nerves. Anxiety about Uncle Alvin's treasure was beginning to tell on me, I thought.

I shook my head as if to clear it, closed my eyes and rubbed them with both hands, then looked once more into the volume of Milton open on the counter, sonnet XIX:

> When I consider how my lute is bent
> On harpy fates in this dork woolly-wold,
> And that dung-yellow witches' breath doth glide,
> Lobster and toothless ...

No use. I was too confused to make sense of the lines at all. It's only nerves, I thought again, and thought too how glad I would be for my uncle's return on Sunday.

I laid the copy of *Al-Azif* aside and determined to put the puzzle out of my mind.

I couldn't do that, of course. The idea had occurred that our particular copy of Abdul Alhazred's forbidden work was changing the nature of Milton's lines. What was it Uncle Alvin had compared it to? An adder, was it? First it poisons, he said, then it devours. Was it indeed poisoning the lines of the great seventeenth century poet? I took up the Milton again and opened to the beginning of his immortal religious epic:

Of a Man's First Dish of Beetles, and the Fat
Of that Forboding Fay, whom Myrtle Trent
Brought fresh into the World, and Hollywood ...

The words made no sense to me, none at all—but I couldn't remember them any differently than how they appeared on the page. I couldn't tell whether the fault lay in the book or in myself.

A sudden thought inspired me to go to my poetry shelves and find another edition of Milton's poems so that I could cross-check the strange-seeming verses. If *Al-Azif* truly was changing the words in the other, then a book untouched by the diary would render up only the purest Milton. I went round to the front and took down three copies of Milton's poems in different editions and used my favorite sonnet as a touchstone. The first one I examined was Sir Hubert Portingale's Oxbridge edition of 1957. It gave me these lines:

When I consider to whome my Spode is lent,
Ear-halves and jays on this dank girlie slide ...

It seemed incorrect somehow. I looked at the poem in Professor Y. Y. Miranda's Big Apple State University Press volume of 1974:

Winnie's Corn Cider, how my lust is burnt!

That line was wrong, I felt it in my bones. I turned to the more informal edition edited by the contemporary poet Richmond Burford:

When I consider how a lighter splint
Veered off my dice in this dour curled end-word
And that wan Talent ...

I shook my head. Was that correct? Was it anywhere near correct?

The trouble was that I couldn't remember how the lines were supposed to read. I had the vague feeling that none of these versions was the right one. Obviously, they couldn't all be right. But why couldn't I remember my favorite poem, more familiar to me than my Social Security number? Uncle Alvin's warning had been: "First it poisons, then it devours."

Now I began to interpret his words in a different way. Perhaps the *Necronomicon* didn't poison only the book it was in physical contact with, perhaps it poisoned the actual content of the work itself, so that in whatever edition it appeared, in whatever book, magazine, published lecture, scholarly essay, commonplace book, personal diary—in whatever written form—a polluted text showed up.

It was an altogether terrifying thought. Uncle Alvin had not warned against placing it with an important *edition*; his warning had concerned an important *book*. I had placed it with Milton and had infected the great poems wherever they might now appear.

Could that be right? It seemed a little farfetched. Well no, it seemed as silly as picturing Milton, the poet himself, in a Shriner's hat. It seemed just dog-dumb.

I determined to test my wild hypothesis, nevertheless. I got to the telephone and called my old friend and faithful customer in Knoxville, Tennessee, the poet Ned Clark. When he said hello, I was almost rude: "Please don't ask me a lot of questions, Ned. This is urgent. Do you have a copy of Milton's poems handy?"

He paused. Then: "Robert, is that you?"

"Yes, it is. But I'm in an awful hurry. Do you have the poems?"

"In my study."

"Can you get the book, please?"

"Hold on," he said. "I have an extension. I'll pick up in there." I waited as patiently as I was able until he said, "Here we are. What's the big deal?"

"Sonnet XIX," I said. "Would you please read it to me?"

"Right now? Over the phone?"

"Yes. Unless you can shout very loud."

"Hey, man," he said. "Chill out, why don't you?"

"I'm sorry, Ned," I said, "but I think I may have made a big mistake. I mean, a heavy *bad* mistake, old son. So I'm trying to check up on something. Could you read the poem to me?"

"Sure, that's cool," he replied, and I heard him leafing through his book. "Okay, Robert. Are you ready? Here goes: 'When icons in a house mild lights suspend, Or half my ties in this stark world have died—'"

I interrupted. "Okay, Ned. Thanks. That's all I need to hear right now."

"That's all? You called long distance to hear me say two lines of your favorite poem?"

"Yes I did. How did they sound to you?"

"As good as Milton gets."

"Did they sound correct? Are those the words as you've known them all your life?"

"I haven't known them all my life," he said. "You're the wild-haired Milton fan. He's too monumental for my taste, you know? I mean, massive."

"Okay, but you've read the poem, at least."

"Yes, indeedy. It's a big-time famous poem. I read all those babies, you know that."

"And these lines are the ones you've always known?"

Another pause. "Well, maybe not exactly," he admitted. "I think the punctuation might be a little different in this book from what I'm used to. But it mainly sounds right. Do you want publication information?"

"Not now," I said, "but I may call back later for it." I thanked my friend and hung up.

It seemed that my surmise was correct. All the texts were now envenomed. I wanted to make certain of the fact and spent the next four hours telephoning friends and acquaintances scattered throughout America, comparing the lines. Not every one answered, of course, and some of my friends in the western states were groggy with sleep, but I got a large enough sample of first lines to satisfy me.

Walt Pavlich in California: *One-eye can so draw my late sow's pen* ....

Paul Ruffin in Texas: *Wind I consider now my life has bent* ....

Robert Shepard in Hawaii: *Wound a clean liver and the lights go out* ....

Vanessa Haley in Virginia: *Wind a gone slider and collide a bunt* ....

Barbara Smith in West Virginia: *Watch a corned beef sandwich bow and bend* ....

These were enough and more for me to understand the enormity of my mistake. All the texts of Milton that existed were now disfigured beyond recognition. I had noted a further consequence of my error. Even the texts as they resided in memory were changed; not one of my friends could remember how the lines of sonnet XIX were *supposed* to read. Nor could I, and I must have been for a decade and a half one of the more constant companions of the poem.

The copy of *Al-Azif* was flourishing. I didn't even need to pick it up to see that. The gilt edge shone like a gold bar fresh from Fort Knox and the morocco binding had turned ruby red and pulsed with light like a live coal. I was curious how the inks would glitter, so now I did pick up the volume—which seemed as alive in my hands as a small animal—and opened it at random.

I was right. The different colors of the inks were as vivid and muscular as kudzu and looked as if they were bitten into the thick creamy pages like etching. However disquieting these changes, they had resulted in a truly beautiful manuscript, a masterpiece of its kind. And though I knew it to be a modern handwritten copy, it also seemed to be regaining some of its medieval characteristics. Most of the pages were no longer totally in Arabic; they had become macaronic. Toward the end pages a few English words were sprinkled into the eastern script.

Oh, no.

As long as *Al-Azif* was in Arabic it was relatively harmless. Most people would be unable to read the spells and incantations and the knowledge to be found there that is—well, the traditional epithet is "unspeakable", and it is accurately descriptive. I certainly would not speak of the contents, even if I were able to read them.

I flipped to the front. The first lines I found in the first page were these:

> Wisely did Ibn Mushacab say, that happy is the tomb
> where no wizard hath lain, and happy the town at
> night whose wizards are all ashes. For the spirit of the
> devil-indentured hastes not from his charnel clay, but
> feeds and instructs the very worm that gnaws. Then an
> awful life from corruption springs and feeds again the
> appointed scavengers upon the earth. Great holes are
> dug hidden where are the open pores of the earth, and
> things have learned to walk that ought to crawl.

I snapped the cover shut. Those phrases had the true stink of the *Necronomicon*. You don't have to be an expert upon the verses of Alhazred to recognize his style and subject matter.

I had read all of the pages that I ever wanted to read, but even so I opened the volume again, to the middle, to confirm my hypothesis. I was right: *Al-Azif* was translating itself into English, little by little. There was only a sprinkling of English in the latter pages; the early pages were English from head to foot; the middle pages half Arabic, half English. I could read phrases and sentences, but not whole passages. I could make out clearly "they dwell in the inmost adyta"; then would follow lovely Arabic calligraphy. Some of the passages I comprehended were these: "Yog-Sothoth knows the gate; in the Gulf the worlds themselves are made of sounds; the dim horrors of Earth; iä iä iä, Shub-Niggurath!"

Nothing surprising, and nothing I wanted to deal with.

I did understand what had happened. When I had so carelessly allowed this copy of *Al-Azif* to batten upon Milton's poetry, it took the opportunity to employ Milton's language in the task of translating itself. With a single thoughtless act, I had given the *Necronomicon*—call it accursed or unspeakable or maddening, call it whatever minatory adjective you choose—both life and speech and I saw the potential for harm that I had set in place.

I flung the volume into my flimsy little safe, clanged shut the door, and spun the dial. I put up the CLOSED sign on my shop door, called my wife Helen to tell her I wouldn't be home, and stood guard like a military sentinel. I would not leave my post, I decided, until Uncle Alvin returned to rescue me and all the rest of the world from a slender little book written centuries ago by a poet who ought to have known better.

Nor did my determination falter.

******

As soon as Uncle Alvin laid eyes on me Sunday morning, he knew what had gone wrong. "It has escaped, hasn't it?" he said, looking into my face. "*Al-Azif* has learned English."

"Come in," I said. When he entered I glanced up and down the empty street, then shut the door firmly and guided my uncle by his arm into my office.

He looked at the desk, at the crumpled brown paper bags that held my meals and at the dozens of empty styrofoam cups. He nodded. "You set up a watch post. That's a good idea. Where is the volume now?"

"In the safe," I said.

"What's in there with it?"

"Nothing. I took everything out."

"There's no cash in the safe?"

"Only that book you brought upon me."

"That's good," he said. "Do you know what would happen if this copy were brought into contact with cash money?"

"It would probably poison the whole economy of the nation," I said.

"That's right. All U.S. currency everywhere would turn counterfeit."

"I thought of that," I said. "You have to give me some credit. In fact, this never would have happened if you had given me a clearer warning."

"You're right, Robert, I'm sure. But I feared you'd think I was only pulling your leg. And then I thought maybe you'd experiment with it just to see what would happen."

"Not me," I said. "I'm a responsible citizen. The *Necronomicon* is too powerful to joke around with."

"Let's have a look," he said.

I opened the safe and took the volume out. Its outward appearance was unchanged, so far as I could tell. The ruby morocco was rich as a leopard pelt and the gilt edge and gold stamping gleamed like a fairy tale treasure.

When I handed it to Uncle Alvin he didn't bother to glance at the exterior of the book, but turned immediately to the latter pages. He raised his eyebrows in surprise, then began reading aloud: "The affair that shambleth about in the night, the evil that defieth the Elder Sign, the Herd that stand watch at the secret portal each tomb is known to have and that thrive on that which groweth out of the tenants thereof: All these Blacknesses are lesser than He Who guardeth the Gateway—"

"Stop, Uncle Alvin," I cried. "You know better than to read that stuff aloud." It seemed to me that it had grown darker in my little office and that a certain chill had come into the room.

He closed the book and looked at it with a puzzled expression. "My word," he said, "that is an exotic and obsolescent diction. What has *Al-Azif* been feeding on?"

"Milton," I answered.

"Ah, Milton," he said and nodded again. "I should have recognized that vocabulary."

"It has poisoned all of Milton's works," I said.

"Indeed? Let's see."

I picked up one of the copies on the desk and handed it to him.

He opened it and, without showing any expression, asked, "How do you know this book is Milton?"

"I brought all my copies in here and stacked them on the desk. I've been afraid to look at them for two days, but I know that you're holding a fairly expensive edition of John Milton's poetic works."

He turned the book toward me. The pages were blank. "Too late."

"It's eaten all the words," I said. My heart sank. I tried to remember a line of Milton, even a phrase or a characteristic word. Nothing came to mind.

"Well, maybe not *eaten*," Uncle Alvin said. "Used up, let's say. *Absorbed* might be an accurate term."

"No more Milton in the world—how am I going to live my life, knowing I'm responsible for the disappearance of Milton's works?"

"Maybe you won't have to," he replied. "Not if we get busy and bring them back."

"How can we do that? *Al-Azif* has—swallowed them," I said.

"So we must get the accursed thing to restore the poems, to spit them up for us, the way the whale spat Jonah whole and sound."

"I don't understand."

"We must cause the manuscript to retract its powers," he said. "If we can reduce it to its former state of weakness, the way it was when I first met it in Columbia, the works of John Milton will reappear on the pages—and in the minds of men."

"How do you know?"

"You don't think this is happening for the first time, do you? It has been such a recurring event that restoration procedures have been designed and are followed in a traditional—almost ritualistic—manner."

"You mean other authors have been lost to it and then recovered?"

"Certainly."

"Who?"

"Well, for instance, the works of all the Cthulhu Mythos writers have been lost to the powers of the evil gods that they describe. Stories and poems and novels by Derleth, Long, and Smith have all been recovered. The works of Lovecraft have been taken into the domain of *Al-Azif* at least a dozen times. That's why his work is so powerfully pervaded by that eldritch and sinister atmosphere. It has taken on some of the shadow of its subject."

"I never thought of that, but it makes sense. So what are the restoration procedures?"

"They're simple enough," he said. "You keep watch here while I go to my car."

He gave me the book and I set it on the edge of the desk, well away from any other written matter. I couldn't help thinking that if Uncle Alvin succeeded in defeating the powers of *Al-Azif* and rescuing the hostage works of Milton, these moments represented my last opportunity to read in the great bibliographic rarity. Simply as a physical object it was inviting: The lush red glow of the binding offered a tactile pleasure almost like a woman's skin and I knew already how the inks shone on the white velvety pages. The *Necronomicon* seemed to breathe a small breath where it lay on the desk, as if it were peacefully dozing like a cat.

I couldn't resist. I picked up and opened it to a middle page. The seductive Persian rose ink seemed to wreathe a perfume around the couplet that began the fragment of text: *That is not dead which can eternal lie, And with strange aeons even death may die.* A large green fly had settled on the bright initial that stood at the beginning of the next sentence, rubbing its legs together and feasting on the ink that shone as fresh and bright as dripping blood. I brushed at it absent-mindedly and it circled lazily toward the ceiling.

That is not dead ...

The lines sang hypnotically in my ear, in my head, and I began to think how I secretly longed to possess this volume for myself, how indeed I had burned to possess it for a long time, and how my ridiculous rabbit-faced Uncle Alvin was the only obstacle in my way to—

"No, no, Robert," Uncle Alvin said from the doorway. "Close the book and put it down. We're here to break the power of the book, not to give in to its spells."

I snapped it shut in a flash and flung it onto the desk. "Wow," I said. "Wow."

"It's an infernal piece of work, isn't it?" he said complacently. "But we'll have a hammerlock on it shortly."

He set down the metal cashbox he had formerly carried the book in and opened it up. He then laid the *Necronomicon* inside and produced from a brown paper bag under his arm a small book bound in black cloth and placed this second book on top of the other and closed the metal box and locked it with a key on his key ring. I noticed that the black book sported no title on cover or spine.

"What are we doing now?" I asked.

"The inescapable nature of this book is to cannibalize other writings," he said. "To feed upon them in order to sustain its ghoulish purposes. If it is in contact with another work, then it *must* try to feed, it cannot stop itself. The method of defeating it is to place it with a book so adamantine in nature, so resistant to evil change, to the inimical powers of darkness, that the *Necronomicon* wastes all its forces upon this object and in exhausting itself renders up again those works it had earlier consumed. It simply wears itself out and that which formerly had disappeared now reappears."

"Are you certain?" I asked. "That seems a little too simple."

"It is not simple at all," he said. "But it is effective. If you'll open up one of your copies of Milton there, we ought to be able to watch the printed words return to the pages."

"All right," I said and opened one of the blank-pages books to a place toward the front.

"The process is utterly silent," he said, "but that is deceptive. Inside this box, a terrific struggle is taking place."

"What is the unconquerable book that you put in with it?"

"I have never read it," he said, "because I am not worthy. Not yet. It is a great holy book written by a saint. Yet the man who wrote it did not know he was a saint and did not think of himself as writing a book. It is filled with celestial wisdom and supernal light, but to read it requires many years of spiritual discipline and ritual cleansing. To read such a holy book one must first become holy himself."

"What is the title?"

"Someday soon, when I have accomplished more of the necessary stages of discipline, I will be allowed to say the title aloud," he told me. "Till then I must not."

"I am glad to know there is such a book in the world," I said.

"Yes," he said. "and you should look now to see if Milton is being restored to us."

"Yes, he is," I said happily. "Words are beginning to reappear. Wait a second while I find our control poem." I leafed through rapidly to find sonnet XIX and read aloud:

> "When I consider how my light is spent,
> Ere half my days—"

"Why are you stopping?" he asked.

"It's that damned pesky green fly again." I brushed at the page. "Shoo!" I said.

The fly shooed, lifting from the book in a languorous circle, buzzing around the office for a moment, and then departing the premises through the open window there beside a broken bookshelf.

"You need to put in a screen," Uncle Alvin said. He wrinkled his nose, pawed at his ear.

"I need to do a lot of things to this old shop," I replied. "Let's see now, where were we?" I found my place on the page and began again:

> *"When I consider how my light is spent*
> *Ere half my days, in this dark world and weird—"*

"Wait a minute," my uncle said. "What was that last word?"

I looked. "Weird," I said.

He shook his head. "That's not right."

"No, it's not," I said. "At first I didn't see it was wrong because the fly covered it, the same old fly that was gobbling up the ink in the *Necronomicon*."

"A carrier," he said slowly. "It's carrying the poison that it contracted from the ink."

We looked at each other and, as the knowledge came clear to me, I cried out: *"The fly!"* Then, just as if we had rehearsed to perform the single action together, we rushed to the window.

But out there in the sleepy southern Sunday morning would be countless indistinguishable green flies, feeding, excreting, and mating.

It used to be that *Necronomicon* hoaxes were limited to bogus ads in book dealer trade journals or fake card catalog entries. No more. Nowadays, various mischief-makers have gone to the trouble of writing and publishing whole books spuriously claiming to be Alhazred's *Necronomicon*. L. Sprague deCamp, biographer of Lovecraft and Robert E. Howard, world traveler, writer, scholar, was party to the first of these tongue-in-cheek tomes, the *Al-Azif*, published by Owlswick Press in 1973. The text was simply page after page of repeated Arabesque calligraphy that meant nothing (which is, of course, pretty darn appropriate! Remember the Introduction to this collection!). Thus there was no question of translating it. But Sprague wrote a Preface, reproduced here, in which he apologized for the untranslated state of the text, explaining that the last few scholars who had ventured the job would not be venturing any jobs again soon! I have also included his later commentary on the project:

> Fourteen years ago, Alan Nourse and I were in Iraq on our way to India. We spent three days in Baghdad, seeing the city and visiting the ruins of Babylon and the Parthian palace at Ctesiphon.
>
> Six years later, when George Scithers published *Al-Azif* (*The Necronomicon*) by "Abdul Alhazred," I concocted a fanciful account of my doings in Baghdad on January 2, 1967. The *Necronomicon* was a sinister unwritten volume of magical spells invented by H. P. Lovecraft for his fantasy stories in *Weird Tales*. The work, he said, was written in the eighth century by a mad Arabian poet, who suffered the spectacular fate of being devoured by an invisible entity before terrified witnesses.
>
> Lovecraft's scholarly use of this fictitious volume convinced many that the book existed, and innumerable people have plagued librarians and booksellers for copies. Having decided that if the *Necronomicon* did not exist, it should, George Scithers hired an artist to decorate blank pages with a series of squiggles vaguely resembling Arabic and Syriac writing.
>
> I composed the preface, telling how the Iraqis sold me the manuscript after three of their savants had tried to translate it and had disappeared under strange and sinister circumstances. George's edition, comprising 348 copies, promptly sold out.
>
> I hope you get a chuckle out of this introduction—but I also trust that you will not take it seriously. I may wish to go back to Iraq some day, and I do not want this little hoax to complicate my visit.

Preface to the *Al-Azif*

by L. Sprague deCamp

Duria* is a village in northern Iraq, on the borders of the Kurdish-speaking part of the country. Otherwise much like hundreds of other Iraqi villages, made of mud huts of the same sad beige or dun color, it is noteworthy in being the last place to speak Duriac. This is the only living tongue descended from ancient Akkadian or Assyro-Babylonian. The traditional written form of the language, of which this book provides an example, was developed in the fourth century of the Christian Era by Assyrian Christian priests and missionaries.

As with other Semitic tongues, this is a very compact script, ignoring unstressed vowels and combining two or three characters into one. This fact makes translation difficult. Like the related Hebrew, Arabic, and Syriac languages, Duriac is written from right to left.

When, in 1967, Alan Nourse and I were on our way to India (my one purpose being to gather material for my book *Great Cities of the Ancient World*) we tarried several days in Baghdad to visit the ruins of Babylon and Ctesiphon. While shopping for antiques to take home, I was approached by a member of the Iraqi Directorate General of Antiquities, with whom I had had correspondence about photographs of archaeological sites. This man said he had a manuscript to sell. This was a strange proposal from such a source, since the Iraqi government tries by severe penalties to suppress unauthorized export of archaeological materials, and most employees of this department are conscientious in the discharge of their duties.

I inquired into this matter but met only polite evasion. Here, my contact said, was an interesting *curiosum* for which the department had no use; did I want it or not? Since the price seemed reasonable and the codex, if it proved worthless, would at least make an amusing coffee table ornament, I bought it, packed it, and thought no more about it until I passed through Beyrut on my way home.

I have several friends in Beyrut. One of these is a successful tourist guide whose name, for obvious reasons, I prefer not to give. When this man learned that I was in Lebanon, he looked me up and spent an evening with me. My friend, I may say, takes a more objective, commonsensical view of the Israeli-Arab conflict than is general in the Arab countries. This time, he felt that his old friendship with me outweighed any duty he might have felt toward the Arab cause.

By virtue of his many connections throughout the Islamic world, my friend was a mine of gossip. On this occasion, he told me what he had heard about my codex.

The sale, it transpired, had been authorized on a high level of the Directorate General. Written on parchment in the little-known Duriac script, this manuscript had been unearthed by a clandestine digger in the tombs of Duria but had by devious routes come into the hands of the Directorate General of Antiquities. One of Iraq's foremost archaeologists, the internationally respected Ja'afar Babili, was assigned the task of translating the book into modern Arabic. This official had scarcely begun when he jubilantly announced that it was a complete—or nearly complete—copy of Alhazred's celebrated *Necronomicon*, or *Kitab Al-Azif* to give it its original title.** The original Arabic version has not been seen for many centuries, albeit rumors of its existence continue to circulate in esoteric circles.***

From study of the script, Babili concluded that this translation antedates A.D. 760. The traditional date of the composition of the original is A.D. 738, which provides a *terminus a quo*. Babili also pointed out that, whereas the script is skillfully executed throughout most of the work, its quality markedly deteriorates on the last eight pages, as if the scribe were working in haste or under severe pressure. It has not yet been established whether the Duriac version includes all of the original Arabic text, or whether, instead, the scribe condensed, abridged, or abstracted the concluding portions of the Arabic text.

Babili went on with his translation until, a few weeks later, he disappeared. No trace of him was ever found; neither was a plausible reason for his vanishment ever adduced. He was a sober, hard-working, conscientious official and a devoted family man; nonetheless, he was gone.

Babili's subordinate, Ahmad ibn-Yahya, was provisionally promoted to his chief's place. He, too, proceeded with the translation of the *Necronomicon*. Ibn-Yahya was a bachelor of more free-living habits than his predecessor; still, nobody had ever accused him of lack of devotion to his profession. After two weeks, ibn-Yahya's landlady reported that she had heard screams from the modest apartment that he occupied on the Musa al-Kadhim. Entering the apartment with her pass key, she found the rooms empty. No more was heard from Ahmad ibn-Yahya.

The next Iraqi scholar to undertake the translation was Prof. Yuni Abdalmajid of the University of Baghdad. He began the task when other members of the Directorate General of Antiquities hesitated to continue the work of their vanished predecessors. Professor Abdalmajid was considered a little eccentric by his colleagues, who nevertheless acknowledge his brilliance. He had broken the secret of the pre-Sumerian Rawson tablets from Ur and thus cast light on the dark places of pre-Sumerian Mesopotamian history.

Professor Abdalmajid had been at work for three days when he, too, disappeared. He lived alone in a small house on the outskirts of Baghdad, in the Kadhmiyya District. Hence his absence was not noted for several days. When, however, he failed to appear for several of his classes, the police were called in. In Abdalmajid's study were found spatters of blood on the floor, walls, and ceiling, but of the missing professor no other trace was found.

Although there is doubtless a rational explanation for these disappearances, they nevertheless display a disturbing similarity to the legendary fate of Alhazred himself. This eccentric literary man is reported to have been devoured alive by an invisible monster before scores of terrified witnesses.

With three disappearances in a row, the Directorate General took thought before entrusting the manuscript to anyone else. Despite its revenues from petroleum, Iraq is far from being an advanced country and could not afford such a drain upon its limited scholarly personnel. At this time, the Directorate was under the domination of Dr. Mahmoud ash-Shammari, a devoted—not to say violent—nationalist. Tension was rising between the Arab states and Israel.

As a result of what Arabs deemed one-sided support of Israel, the United States was unpopular in Iraqi political circles, and Doctor ash-Shammari was one of the most extreme anti-Americans. His plan was to smuggle the manuscript into American hands. Then, if the coming Six-Day War—which he foresaw—took the course that in fact it did, the manuscript should be left in America, to wreak its woes upon American scholars. Doctor ash-Shammari considered any harm done to individual Americans as but a just requital for what he viewed as America's crimes against the Arabs. If the American government improbably changed its policies to favor the Arabs, the Iraqis could pass a word of warning to their American colleagues and thus save them from the fate of Doctors Babili, ibn-Yahya, and Abdalmajid.

Thus I learned of the true nature of my purchase. My friend advised me to destroy the book, but I scoffed at his fears. After all, I have been known for decades as an uncompromising rationalist and materialist, with no belief whatever in gods, ghosts, demons, or other spooks. I was familiar with the allusions to the *Necronomicon* in the stories of H. P. Lovecraft but was not prepared to admit the reality of his Ancient Ones or other supernatural entities. In fact, I long disbelieved in the existence, even, of Alhazred and his portentous *Necronomicon*.

Still, I left Beyrut with the sensation of traveling with a ticking package in my gear. Back home, I have pondered what to do with my sinister little codex. I could not translate it myself, for I am no learned Semiticist; it is all I can do to manage a few sentences of tourist's Arabic. I finally decided to let my colleagues publish the facsimile of the original manuscript, which you have in your hands. Then, if somebody wishes to dare the fate of Doctors Babili, ibn-Yahya, and Abdalmajid, he has been warned.

My only further suggestion is this. While the disappearance of the Iraqi savants is probably a matter of coincidence, with prosaic, mundane explanations, a rational man must be prepared to draw logical inferences from the evidence, even though they contradict his long-held beliefs. Let us assume that this book is in truth the *Necronomicon* and that it is indeed possible, by reciting the spells herein, to invoke entities from Outside. On this assumption, a possible answer to the disappearances of the Iraqi scholars is that, in making their translations, they unconsciously subvocalized the passages as they wrote them. Hence the spells took effect and the spooks appeared, as if they had been purposefully invoked. But, since these scholars lacked the arcane knowledge required to keep these beings under control, the entities destroyed the unwitting sorcerers.

So if any reader be so rash as to undertake the translation anew, let me urge that he have a care not to move his lips or mutter as he does so. We have all, I am sure, been annoyed in libraries by people who mumble as they read; but never before has this petty offense been punished by the fates that befell Doctors Babili, ibn-Yahya, and Abdalmajid.

L. Sprague deCamp
S.S. France, on the high seas
March 11, 1973

*Also spelled Douria, Douriyya, &c.

**The name "Abdul Alhazred" is a corruption of a lost original, which passed through several languages before it reached its present form. Philetas spelled it Αμβδνλ Αλχαζρηνδ. Its original form may have been Abdallah Zahr-ad-Din, or Servant-of-God Flower-of-the-Faith.

***For existing editions of the *Necronomicon*, see H. P. Lovecraft: "History and Chronology of the *Necronomicon*", Oakman: Rebel Press, 1936; in *Beyond the Wall of Sleep*, Sauk City: Arkham House, 1943; and in Mark Owings, *The Necronomicon: A Study*, Baltimore: Mirage Press, 1967.

One of the most intriguing facts about the *Necronomicon* is its association with the Elizabethan Magus Dr. John Dee, Court Astrologer to the Queen. He employed a scrying crystal to communicate with angels, from whom he learned the Enochian language. (Why "Enochian?" Because a long Jewish and Christian tradition made the antediluvian patriarch Enoch a great revealer of heavenly secrets.) The Dee connection was the brainchild of Lovecraft's pal Frank Belknap Long. In his early tale "The Space Eaters" (1928), Belknapius headed the tale with an epigram from "John Dee's *Necronomicon*" and featured the book later in the story, as a *deus ex machina*. I have always had the impression that Frank intended Dr. Dee as the actual author of the dreaded volume, despite Lovecraft's ascription of it elsewhere to Abdul Alhazred. Maybe we have a parallel here to the time Lovecraft's imagination ran ahead of him, filling in bibliographical lore for Richard F. Searight's creation *The Eltdown Shards*, unaware that Searight himself had simultaneously dreamed up his own version. Lovecraft did incorporate Long's mention of John Dee by making him the translator of Alhazred into English. The fragment that follows first appeared in *Crypt of Cthulhu* #23, St. John's Even, 1984.

John Dee's *Necronomicon*: A Fragment

contributed by Frank Belknap Long

(who refuses to discuss how these few lines came into his possession)

(Retranslated into slightly more modern phrase patterns here and there, but without the slightest departure from the original text otherwise.)

Paragraphs Seven and Eight—Page 30, Book Three

It must not be thought that the powers capable of the greatest wickedness appear to us in the form of repellent familiars, and other, closely related demons. They do not. Small, visible demons are merely the effluvia which those vast forms of destructiveness have left in Their wake—skin scrapings and even more tenuous shreds of evil that attach themselves to the living like leeches from some great slain leviathan of the deep that has wreaked havoc on a hundred coastal cities before plunging to its death with a thousand hurled harpoons quivering in its flesh.

For the mightiest powers there can be no death and the hurled harpoons inflict, at most, surface injuries which heal quickly. I have said before and I shall say again until my tardily earned wisdom is accepted by my brethren as fact—in confronting *that which has always been and always will be* a master of magic can know only self-reproach and despair if he mistakes a temporary victory for one that he can never hope permanently to win.

In a letter to Clark Ashton Smith (November 18, 1930), H. P. Lovecraft noted in passing that according to his conception of the imaginary *Necronomicon*, the mad Arab Abdul Alhazred had recounted various "adventures of his" in Irem the City of Pillars (of Koranic fame) and elsewhere. With his characteristic sharp exegelical eye, Lin Carter noticed this intriguing tidbit and realized what a fine idea HPL had left undeveloped. While researching his *Lovecraft: A Look behind the Cthulhu Mythos*, Carter began writing up some of the mad Arab's adventures just for fun and then started adding to them some years later once he began to contribute regularly to *Crypt of Cthulhu*.

One of Lin's doomed Lovecraftian protagonists (in "Zoth-Ommog") peruses the *Necronomicon* and notes that "[t]he narratives contained in the first book [were] personal accounts from the early years of Alhazred's own career of various uncanny experiences and magical or occult experiments." As Lin explained further to me, the idea is that all the episodes were intended as lessons and cautionary tales for the benefit of the too-eager reader of Alhazred. Thus the stories all end in pretty much the same manner: Alhazred is horrified and mortified by what he sees! The repetitiveness will at first strike the reader as a mark of Carter's lack of imagination: Can he not come up with any other ending? In fact, Carter's creativity is manifested elsewhere in the story; once he decided what sort of narratives Alhazred must have written, i.e., cautionary tales, he was stuck with the "I-learned-the-hard-way" ending and had to apply his creativity to what came *before*. How different and how interesting could he make several stories which had to share essentially the same climax?

The order of the episodes follows as closely as possible the cross references within the stories themselves. Lin had planned on reshuffling the order per a note originally at the end of "The Madness out of Time." The new sequence would have entailed rewriting parts of several of the stories, which Lin perhaps intended but never got around to doing. You will notice, too, that he intended to add two more episodes, but he never got around to it.

The *Necronomicon*:
The Dee Translation

annotated by Lin Carter

Introitus

The Book of the Laws of the Dead, which was writ by the poet Abdul
Alhazred of Sanaa, in Damascus, the Year of the Hejira 113, so that all
Mankind might know of the Horrors of the Tomb and of those greater
Horrors which await Beyond.

I. The Book of Episodes

The First Narrative: The Doom of Yakthoob

As a youth I was apprenticed to the notorious Saracen wizard,
Yakthoob, among many others, of whom the languid and dissolute
Ibn Ghazoul became my closest friend, despite his voluptuous and
immoral habits. At the behest of the Master we learned the summoning-up
of Evil Things and conversed with ghouls in the rock tombs of Neb and even
partook of the unnamed Feasts of Nitocris in loathsome crypts beneath the
Great Pyramid. We went down the Secret Stair to worship That which
dwelleth in the black catacombs below the crumbling ruins of elder and
ghoulhaunted Memphis, and in the noxious caverns of Nephren-Ka in the
sealed and unknown Valley of Hadoth by the Nile we performed such
Blasphemous Rites that even now my soul shuddereth to contemplate.

Ever we begged of the Master that he instruct us in the calling up of
the Great Princes of the Pit, the which he was fearful to do, saying that the
Lesser Demons be easily satisfied with the Red Offering alone, having a horrid thirst for the Blood of Men, but that the Great Ones demand naught less
than the offering up of a Living Soul, save that thou hast a certain Elixir,
compounded according to the Forbidden Books from the ichor of holy
angels, the secret of which is known but to a certain Necromancer who
dwelleth amongst the dead tombs of accursed and immemorial Babylon.

For a time the Master sated our lust for daemonic knowledge with Rites and Horrors terrible to think upon, but ever and again we did beseech for that Great Secret whereof I have spoken, and at length he was persuaded and dispatched the youth Ibn Ghazoul to crumbling and antique Babylon with much gold to purchase from the Necromancer the terrible Elixir. In time the youth returned therefrom and bore with him, in a flask of precious orichaic from dead Atlantis, the Elixir, and we thus repaired to sealed and hidden Hadoth where the Master did That of which I dare not speak, and Lo! a great Thing rose up tall and terrible against the stars. Scarlet and wet and glistening was it, like a flayed, tormented thing, with eyes like Black Stars. About it hovered a burning cold like the dark wind that blows between the Stars, and it stunk of the foetor of the Pit.

In a slobbering voice the Abomination demanded its price, and bore the flacon of orichalc to its snout in one scarlet Claw, and snuffled thereat, and then to our immeasurable Horror howled forth a braying Laughter and hurled the Flask from it, and caught up the Master in one Claw of horrible cold and plucked and tore at him, all the while making the Night hideous with terrible laughter. For a time the hapless Yakthoob squealed and flopped in the clutches of the Claw, but then lay still, and dangled therefrom, black and shrivelled, as the laughing Thing ripped at it until it raped forth the Spirit of Yakthoob, which it Devoured in a Certain Manner which made my dreams hideous with Nightmares for twenty years ....

We screamed and fled from the accursed gloom of Hadoth where a Scarlet Thing howled and fed abominably under the shuddering stars, all but the vile and horrid Ibn Ghazoul, that wretched voluptuary, who had squandered the Master's gold on the lusts of his flesh during his travels to Babylon, and had substituted *naught but wine* in place of the rare ichor. ... Him we saw never again, and to this day I quake with nameless terror at the thought of summoning forth the Great Ones from the Pit, mindful of the horrible Doom of the wizard Yakthoob.

Notes

Most editions of the *Necronomicon omit*, for some reason which I shudder to conjecture, the little-known "First Narrative", going straight from the "Introitus" to the famous "Second Narrative", that of the Thing under Memphis. My own copy of Alhazred—a virtually priceless manuscript in Dee's own hand—luckily contains this rare episode, which I have transcribed here for the use of the serious student.

In publishing the ten narratives which comprise the first book of the *Necronomicon*, I think I should clarify the correct sequence of the individual titles. The sequence is as follows: I. "The Doom of Yakthoob"; II. "The Thing under Memphis"; III. "In the City of Pillars"; IV. "The Ghoul's Tale" (awaiting transcription); V. "The Vault Beneath the Mosque"; VI. "Mnomquah"; VII. "The Madness out of Time"; VIII. "Dreams of the Black Lotus"; and IX. "The Shadow from the Stars." Narrative X at present is also awaiting transcription.

Von Junzt and other commentators, including Laban Shrewsbury, have pointed out that the ten narratives of this first book of the *Necronomicon* seem written in
imitation of the second portion of the *Book of Eibon*, which is called "Episodes of
Eibon of Mhu Thulan." Therein, Eibon sets down what purport to be actual episodes
from his own career as a sorcerer, precisely as Alhazred does in *Necronomicon* I, i-x. In
both instances the episodes (or, in Alhazred, "narratives") seem to serve the purpose
of precautionary fables or teaching parables, designed to warn the student away from
some of the hazards of the sorcerous career.

The Second Narrative: The Thing under Memphis

Innumerable and noxious are those secrets still surviving from this planet's unmemoried and mythic Prime; and in malodorous gulphs beneath
the earth's crust, where seethe the mephitic vapours of the Vault and
Sepulchre, there yet lurk on into our day, suspended betwixt sleep and
death, a madness out of time and a horror from beyond the spheres; and
rash indeed is he who would dare arouse them from their deserved rest.[1]

Alas, the greedy lust which ever goadeth such as we to ferret out forbidden wisdom from the adyts of the Past, to pry into the profoundest and
most fearful arcana of cycles anterior to our own, to search for secrets better left deep-buried and unknown, and to awaken from this sleeping death
That which even the endless ages have forgot and which were by men also
best left alone and unremembered.

All this is dreadful truth, as well did I, Alhazred, know; and yet I could
not yield to the inevitable defeat of my desires, which the demise and doom
of Yakthoob forced upon me; and in the fullness of Time it became my
firmest resolve to pursue withouten guide nor mentor the secrets of those
Mysteries concealed from men for aeons in the subterranean abyss and in the
darksome and unwholesome places of the Elder World.

And thus it eventuated that, at length, I rose up and went forth from
the sealed and hidden Vale of Hadoth amidst the sombre, stony hills of Neb,
which rise anear the crawling floods of the immemorial and mystic Nile,
together with those few who followed me and who, with me, had learnt the
Elder Lore from the lips of the Saracen wizard, our aforetime Master.

Erelong our journey led us to that desolate and lonely waste of shifting
sands which stretched under the cold mockery of the leering Moon, not far
from the immense and antique wreckage of riven shards and sundered stone
by men called Memphis. Here of old the pshent-crowned Pharaohs reigned
and revelled, the same that now sleep long, slow ages by, soaked in bitter
natron and wound in spiced winding-sheets, in secret crypts burrowed
beneath the tall cliffs of the Valley of the Kings.

And here, amidst the desert sands, there croucheth that elder eidolon
of shapen stone fashioned by our forefathers into the likeness of a Crouching

Beast. And when my followers beheld the fearful thing they faltered and fell back; hence, disdaining to bemock the folly of their fear, I forward went alone, with but the boldest of my fellows at my heels, a valiant youth called Ibraheem. And thus it was that we went through that Secret Door that lieth between the out-stretched paws of the mighty Sphinx, that sinister and brooding thing of stone that hath from of old made of the bleak and barren waste its lair, and which looks ever into the visage of Eternity with unblinking and with cryptic gaze, smiling its light, its knowing, and its sardonic smile.

Through the portal we passed, and by the Hidden Stair that leadeth down and down to profound and nighted crypts that lie long-hid beneath the vast necropolis of Memphis. But once before, in years long antecedent to this, had the learned Yakthoob led us hither by this gloomy way, to grovel before That which may by subtle craft be summoned to the Pits below time-ruined Memphis from dark realms contiguous to our own. And thus at length came Ibraheem and I into a vast and high-roofed Vault, where by the feeble luminance of flickering tapers did we draw twin Circles on the pave thereof, both the Circle of Protection where amidst we twain would stand, and the Circle of Protection that should hold ye Thing (and these Two be needful, lest ye Thing be untimely loos'd and come Ravening against us), and touched to malodorous fumes certain Suffumigations as were requisite, and howled the Words and the Name. Thus did we dare invoke Great Tsathoggua, who was old when the very stars were young, and who came down from remote, trans-cosmic gulfs when this earth was but newly-formed and bore as yet no life, save for the formless and mewling efts of the Prime.

Black and plastic was the quivering Bulk thereof, befurred, swag-bellied and obscene, and in His awful visage there were blent the salient characteristics of Bat and Toad and Sloth; and He squatted there in the centre of the Circle and in a deep and sleepy Voice bade us speak wherefor we had call'd Him from His age-old slumbers. Now, Ibraheem was palsied with terror and sick with loathing of the Stench, but I, who was made of sterner stuff, made bold to speak the desires that seethed within my heart. Wherefore the Black Thing taught us the Mao Games and the wording of the Uthgos Chant, and spake of the Secret Parable of Byagoona the Faceless, and of very much more.[2] Aye, 'twas from the very Lips of Tsathoggua that I learnt those formulae by which thou mayest command the demons; all of the formulae between the Yr and the Nhhngr became thus mine, and great Power thereby, for those demons dwell in spheres apart from this, upon the far side of Kadath itself.[3]

All of these secrets and many more I mastered in the darkness of that malodorous and mephitic Vault 'neath the ancient city, but when it came to pass that I had gained all of the Knowledge that I sought, and that mine over-wearied brain could learn no more, and I uttered aloud the Rites of Banishment, the toadlike and squatting Thing only grinned, and licked its lips with a long tongue like a slimy white Worm, and stirred not from its coign, neither did it vanish.

Then it was, in very truth, that fear gnawed at my vitals and my companion gazed at me with terror in his eyes, for we both perceived that the Thing which we had summoned hither with such ease was not with such ease sent back to the place of its abiding. Wherefore have I aforetime said, and here repeat again, Do not call up Any that thou canst not put down.[4]

Now we had summoned hither Dread Tsathoggua by means of the Voola Ritual[5] which summoneth up from the nighted caverns under earth That which lurketh far beneath the crust, and the Banishment we had in vain performed was as pertaineth to that Ritual. Howsomever, as it seemed notably lacking in efficacy, did I strive with every rite of Banishment and Dismissal known to me to send the Black Thing back to lightless N'kai; but it did not seem within my Knowledge or my Power to effect that which I so devoutly wished.

And all the while mine acolyte stared at me with eyes wide with terror in a face as pale as whey ...

At length I resolved, in the uttermost extremity of my Fear and Peril, upon a desperate recourse. Seizing up the slight form of my disciple, the hapless and affrighted Ibraheem, I flung him squalling from the precincts of the Circle of Protection and in such wise he fell prone and helpless upon the pave betwixt the toadlike feet of the squatting Thing (the which bent its loathsome Head to investigate this unexpected Offering, which mewled and slithered 'neath the questing Tongue thereof, and the drooling Lips; and, as the Screaming commenced and I saw that Tsathoggua was otherwise occupied, I then prudently took to my heels and fled from those accursed and noisome Vaults, and up the Secret Stair, and henceforth into the clean air and wholesome light of dawning, and departed forthwith from that place with my Followers at my heels, and we betook ourselves by slow and easy progress towards the deserts of Arabia Felix and that City of the Pillars, even ill-rumored Irem, the which lieth thereamidst.

Notes

Title. Lovecraft refers to "that Dark Thing below Memphis" in his novel, *The Case of Charles Dexter Ward*.

1. Lovecraft employs this phrase "a madness out of time and a horror beyond the spheres" in *Charles Dexter Ward*, although without identifying it as a quotation from Alhazred.

2. "The Mao Games" were first mentioned by Arthur Machen in one of his fine stories; the "Uthgos Chant" is referred to by Ramsey Campbell in his tale "The Render of the Veils"; the only mention I have seen of the "Secret Parable of Byagoona the Faceless" was in Robert Bloch's story "The Grinning Ghoul."

3. According to Lovecraft (in "The Dunwich Horror"), the Yr and the Nhhngr are *formulae*, but in *The Lurker at the Threshold*, Derleth mentions them as places beyond Kadath where certain demons dwell. My clearer reading of the disputed passage, given above, seemingly reconciles the apparent discrepancy.

4. This phrase appears in *Charles Dexter Ward*, although not as a quotation from Alhazred.

5. The Voola Ritual is employed in this same manner in Ramsey Campbell's story, "The Mine on Yuggoth."

The Third Narrative: In the City of Pillars

Hast thou not heard how Allah dealt with Ad, the people of the many-columned city of Irem, whose like hath never been built in this land, and with Thamood, who hewed out dwelling-places amidst the rocks of the valley? Their lives were filled with sin and because of them the land teemed with wickedness; therefore didst Allah let loose upon them the scourge of His Punishment.

—The Koran: The chapter called "The Dawn"

There is a dark thirst rageth in the hearts of certain men like a black flame, and the fires thereof consume them with the unholy lust for forbidden knowledge and the secrets of Elder Time; and in their quest for this lore, which hath lain hidden for endless aeons from the light of day, they all too often call down upon themselves the wrath of Heaven. These things I know to be the truth, yea and verily, for alas! I too am one with them and that dark thirst that consumeth them rageth within mine own heart to this very hour.

I too have delved into the forbidden books, which wiser men than I deem blasphemous, and I have done things which memory forbids me to recall lest my reason founder, but whose shadows arise within my deepest dreams and rouse me shrieking from my rest and thrust me shuddering into that hell of self-loathing wherein I pass my days.

Once when I was young and my heart was full to the brim with pride and vanity and seethed with the black thirst for forbidden wisdom, I went through the Secret Door that lieth between the two paws of the Sphinx, that elder eidolon of stone fashioned in the awful likeness of a Crouching Beast ... that sinister and brooding Thing that hath from old made of the bitter desert waste its lair and which stares ever at Eternity with unblinking, cryptic gaze, smiling a small, sly, knowing smile. Through the door I passed, and down the ancient stair into those nameless catacombs and into that gloom-enshrouded Crypt by all the world save us forgot ... and Him Who Dwelleth Below I begged to know that which I could do in barter for that lore for which my heart thirsted.

From this colloquy I emerged at length into the upper world again, and from thence passed into the deserts of Araby and into that vast and trackless waste men know as Roba El Khaliyeh, the Empty Places; and for many a day and a night I ventured through the shifting sands, I and my followers, amongst the which were many who with me had knelt aforetime at the feet of Yakthoob the Saracen and had learned the Forbidden Secrets from his lips ere Doom silenced them forever. They asked me whither were we bound, seeing they had followed me into this desolate and unwholesome bourn that was far from the habitations of men: and I made answer unto them, saying: There be three Secret Cities amidst the sands, whereof the eldest be that Nameless City of the pre-Adamites, wherein dwelt of old the Children of the Serpent; and also that Black City of the legends, wherein sits the mummy of Xulthltan enthroned, a shimmering Gem clenched in his bony fingers: but (said I) we seek the third of them, the which is even Irem.

And they asked me concerning Irem, this City of the Pillars, and I spake unto them of the Elder Days and of the four nations had ruled this land of old, Thamood of the north, and Ad of the south, and Tasm, and Jadis: and I spake of many-columned Irem and of Shaddad the Accursed who had raised up its walls and who hath builded therein an thousand pillars to Those Ones better left unnamed. At length we passed into the Inner Lands where men come not and where stones yet stand that were reared up by limbs other than human hands, and where Old Things lurk yet that were of an age incalculable when even dim Chaldea stood new-builded in the mists of primal dawn.

Now the way we followed thither was not withouten peril, for hereabouts there be a plenitude of elder tombs and crumbling old sarcophagi whereamong yet linger certain repulsive and shambling and canine-muzzled Ghouls. But of the Loathly Feeders I summoned forth their leader, even Nug, whom certain books do term The Prowler Amongst the Tombs, and concerning whom rumor whispereth naught that be wholesome. Father of all the Ghouls is Nug, and chief of all such who dwelleth on the Earth plane, and he be also the minion and servitor of the abomination Nyogtha, the Dweller in Darkness.

And unto this gaunt, and loping, and hideous Nug I paid a fearful Price for our safe-passage through the gloom-fraught Waste that is the dominion of Nug and his awful Kind ... a fee I shall not name here ... but a fee the which must be paid by all who would venture through this land to the City of Pillars.

This having accomplisht, on through the illimitable Waste we wandered and through dead lands as drear and desolate as even the fiend-inhabited desert of Kaf which old tales relate lieth at the world's ultimate and darkling verge: And at the Hour of Subhi Kazib we drew nigh unto a vast mound, whereupon my disciples cried out to see the image of a mighty city form slowly out of the wan luminance of false-dawn like unto some ghostly apparition or mirage.

Thus came I, Alhazred, unto that ancient City of Evil that was smitten of old by Heaven and lieth still under Heaven's curse. A somber and silent city of red stone, lost in the drifting sands of the limitless Waste, was fabled Irem when first I looked upon it. All ringed about with broken walls it lay, and battlements of Cyclopean stone, and through the empty gates sand had slithered and the portals of Irem gaped like the blank and empty sockets of a skull. Thus and so was Irem: And with fearful awe we looked upon the forest of stone monoliths that thrust up from the sand, and at the dread Images which squatted loathsomely atop each of the Thousand Pillars.

At the centre of this ruin we beheld one vast pile of masonry time had not touched, and therein we dwelt throughout the days which followed, and the which were devoted to those Ceremonials whereof the Nightmare Thing which Dwelleth beneath the Sphinx had spake of, and those Litanies preserved in the rotting pages of the last surviving copy of the accursed and abhorrent *Rituals of Yhe* the which had been a possession of the Saracen magician, but had not been buried with the torn and mangled remnants of his corpse what time he met that Doom whereof I have aforetime writ.

These rites we droned and wailed under the cold mocking eye of a distant and uncaring Moon, and with great trepidation and fear, but withal in the expectation of mighty things to come; for it was even my purpose to ope in this time-forgotten city a Door to Outside, so that They Who dwell Beyond and Who are beknownst to men as the Old Ones might enter this world again, wherever to rule again as They did reign aforetime; and in that dark Empire to Come vast authority and power and the mastery of many Secrets had been promised unto me. For that this City of the Pillars lay at a nexus of strange forces and it was to Them whereof I speak like unto a pole of Power; therefore was it easier in this place to open the Gate than elsewhere upon Earth. Thus it was even I, Alhazred, was first to open the Portal in this very Irem on one black night when the cold Moon shuddered and hid her face and weird red stars blazed in a mighty Sign.

Then raised we up tall pillars of graven stone and afore them was the Red Offering made, and certain Names we uttered in that place that are not lightly spoken by the lips of men; and betwixt the pillars a Darkness grew, from the which there came a bitter wind and cold, and the place whereat that wind riseth was not of this Earth; and into this Darkness I looked long and deep, whilst all about me my disciples cowered and squealed and hid their eyes, for that they were wiser than I, mayhap, or less brave, or less maddened with desire of unknown and terrible wisdom.

Long, long I gazed upon That which peered forth from the Darkness laughing, laughing; and then, as the Earth trembled and as the lightnings of Heaven poured down in strokes of livid and cleansing flame, and the great pillars fell, slowly, one by one, and all they who had come hither at my side were crushed in the falling of the great stones, saving only I alone; and as the Gate thus opened was closed for all time to come, and by a mighty and terrible Hand, I who yet lived rose up and fled from that place accursed of old, and now accursed anew, and fled forth into the wilderness with the image of That which I alone had dared to look upon seared deep into my brain, never to be forgotten. Thus I fled from Irem, knowing my soul damned, and that utterly and beyond all forgiveness; knowing my soul damned, as all be damned who, even as I, have dared to look for an instant only upon That which lurketh on the threshold between this world and the next. *Iä! Yog-Sothoth!* It is written Their very shadow blights the Earth, and one glimpse of Them can make thee mad. And I am damned forever, and cannot even find forgetfulness in red howling madness; for I have looked upon the Lurker on the Threshold, and know the doom unspeakable that awaits me ever beyond the grave.

The Fifth Narrative: The Vault beneath the Mosque

There is a mode whereby mortal Life may be preserved unto infinite Time, and the mages of the Past knew it as the Formula of Nnh; but very dangerous is this Formula of Nnh and the failure to utter aloud a single vocable according to the proper way may end in an horrible and unmentionable Doom, wherefor do I deem it exceeding rash and imprudent of the sorcerer who attempteth it.

- - -

And we rose up and departed out of shunned and legended Irem, those of us who had looked upon the very Face of Yog-Sothoth; and I sent my disciples ahead to procure suitable lodgings for us in the great metropolis of Alexandria, whilst I journeyed on to a certain Nameless City where for some time I abode among the denizens thereof and to which I determined at another time to return.

Now in this great city of Alexandria had my followers found an old house in that quarter which lieth beneath the shadow of the Black Mosque, for by that name do the Alexandrians becall the edifice, which is of frightful and unguessable antiquity, and whose precincts are shunned and avoided by wholesome men. This house which my disciples had procured for our dwelling place was eminently suitable to my purposes, albeit that I did not enjoy our proximity to the Mosque, whose ebon spires soared aloft like the black tapers lit by necromancers in their abhorrent rites.

And there came to my door a deputation of the Faithful of that city to beg the assistance of my wisdom, for know that the reputation of Alhazred as a wizard had waxed mightily in the years since first I sat at the feet of my mentor, Yakthoob, the Saracen. These personages I received with every honor and hearkened to their plea, which was that the Black Mosque might be cleansed of the Evil Presence that inhabited it. While it had been years agone since last were the ritual prayers of the Faith performed in that awful place, still were fearful rumours whispered thereof: how it was that cruel and mocking laughter echoed to drown out the most solemn ceremonies of the Prophet; and that the sweet smokes of incense, under some malignant spell, were wont to turn to foul and foetid stenchfulness; and how even the sacrosanct pages of the Holy Alcoran were found besmirched with vile filth and bescribbled with loathsome obscenities.

On the day following upon this, I eloigned with my disciples to the sealed Mosque, whose portals were reluctantly unlocked by the trembling hands of the most venerable of the Imams. Within, all was neglect and decay, and the dust of very many years overlay every surface. Torches were struck to fire, and by their source of luminance I at length perceived that mine apprehension as to the antiquity of the Mosque had been accurate: far more ancient was this gloom-enshrouded edifice than even the very Faith of the Prophet. Once, ages before, had it been the fane of the Idolatrous Ancients, for it could be seen that many chisels had ruthlessly hewn away the images and hieroglyphics of the forgotten past, now over-painted with flaking and rotting plaster.

It might well prove, or so I reasoned in mine own heart, that when this temple of the Idol-worshippers had been purified by the Musselmans and consecrated to the usage of their own Faith, that the rites of exorcism had been performed with undue haste or unwise carelessness, and that some-what of the Power of the beast-headed Gods of ancient Aegypt lingered on to mock and confound the present worshippers herein.

Now it was well and fully known to me that the Idolaters of old were wont to dig certain secret crypts beneath the temples of their Abominations, and so we made search by torchlight for an entry to the adyts beneath the temple; and in the fullness of Time I came upon one place where the tiles upon the floor had crumbled with age and desuetude, revealing the outlines of a mighty slab of stone that once had served the priests of Aegypt in the man-ner of a trapdoor. There was a great bronze ring sunken into the stone and much gnawed with vertigris but still sound, and there was amongst them who followed at my heels a youth of prodigious strength, aye, a veritable Rustum was he, whose great thews pried open the slab from out the stony floor. And we discovered then a flight of steps hewn from the very bedrock upon which had the City been reared, a flight of stone steps the which descended into the unbroken darkness below. Now in sooth didst fear and trembling assail the valor of our hearts, for that the mephitic vapours of the Vault panted forth into our very nostrils, loathsome with the putrescence of the Pit itself. Natheless must we descend into the depths, for having once taken up the burthen of the task we might not, on our Honour, avoid the Perils that might ensue ...

- - -

The Vault beneath the Mosque was Stygian in its gloom, and here even the light of our many torches did little to dispel the Dark; moreover the very air itself was vitiated and stale with the passage of long ages that had passed since the day when last was the great stony slab set to seal in the Secrets below, whereby did our flames burn but feebly.

Yet was their light enough for us to see with shudderings that small, squirming, pallid shapes squealed and scurried from the unwonted luminance; larger than any rats were these and almost did their repulsive lineaments bear the stamp of humankind, although of a stock long turned vicious and depraved, through what unspeakable Practices we could but conjecture. Deformed and dwarfish were these squeaking, timorous troglodytes, with weak small eyes, and hideously *pink* were these eyes, as even was the lank hair of these misshapen Creatures as pale as be the hair of albinos.

Through the gloom and the dreadful Stench of these Vaults did we make our slow and stumbling way, squeamishly avoiding, after one horrified glimpse, that upon which our feet trod: the gnawed small bones and corpses of rats, and of vipers, and, betimes, of the bones of stolen children ...

We came at length and in the fullness of Time to the discovery of That which the abominable dwarflings worshipped as had their ancestors for uncounted ages: it was an Idol in the likeness of a man, clad in the vestments of a priest of antique Aegypt, and so true to man's veritable eidolon was it that for a terrible moment we feared it lived and drew breath; but, nay, it was only a dead thing, hard as stone to the touch, and thick with the dust of aeons. Then it was that rash and imprudent curiosity bade me take up the hem of my garment to wipe away the dust from the features of the Idol so that I might discern their nature ... and I cried out and let my torch fall from palsied hands, and we turned and fled back through that ghastly carpeting of gnawed little bones, and up the stone stair and back to the blessed light of Day, letting fall the stone slab upon the opening to those nether horrors, sealing them up forever, as we hoped.

- - -

And I did not for very long continue to abide in this dark quarter under the grim shadow of that accursed Mosque of Abominations, and, indeed, soon left the city of Alexandrians to embark upon a long and difficult journey, never to return to the mighty metropolis where the Black Mosque stood ancient, unhallowed, and regrettably unburnt. For I had read in crumbling papyri of the awful Formula of Nnh[1], which no wizard recites save at his Peril and whereby may a man be frozen forever in one infinite moment of Time, and I knew the dreaded horror of the Thing the abominable dwellers beneath the Mosque worshipped in their degeneracy, and knew as well the terrible Secret thereof ... the which had burst upon my horrified mind the instant I wiped the centuries of dust from those *living, staring, mad and desperate eyes* of the Idol beneath the Mosque.

Notes

In a letter to his friend Clark Ashton Smith, dated November 18, 1930, Lovecraft mentions the Fifth Narrative thusly: "some timid reader has torn out the pages where the Episode of the Vault under the Mosque comes to a climax—the deletion being curiously uniform in the copies at Harvard & at Miskatonic University" (SL 11.218-219). The copies of the *Necronomicon* that I have checked at these two great institutions of learning (and also the copy preserved in the library of the Field Museum in Chicago, to which August Derleth called our attention in his story "The Evil Ones", *Strange Stories*, October 1940) bear an identical mutilation. However, the Dee Manuscript from which I have made this redaction is whole and unimpaired. The extirpation begins with the words "Yet was their light enough for us to see."

1. It is probably significant that the concluding books of the *Necronomicon*, which are compilations of spells, formulae, recipes, pentacles, sigils, incantations, spells, and the like, do not contain the Nnh Formula, which is conspicuous by its absence. In view of the gingerly and trepidatious manner in which Alhazred treats this Formula, however, his refusal to set it down seems excusable and quite understandable.

The Sixth Narrative: Mnomquah

I.

After my sojourn in the city of the Alexandrians I removed myself apart from the habitations of men, and repaired at length into the trackless deserts of Arabia Felix, alone but for two of my students in the Art Sorcerous, the youth Mouli, who was of prodigious strength and as fearless as any lion, and the more studious Ismail; together we contemplated the desolation of the sandy wastes and studied the wheeling of the constellations in the measureless firmament, and sought into the secrets of Nature.

I was consumed by an avid thirst to uncover the lore of age-forgotten Antiquity, and for this purpose we guided our camels across the sands of that immense desolation known to the Ancients as the Roba El Khaliyeh, the Empty Space, for that on the maps of the geographers it is naught but a blank on the written page; for in the vastness of the southern parts of that Desert there protrude from the sands the hoary bones of an Elder city that was old ere the first stones of Memphis were laid and whilst the bricks of Babylon were yet unbaked.

Thither did I wend my way, in fullest cognizance of the fact that there are terrible primal arcana of Earth that are better left unknown, and dread secrets unhuman that none may know and yet have peace, and Secrets beyond even these that render whomsoever unriddleth them as forever alien unto the tribe of Men and doom him to walk alone on Earth, for he who learns such Secrets must pay the fee thereof.

And we came at length, and in the fullness of Time, to where the nameless city stands, its colossal wreckage knee-deep in the drifting sands. Nameless it is in very sooth, for there is no legend so old as to give it a name, or to remember it in the bygone ages of its greatness, and even the fearless desert tribes shun it as did their sires and grandsires before them, unto that forgotten time when first the Children of Men came drifting into these desolate parts of the World, as the sand drifts beneath the desert wind.

That first night did we camp beneath the glitter of the stars and the cold glory of the Moon, and ere I sought my rest an urging o'ertook me and I scribbled down a line or two of verse, as I had not done these many years aforetime. The next day, and for days thereafter, we traced the crumbling foundations of houses older than the First Pyramid, and of streets that once had known the tread of beings that were not men, but nowhere did we discern aught in the manner of carving or ornamentation of charactery that mighty yield up a clue as to the nature of Them that had raised this mighty ruin: but that they were not the Children of Men was horribly apparent, for doorways and portals were taller and narrower than afford easy access to humankind, and in lieu of flights of steps there were to be found queer sloping planes and descending ramps.

Old beyond the dreams of humankind were these sombre ruins, whose shards of wall or broken stumps of colonnades thrust out of the drifted sand as might dead bones from an ill-made grave, and empty windows leered and mocked us as forlornly as would the empty eyesockets of a skull. I had visited this nameless city amidst the sands once before, and knew somewhat of its mysteries, but not all of them, wherefor was I eager to plumb these mysteries to their uttermost depths. And it became ever more apparent, as we scratched away the sand and laid bare the mouldering and age-rotted stones, that here were the remains of an antiquity that transcended History and even Myth, and the sense of utter *alienage* grew ever more frightful the more we searched: and I became possessed of the desire to prove this wreckage of more wholesome age than so it did appear to be, but nowhere could I discover some sign or device to prove that the city had been fashioned by men like myself, and even something in certain of the *proportions* and *dimensions* of the ruin hinted at a frightful, and incalculable, and prodigious, and pre-Adamite age.

II.

Now neither of my young companions, not Mouli nor Ismail, seemed able to sense the utter and horrible alienage of the nameless city, for to such as them a ruin was but a ruin and stone was stone, by Whomever set in place or however many aeons ago. In part this insensitivity of my disciples pleased me, for I found it comforting, and betimes I cursed mine own imagination that, mayhap, painted horrors where horrors were not found. But I bethought me of certain other primordial cities that I had seen and visited during the years of my wanderings to and fro upon the Earth, of that dreadful City of Evil under its ancient curse, that city the Bedoines of the desert whisper of as Beled-el-Djinn the City of Devils, which the Turks call Kara-Shehr the Black City, where a gem of nameless ancientry goeth ever clutched in the withered claws of a Mummy crouched upon a centuried throne; and I bethought me, too, of Irem the City of Pillars, and of my wanderings in Mesopotamia where stand the ruins of Sarnath the Doomed the which is amongst the eldest of the cities built by men, and of its ill-rumoured neighbor, the gray stone city Ib, which was never raised by the hands of men.

And there came to me one day the youth Ismail with a discovery that might well prove the key to the mysteries of the nameless city, for he had found portions of the colossal wreckage where the very bedrock upon which had the city anciently been reared rose clear of the clinging sands that else choked and smothered so many of the ruins. And here I perceived with elation the facades of houses or temples whose interiors might well preserve many carvings, else eroded by the whispering sands; and by the light of our flaring torches beheld certain signs chiseled into the naked stone of what had perchance been a temple or shrine of the Antediluvians whose hands had reared the ruins. And there were tunnels hewn deeper into the rock which bore obscure shrines or tables of cryptic nature, but whose runnels, hideously stained rust-red, hinted at abominable rites of living sacrifice to black gods of madness out of the abysm of Time.

For days and nights we searched on through this veritable labyrinth of rooms and chambers of uncertain and dubious nature hewn by centuries of unthinkable labour out of the solid stone. And we came at length into a vast rotunda whose sloping walls and oddly-angled roof and strangely-shapen buttresses seemed designed according to the precepts of some geometry not remotely Euclidean, like unto a chamber from some distant sphere or alien dimension of space. Here blew from unguessable recesses beyond a stinking wind of super-Arctic rigor, uncanny and inexplicable in this southern place; and here, too, I found for the first time the age-gnawed remnants of prehistoric art, for faded traces of flaking paint adorned the sloping walls, and the misshapen stone altars or tables that held a mass of curvilinear grooves or markings, which charactery (if charactery indeed it was!) bore little or no resemblance to any form of writing known to me, save for the more ancient

and indecipherable portions of the crumbling *Pnakotic Manuscripts*, those
parts thereof that are far too ancient to be read.

And ever there blew that cold and fetid wind ...

III.

We came at length through those winding and labyrinthine ways into a
vast, arch-roofed chamber like a tomb, wherein were many stone coffins
arrayed about the walls; but these were not contrived after the manner of
ancient Aegypt but were longer and narrower, and the stone Faces upon the
coffin-lids were hideously suggestive of a reptilian ancestry, in that they bore
one and all the scaly and rugose hide and elongated saurian muzzles of *horribly sentient crocodiles*. And I bethought me then of that crocodile-headed
beast-god of old Aegypt, even of Sebek, and wondered within the adyts of
my heart whether or no that grim, cruel cultus of Antiquity had not found
its primal roots here, in these fetid stone labyrinths of the nameless city.

And in the very midst of this chamber of stone coffins stood an uncouth
idol of green stone, hewn very much in the likeness of the lids of the coffins,
save in that it stood balanced on clawed feet, with bowed legs, balancing
upon a long, sharp-ridged spine: and its head was saurian in lineaments,
with black, cold, unwinking gems for eyes. And there was a sign hewn on
the base of the statue that I had seen graven in green stone once before, and
that in immemorial Ib: and I knew the meaning thereof, and shuddered
within my soul at the knowing, for it was the name of *Mnomquah*; the Ib-
things worshipped Him once, they whom we call the Thunn'ha and who are
among His minions, and whose leader is named Bokrug.

Ever was He among those enemies of humankind we call the Old Ones,
They who came seeping down from the stars when the Earth was young,
They who ruled it once in another space and time, and who hunger always
to repossess Their ancient dominion; and when the Elder Gods came voy-
aging hither to wreak Their vengeance upon Their rebellious Servants, it
was Mnomquah They sealed up in the Moon's cavernous heart, and there to
this day He walloweth loathsomely amidst the sluggish waves of the Black
Lake of Ubboth in the unholy and unlitten abyss of Nug-yaa.

Now the Ib-things, the Thunn'ha, were squamous and batrachian,
although they went upright on their hind legs like unto the Children of
Men, whereas the former inhabitants of this nameless city, as it would seem
from their likenesses hewn upon the lids of the prehistoric stone coffins,
were saurian rather than toadlike: but more than a few of the Old Ones have
as Their minions or servitors many dissimilar Races, as Him Who Is Not To
Be Named enjoys the service of the Byakhee and of the Abominable Mi-Go,
and Yet Others; wherefor it seemed very likely to me that this nameless city

had once been an outpost or fortress of Mnomquah in the dim-far-forgotten days when the World was very young and all of this Earth was under the heel of the Old Ones, of Mnomquah and His Brethren. And I breathed silent thanksgiving to Yog-Sothoth and to Tsathoggua that those days were long over, when the squalid, reptilian servitors of Mnomquah ruled over the quaking fens and steaming seas of the new-made Earth ...

And we rested that night amidst the noisome caverns, being too wearied in flesh and spirit to return to the more wholesome air of the upper world; and I would that we had not been so wearied, but had gone back to the surface, where the dead bones of the nameless city stare at the cold eye of the Moon.

IV.

And then there came to me my disciple, Ismail, with word that a vast stone slab had been found in one of the nethermost adyts of these endless caverns, and that there was set in the midst thereof a massy ring of age-eaten bronze; and I bethought me of just such a slab that we had found in the flooring of the Black Mosque, whereof I have aforetime writ; and trepidation came upon me, aye, and fear and trembling, and I rose up and bade Ismail that we should not disturb whatever Nethermost Secrets might lurk beneath the base of this great hill of rock; but he made relation that even as we spoke the mighty thews of stalwart Mouli were to work at prising up the slab to discover What lay beneath ... then did I know fear and trembling in very sooth; but by then it was too late for fear.

And there came to our ears from some distance a noise like the sounds of a Battle, and the shouting of strong Mouli rose above the clamour; and all the while there was another sound which liked me not, and it was even as the clicking of clawed feet, and the slithering of saurian tails, and a hissing like unto the voice of reptiles. And then I knew, and caught up Ismail and led him forth from that darksome and accursed place of fetid caverns, where ever and forever there blew from unguessable depths beneath our feet the noisome breath of the panting Pit.

And we came at length forth through the labyrinth and out into the blessedness of the open air in a pale, wan dawning; but at our very heels, from the gloomy caverns beneath, came That which pursued. And a crawling, hideous, loping horde of deformed and dwarfish degenerated creatures, with great cruel claws on hindlimbs and forelimbs, and a rugose, green hide upon their loathsome bodies, and the great snouts of saurians grinning with white, sharp, pointed fangs. And I shrieked and knew the red, mangled, pitiful thing they bore upon uplifted claws like a dreadful banner to be all that remained of Mouli, young Mouli ... and I knew then that the Elder

Age has not perished from the Earth, and that likewise there are dread, unhuman Survivals that have straggled down through the aeons, none knoweth how: monstrous, blasphemous Entities that have slept or lain in secret crypts and in remote places for unhallowed ages, governed by neither logic nor reason as we know it, to be awakened from their age-long sleep by whomsoever knoweth the Rites, the Signs, and the Words (for they die not but shall be until the Ending of all things), or roused to wakefulness by the rash, unknowing intruder.

And this hissing, chittering, hideous horde would have flung themselves upon us, gnawing, rending, and tearing with those cruel white fangs, had it not been for the merciful light of Day, the which the antediluvians, who had dwelt in the dark bowels of the earth for countless aeons, could not endure. And as we fled on our camels from that accursed and nameless city where an ancient Foulness yet lives and hideously thrives, did I bethink me of that scrap of verse that I penned that first night when we came nigh unto the nameless city; and my soul shuddered at its prophecy:

> *That is not dead which can eternal lie,*
> *And with strange aeons even Death may die.*

Notes

It has become apparent that the early members of the Lovecraft Circle made extensive use of the Sixth Narrative. Lovecraft himself used it as his source for "The Nameless City", and it is interesting to compare the two texts and see how very little he actually took from Dee's English version: virtually no more than an image here and there, a line or two elsewhere. Under Lovecraft's hand the plot diverges considerably from the Alhazredic text; also, Lovecraft made a slight error when in the tale he wrote ,"It was of this place that Abdul Alhazred the mad poet dreamed on the night before he sang his unexplained couplet." (The text clearly states that Alhazred wrote the famous couplet on the night he and his two followers *arrived* at the Nameless City.)

It had puzzled me that Lovecraft made no use whatsoever of the Old One, Mnomquah, either in "The Nameless City" or anywhere else. The explanation may lie in the fact that the English *Necronomicon* was never published, but laboriously copied in longhand, generation after generation; it is more likely that whatever copy Lovecraft used was either fragmentary, or that age and neglect had obliterated many words, passages, even entire pages.

Lovecraft also made an oblique reference to the Sixth Narrative in his "History and Chronology of the *Necronomicon*", in which he states Alhazred "spent ten years alone in the great southern desert of Arabia ... and found beneath the ruins of a certain desert town the shocking annals and secrets of a race older than mankind."

Two other of Lovecraft's colleagues (at least!) also had access to the Sixth Narrative, Robert E. Howard and William Lumley. Howard remarks in his story "The Fire of Asshurbanipal" on "the ancient, ancient City of Evil spoken of in the *Necronomicon* of the mad Arab Alhazred—the city of the dead on which an ancient curse rested. Legends named it vaguely: the Arabs called it *Beled-el-Djinn*, the City of Devils, and the Turks, *Kara-Shehr*, the Black City."

William Lumley, Lovecraft's friend and sometime revision client, also saw the Sixth Narrative, or quotations from it, at least, for in his story "The Diary of Alonzo Typer" (which Lovecraft later revised for publication), Lumley quoted almost verbatim two passages from the Dee version: the first beginning with the phrase "There are terrible primal arcana of Earth", and the second beginning, "Likewise there are dread unhuman survivals that have straggled down through the aeons.."

It is important to note here that these quotations from the Sixth Narrative were *not* inserted into the text of "Alonzo Typer" by Lovecraft, since they appear in Lumley's original version of the story, recently unearthed and published.

The Seventh Narrative: The Madness out of Time

I.

There is a madness beyond Time and a Foulness beyond space, and may heaven help him who dares arouse the Wrath thereof, and the nameless Doom that ever lies in wait for all who do be rash enough to risk such horror. Knowest thou that in the ten years that I, Alhazred, did spend in the trackless wastes of Arabia Felix, after what time that I rose up and departed out of the city of the Alexandrians, many and strange were the happenings that befell me, but none there was that was strangelier than this which now I would relate.

In the fullness of time did I betake me to that place in the Waste beknownst unto men as the Valley of Tombs, for that in its desolation there stood the empty fanes and desecrate of an old necropolis abuilded in the days of Ancientry, and by men now forgot save for us sorcerers; ravaged and open stood these tombs, and hewn were they out of the very fabric of the cliffs, which cliffs line the Vale to either side, like walls; and here it came to pass that I took one of these for mine abode, a tomb that stood up amongst the hills and from which coign had I the broad vantage of the Vale and the oasis that stood amongst the rocks that bestrew the floor of the valley.

And here it was, in solitude and silence, under the wheeling constellations that jewelled the desert night like handsfull of gems strewn on black velvet, that I pondered the Elder Books and scanned the stars, studied the epicycles and meditated upon the arcana of mine Art. Erelong it chanced that I discovered myself not to be the only eremite who dwelt here in the Valley of Tombs, for there was even another: an older man than I was he, and lean and furtive, overgiven to secretive ways, and I but glimpsed him from afar betimes, for we did share the same small oasis amidst the sands, and the fresh, lifegiving waters thereof. Betimes did I observe him as he came and went below the height of my dwelling, as he sought the rich fruit of the date palms and the sweet waters of the pool, but long and long it was to be ere that we exchanged Words, and when at length this came to pass I did learn that he was one Sargon, a Sorcerer who from of old had made his place of abiding within the wastes of that land to the East that was formerly the realm of the famous Chaldaeans, from whose ancient blood was he sprung.

Now in time from the lips of this Chaldaean heard I a frightful Tale of Terrors, but for a while I but watched him as he came and went, and that mostly in the dim gloaming; and I observed of him a curious behavior, in that in these peregrinations he did not progress from point to point in a straight line, as did other men, but in a manner circuitous and serpentine, as meandering in curved paths, which was to me most marvelous strange, as I could imagine no reason for this peculiar mode of locomotion.

And I bethought me then of that which was written of old: that men shouldst tread the Straight and Narrow Path, for the salvation of their Souls; but he was one man whom I have known who trod the same straight and narrow Path to the ultimate and unspeakable Damnation of his soul, whereby had I great cause to Marvel thereat. ...

II.

In the passage of time we became friends, we two lonely Sorcerers who shared betwixt us this barren and bleak Valley of the Tombs; and it was from the lips of this Sargon the Sorcerer that I had the tale which follows.

Now he was gaunt and wasted, this Chaldaean, and it demanded no great shrewdity of mine own to discover that a dreadful Fear rode him as a man bestrideth a Camel, for that Fear thou couldst discern in his shifting and red-rimmed eyes, and in the shaking of his palsied hands, and in the nervous twitching of his Visage. But as to *that* of which he feared I knew not, nor did I care to guess: and the Truth of it all, when at length I gained the knowledge, was strange and strangelier than ever I could have dreamed ...

Once, O Alhazred (said he unto me), I sought in my rash and imprudent youth to attain to the Vision of the All beknown to Mystics and Philosophers and by such deemed admirable beyond the boundaries of ordinary Experience. The attainment of this Vision I sought by the means of a powerful drug called the Liao, the which is even a derivative of the Black Lotus of much frightful lore and legend; and the drug Liao I in time acquired, purveyed unto my hands by the Divers Ways from the wise and learned apothecaries of Far Cathay. Now it is one of the properties of this drug Liao that it doth dissolve the strictures placed upon the mind of Man by time and space, the both of which cease to exist, thus permitting the Intellect, together with a swift and all-encompassing sense of Perception, to range afar; and when that these strictures of Time and Space are removed there be thus stripped from the eyes of men those Veils of illusion that time hath thrown over them, the myth of Now and Then, when in reality there be only *forever*.

And thus, having imbibed of the drug Liao, after the prescribed manner, it seemed to me that I did view all Lands and all Ages in one endless and eternal instant, and very wondrous strange was this Marvel: aye, in one and the same flashing Instant of time I saw myself a hairy, bestial creature, squatting in a filthy cave, wrapt about with dirty hides, gnawing on a thighbone ... and a thousand naked slaves grovel before me as I pass in a litter of gold and ivory drawn by a night-black oxen from Thebes; I am a priest, and I exalt with painted palms the beast-headed stony idols of Aegypt ... and a howling savage from the wind-scoured plains of Parthia, riding to ambush a Roman legion; I am a half-naked Vandal, sacking the desecrated temples of Greece ... and in India I am an humble acolyte, and I hearken to the teaching of the mystic Masters, and run screaming from their presence, for their revelations are as salt on wounds that bleed ...

And I am the first man arising from the steaming fens and the quaking bogs of the new-made Earth, and I am fled squealing from between the trampling feet of the vast Reptiles that roved and ruled before the coming of man; and I penetrate further, into the very backward and Abysm of Time, for in the impatience of my Folly I strove to probe even beyond the very bournes of Time and Space, to That which existeth forever, and the which was before ever Time or Space was.

And I, who had lived in all men as all men live in me, I, who had perceived the entirety of human history in one vast moment, one all-pervading Now, sought to go Beyond ... into that gray and featureless phantasmal bourne that knoweth not the strictures of Where or When, but only Is: and, for a moment (as mere men may measure a moment) I stood upon the pale colourless shore beyond Time, where mist-waves lap at sandless sands, and darkness dwells instead of light; and *They* scented my presence—those shadowy and furtive and implacable Things that dwell in that terrible Realm—That which is begotten of the Madness out of Time and the Foulness that reigneth beyond Space. There, on that dim and hueless shore of shadows, They prowl ever, lean and athirst; and now, O Alhazred, that I have in my folly dared attract Their attention by mine uninvited presence in Their realm, They hunt me down all the paths of Time and Space, and never will I be free of Their unrelenting pursuit.

III.

And I, Alhazred, then roused mineself and spake unto this Sargon the Sorcerer from out of the fullness of my daemon-wrested lore, saying:

Beware, O hapless Chaldaean, for once in the sealed and hidden Vale of Hadoth beside the immemorial Nile saw I in my youth the likeness of Those thou fearest; aye, graven it was in an amulet of curious and exotic design, the oddly angular and strangely stylized representation of a winged and couchant Hound, exquisitely and loathsomely carven from a thin wafer of lucent jade. And it was the hand of my Master that held it, the Wizard Yakthoob, for amongst his collection of rare and obscure periapts had he this, that was the ghastly soul-symbol of the corpse-eating cult of forbidden and inaccessible Leng—but of this talisman, of its properties and of the horrible relation of the souls of the dead to That which it symbolizes, I shall speak more fully at another time.

Suffice it to say, O Chaldaean, that stamped upon the semi-cany face of that jade amulet was an expression so repellent in the extreme, savouring at once of death, of bestialism, and of utter malevolence, for that those sinister lineaments were drawn from some obscure manifestation of the souls of those who vexed and gnawed at the dead, that never have I forgotten it, or That which it represents. Aye, I speak of the very Hounds of Tindalos themselves, those Hunters From Beyond that be the Spawn of Noth-Yidik and the effluvium of K'thun, and that howl forever in the maelstrom that is dread and fearsome Azathoth; aye, They be none other than the very minions and servitors of the Daemon-Sultan[1], under Their ghastly sire and dam, Noth-Yidik and terrible K'thun. Aye, They bay and slaver forever in that shadowy and indistinct realm of Chaos that lieth beyond all bournes of Time or Space, wherein also dwelleth from of old Their Dread Master, Azathoth; and it was writ of old that men awake within Them cosmic hungers: yet are even such as They bound by the Elder Gods with certain strictures, even as we be weak and timorous mortals, for our space is curved whilst They move only in *straight lines* or through *right angles*, for such be the limitation of Their nature which are obedient to the biddings of the Elder Gods that rule all that is; wherefore are They hampered in Their pursuit of thee, O Chaldaean; and if thou canst contrive to elude Them long enough, peradventure They will slink back, snarling and ravenous and unsatisfied, to that Foulness wherefrom They came in the beginning, before Time and beyond Space.

Now somewhat of the import of my words had this Sargon already guessed, which explaineth his circuitous and meandering manner of locomotion, for the Sorcerer well knew of this Difference between curved and angled space; and in the days that followed hard upon the heels of our converse did we extend modes of protection new and novel: with clay dug from the marge of the font amidst the oasis did we smooth into sleek curves the sharply-angled jointures of his stony cell, even the corners of the walls and the roof thereover; and long did we strive with the Exorcisms of Pnom (both the Lesser and the Greater) to free him of this Curse, but, alas! to no avail.

And nightly did I peruse those tomes of the Elder Lore which I had borne hither with me into the fastnesses of the desert for my study, seeking the text of that Great Invocation to Azathoth that might sever the shackles that bound the hapless spirit of my Chaldaean friend to the Hunters from Beyond, who all the while did hunt him down the byways of Time and Space, howling and an-hungered. But nowhere in the texts didst my perusal disclose this Liturgy and I found it naught, although I searched through those portions of the *Pnakotic Manuscripts* which may still be decyphered by men. And at length I did despair for the Chaldaean, for many and dread are the Forces that be leagued with those gaunt and famished Hunters from Beyond, and the Dholes may aid Them, and the Little People of the Wood (for these are the servitors of Shub-Niggurath, the Mighty Mother), and by whose aid even the Hounds of Tindalos may move through the Scarlet Circles and encroach upon that region of curved space whereunto be native our mortality.

And yet were all my searchings in vain, for I found not that grand invocation that was the object of my Quest; and daily, as I consulted with this Sargon the Sorcerer, I could not help but observe how ever more gaunt and hag-ridden was the unhappy Chaldaean, for that he sensed that the Hunters from Beyond were snuffling at his traces even through his far-wandering Dreams, the which he could not control, no more than may any ordinary man, Sorcerer or shepherd. And there was naught that I could do to succor him in the direst extremity of his Need; and it became apparent to me that some grim doom hovered near unto our dismal Vale, for the skies even of Noon were enshadowed with veils of darkness, through which the stars burned bright as bale-fires at a Witches' Sabbath, and a chill, uncanny breeze, as stenchful as one come panting up from the very Pit, made all that bleak and stony Vale as noisome as an abattoir.

And then there came a day whereupon all of these matters came to a head, as 'twere: a gloaming, when the gibbous Moon rode high in a sky where scudding cloud-wraiths fled before a whining wind, and I shuddered and wrapt more tightly about me the folds of my robe, for as the wind went whistling through the naked fangs of rock over my head, they made a thin, shiversome sound not unlike the howling of hounds, far-off and faint to hear … like the baying of those grim Hounds that howl forever at the heart of that black Maelstrom that is even Azathoth, the Daemon-Sultan …

Now, as it had chanced, the slumbers of Sargon the Sorcerer had nightly been fitful and much broken, haunted as he was by dire and grisly Dreams, so that he got of Nights little or no sleep, wherefore had I counselled him to seek his cot during the long afternoons when still the Earth basked in the fullness of the light of day, and Night, and the gruesome creatures that prowl its darksome Deeps, be yet afar-off. But on this very day of days had he sunken deep into the bottomless slumbers of exhaustion, from which he woke asudden, with a fearful start, as the dark shadows crept across the dusty flooring of his stony cell and heralded the Coming of Darkness. And up sprang the Chaldaean, suddenly stricken to the roots of his soul with a nameless Fear, and ran forth from the open portal of the tomb that was his habitation, crying aloud my name, and as I came forth from mine own abode to answer him I beheld beneath me the dark floor of the Valley of Tombs where he fled—*and the gaunt, lean Shapes of darknesses even darker than the shadows that closed upon him from the four points of the compass*—and ripped and tore as I stood, fear-frozen, helpless to do aught.

And I realized that, in his terror, Sargon the Chaldaean had for once forgot to take great care in progressing by curving paths, but had run for mine abode *in a straight line* … wherefore do I say that once I have known a man who followed the Straight and Narrow Path to his detriment and very Doom, for all that the Scriptures and the prophets preach … aye, ye that scan my words, beware! lest ye incur the wrath of the Hunters from Beyond that are the very Hounds of Tindalos!

Notes

Title. The actual title of this narrative in the Dee text is "The Hunters from Beyond"; I have changed the title so as not to confuse my readers, since Clark Ashton Smith wrote a story with that title, published in 1932. At this late date, it is beyond conjecture whether Smith borrowed the title from Dee or arrived at it by independent invention.

Whether or not Smith read the Seventh Narrative, Frank Belknap Long certainly did, for he used both the Liao drug and the Hounds themselves in his famous story "The Hounds of Tindalos" (1929). However, he did not imitate the plot structure of the Sevenhth Narrative, only letting it stimulate his own imagination. He did, however, borrow a few phrases therefrom.

The title I have substituted here for the original was coined by H. P. Lovecraft, but never used on a story. "The Madness out of Time" was the original working title for the story eventually published as *The Case of Charles Dexter Ward*.

That this narrative is the source of the allusion which Lovecraft makes to a passage in Alhazred given in his story "The Hound" (1922) is certain from a comparison of that story and the text of the narrative.

1. Lovecraft nowhere identifies the Hounds of Tindalos as the minions of Azathoth in explicit terms, but apparently he was familiar with the fact, to which he alludes directly in "The Horror in the Museum" ("Spawn of Noth-Yidik and effluvium of K'thun! Son of the dogs that howl in the maelstrom of Azathoth!"), and hints at in "The Whisperer in Darkness" ("I was told the essence [but not the source] of the Hounds of Tindalos … and I started with loathing when told of the monstrous nuclear chaos beyond angled space, which the *Necronomicon* had mercifully cloaked under the name of Azathoth.") Mentioned in the same breath, as it were, Lovecraft here seems to suggest a connection between the Hounds and Azathoth that, perhaps, he dared not speak boldly upon; note also the mention of "angled space" in this context.

The Eighth Narrative: Dreams of the Black Lotus

I.

Now, it came to pass, after our brief and calamitous sojourn in the Nameless City, and following upon my hearkening to the Ghoul's Tale, as I have aforetime writ, that my Disciple, Ismail, and myself, whilst traversing the endless wastes of the Desert Sands bestride our Camels, came at length and in the fullness of time into an Oasis amidst the desolation of the wilderness. Here, palms of sharded emerald were mirrored in a calm pool of lucent sapphire, mercifully shielded from the intolerable radiance of the noontide Sun; and here tents and small hovels and pavilions had reared somewhat very like unto a Town amidst the desert, for that this Oasis was become a crossroads in the burning and trackless sands where many caravans of traders paused betimes to refresh themselves in the coolth thereof, and to rest and water their beasts, ere that they took up yet again the long journey overland to the populous cities of the Coast.

And here didst Ismail and I erect our tent and here we bided for a time, glad for once of the bustle and the clamour of ordinary men and of the common ways of the Mundane Sphere, after the shadowy and sepulchral silence of the tomb-city of the pre-Adamites, from the which had we fled into the dolorous whispering of the shifting sands with such precipitous Haste. And here, too, did I fall in with one Abdoullah, a merchant of Bassorah, who had journeyed hither halfway adown the wide-wayed World with his burthen of curious articles, and shimmering silks, and rare spices, and apothecary-goods, fetched hither from afar, aye, even from the famous kingdom of China, even from the Empire of the Grand Cham. And it was from this Abdoullah of Bassorah that I, Alhazred, procured at length a modest sufficiency of the Black Lotus, that ill-rumoured and most elusive blossom from the which an uncanny and malignant Potion may be brewed, but only by the hands of the rash and imprudent, for naught that is wholesome is reputed of this Black Lotus, of the which no man knoweth where that it blooms or where it is gathered, nor by what Hands.

But sorcerers whisper that to imbibe of its potent fumes doth expand the mind to new dimensions beyond every known limit of the Flesh, even beyond the accustomed boundaries of the Spirit, whereupon will the mind of him that dares imbibe thereof drift languid as a lily afar through weird, uncanny bourns of Dream, whereamongst the which may full oft be found the secrets of an Elder arcana by all the waking world forgot, and only unto him who dares to dream beknownst.

Now, it was of this same Black Lotus that the misfortunate Chaldaean, Sargon the Sorcerer, partook, and to his eternal detriment, for thereby fell he hapless victim to an awful Doom; and so it may seem to thee both rash and exceeding imprudent of me in this wise to risk the imbibement of that same dire and dreadful Narcotic whereby was the ill-starred Chaldaean brought to the brink of Terror and beyond; and yet this pause to rest amidst the shady coolth of the Oasis, and our encounter with the merchant of Bassorah, did occur long years before mine abiding in that hermitage amidst the Valley of the Tombs, and as yet I had not met with the doomfraught Sargon. However, even hadst it been otherwise, I little bethink me that I would fade and falter before the experience of the Lotus, for faint hearts do not wise wizards make, and to risk naught is to gain naught. And there is much to be learned from the dreams of the Black Lotus, say the sages.

And so it came to pass, that, one evening as the Sun perished on a fiery funeral pall in all the gold and purple of his Imperial pomp, I sought out the seclusion of my tent and prepared a decoction of the Drug according to certain and several Precepts I had learned by odd, and obscure, ways, and from Sources far better left unnamed. But in a different strength and according to a different manner of preparation, and by yet another mode than that to be employed at length by the pitiful Chaldaean: for knowest thou that there be a full many of means whereby that thou mayest partake of the Black Lotus, and that each and every one leadeth to an other and quite different Resultancy: which is to say, the Drug may be eaten in its raw form; or reduced to flakes and smoked in a *nargeelah*; or ground to a powder with mortar and pestle and then dissolved in an admixture of wine and drunk down; or the powder thereof may be inhaled into the Nostrils; and thy choice of the Mode whereby wouldst thou imbibe of the opiate dependeth greatly upon the form and nature of That which thou wouldst experience under the influence of the Black Lotus.

And so it did eventuate that, having encompassed both mineself and my disciple, the youth Ismail (whose role in that which would ensue was to keep record of all that should chance to occur during the course of this Experiment) within the Triple Circle of Protection, the which I traced upon the flooring of the carpet of my tent with blue luminous Chalk, prepared according to the wise precepts of the ancient Pnom. I did with all due care and caution partake of the Black Lotus after a certain manner.

II.

At the first naught occurred to betid me in any wrong; however, at length I felt a *peculiar disassociation* from my body, and seemed to float free and bodiless betwixt the flooring and the roof of my tent. Erelong, all vision blurred into a many-colored haze, and it seemed to me that I passed through the fabric of my tent and dispersed, like a shapeless Vapour, into the infinite Element. Upon the heels of this there passed an unmeasurable Time in which I but vaguely drifted idly to and fro, as if tossed upon the currents of the surface of the River of Time; erelong, however, I was seized and caught in the remorseless grip of that Current and found myself borne helplessly as a chip in a torrent into the immeasurable Past.

The swirling mists that cloaked my vision cleared—I saw a sweeping panorama of those Wars betwixt the Crescent and the Cross, when grim-faced giants clad in merciless iron, those Frankish dogs, broke the strength of the stalwart Saladin, and stormed and seized the soaring ramparts of Acre, and aspired even to Jerusalem the Golden; then the mists closed about my stunned gaze for an immeasurable time, and when again they cleared I had journeyed further backwards in the black abysm of Time, and, centuries earlier, ecstatic, God-drunk hordes followed on the very heels of the Prophet as he entered into Holy Mecca ... and again the mists of time gathered as a veil before mine eyes, and when at length they cleared, and centuries earlier still, I watched enthralled at the heroic last stand of a Roman legion against the howling and half-naked wolfpacks of savage Parthia ... and watched as the yelling horsemen overwhelmed the iron Roman square, broke it and tramped it down underfoot, treading into the mire the gallant centurions, aye, and watched with awe as their sacred standards, the bronze Eagles, swayed and tottered and went down under the screaming red wave of utter savagery.

Now the sheer velocity of mine adventure in time quickened to a giddy speed—centuries flickered before my gaze as swiftly as a sage flips through the pages of a book ... I looked on as the numberless hosts of the invincible Alexander of the Two-Horns[1] crossed over the Hydaspes into Hindoostan, leaving all of mighty Mother Asia prostrate and whelmed and conquered behind them ... another sweeping together of the Veils of Time to shroud my vision, and when they parted at last I stared upon an even earlier scene, for the topless towers of kingly Troy stood standing in the Sun, with the curved glitter of the Scamander like a steely scimitar behind them, and the forces of the Achaiai drawn up in ten-years' siege before those fabled and impregnable walls ... again the mists gathered, then swirled apart, laying bare before me a scene of scorched granite desert, and I watched in wonder as naked brown *fellaheen* hewed, and cut, and then hauled with infinite slow labor into place, the very cornerstone of the Great Pyramid of Cheops ...

Again the mist-veils curtained the scene before me, then parted to disclose a wonder beyond all wonders, as my bedazzled eyes beheld in awe the magnificent spectacle of Lost Atlantis as its shining cities were drunk down by the emerald gullet of the thirsty seas ... and, e'en earlier yet, I stared upon the age-drowned glory that was timeless Valusia[2], that myth-forgotten City of Wonder ...

III.

Swifter apace the visions grew, and now my dazzled gaze beheld vistas not of ancient time but of infinite space, as well, for I looked with wonder and amazement upon realms and regions far and farther still from Earth's environs—but whether they stood on the worlds of distant Suns, or in Earth's Dreamlands, or in regions contiguous to alien spheres and dimensions, I yet remain uncertain.

And thus it was that I looked upon those weird and phosphor-litten woods of quaint and gnarled trees wherein the furtive and elusive and unwholesome Zoogs lurk, and from whose deeps and glooms they slink and creep and gibber ... and saw, amidst that desolate, that daemon-haunted Waste, the mystic heights of Kadath rear up her onyx-castled crest against strange stars in alien-constellated skies made far and fabulous by the cold fires of shuddering and unearthly aurorae ...[3]

Again, my vision blurred, and when it cleared I was far and farther still from the known, familiar Earth: and I glimpsed amidst the landscapes of Nightmare the terrible kingdom of the Gugs that are the minions of The Nameless Mist that engendereth the dread Lord Yog-Sothoth[4] ... and my vision blurred again, but when it cleared at length, I looked upon fabulous and age-deserted and pre-human Sarkomand, whose winged, prodigious lions of glinting diorite guard black nitrous stairways, the which go down and down and ever down into The Gulf ... and then the slimy waves of the Black Lake of Ubboth washed before my shuddering sight, and I knew, there in the Stygian glooms and bottomless silences, that I paused in the ghastly deeps of Nugg-yaa, deep beneath the Moon's ancient crust, where slumbers from of old under the Elder Sign the dreadful, and the dreaded, Mnomquah ...

And then, and at length, there flashed upon my vision one glimpse of a depth and of an abomination more horrible than any that I had glimpsed before: I looked upon a foul black pit, with a carven rim of beslimed rock about it, all drowned in Plutonian gloom, litten only by the vile phosphorescence of the primal white jelly of the proto-Shoggoths[5] ... and amidst the hideous slime and the obscene stench I saw the bubbling, quivering, plastic horrors, those shuddering towers of gelatinous, liquescent filth, studded with naked and protruding and staring eyeballs ... and I shrieked, and fled, back down the pathways of space and time and dimension, knowing in that last, soul-blighting glimpse the nodding flowers that blossomed in the scummed shallows of that lake of bubbling filth—*and shrieked, and fled, knowing at last where the Black Lotus bloomed, and upon what unspeakable slime it feeds.*[6]

Notes

Robert E. Howard, Robert Bloch, Clark Ashton Smith, and other members of "The Lovecraft Circle", who obviously had access to a copy of Dee's *Necronomicon*, wrote knowingly of the "Black Lotus." It is, I would say, beyond question that they all knew of the Eighth Narrative, and of its revelations.

1. In his original Arabic text, Alhazred would have written *Iskandar Dhoulkernein*, "the two-horned Alexander", which is the name by which the lore and legend of Islam knew the mighty Macedonian.

2. Robert E. Howard made reference to Valusia, "the City of Wonder", in his King Kull stories, but this is the first reference I find to Valusia and its age in the *Necronomicon* (if, indeed, I am correct in identifying Dr. Dee's Falushyaa with what Howard termed "Valusia").

3. Lovecraft referred to the wood of the "furtive Zoogs" in much these same terms in his *Dream-Quest of Unknown Kadath*, and also to Kadath, the kingdom of the gugs, Sarkomand, etc., in much the same terms employed here in the Eighth Narrative. Obviously, HPL derived them from this narrative. Some of the very phrases used are identical.

4. Although "the Gugs" have been named as among the minions of the Great Old Ones, in a fragment from the *Necronomicon* quoted in the posthumously collaborative novel *The Lurker at the Threshold*, it has not previously been discovered which of the Old Ones the gugs serve as minions. A glance at the "Descent of the Old Ones" genealogical chart on page 183 of *Selected Letters* IV identifies "The Nameless Mist" as the direct progenitor of Yog-Sothoth. Now it is known that the little-known gugs are the servitors of this little-known Old One.

5. That Lovecraft was well acquainted with the Eighth Narrative can easily be proven from a comparison of the two texts. In the last page of *At the Mountains of Madness*, Lovecraft quotes directly from this Narrative: Such phrases as "the black pit", "the carven rim", "the primal white jelly", and "the proto-Shoggoths" are unmistakable.

6. While it cannot yet be made quite clear what particular horrible abomination lies cloaked beneath the term "the Pit of the Shoggoths", now at last it is possible to understand in full the concluding lines of Sonnet XX, in the sonnet sequence of the late Wilbur Nathaniel Hoag (which I edited under the title of *Dreams from R'lyeh*, and guided through press in 1975), which reads as follows:

My dream-self roamed the cosmic gulfs profound,
Past daemon-haunted Haddith, where in deeps
Of foul putrescence buried underground
The loathsome shoggoth hideously sleeps,
I saw—and screamed! And knew my doom of dooms,
Learning at last ... *where* the Black Lotus blooms.

The Ninth Narrative: The Shadow from the Stars

I.

After that doom which befell Sargon the Sorcerer, that most misfortunate Chaldaean, I in time rose up and departed hence from mine abode there in the ancient Valley of the Tombs, and repaired to the famous city of Damascus in the land of the Syrians, for in that country there were a few of my former disciples who yet dwelt therein and abided together, having eloigned thither from the city of the Alexandrians some years before.

Long was my journey thereunto, and not withouten certain mishaps and adventures, the which I will not set down in this record, since that they bear not upon the matter thereof; but suffice it to say that I, Alhazred, did traverse the Three Arabys and, at length and in the fullness of time, found myself at a certain Place within the dominions of the Grand Caliph, a place that was in the long-gone days of ancientry well beknown unto Men, for these were the time-gnawed ruins of Elder Kuthchemes, a city that has not gone unremembered of Time, and that lingers on yet from the primal age of the Hyboreans, which people be by all the world save wizards well forgot.

But it is not of these crumbling shards of stone that I would speak, but of that dark eminence the which riseth hard by these aforesaid ruins, the which is known to certain of the sages as the Black Mountain[1]. Now, it was written of old in the annals of Pnom the Exorcist, and also in the texts of Eibon the Hyperborean, that it was within this Mountain of old that the Elder Gods prisoned beneath their Sign even the Great Lord Yog-Sothoth, after what time the Old Ones had been utterly whelmed and cast down from power by the Elder Gods at the terminus of that frightful War wherefrom the very extremities of the Cosmos yet reverberate to the thunders thereof.

And here in the very shadow of the Black Mountain did I dare linger for a time, wondering full greatly thereat: for the Lord Yog-Sothoth, who is All-in-One and One-in-All, and who was begotten by the Nameless Mist[2] out of its very substance, and after a certain Manner most peculiar to the Old Ones, and known only by Them; and that the time of that monstrous Begetting (sayeth Pnom) was even in the Hour of the Spiral Wind[3] from Nith—whereof the which do I, Alhazred, know naught that I would dare impart to mere mortal men: for there are things it is unwise to speculate upon and unwholesome even to know.[4]

And it is further written in the Elder Texts that the Nameless Mist was among the first-begotten of Azathoth the Daemon-Sultan, and very brother to The Darkness[2], from whose womb was birthed that hellish, cloud-like Entity[5], even Shub-Niggurath, in whose honor nameless cults yet hold the shocking rites of the Goat with a Thousand Young; and Shub-Niggurath was herself begotten at the place called Shumath-Ghun, the which lieth amidst the trackless mystery of the Black Nebula[6] ... but of these Matters I know little and should speak even less.

II.

Now, as I abode there in the very shadow of the Black Mountain, pondering upon the mysteries of Antiquity, I at length became aware that a host of the desert people shared with me this desolation, for I beheld their black tents from the heights whereon I dwelt; and erelong I made the acquaintance of the leader of this tribe, who were most strangely named, for they were called The Nameless Ones; and he was the Sheik Fakhreddheen that was the chieftain thereof.

It was from his bearded lips that I learnt at length why that his people bore their nameless name, and that reason was that they were outcast from the nations of their kind, for that they had abjured the worship of Allah and His Prophet to grovel before the Old Ones, whom their ancestors had served in the Elder Days. For these were no less than the descendants of those human servitors of his that had freed Yog-Sothoth from the bondage of the Elder Sign aeons before, in the days when Great King Rhampsinitus sate him upon the throne of Aegypt and the Children of Israel were not long since departed up out of their bondage and had crost the Red Sea into the land promised into them.

It beseemed that, even to mine own day, were the begotten of the begotten of those human minions of Yog-Sothoth yet faithful to their awful Liege, and were wont to foregather once each lustrum here at the Black Mountain to celebrate with certain Rites the liberation thereof. I had ere this known from my perusal of the Elder Texts that it had been mortal men had set free the Lurker at the Threshold, but what I had not known heretofore was that Yog-Sothoth still numbered men among his minions, for all that I had known hinted that it was the frightful Gugs who were his servitors[7], and they dwelt not here in the Waking World of Malkuth, but in the Dreamworld of Yesod.[8]

And long didst we converse there under the glory of the wheeling stars, for the Sheik Fakhreddheen was of the few who knew that it was even I, Alhazred, had been the first of men to open the Door to Outside, to where dwelt Yog-Sothoth in the Chaos beyond Space and Time, and for that goodly reason did he hold me in some certain Honor. We talked concerning many things, of the vaults of Shuggon[9] beneath the waves, which was the age-lost homeland of the prehuman Valusians, the Serpent-folk, which continent had been reft asunder in the grip of titan forces and sunk beneath the ponderous weight of sprawling waves in the dawn of time; and of crimson Haddoth[10] did we speak, from the which came down to Earth hideous and unspeakable Shudde-M'ell; and of many another marvel, but of none other that are for the inscribing on this page, for it is not meet or seemly that any save for an initiate should even hear a whisper of such arcana.

It was nigh unto the hour of false-dawn afore I returned to my tent in the shadow-drowned foothills that hunched furtive shoulders under the height of the Black Mountain, and I liked me little this discovery that I had made, and heartily wished that I might rise up and get me gone from amongst The Nameless Ones, and hie me on the long road to Damascus. For it liked me not, this unwholesome proximity to the hollow mountain in whose very gulphs had Yog-Sothoth himself brooded the ages by, under the prisonry of the Elder Sign ... hating the very stones about him from the bottomless depths of his infinite malignancy!

III.

And so it came to pass that upon that very night that I had talked long and long in his tent with the sinister Fakhreddheen, I resolved to quit the precincts of this accursed and ill-rumored Mountain, and as the gold fires of dawn washed the skies I had packed my belongings, struck my tent, mounted my camel, and fled towards Damascus upon the old stone causeway amidst the sands, whose length ran true as a die to the horizon, and the stones of which had been set in place (it might well be) by the Romans in their bright days of conquest and empire. And gradually did the gloomy heights of the Black Mountain recede behind me, until, by nightfall, the mount was but a mere notch on the black horizon against the glory of sunfall.

Now, thou must understand that I, Alhazred, who had once been a worshipper amongst the worshippers of Yog-Sothoth was now apostate therefrom, and accurst, for all I knew, by the dread Lord to whom once I had grovelled upon my belly, and to whom, what time that I had made my sojourn in Irem, the City of Pillars, I had even made the Red Offering ... thus it was that I dared not to linger over-long in the vicinity of the Black Mountain, on those nights when The Nameless Ones howled their horrible chantings to the leering stars and lit their awful fires and held their grisly rites before that congeries of iridescent globes, half-seen but stupendous in its malign suggestiveness, upon whose terrible and unhuman and naked Face I once had looked.

When that at length I had entered into the famous city of Damascus, and had congreeted with my disciples, I felt at last secure, and put the memory of the Black Mountain and of The Nameless Ones behind me, and well out of mind. Together that eve we feasted, for my former students had prepared an repast before me, and there was roast lamb with mint, and steaming rice, and figs and dates and onions, and a plenty of the good red wine of Schiraz and of the sweet white wine of Kirmische[11], and I slept that night with a full belly. But my dreams they were not pleasant dreams.

It seemed to me that I stood upon a height, and saw the Black Mountain loom up against the stars, and knew that this was even the night of the Foregathering. And as I watched from my coign of vantage, I saw The Nameless Ones in an endless file, clad all in robes of black and of scarlet, with torches borne aloft, as they filed in an endless file through a secret door in the cliffy wall of sheer, and seemingly unbroken, stone; and I knew in my heart of hearts that they sought within the mountain that ominous gulph that had for measureless aeons been the durance of Yog-Sothoth, who upon this night of nights awaited their gathering.

And then I saw his shadow descending from the stars ... for there was no forgetting that congeries of phosphorescent bubbling spheres of slime[12], those writhing and gelatinous tentacles, and, thrusting from the midst of this horror, That Unthinkable Thing that was the very face of Yog-Sothoth—

And I shrieked aloud, and woke gasping upon my sweat-soaked pallet, while yet the gaunt walls of the room reverberated with my shrieking, and found upon the wet pillow this note, pinned to the bed with a slim curved dagger, whose hilt of smooth mellow old ivory I had seen once thrust into the very girdle of the Sheik Fakhreddheen, and the message thereof was even thus:

> *Know, O Alhazred, that it doth thou no good to flee, for the*
> *Lord Yog-Sothoth will seek thee out, aye, even in the city of the*
> *Damascenes, and in the very hour foretold[13] shalt he rend thee*
> *asunder, for thine apostasy.*

This note bore the signature, *Fakhreddheen*. And upon the hilt of his dagger was graven the very seal and sigil of Yog-Sothoth, the One-in-All and All-in-One.

Notes

1. In antiquity, around the time of Moses, Yog-Sothoth was released by human agents from immemorial imprisonment beneath a black mountain near the ancient city of Kuthchemes, as Richard Tierney wrote in *The Winds of Zarr*, Albuquerque, NM, 1971. Robert E. Howard made mention of Kuthchemes in certain of his Conan stories.

2. *Nameless Mist and The Darkness*: I hope that I am correct in so rendering these two names, which Doctor Dee left untranslated. He gave them as "the *Magnum Innominandum*" and "the *Magnum Tenebrosum*", which actually mean "The Great Not-To-Be-Named" and "The Great Darkness." However, in his brief genealogical chart of the Old Ones published on page 183 of *Selected Letters* IV, Lovecraft gives the parents of Yog-Sothoth and of Shub-Niggurath as "the Nameless Mist" and "The Darkness." In this context, please note that the name or term *Magnum Innominandum* appeared in Robert Bloch's story "The Shambler from the Stars", in a brief quotation from *De Vermis Mysteriis*—which quote, in Latin, we now know from *Selected Letters* V (p. 88) to have been supplied to Bloch by Lovecraft.

3. Lovecraft mentioned "the Hour of the Spiral Wind from Nith" in a letter to Clark Ashton Smith dated 29 June 1933.

4. As can be seen, the text of this paragraph is so very corrupt as to be almost incomprehensible. I have done the best I can to untangle it, without actually rewriting the passage.

5. The phrase "that hellish, cloud-like entity ..." appears also in one of Lovecraft's letters quoted on page 92 of *Lovecraft at Last*.

6. The place called "Shumath-Ghun" amidst "the Black Nebula" is mentioned by Lovecraft in a letter to Clark Ashton Smith dated 26 July 1932, without, however, any reference to Shub-Niggurath.

7. The Eighth Narrative contradicts this, curiously, and states that the gugs are the minions and servitors of The Nameless Mist. Perhaps it is not for nothing that Alhazred was called "the Mad Arab"—the "Forgetful Arab", at any rate!

8. *Malkuth and Yesod*: In the Kabbala, the stations upon the Sephirotic Tree which represent the physical plane (the earth) and the astral plane (the realm of dreams) are named Malkuth and Yesod; Doctor Dee has spelt these names in a peculiar manner, "Malqooth" and "Yetzod", which is neither good Hebrew nor good Kabbalah. I have taken the small liberty of correcting his transliteration in line with spellings currently in use by students of ceremonial magic in the O.T.O. and similar occult fraternities.

9. This name for the continental home of the Serpentmen of Valusia, submerged before the rise of man, is not previously known in the literature of the Mythos. The line "vaults of Shuggon beneath the waves" does, however, appear in certain lines by Lovecraft from a discarded early draft of one of the *Fungi from Yuggoth* sonnets.

10. The line "crimson Haddoth from which Shudde-M'ell came to Earth" appeared in a story by Llewelyn M. Cabos in *Eldritch Tales* #4, as being quoted from the *Necronomicon*.

11. *Red wine, white wine*: Note that Alhazred, an apostate from Islam as he was from the secret *cultus* of Yog-Sothoth, here ignores the precepts of Mohammad, who forbade the Faithful to partake of the fruit of the grape.

12. The line "a congeries of iridescent globes, yet stupendous in its malign suggestiveness" appeared in Hazel Heald's story "The Horror in the Museum", which was one of Lovecraft's ghost-writing jobs.

13. *In the very hour foretold*: Abdul Alhazred is known to have spent his last years in Damascus, where, about the year A.D. 730, he composed the *Necronomicon*. In 738 he perished, torn apart and devoured by invisible monsters in mid-air in the sight of many witnesses, according to his biographer, Ibn Khallikan; perhaps this was the vengeance of Yog-Sothoth, after all.

II. The Book of Preparations

I. Of the Powers of the Sorceror

Knowest thou this, that of all of the arts and crafts and sciences whereunto may mortal men aspire, supremest and most potent of them all be the practice of Magic. Yet indeed, as *Ibn Shoddathua* sayeth in his commentaries upon the Papyruses of Mum-Nath: Many are they who lust for the Mastery thereof, but few indeed are they who succeed therein. For the wise magician is the Master of Nature and the archpriest of

all her Mysteries; at his command there openeth forth the Grave of Sod or
the shutten Sepulchre of Stone, to admit forth they who slumber therein;
before the utterance of his will shall storms becalm themselves, and floods
retreat back into the secret fountains of the Deep, and conflagrations extin-
guish their fiery flames.

Aye, and verily can he call down from beyond the stars That which
abideth in the dark and freezing spaces of the Void, or forth from the Pit
may he summon That which resideth in the black and frightful abyss; spells
and enchantments may he cast upon even the holiest of men or they that be
purest of heart. I say unto thee that such power may the accomplished
Initiate command that nations shall grovel before his awesome might, and
that the very Kings and Princes of the Earth shall flock to do him homage
and obeisance. Even the very life of the Sorcerer may be by his Art extended far beyond the ordinary limitations set upon mortal men, aye and verily,
for untold centuries may he thrive, untouched by Time. For, behold! doth
he not wield the keys of Life and Death? wherefore shall all mere mortal
men exalt the Master thereof, and grovel at his feet, *iä Nyarlathotep*! The
Wise Magician is a very mighty god.

Of these matters and yet others, too, may I speak with certainty, who
have proven them within the circuit of mine own experience. Yea, and I have
even found how one may, be he an Adept and his familiar spirits powerful
enough, control the very wanderings or migrations of his Essence into all
manner of beings and creatures—aye, even from beyond the Grave of Sod
or the door of the Sepulchre of Stone.

II. Of That Which Is Needful to Sorcery

Now if thou wouldst even become such a One as this whereof I speak,
be heedful and hearken well unto my words, for it be most necessary
that the Sorcerer shouldst prepare himself well and carefully for the practice
of the Art, and so thou shouldst attend to my Teachings as given forth here,
and obey my precepts in each and every particular thereof.

First must thou seek out a bleak and solitary place far off from the
crowded and noisy habitation of men, where thou shalt prepare thyself for
thine Art withouten interruption or distraction therefrom. In this I counsel
thee to seek out the savage wilderness of the gloomy forest, or some desert
cave or grotto apart from the busily-trodden ways; and therein thou must
meditate upon the purposes of thine Art, to the exclusion of all other and
lesser matters from thy mind.

Search, then, into the secret recesses of thine own soul to discover
therein That which thou the most desirest to attain through the practice of
the Art Sorcerous. There in thine humble cell far in some dark and obscure

region amidst the desolation of the wild, thou mayest ponder the Craft and discover that which lieth hidden within thine own heart. Having accomplished this to thine own satisfaction, thou must next determine which Being or Entity of the Dark Forces may best and wiseliest be evoked to thine aid and to the attainment of That which thou desirest to achieve.

III. Of the Old Ones and the Favours They Bestow

Now let it be known to thee, that the Lords of Darkness be full many and numerous withal, and that there be Some which be friendly unto men and Some forever the implacable enemies of men; wherefore thou must be wary in the choosing of That which thou wouldst implore assistance from; and here will I set before thee somewhat that may guide thee in thy choosing, for, as *Eibon* sayeth, Better the right teacher than no teacher at all.

Knowest thou, then, that the Dark Forces that be otherwise known as the Old Ones, or the Great Old Ones, hold empery and dominion over the several Elements whereinto all of Nature be divided, and therefore the Lords of the Air may not aid thee in the Operations of the Earth, neither can They of the Earth assist thee in Operations of the Air. Now here is the Matter of these things that I would set before thee.

The dread *Cthulhu* that is Lord of the Watery Abyss, even *He* Who Was Before and Who Shall Be Again, who commandeth all of the seas of the Earth and everything that be therein; He presideth over storms and shipwrecks and can demolish the vessels of thine enemies to their undoing, or, conversely, He may afford unto thee and unto those that have bought thy favour calm seas and steady winds. Fish will flock into the nets of thy friends and the same will desert the nets of thy foes, even as thou wilt; and moreover, He doth know the treasures lost beneath the waves: as bars of gold, inestimable gems, bales of spice, and suchlike goods beyond worth and reckoning; and He knoweth where there lie buried in the oozy slime the records and the wisdom of the Sunken Cities and the loot and plunder thereof, and works of antique art, or carven stone and precious metal. Seek of *Cthulhu*, then, or of His Spawn and Their Minions, if these matters be thy choice.

And dark *Hastur* the Unspeakable, Him that abideth on Carcosa in the Hyades, is first and foremost of the Powers of the Air; with His aid canst thou whelm the forest and smite down the walls of cities, bringing storm and pestilence and whirlwind forth, to the confounding of thy foes; or, conversely again, thou mayest calm the winds of heaven, quell the tempest, bid the whirlwinds be still. Moreover will He, and His Spawn and all Their Minions, transport thee to the far corners of the Earth, or distant worlds among the stars, even as thou wilt.

Of the Powers of the Earth, it is even *Shub-Niggurath* the Mighty Mother ruleth the woods and all that dwell therein, and knoweth the site of many buried things; moreover doth She command the fertility of women and the potency of men, and may render fertile whom She wilt or sterile whom She wilt; and She may blight the harvest and the orchard at desire, or increase the richness thereof. And of Her Brethren it is *Black Tsathoggua* and His servants guard the secret catacombs beneath the Earth and have knowledge of all buried treasures, or of mines of gold and silver, and of precious gems, where that they be hid within the recesses of the Earth, and of the secret tombs of mighty Sorcerers of yore, the which may be summoned up to hold converse with thee by arts of vile Necromancy, to the enhancement of thine own knowledge.

And of the Powers of Fire, the prince of these is *Cthugha* the Burning One, He who dwelleth afar on distant Fomalhaut; and He and His Spawn and the Minions thereof, hold power over fire itself, and with Their favour mayest thou bid the flames consume the dwelling-place of thine enemy, or the cities of the foe, or thou mayest still the flames of any holocaust at thy will. Moreover do such as *Cthugha* hold the secrets of mystic Alchemy and of the transmutation of metals, whereby in the crucible of fire may leaden dross become purified to fine red gold. And know that these be the four Elements whereof is the Earth and all of Nature composed, and These be the rulers of those elements.

Now there existeth even a Fifth Element, as of old the philosophers had cause to theorize, and this be Aether: tenuous and insubstantial is this Aether, and its powers and qualities be yet unknown to all save the most abstruse initiates. But it is not true, and many of the Ancient Scriptures would attest, that such of the Old Ones as *Yog-Sothoth* or *Nyarlathotep* the Mighty Messenger or *Azathoth* Himself, the Daemon-Sultan, be mere Earth elementals; nay, They be even Aether elementals, and the powers They command are awesome in their might: for They know all that hath ever been, that which is, and all that will ever be, since They dwell beyond time and outside of space, and there is very much thou hast to learn from Them.

IV. Of the Times and Seasons to Be Observed

As thou hast seen, Those thou mayest wish to call upon may be ordered under the four Elements of space and matter and the Fifth Element of infinite and eternal nonexistence. Thou must be mindful of the starry sciences, therefore, that the Rituals of Summoning be properly performed by thee at the times and seasons most propitious thereunto. Therefore do I say unto thee, whenever thou wouldst call forth Them From Outside or Their Spawn or the Minions Thereof, thou must mark well the seasons and the times in which the spheres do intersect and influences favourable floweth forth from the Void. Wherefor thou wouldst be wise to observe the cycles of the Moon and to mark the movements of the Planets, to note the Sun in his course through the Zodiac and the rising or decline of constellations in the Firmament of Heaven. Now the Ultimate Rites themselves shall be performed only in the Seasons most proper to them, and these be as the followeth next: at Candlemas, the second day of the second moon; at Beltane, or the Eve of May; at Lammas, the which falleth upon the first day of the eighth moon; at Roodmas, the fourteenth day of the ninth moon; and at the Mass of All-Hallows, the which is November eve.

Of Operations of the Aether
Thou mayest call out to dreadful *Azathoth* most propitiously when that the Sun sitteth in the Sign of the Ram, or the Lion, or the Archer; and in those seasons when the Moon decreaseth and Mars and Saturn conjoin their powers. Also, mighty *Yog-Sothoth* called upon will rise to thine incantations when Sol hath entered the House of Leo and the hour of Lammas is nigh upon thee. And there be another mode of summoning *Yog-Sothoth* the which I shall reveal in another place.

Of Operations of the Air
In general are the Lords and Princes of the Air wiseliest evoked when the Sun is in Libra, Aquarius, or Gemini. But thou mayest evoke the terrible *Hastur* on Candlemas Night, when Sol hath entered the House of the Water-Bearer and Mercury is in trine. The which season be also wise for summoning *Ithaqua* the Wind-Walker and His Spawn, *Zhar*, and *Lloigor*.

Of Operations of the Sea
Thou mayest call upon the Princes of the Deep when the Sun be in the Watery signs of Cancer, or Scorpio, or Pisces; and thou shouldst supplicate *Great Cthulhu*, His Spawn and Their Minions, at Hallowmas, when Sol reigneth in the House of the Scorpion and Orion be in the ascendant. And when that All-Hallows doth fall within the cycle of the New Moon, the Power shall be all the more strong.

Of Operations of the Earth
The Earth Elementals be the most amenable to the bidding of the adepts when the Sun sitteth in Taurus, or Virgo, or Capricornus, for that these be Earth signs. But thou mayest best conjure forth *Shub-Niggurath* when the Beltane fires blaze forth on the hill; with Sol in the Second House, repeat the Rites at Roodmas, which be when the Black Goat appeareth most frequently before men.

Of Operations of Fire
They that be Powers of Flame hearken most to the invocations of Sorcerers
when that the Sun resideth in the Signs of Aries, or of Leo, or of Sagittarius,
for that these be Fiery signs; in those seasons thou mayest best supplicate
Cthugha, or the Fire-Vampires that be His minions, or their leader, *Fthaggua*,
or *Aphoom Zhah*, His Spawn.

V. Of the Powers of the Moon

Albeit that the Sun ruleth through the Signs Zodiacal, yet hath the
Moon great powers withal, nor is her influence to be held lightly nor
ignored. If thou wouldst attempt invoking spirits, or calling up the Dead,
or for the recovery of lost treasure, or for all works of Necromancy, thou
wouldst be wisest to employ thine Art when that the Moon be in one of the
Terrestrial signs, such as Taurus, or Virgo, or Capricornus. And, likewise, if
thou wouldst bless with fertility, or curse with sterility, or if thou wouldst
evoke lust and lascivious passion in the hearts of women, or if thou wouldst
render thyself viewless as is the circumambient air with Operations of
Invisibility, thou mayest best cast thy spells when the Moon riseth in one of
the Fiery signs, as Aries, or Leo, or Sagittarius, excepting only when thou
wouldst call upon *Shub-Niggurath* for the accomplishing of these ends: for
She be most favourably supplicated under the Signs Terrestrial, as I have
aforetime writ, being one of the Powers of the Earth and an Elemental
thereof.

And in all works of hatred, or discord, or destruction, thou mayest
wisely cast thine enchantments when that the Moon ruleth in one of the Watery
signs, such as Cancer, or Scorpio, or Pisces. And be ever-mindful that all
operations of Sorcery which take especial caution of the Moon Signs be most
propitiously accomplished upon Monday, for that day is sacrosanct to the
Moon; but of this I shall speak at greater length in another place than here.

VI. Concerning Them from Outside

Now as I have said unto thee, the Old Ones bestow great and potent
powers upon those of men that please Them; and these dread and
awful Entities be neither gods nor daemons, but are beyond all limitations
of Good or Evil even as They dwell beyond all boundaries of time or space;
They are immortal and eternal and undying, and They abide from everlasting to everlasting, for They are not constructed of Matter as we know it, and
neither are They in Their origins true inhabitants of this Universe at all, but
in the beginning were native to Another. There it was that They were
brought into being by the Elder Gods to be the servants and the thralls

thereof; but the Elder Gods wrought better than They knew, and in the fullness of time did They wax exceeding great in Their Power, and wise and subtle and crafty in Their Thought. And in the time that followed, it came to pass that They rose up in rebellion against Those that had made Them, who were even the Elder Gods, and They fled forth from that region of existence, or dimension of space, or plane of being, wherein had They been created by Their erstwhile masters; and They came hither and entered into this Universe, and made of it Their empire and dominion.

Now few They were in number at the time of Their coming-hence into this Universe; but as They had good cause to fear that They should even be pursued by the Elder Gods, They did spawn exceeding vile and potent Beings to swell Their ranks and to strengthen Their might. Such of these, the latter-born, was even *Great Cthulhu*, Who was spawned by *Yog-Sothoth* upon shadowy Vhoori deep in the twenty-third nebula; and Whom in turn, upon remote and ultra-telluric Xoth, the dim green double sun that gleams like a daemonic eye in the blacknesses beyond Abbith, mated with *Idh-yaa* to the Begetting of His Spawn, *Ghatanothoa*, and *Ythogtha*, and *Zoth-Ommog*, and One Other, concerning Whom I dare not speak. And it is whispered that the last and latter-born of Them All was even *Vulthoom*, Who now resideth upon the World of the Twin Moons.

And many there were Who chose to make Their empery upon the several stars and worlds of this Universe, but many Others there were that came hither and descended upon this Earth, which some say had once, untold aeons of time before, been even a part of that Place wherein had They formerly dwelt under the dominion of the Elder Gods. And, Lo! the Elder Gods were waxed exceeding wroth to be thus deserted and deceived by Their Slaves; and They vowed to pursue Their rebellious Thralls into whatsoever region of existence They had fled, and there should They fall upon the Old Ones and seize and bind Them with mighty spells, and cast Them into everlasting prisonment, Who had durst defy Their Creators. And thus it came to pass that the Elder Gods, abandoning the Universe which They had ruled from everlasting to everlasting, and They came hither in Their Wrath and followed into this Universe Those that had been Their Servants; and They paused upon that sphere They called Glyu-Vho, which is of the stars of space, therefrom to reconnoiter; and They beheld to Their Rage that the Rebellious Ones were arrayed against Them as if for war; wherefore did they wax exceeding wroth, and They chose One of Them to be the leader of Their host; and He bade Them to assume an awful Shape, even the likeness of Towers of Flame, that in such form They should fall upon the Earth to punish Those that had transgressed against Their Creators.

VII. The Punishment of the Old Ones

And it came to be known by the Elder Gods that He that had unwisely and rashly counselled His Brethren to stand fast and to oppose with all Their Might the coming-hence of the Elder Gods was even one *Cthulhu*. Aye, and it was so, true and veritably: for *Great Cthulhu*, Who had by this epoch of time firmly established His dominions over all of the seas and oceans of the Earth, and over all that dwelt therein, had urged his Brethren that They flee no further from the wrath of the Elder Gods, but take a stand and match Their Might against Them from Glyu-Vho, for in that conflict mayhap the Old Ones should have the triumph. When that this was known, He of the Elder Gods that had the commanding of the Host Thereof, and to Whom was assigned the punishing of the Rebels, sware Him a mighty oath that *Cthulhu* in especial shouldst be whelmed utterly, and cast down, and chained in the unbreakable fetters of Power. And whether this One was *Lord Kthanid*, which Name the Scribe rendereth as The Veiled Eminence, or some Other, as hoary *Nodens* the Lord of the Great Abyss, none there be can say for certain.

And so They descended upon the Earth in Their might and majesty, and They smote down the Old Ones, and brake Their power, and scattered Them afar, and chained Them on distant worlds and stars or in the black, unwholesome chasms of the Deep; and against those bonds the Old Ones raged in all Their impotence, but could not burst them asunder. Nor did the Veiled Eminence forget His oath to whelm and fetter *Cthulhu*, for They came face to face, these two, and They did battle, and it was *Lord Kthanid* bore away the victory.

And it was done then as it had been promised aforetime, that He was taken by Those Whom He had defied, and was plunged into the nethermost depths beneath the Sea, and They placed Him within the Barnacled Tower that is said to rise amidst the great ruin that is the Sunken City, and He was sealed within by the Elder Sign; and, raging at Those who had imprisoned Him, He further earned Their wrath, and They, descending upon Him for the second time, did impose upon Him the semblance of Death, but left Him dreaming there beneath the Great Waters, and returned to that place from whence They had come, which is named Glyu-Vho, or Ibt al Janzah as we would say, which is Betelgeuse, and which is amongst the stars, the which looketh upon Earth from that season when the leaves fall to that season when the sowers-of-the-soil are accustomed once again to their fields. And there shall He lie dreaming forever in His House at R'lyeh, unto which withouten pause they who served Him swam, and did strive against every obstacle, but then disposed themselves to await His Awakening, for that they had no power against the Elder Sign and were fearful of its great potency; but they knew that the Cycle returneth, and that He shall be freed to seize upon the Earth again and make it His Kingdom, and thus to defy the Elder Gods once more. And to His Brethren it chanced likewise, that They were taken by Those whom They too had defied and were hurled into banishment; Him Who Is Not To Be Named was thrust into the Outermost Emptyness that is beyond the Stars, and with the Others it was the same, until at last was the Earth free of Them, and Those who had come hither in the form of Towers of Flame returned whence They had come, and were seen on this world no more, and on all of the Earth peace came and was unbroken; yet ever the minions of the Old Ones gathered and planned and sought ways whereby to free their Masters, and lingered whilst men came to search into the secret and forbidden places and fumble at the Gates. And thus He slept unbroken ages by, whilst in the Dark City, against whose dim shores the cloud-waves break, Him Who Is Not To Be Named roared and writhed in His fetters, and in black, lightless N'kai, deep within the secret places that gape and yawn beneath the Earth, the *Black Thing* lay enchained and *Abhoth* too, the Unclean One, even as did They all, nor was it within Their power to free Themselves from the strictures imposed upon Them by the Lords of Glyu-Vho, aye, and thus while aeons lapse *Ythogtha* howls ever from His Abyss, and *Ghatanothoa* from His Mount, and *Zoth-Ommog* from His Deep, which is under the Great Waters off the Isle of the Sacred Stone Cities, and all Their Brethren, helpless as are They to free Themselves, and hungry for that freedom to which in the passing of ages They shall attain. In the meanwhile They lurk ever just beyond the threshold which They cannot pass, and hideous beyond the comprehension of mortal minds is the Vengeance that fills Their troubled dreams.

VIII. Of That Which Is Foretold of Their Return

But it shall not be always thus, for it is written that the Cycle shall in time return in its appointed Round and They shall cast off Their bonds and even rise again; but the time is not yet, meanwhile against these bonds the Old Ones rage in Their impotence, and strain against the adamantine fetters and They would be free to rule again as once They ruled before; and of Them, some were chained on worlds and suns far distant from this Earth, and some were thrust into the black, unholy chasms which gape and yawn beneath the Earth's crust, and Others were flung beyond the Universe itself, and hurled forth into that mad Chaos which seethes and roils forever in its nightmare turbulence beyond the borders of matter and energy, of time and space: and These be the greatest and most powerful of the Potentates that ruled and led the Great Old Ones, saving only *Ubbo-Sathla*, that walloweth in Y'quaa, bereft of intelligence even as was His Brother, *Azathoth*, the blind, idiot god of Chaos.

And thus were the Great Old Ones punished for Their iniquitous rebellion against Their Masters, Who linger yet on Glyu-Vho and watch with vigilance and unsleeping wariness lest that the Old Ones should break free of Their fetters, shrug aside the Elder Sign, and burst forth to ravage and Feed.

And it is written that the Old Ones will, betimes, aid those men unwise enough or desperate enough to give Them worship, for They seek ever to break through from Outside to resume once again Their ancient dominion, that all shall be again as 'twere in the Elder World; but until the time of Their redemption be at last come nigh, and the stars are right for Their return, knowest thou that They lie in wait just beyond the portal, and that the Liers-in-Wait be strong beyond the strength of mountains, aye, and Their power is potent and terrific to bless and exalt or to curse and to doom the Children of Men.

IX. The Liers-in-Wait

And even *Azathoth* is Their Father; aye, and *Ubbo-Sathla* that Unbegotten Source from whence came Those who durst oppose the Elder Gods that rule from Betelgeuse, the Great Old Ones who fought against these Elder Gods; and these Old Ones were instructed by *Azathoth*, Who is the blind idiot god, and by *Yog-Sothoth*, Who is the All-in-One and One-in-All, and upon Whom are no strictures of time or space, and Whose aspects in Earth are *'Umr At-Tawil* and the Ancient Ones. The Great Old Ones dream forever of that coming time when They shall once more rule Earth and all that Universe of which it is part; then shall Azathoth rise up from His throne at the centre of Chaos; *Ubbo-Sathla* shall rouse Him from the slimy gulf of Y'quaa wherein He walloweth from the Prime; *Nyogtha* the Dweller in Darkness shall walk the Earth again; *Daoloth* shall rend asunder the Veils; *Byatis* shall come forth from His imprisonment; *Ghatanothoa* shall rise from Yaddith-Gho beneath the waves; *Chaugnar-Faugn* shall wake to Feed again, and that abominably; *Glaaki* shall come again through the reversed angles to Tagh-Clatur; *Great Cthulhu* shall rise from R'lyeh; *Hastur*, Who is even Him Who Is Not To Be Named, shall come again from the dark star which is near Aldebaran in the Hyades; *Nyarlathotep* shall howl forever in darkness where He abideth; *Shub-Niggurath*, Who is the Black Goat with a Thousand Young, shall spawn and spawn again, and shall have dominion over all wood nymphs, satyrs, leprechauns, and the Little People; *Lloigor, Zhar*, and *Ithaqua* shall ride the spaces among the stars and shall ennoble those who are Their followers, who are the Tcho-Tcho; *Cthugha* shall encompass His dominion from Fomalhaut; *Tsathoggua* shall come from N'kai; *Aphoom Zhah* shall come forth from Yaanek at the Pole; *Ran-Tegoth* shall arouse Him and rise up; *Father Yig* shall come forth from subterranean

K'n-yan where He abideth; unclean *Abhoth* shall come forth out of Voormithadreth; *Yigg-Tsil* shall likewise come up from Below; *Han* shall rise from obscure and frozen Leng; *Atlach-Nacha* shall arise and leave His webs; also shall *Y'golonac* come back again; and *Vulthoom* shall come up from Ravormos; and all of that Race whereof *Vulthoom* is but the youngest Child.

III. The Book of the Gates

I. Of the Worlds beyond This World, and the Modes of Travel

Knowest thou that this world of ours be not alone in the Infinitude of space, for there be myriads of other worlds amongst the stars, and that life clingeth tenaciously wherever it hath found a foothold; and while there be wise men upon the Earth, both in our day and in the ages gone to dust, there be far wiser than they elsewhere; and the Sorcerer must search out the wisest teacher ever he may find, albeit needful he seeketh afar in remote and fabulous bourns beyond the world we know. And Intelligences deeper and older and wiser than men reside on Yaddith of the Dholes, and on Ymar, and Yith; on Zaoth of the Metal Brains, and Abbith, and horrible Shaggai; on Kythanil and Xoth and trans-galactic Stronti, aye, and on the benighted Yuggoth where she rolleth at the Rim: but which of the Children of Men hath seen even Yuggoth, much less the worlds that lie beyond in the vertiginous and sickening abyss of endless inimical space?

It is on Yuggoth that the Outer Ones dwell, they whose leader is even *N'gha-Kthun*, and who be the minions and servitors of Him Who Is Not To Be Named. On Earth are they beknown to men as the Abominable Mi-Go, and have the form of lizard-crustaceans noxious to the eyes of men; but on dim Yuggoth they rear nightmarish cities of monolithic stone, riven through and through with deep canals like terrible chasms wherethrough flow, and sluggishly, rivers of viscous black ooze like unto liquid pitch. Betimes they visit this Earth and have commerce with men, they who serve *Great Hastur* in the star-spaces, and some say the lizard-crustaceans arrive on Earth through their Towers, which are of the imperishable *lagh* metal that feeleth not the bite of the black and frigid winds that blow between the worlds, while others say that they fly hither wearing artificial wings that beat against the particles whereof light is formed, as do their brethren, the Byakhee.

But we are not Mi-Go, but mortal men, and cannot traverse the gulfs between the stars with impunity or ease. Now there are other ways to visit the worlds that roll forever in the darknesses beyond this Earth, and some there be that men may comfortably take. In Thenoph, that was of old a great metropolis in Mu before the foundering thereof, a mode was found to harness the D'horna-ahn Energies, whereby could the bodies of men be shielded in envelopes of folded space, thus venturing to the stars; and on Tond they speak of the Maze of the seven thousand crystal frames and of the faces that peer from the fifth-dimensional gulf, but few there be of mortals that may safely pass the three thousand, three hundredth and thirty-third frame, where the Dead Mouths gape and gulp; and who knoweth aught today of the Maze whereof they of Tond spake.

And there is also a way to Yuggoth that doth not pass through the star-spaces, but *between* them; by the planes between the star-spaces, it mought well be, came hither of old *Tsathoggua*; but little there is beknownst for certain of this mode, save that it lieth beyond the Zone of the Thirteen Faveolate Colossi. There be also the reversed angles of Tagh-Clatur, whereby mayhap *Glaaki* visited Earth in the Prime, descending hither by way of Shaggai, Yuggoth, and Tond: nor may the way therethrough be lost in its entirety to the knowledge of living men, even in the benighted ignorance of our own latter day; for the secret priests of *Sebek* and hierophants of olden Karnak were once conversant with the Mystery of the Tagh-Clatur in their ancient time, and the mode and the methods thereof may yet be decyphered from some crumbling papyrus thieved out of the nighted tombs of black and elder Ægypt.

II. Of Foul Necromancy

Yet do there exist other and far safer modes whereby may the Sorcerer acquire wisdom of the Forbidden Lore, to the mastery of his Art, than by risking sanity of mind and life of body in venturing forth into the howling chaos of the black abyss that gapes hungrily between the stars and worlds of the Infinitude; for thou mayest even summon forth out of the Grave of Sod or the sealed and shutten Sepulchre of Stone the wise and learned Dead who must yield to the imposition of thy will, aye, even unto the revealing of their most jealously guarded secrets and most deeply cherished lore.

And be thou not afeared to search after wisdom in those places wherein may wisdom easiest be found, for as old *Zosimus* sayeth, The seeker after forbidden things must hunt in the dark places, for only out of the womb of darkness is born the light of knowledge. Wherefore I say unto thee, in the questing for the most deeply-hidden Secrets, thou wert wise to learn from the wisest masters, the which be among the Elder Magi that have gone down before us into the Mystery of Death; for knowest thou that even the Black Gate Itself affordeth no barrier to him that hath achieved mastery over the unhallowed arts of dire Necromancy.

Now there do be some that shrink back shudderingly from the Calling-up of the restless Dead, and those that would turn to other and less dubious arts whereby may the secrets of the deepest and most hidden Arcana be acquired. Some there be the which employ the Dho formula which doth, with a full many repetitions thereof, permit the Inner Eye to penetrate to realms remote and far away, contiguous to ultra-mundane spheres and to abysmal gulfs profound. Yet others there be that imbibe of the juice of the Black Lotus and meditate upon the Sign of Koth, whereby the very gates of dream be made to ope on stranger regions, aye, and alien gulfs profounder far; while there be some few that use the Liao drug, the which dissolveth all strictures of time or space, and, by thus doing-so, permit the liberated mind to peer beyond the Veil. And 'twas even by this mode, some say, the wisest of the Sages of old Cathay first grasped the Key to the mystery of the all-encompassing and circumambient *Tao*. And of all these matters shall I speak more fully in this my III Book: of the Liao drug, and of the peril into which it may lead the unwary; and of Koth and of the Sign thereof and of the dangers which adhere thereunto; and of yet other arts and practices whereby may the Sorcerer obtain entry into the profundities of the Forbidden Wisdom: of each will I speak further in the proper place, and at the time appointed.

For truly each and every mode or method hath its own peculiar hazard withal, as they that deeply drink of the Black Lotus do so imprudently, and at the peril of their immortal souls—or mayhap they be ignorant of *Where* the Black Lotus blooms!—and as for them that risk the abhorrent Liao drug, they walk in danger of the ultimate and terrific Hounds of Tindalos, wherefrom the very inking of that Name my soul shuddereth and my hand palsies: yet it must be told.

III. The Peril That Lurketh beyond Time

Aye, be thou warned, for in all such voyages and venturings of mind or soul or spirit there be very great and terrible dangers, by mortal men undreamt-of and unknown. Beware then, lest thou penetrate too deeply into the blackest backward and depthless abysm of the womb of infinite time. For beyond the very Beginning thereof, and on the Other Side thereof, there dwelleth That of which man suspecteth not; and there thou wilt find a strange and ominous Realm where hidden horrors lurk and naked Terror hunts unseen; which dim, uncanny bourn hath the seeming and the semblance of a pale, and grey, and indefinite shore, lapped by the sluggish waves of unmeasured and unthinkable Time. And it is even there, in an awful Light that is beyond all darkness, amidst a profound Silence that shrieketh beyond all sound, that *They* slink and prowl in all their ghastliness, slavering with a loathsome and an unspeakable hunger for all that is clean and whole and unsullied.

Yea, but it lieth beyond the powers of my pen to limn their true and veritable likeness, the lean and ravenous Hunters, the famished and unnamable Devourers, and yet in certain ancient myths are they symbolled forth if but in vague and ambiguous fashion: even the Greeks of old had a name for them, albeit one which veiled and hid their essential and unclean vileness. *Iä! Hastur!* They are lean, and hideous; and men awake in them cosmic hungers; and all that be foul and vile and abominable in Nature is but their shade, and echo, and memory. Dreadful are they when the Hunt is on, and tenacious and undeviating as they are unwearying and unavoidable.

Through angled space they lope and slither, furtive yet unswerving from their course, aye, and unappeasable; for they are the Hunters from Beyond, concerning the which but little there be that the wise men and sages of olden-time dared to set down for men less wise and prudent than they to read. For even to know of them is to have their gaunt and slinking shapes to haunt thy dreams; and even to dream of them is, as *Eibon* sayeth, to lure them hither. Through angled space they glide and lope with ease, I say: and yet they can but with difficulty transgress into curved space, of the which be our Universe composed.

IV. Those That Aid the Unnamable Devourers

There be strange affinities beyond our mortal comprehension that link and bind such Things together in unholy amity, to the perpetual and eternal peril and damnation of men. And in the matter of these, the Unnamable Devourers of the Abyss Beyond Time, there be those that will help the lean and ravenous ones through the barriers of curved space, to track down their hopeless prey. The Dholes of Yaddith be even such, for the Dholes will aid them to break through unto wheresoever thou art hiding, if that the Hunters be on thy trail. They, the Dholes, and the Nug-Soth, that be savants and wizards, the both of which inhabit far, nightmarish Yaddith of the Five Suns, be the servants and minions of *Shub-Niggurath*, the Mighty Mother, the Black Goat of the Wood with a Thousand Young.

And there be even others that dwell in the hidden and the secret places of this Earth of ours that will give the Hunters from Beyond assistance in traversing the dimensions and entering in to curved space; and these are the Little People of the Wood, that serve the Mighty Mother on this sphere; aye, all they that do give fealty and service to *Shub-Niggurath* will help them trace thee to thy lair. And in especial will the Satyrs aid them to gain entry unto thee, for the Satyrs can traverse space through the Scarlet Circles even as few of the Begotten of the Black Goat can do, whereas the Nug-Soth can travel the black gulfs between the star-worlds and the uncanny distances between the planes and the dimensions of space in their light-beam envelopes, whereof but little is known to mortal men; and, as for the Dholes, it was writ of old in the Forbidden Books that they hunt the sleeping minds of men and trace them through their very dreams, for they, too, have strange hungers and feast abominably, but in a manner that haply remains unknown by men. But of such things as these, it is unwholesome to speculate.

It is said there was once a way known of old whereby to prevent the coming of such as the Hunters from Beyond, but the way, which once the wisest of the wise men knew, hath become lost to us in the lapse of interminable ages, and forgotten among men. Nevertheless, I will trace it for thee here, as Sorcerers know the form and lineaments thereof, but not the mode or method of its use.

[Illustration: The Tindalos Seal]

The Seal of Tindalos, men call it, after that strange bourn beyond Time wherefrom the Hunters come; but how the talisman was employed of old hath perished in the ruin of anterior cycles. Therefore, be on thy guard, for once they have caught the scent of thee they will hunt thee down the aeons and through the dark spaces between the stars. *Iä! Hastur!* They are lean and athirst: bewarest thou of the Hounds of Tindalos!

V. Of Tindalos, and the Hounds Thereof

And in that Place beyond the backward abysm of Time whose secret nature the Sages have cloaked behind the name Tindalos, there was done once a terrible and unspeakable Deed: before ever time was and before even the Beginning thereof, was this Deed done; and from that awful and unnamable Deed was sprung the evil things that are the Hounds of Tindalos. And all of the evil in the Universe is concentrated in their lean and hungry bodies, and they will scent thee if thou comest too near and they will hunt thee down, for they thirst for that in us which is clean and untainted. Beyond all good or evil are they, for they are of That which in the Beginning of things fell away from cleanliness; and through the Deed whereof I dare not speak they became bodies of living death and receptacles of all Foulness. In the spheres through which they lope untiringly there is no thought or action, no moral or meaning, no right and no wrong: merely That which is pure and That which is foul.

And the utter vileness of that Place expresses itself through angles while the pure gains expression through the curves of space: wherefore they but slowly slink through curved space, aye, and slowly, too, through angled space. For they have no bodies according to our interpretation of the word; and they move interminably through outrageous angles of space and they will pursue thee if once they scent thee in thy trespass beyond time.

Aye, they will even hunt thee down, ravenous and snarling and unsatisfied, flee however far thou wilt: and they will return again from their unholy Feasting still ravenous and snarling and unsatisfied forever, to that Place of Foulness that was in the Beginning, before ever time was or space itself was fashioned by That which fashioned space. Bewarest thou, then, of the Liao drug that dissolves all barriers of time and space and permitteth thee to peer Beyond, that thou imbibest of it not so freely that thou needs must fall prey to the cosmic hungers of the Hounds of Tindalos. But thou mayest employ the repetitions of the Dho formula the which doth enable the Sorcerer to extend his inward vision to the comprehension of far and fabulous bourns beyond the worlds and stars we know.

VI. If Thou Wouldst Raise the Dead

Wherefore I say unto thee, that if thou wouldst learn from the unresting Dead, seek them not by such modes as these. Thou canst summon up for converse certain Ones by that ritual we call the Aklo Sabaoth; howbeit this rite be futile withal for some purposes as it is unanswerable only from the Hill, not from the Air. And the formulas between the Yrr and the Nnnyrr will ope these Portals to certain regions where Time existeth not and all that hath ever been spake of old yet echoeth still, but in a monstrous cacophony whereof but little can be discerned amongst the infinite and unending babble. Yet of all modes whereof I have certain knowledge, the supremest and least perilous be the unhallowed arts of dire Necromancy; wherefore hearken thou well and attend my words, for I shall unveil a mighty Mystery beyond the wisdom of wizards lesser than I.

Seek out the tomb or sepulchre of him thou wouldst raise-up, and see that thou hast with thee in that lonely place an assistant or acolyte, and bid him to partake of an sufficiency of the Golden Mead so that he be entranced. Thou wouldst be wise to see to it that him thou hast chosen to companion thee in this Deed be not one endeared to thine heart, but one with whose accompaniment thou canst easily and withouten pain or loss dispense: for him thou wouldst summon from beyond the Black Gate shall have dire need of the life-force of thine associate, and may well drain him dry.

This done, encircle the tomb of him thou wouldst raise with a band of the blue Voorish powder, the which thou must then set aflame; and next thou must trace with the Scimitar of *Barzai* in a Greater circle around about the resting-place of the dead all of the Signs of Hnaa between the Third and the Thirtieth thereof. These things accomplished all as set forth upon this page, next situate thyself at the Eastern Node of the outermost Circle, with thy companion or acolyte situated within the Voorish Circle, face the head of the tomb and utter the Ritual which followeth:

Him who knoweth the place of R'lyeh,
Him who knoweth the secret of far Kadath,
Him who keepeth the key to Cthulhu;
By the five-pointed Star,
By the Sign of Kish,
By the assent of the Elder Gods:
Let him come forth!

VII. To Send Back Down That Which Thou Hast Called Up

If thou recitest the above Ritual of Summoning thrice, and if upon each
Adjuration thou completest thou drawest upon the floor with the
Scimitar of Barzai the Kadishtu Symbol before the sepulchre, the Apparition
will slowly form above the tomb, taking on flesh and substance and shap-
ing itself slowly as a thing of mist of Vapour, drawing betimes at need upon
the vital force of thine acolyte. And when it hath completely formed itself,
then and then only mayest thou address it; and it will answer all of thy questions to the extent of its knowledge. When thou hast learned of the
Phantom all thou desirest to know and all that it be able to impart unto thee,
utter this Dismissal:

> *Return now whence thou came, N_____, by the Power of*
> *the Sign of Kish and by the Authority of the Elder Gods;*

and shew before it the Elder Sign which thou wilt have previously prepared
as I have aforetime instructed thee. Whereupon the Apparition will slowly
disperse again into the primal elements and the blue flames of the Voorish
Circle will die out.

It is true that this mode of summoning-forth the Dead may be
employed only when thou knowest, and may come unto, the place where
the one thou wouldst question is entombed; perchance thou wouldst raise-
up one whose burial-place is not known to thee, or lieth in a place so situated that thou canst not easily journey thereunto. In that matter I can
advise thee naught, but to say that, with judicious choosing from amongst
the famous and the celebrated Dead, there will be, as thou wilt find, full
many whose raising-up thou mayest accomplish to great profit and with
much augmentation of thy store of wisdom. *Iä! Nyarlathotep!* the Dead keep
many secrets from the living, to their peril and our impoverishment.

[Illustration: The Amulet of Alhazred]

VIII. Of the Signs of Hnaa

Now concerning these Signs of Hnaa, it is said by the ancient Sages that they were copied down by the Spawn of *Ubbo-Sathla* the Unbegotten Source in the days of the dim and misty Prime; and that they were engraven upon the stones and tablets of the Elder Records, the which did *Ubbo-Sathla* thieve in the remotest of aeons from that library of the Elder Gods which hath from of old stood upon a lightless world near the star Celaeno in the Pleiades; and it was for this Theft that the Elder Gods came hither in Their Wrath to do the destruction and undoing of the Great Old Ones, whereof doth *Ubbo-Sathla* share with *Azathoth* the Daemon-Sultan the begetting of Them.

And it was in Earth's dreamlands, or some extension thereof, that the priests of *Ubbo-Sathla*, or of some Other of His Spawn, did first bequeath them to moral men. They were written down in the Seven Cryptical Books of Hsan but who had found a copy of that elder scripture? It was the Prophet *Hnaa*—even him who succeeded the Prophet *Kish*, and who led forth out of the doomed city of Sarnath in the Land of Mnar the followers of the Elder Gods from whence he sprangeth—who did pass the Signs into the possession of the Children of Men.

And there be those that say the Chaldaeans knew the Signs of Hnaa from of old, and that *Zoroaster* calleth them, in his Scriptures, The Fifty Names; however the truth of this matter may be, the Sages have written that they be certain Sigils of the Elder Gods, verily potent and terrific Names the which They did bestow upon Him of Their Number that did whelm and trample down the Old Ones when the Earth was young. If this be true or untrue, I cannot dispute it: for who of us knoweth aught of the Elder Gods, Who abide remote and far-off, and Who meddle not often in the Affairs of men? But there be those, and they be accounted wise, who name the Signs of Hnaa the Sigils of Kthanid, given unto that Lord for His triumph over the Spawn of Chaos, for that They were a fearful and a mighty foe; and, as it was writ of old,

> The Chaos Spawn exact a fearful price,
> A slaughtered babe or virgin sacrifice,

and thus were They the detested and the loathly Enemies of men as well as the foes of the Elder Gods, and men and Gods rest happier in this very hour that the Spawn of *Azathoth* were whelmed and trampled down, whether it be by *Kthanid* or by some Other.

Here follow the Signs of Hnaa, which some have called the Sigils of Kthanid.

[Illustration: The Signs of Hnaa]

IX. Of the Dream-Gates

And there are those among the Sorcerers of this Earth who shrink back from the practice of the arts of vile Necromancy, and searchers-after-wisdom who would rather seek their goal beyond the waking world, amidst the dreamlands contiguous thereunto. And the secret of this art is one that may be given only to the adept but is withholden from the novice and the student; therefore must I now veil my message in terms ambiguous and symbolic, the Truth of which will be discernible only by the Initiate. But if thou art one of them that would pass the dream-gates and venture beyond the waking world, thou must go down the Seventy Steps of Sleep into that cavern-temple of the Dream Gods where the two priests Nasht and Kaman-Tha forever tend the Pillar of Fire that burneth amidst the sepulchral glooms thereof: and be thou warned that these priests are not and never were true men.

For this temple lieth not far from the gates of the waking world and is easily reached therefrom; and from thence thou must go down the Seven Hundred Onyx Steps and pass through the Gates of Deeper Slumber, wherefrom thou shalt emerge into a gloomy forest that is known to dreamers as the Wood of the Zoogs. From that enchanted wood thou must henceforth find thine own way; but be thou wary, for the Zoogs and the other denizens of that dubious land, as the Wamps and the Gugs and the Ghasts of Zin and the Ghouls, and all other manner of Thing that dwell thereabouts, be neither friendly nor unfriendly to man, and there are Those amongst them that regard him as but a tidbit.

And also be thou herewith warned that in those dreamlands beyond the Gates of Deeper Slumber distance and measurement have little meaning, and that it is beyond the abilities of the flesh to go from one point to another by means of a straight line, for all is curved there, and circumambient; step warily and seek the path, and thou shalt find it.

And alsoe there remaineth yet Another mode by whiche thou mayest at least perceive That which is beyond the strictures of the Naturall Worlde, withouten ye risks attendant upon thine entry thereunto in the Bodie; a means whereby thou mayest thrust aside the Veil and peer into those oth'r Realms of Beinge which pervade and interpenetrate with our owne Plane, yet which remaine invisible and imperceptible to mortall Men, and by them Unknown. Ye Ritual of ye Bell this mode is call'd, and it employeth a certaine Bell of Silver inscrib'd about ye Rim thereof as with ye X Spatial Key, the whiche shouldst be writ accordingly in either ye Runes of ye Nug-Sothe or ye antient Aklo letters. Yet be wary that thou not over-doe thine usage of this Mode, for him who sees Beyond can betimes also be seene by Them that make of that Realm the place of Their abiding.

X. Of Koth, and the Sign of Koth

There is a Sign some dreamers wandered far afield have seen affixed above the archway of a certain Black Tower which standeth alone in the twilight, and this is the Sign of Koth. It affordeth strong protection to him who would pass the dream-gates unmolested; also, it is as a Key that opens forth unto dim worlds penumbral certain of those gates. Of old there was a city named with the name of Koth, Who is even one of the Little Gods of Dream. But by whom builded, or in what forgotten age, no man can truly say: but it is dead and gone to ruin long since: aye, and the black Cyclopean walls thereof, and the evil black citadels thereof, to which no mortal man save one shall ever attain, and that to his undoing.

In Earth's dreamlands stood once ill-rumoured Koth, or in the Netherworld thereof, beyond the grey and ominous pinnacles of the fabled Peaks of Throk that glimmer in the cold colourless death-fires of an uncanny aurora. Awful and sinister they stand in the haunted dusk of those sunless and eternal depths, higher than a man may reckon, guarding terrible valleys where the enormous Dholes crawl and burrow nastily. Beyond the Peaks of Throk, I say, and beyond the gloomy Vale of Pnath where Shuggob dwells; and beyond the dreadful kingdom of the Gugs, those hairy and prodigious giants who rear stone circles in the wood and strange sacrifices make to That which the Gugs worship gruesomely, and which they be the minions and servitors thereof; and beyond the Vaults of Zin where the furtive and fearsome Ghasts hide, that shun the light of day; beyond all these the Tower of Koth riseth.

If ever thou wouldst venture into these dubious lands, and would see the Black Tower for thyself, and the cryptic Seal thereupon, thou wouldst be well advised to leave the Abyss at Sarkomand, that deserted city in the frozen valleys below Leng, where black nitrous stairways guarded by winged lions of diorite lead down from dreamland to the Lower Gulfs. There must thou creepest past the great wall that girdles the kingdom of the Gugs roundabout, and slink through that twilight realm at an hour when all of the dreaded and gigantical Gugs would most like be gorged and somnolent, and seek out the centralmost of the towers, which is even that of Koth. Thou shalt know it when once thou seest it, for in all that forest of vast and lichen-crusted monoliths, and amidst all of that stupendous vista of colossal, round, windowless towers mounting up illimitable into the grey dusk of the Netherworld, it is a Tower even more vast, above whose colossal doorway is fixed a monstrous symbol in bas-relief that is the Sign of Koth.

[Illustration: The Sign of Kith]

XI. The Ritual of the Silver Key

And some of them that dare to venture into Earth's shadowy and ambiguous dreamland prefer not to employ the Sign of Koth but, instead, the Ritual of the Silver Key, and the Gates thereof. Far beyond the Veil of Wakefulness and Sleep which separates this Earth from those dubious and adumbrative regions contiguous thereunto, are realms which are in some measure coterminous with certain Spheres and Gulfs and Regions transmundane, and infinitely remote in time or space beyond all measuring of mortal man. And if thou hast the courage withal, performest thou then the Ritual of the Silver Key, the which thou wilt find written out at length in my Book of the Rituals; and thou shalt even pass through the Gates of the Silver Key, as legend names that Dubious Portal. They are as a turbulence in time and space, a roiling and a vortex within the viewless fabric of the Aether, a Door which opens to Beyond, and to that region where lieth a Land unknown and unguessed-at by Earth's geographers, and an age and epoch whose date no historian may establish.

Thou wilt have thus opened into that world a Gate, but it is not the Ultimate Gate; nay, naught but a little and a lesser Gate that leadeth out of Earth-time and Earth-space into that extension of Earth which is outside of time and beyond space; and from which, even in its appointed turn, doth the Ultimate Gate Itself open fearsomely and perilously upon the Outer Void which lieth beyond this Earth, and all other Earths, all Universes, and all Matter itself.

And at the Portal thereto thou wilt find that there awaits ever and eternally a certain Guide, whose face—if face indeed *He* hath!—goeth perpetually veiled from thy vision. Very awesome and terrible is this Guide, beyond the imaginings of men; for *He* was an Earth-entity many millions of years ago when the world was but newly-molded from the formless Stuff of Chaos. And this was aeons before man was even dreamt of by Them that made man, when unthinkable and terrific Shapes lumbered through the steaming fogs of the Elder World, to rear strange Cyclopean cities among whose last, neglected, and crumbling ruins the first mammals of the Dawn would someday play.

And mighty and potent Mage and Sorcerer of the Elder World though *He* doubtless was, in those dim, remote, and dubious ages whereof we know but little, and nothing that be Wholesome, I know within my heart that all His vaunted magistery availed Him naught once He had dared to venture beyond the Gates of the Silver Key, and came face to face with That which lieth in wait for the unwary and the uninvited Intruder.

[Illustration: The Symbols that are Carven upon the Gates of the Silver Key]

XII. 'Umr at-Tawil

Not lightly, then, neither from thine idlest whim or merest curiosity, shouldst thou dare pass beyond the Veil in this manner, for the Veil whereof I speak was set in its place for a reason, and the reason is this: to afford a barrier between this Earth and the dwellers therein and That which awaiteth in the regions Outside. And somewhat of That Which Awaited Beyond have I aforetime spake; and even more will I yet reveal concerning That.

Not lightly shouldst thou venture thence, I say, for here again, as in other Matters whereof I have already given thee knowledge and warning, the venturing-forth hath many Perils unwritten and unknown.

And neither shouldst thou accept the services of this Guide, however much thou needest *Him*; for better would it be by far for thy health of body and of soul and for the sanity of thy mind that thou shouldst become lost, to wander ever amidst the dim and dubious regions of Earth's extension into super-time, than that thou shouldst dare accept *Him* as thy Guide. Be thou warned by me in this, I pray, and hearken unto my words of warning: for while there are those that have done so and that withouten peril, yet mayest thou not come away from thence as easily as did they.

And while there are those who have dared to seek glimpses beyond the Veil, and to accept *Him* as guide, they would have been more prudent had they avoided commerce with *Him*; for it is written in the Book of Thoth how terrific is the price of a single glimpse. Nor may those who pass ever return, for in the vastnesses transcending our world are Shapes of Darkness that seize and bind. The Affair that shambleth about in the night, the Evil that defieth the Elder Sign, the Herd that stand watch at the secret portal each Tomb is known to have, and that thrive on That which groweth out of the tenants thereof: all these Blacknesses are lesser and less terrible than *He* who guardeth the Gateway: *He Who* will guide the rash one beyond all the worlds into the Abyss of the Unnamable Devourers. For *He* is *'Umr-at-Tawil*, the Most Ancient One, which the Scribe rendereth as The Prolonged of Life.

[Illustration: Seal of 'Umr-at-Tawil]

In that forgotten abysm of time, in the vague prime of the Elder World, *He*, like thee, dared venture beyond the Veil that separates this world from the next, and passed through the Gates of the Silver Key, and it was there, in those bleak and drear and ambiguous regions that lie beyond Earth's gates, in those shadowy and illusive realms which border upon worlds and regions and planes of being further yet and stranger still, was *He* confronted by Those who serve the Beyond One, Who is even ultimate and unthinkable *Yog-Sothoth*, the All-in-One and One-in-All.

There they brood eternally upon multi-angled thrones atop sheer pedestals of ultra-telluric stone, Who be the minions and servants of the Lurker on the Threshold: even They whose name the Scribe rendereth as

The Ancient Ones. No guide nor guardian had *He* in that terrible hour of *His* most dreadful peril; yet did *He* escape the Doom decreed by Them that guard forever the Ultimate Gateway which leadeth beyond the universes of Matter, for *He* yielded up *His* inmost self to the servitude of *Yog-Sothoth*, and became at length and in the fullness of infinite time the foremost of the Ancient Ones, and Their leader. And forever doth *He* stand ready at the Gate to serve them who rashly and imprudently would pass therethrough; and awful beyond the power of words to describe is the Fate of those who dare accept *Him* as their guide!

XIII. Of Opening the Door to Yog-Sothoth

Therefore of this mode of mastering the profundities of Wisdom shouldst thou be cautious, for the many and good reasons whereof I have spake, for those who venture through the Gates of the Silver Key come not often back into Earth's fields. And again I say unto thee that of the many modes and means whereby thou mayest approach the Forbidden Wisdom, the least hazardous to thy life and the least perilous to thy soul is even foul Necromancy. Albeit there be some, and they be many, who prefer the scrying-glass or wizard's crystal, wherein may ghostly apparitions be conjured forth and converse had with the wise and mighty spirits of men long dead and buried. But there is yet another way, and I advise that thou hearken closely to my words.

For if thou must venture Beyond the Gate to seek wisdom at its very Font, and to inquire after it of That which abideth in those places, be thou well advised by me to take full and good preparation. For verily do we know but little of the other Universes beyond the Gate which *Yog-Sothoth* guardeth. Of Those which come through the Gate and make Their habitation in this world none can tell, although *Ibn Schacabao* telleth of the Beings which crawl forth from the Gulf of S'glhuo, that They may be known by Their sound. In that Gulf the very words are of sound, and matter as we know it is but an odor unto Them; and the notes of our pipes in this world may create beauty or may bring forth abominations in S'glhuo. For the barrier between haply groweth thin, and when sourceless sounds occur we may justly look to the denizens of S'glhuo. They can do little harm to those of this Earth, and fear only that shape which a Certain Sound may form in Their Universe. And if thou wouldst aid Them of S'glhuo to reach through the Gate, thou mayest best employ that formula that Sorcerers know of as the Mao rite, and by the letters of Nug-Soth, and by the power of the Black Seal of Irahn.

[Illustration: The Letters of Nug-Soth]

But be thou wary of Them that lie in wait just a little ways beyond the portals of time and of space, and be thou wary, also, of them that be Their servants and minions: as the Gugs, and the Ghasts, the Byakhee that flieth hither from dark Yuggoth on the Rim, the Ancient Ones and the Little People of the Wood, the Dholes and the Nug-Soth; for such as they be ever and eternally the enemies of Man, and of all the works and dreams of Man, and such as they ever bring doom and death and destruction in their wake.

In the city of Thenoph as in the city of Koth, in horrible Yaddith as in Tond, at the Peaks of Throk as in the Vaults of Zin, in the Gulf of S'glhuo as in the Vale of Pnath, at the Gates of the Silver Key as in Tindalos Beyond Time, ever hath the Fearful weight of Their Hand been laid against such as thee and I, even unto a grim and dreadful Reckoning; wherefore, be thou warned.

[Illustration: The Black Seal of Irahn]

XIV. The Ninth Verse That Summoneth Yog-Sothoth

The seeker after wisdom would be advised to search for it among Those that be older and wiser than men. Wisest and foremost amongst these Ones whereof I speak, is He of whom '*Umr at-Tawil* is but the slave and minion: even *Yog-Sothoth*, Him Who Knoweth All, for that He is All: aye and verily, the All-in-One and One-in-All.

As a congeries of shining Globes is He, stranger far than aught envisioned by the imaginations of men. But if thou darest, then when that thou wouldst call forth *Yog-Sothoth* thou must await until that time when the Sun sits in the Fifth House, with Saturn in trine; drawest thou then the Pentagram of Fire upon the Earth and chant the Ninth Verse thrice. This verse thou shalt repeat each Roodmass and Hallows' Eve, and the Thing will breed in the Outside Sphere, and there shall come round the hour appointed.

<u>The Ninth Verse</u>
Iä! Iä! Yog-Sothoth!
Ygnaiih, ygnaiih, thflthkh'ngha
Yog-Sothoth y'bthnk h'ehye—
N'grkdl'ly eh-ya-ya-ya-yahaah!
E'yayayayaaaa ngh'aaaaa
Ngh'aaa h'yuh, h'yuh
Yog-Sothoth ngh'aaa!
N'gai, n'gha'ghaa, bugg-shoggog,
Bugg-shoggog, y'hah;
Yog-Sothoth, Yog-Sothoth,
G'nnha 'nyaaa!

If the Ninth Verse should fail thee, turn then to the Long Chant in my Book of the Rites.

XV. Of Them from Outside and Their Spawn

Aye, long before there were ever wise men on this Earth, as I have said, there were yet Those Others that were not men and that were infinitely wiser, for never is it to be thought that man is either oldest or last of Earth's masters; nay, nor that the greater part of life and substance walks alone. The Old Ones were, the Old Ones are, and the Old Ones shall be. Not in the spaces we know, but *between* them, They walk serene and primal, undimensioned and by us unseen. *Yog-Sothoth* knows the Gate, for *Yog-Sothoth* is the Gate; *Yog-Sothoth* is the Key and Guardian of the Gate. Past, present, future—all are one in *Yog-Sothoth*. He knoweth where the Old Ones broke through in time gone by, and where They shall break through again in time to come until the Cycle is complete. He knoweth where They have trod Earth's fields, and where They tread them still, and why no man may behold Them as They tread. By Their smell can men sometimes know Them near, but of Their semblance can no man know, saving only in the features of those They have begotten upon mankind; and of those Offspring there be divers kinds, differing in likeness from man's truest eidolon to that Shape without sight or substance which is Them.

They walk unseen and foul in the lonely places where the Words have been spoken and the Rites howled through at Their Seasons. The winds gibber with Their voices; the Earth mutters with Their consciousness. They bend the forest, and crush the city, yet may not forest or city behold the Hand that smites. Kadath in the Cold Waste hath known Them, but what man knoweth Kadath? The ice desert of the South and the sunken isles of Ocean hold stones whereon Their seal is engraven, but who hath seen the deep frozen city or the Sealed Tower long garlanded with seaweed and barnacles? Great *Cthulhu* is Their cousin, yet can He spy Them but dimly. *Iä Shub-Niggurath!* As a foulness shalt thou know Them. Their Hand is at thy throat, yet thou seest Them not; and Their habitation is even one with thy guarded threshold. *Yog-Sothoth* is the Key to the Gate whereby the spheres meet. Man rules now where once They ruled; They shall rule again where man rules now. After summer is winter, and after winter summer. They wait patient and potent, for here shall They reign again, and at Their coming again none shall dispute Them and all shall be subject to Them. And those who know of the Gates shall be impelled to open the way for Them and shall serve Them as They desire, but those who open the way unwittingly shall know life but a brief while thereafter.

Now of this Gate whereunto *Yog-Sothoth* is both Key and Guardian, and whereby are all Spheres coterminously linked, is it not that one, same and eternal Gate wherethrough the Old Ones shambled in the remotest of the forgotten ages of this Earth? For, concerning the Old Ones, it is written in the Secret Books that They wait ever at the Gate and the Gate is all places and all times, for They know naught of time nor of place, but are in all times and in all places together and without even the Appearance of so-being. And the Opener of the Way is even *Yog-Sothoth*, who reigns from everlasting to everlasting; and of Whom sayeth *Eibon* in his Book, What has been, what is, what will be: all are one in Him.

[Illustration: The Seal of Yog-Sothoth]

XVI. Somewhat of the Gates That Open to Beyond

As a foulness shall They be known to the Children of Men, sayeth the Sage; and also it is written concerning Them From Outside that while there be Those amongst Them which can assume all manner of different Shapes and Features, and any given Shape and any given Face, that thou mayest guess betimes at the horror of Their true semblance and likeness in the lineaments of those that They have spawned upon mortal flesh, and of such Spawn that while they be most awful to behold, yet are they not so awful as be the faces of Those that sired them. And that Their stench, which is strange to the nostrils, and like unto a thing long dead and far gone in rottenness, is not easily disguised, whereby at times thou mayest know that one of Them be near.

Yet do they wait beyond the Portal and patient are They in Their abeyance, for full well They know that the time will come when the ancient stars return again into their sphere and the Hour of Their liberation be nigh at hand. Now of these Portals, or Gates, they are for Them everywhere; but the first was that Gate which I, *Alhazred*, did cause to be thrust ajar as I have related aforetime, in Irem, the City of the Pillars, the City Beneath the Sands. But wherever the Children of Men shall set up the Stones and shall say thrice the Forbidden Litanies, there shall they cause a Gate to be established and the Portals thereof to be set ajar; and they shall serve Them Who Come Through the Gate, even as do the Dholes of Yaddith, and the Abominable Mi-Go, and the Tcho-Tcho people, and the Deep Ones, and the Gugs, and the Na-hag, the Voormis, the Aihai, the Ghouls, and the Ghasts that dwell in the primordial Vaults of Zin.

For many and multiform be those who serve the Great Old Ones as Their minions, and they lurk ever near the Gates and in the secret and the hidden places where Those of their Masters as be prisoned within the dark and secret places of the Earth lie chained and slumbering, striving ever to put asunder the chains that bind Them. Aye, they swarm within the nighted and accursed places of the Old Ones' imprisonment like teeming maggots in a festering wound, the Valusians, and the Gaunts of the Night, and the Yuggya, and the Miri Nigri, and the Cold Ones, and the Byakhee that with their mighty wings traverse the star-spaces, and the Little People of the Wood, and the foul Shantaks which guard Kadath in the Cold Waste and the Plateau of Leng.

XVII. Of Leng and the Mysteries Thereof

Concerning this Leng, 'tis said by some to lie in Earth's dreamlands to be thus only visited in sleep by power of the Sign of Koth, but I have heard yet others tell that it lieth afar off in the frozen wastes of the anti-boreal Pole, and there be those that hint of Leng that it may be found within the black and secret heart of Asia. But, while many differ on the place thereof, I have heard no man say aught of Leng that is wholesome to the ears of men.

Now of this Leng, 'tis written in that dark and frigid land many worlds meet, for it is coterminous with dimensions alternate to our own; and amidst those bleak, untrodden sands, and frozen hills, and black and horror-haunted peaks, there be strange Portals to Beyond; and Things from Outside that sometimes stray through the Gates to stalk through earthly snows, returning thence to Their unknown and nameless Spheres, glutted on horrid feasts whereof I dread to think upon. So they say: but, as for myself, I believe me well that cold and frightful Leng as much be part of other worlds as part of this, and representeth but a half-world, as it were, a bridge between the worlds.

They say of old ventured Ilathos there, a wizard of Lomar, beyond the Bnazic Desert and through the Vale of Pnor, taking great care to avoid the dreadful Vaults thereof, and that in time he came upon a crude stone tower amidst the Waste wherein there dwelt from of old a certain Priest whose unseen visage went ever veiled behind a mask of yellow silk. It is written upon the Cylinders of Kadatheron that long they conversed together there in that lonely and ill-rumored tower, the Lomarian mage and Him they call the Elder Hierophant, but of that which was spoken all record has been expunged therefrom, and the Cylinders of Kadatheron are blank, and no man knoweth why.

But I have not seen Leng in all my wanderings or travels, save only in my dreams, and but repeat here the idle tales which others have hinted at within my hearing. He who would know the secret of Leng, he who would walk the bleak and lonely paths of Leng, let him venture thereunto if he knoweth the Way.

[Illustration: The Seal of Leng]

XVIII. Of the Coming-Hence of the Old Ones

In another place I have already writ of how this Earth of ours fell into this Universe or plane or state of being from Outside, and of how it was contested for in long and direful contention betwixt Them from Yith and the Polar Ones, ere the descent of the Great Old Ones from Beyond. All are alike the Children of the Elder Gods, but the Great Race of Yith and the Old Ones failing to agree, one with another, and both with the Elder Gods, separated, leaving the Great Old Ones in the possession of the Earth while the Great Race, returning from Yith, took up their Abode forward in Earth-time not yet known to those that walk the Earth today; and there await till there shall come again the Winds and the Voices which drave Them forth aforetime: and That which walketh forever on the winds above the Earth and in the spaces that are between the stars.

Not long thereafter did the Great Old Ones retain the mastery of this planet upon the departing-hence of Them from Yith, for the Elder Gods in time descended upon this Earth in all Their terrible wrath: but of this, too, have I spoken in an other place, whereas of the advent of the Old Ones I have not yet spake.

Now the coming-down of the Great Old Ones from the stars, it is written in the Book of *Eibon* that the first who came hither was the Black Thing, even *Tsathoggua*, who came hence from dim Cykranosh not long after the creation of life on this planet. Not through the starry spaces came *Tsathoggua*, but by the dimensions that lie between them, and of His advent upon this planet, the place thereof was the unlitten and subterraneous Gulf of N'kai, wherein whose gloomy depths He lingered for innumerable cycles, as *Eibon* saith, before emerging into the upper world. And after this it was the Great *Cthulhu* came hither next, and all His Spawn from distant Xoth, and the Deep Ones and the loathsome Yuggs who be Their minions: and *Shub-Niggurath* from nightmare-rumoured Yaddith, and all they that serve Her, even the Little People of the Wood.

But of the Great Old Ones begotten by *Azathoth* in the Prime, not all came down to this Earth, for Him Who Is Not To Be Named lurketh ever on that dark world near Aldebaran in the Hyades, and it was His Sons who descended hither in His place. Likewise, *Cthugha* chose for His abode the star Fomalhaut, whereupon He begat dread *Aphoom Zhah*; and *Cthugha* abideth yet on Fomalhaut, and the Fire-Vampires that serve Him; but as for *Aphoom Zhah*, He descended to this Earth and dwelleth yet in His frozen realm. And terrible *Vulthoom*, that awful thing that be brother to black *Tsathoggua*, He descended upon dying Mars, which world He chose for His dominion; and He slumbers yet in the Deep of Ravormos 'neath aeon-crumbled Ignarh-Vath; and it is written that a day or a night to *Vulthoom* is as a thousand years to mortal men. And as for great *Mnomquah*, He took for the place of His abiding those cavernous spaces which yawn beneath the Moon's crust; and there He abideth yet, wallowing amidst the slimy waves of the Black Lake of Ubboth in the Stygian darknesses of Nug-yaa.

Now it is also written of those of the Begotten of *Azathoth* who abide not within the secret places of the Earth, that when the Great Old Ones came down from the stars in the misty Prime, They brought the image and likeness of Their Brethren with Them. In this wise, it was the Outer Ones that serve *Hastur* the Unspeakable, brought down the Shining Trapezohedron from dark Yuggoth on the Rim, whereupon had it been fashioned with curious art in the days ere the Earth had yet brought forth its first life. And it was through the Shining Trapezohedron, that is the very talisman of dread *Nyarlathotep*, that the Great Old Ones summoned to Their aid the might of the Crawling Chaos in the hour of Their greatest need, what time the Elder Gods came hither in Their wrath.

Likewise, it was the Deep Ones who carried down to this world the awful likeness of serpent-bearded *Byatis*, the son of *Yig*, whereby was He worshipped, first by the shadowy Valusians before the advent of man on this planet, and yet later by the dwellers in primal Mu. For the Great Old Ones had foreseen the day and the hour of Their need, when that They must summon to Their side those of Their awesome Brethren who had taken far worlds for the place of Their abiding, and had brought hither these images for this very purpose. Now of these star-made eidola, little there is that is known to men; it is said they were wrought by strange talismanic art, and that the sorcerers and wizards of this Terrene sphere are not deemed worthy by the Great Old Ones to be instructed in the secrets thereof.

But it is whispered in certain old, forbidden books an awesome power lurks within such images, and that through them, as through windows in time and space, Those that dwell afar can sometimes be evoked, as They were when that it came to pass, in the fullness of time, the Elder Gods descended on this world in Their wrath. And there be those that worship the Great Old Ones through Their image and likeness, but of this thou must be wary, for such eidola be uncanny, and betimes are known to drink the lives of them that handle them unwisely, or who seek through such images to summon to this sphere Those far off and better left undisturbed. Neither is it wholly within the knowledge of men to destroy such images, and many there be that sought the destruction thereof, who found their own destruction; but against such images from beyond the stars the Elder Sign hath very great power, although thou must beware lest in the conflict betwixt That which thou evokest to destroy the likeness of That which slumbereth afar, thou be not consumed and swallowed up, or be thyself destroyed thereby, and that utterly, even to thine immortal soul. For like unto all things that did belong once to the Old Ones, or that knew the touch of Their Paws, they be unwholesome and infectuous and will disturb and make vile the dreams of men; for eternal is the Power of Evil, and infinite in its contagion; as the *Great Cthulhu* yet hath sway over the minds and spirits of men, yea, even though He lieth chained and ensorcelled, bound in the fetters of the Elder Sign, and His malignant and loathly Mind spreadeth the dark seeds of madness and Corruption into the dreams and nightmares of sleeping men, so may the star-wrought eidola infect thy nocturnal hours with visions of horror, and fearfulness, and despair. *Iä! Cthulhu!* It is written they seduce and destroy men through their very dreams.

XIX. The Openers of the Way

Wherefore again do I say unto thee, that in all dealings and Commerce that thou wouldst have with such as These, be certain to take exceeding great care. For They be ever the foes of men and the enemies thereof, in Yaddith as in frigid Leng, in ruined Ignarh-Vath as in ruined Irem of the Pillars, in the Deep of Ravormos as in the Deep of Nug-yaa, in Ephiroth as in Yith; and even now it shall be seen that,

> They lurk ever just beyond the Gate,
> And for unwary fools They lie in wait.

IV. The Book of Dismissals

I. Of Calling Up That Which Thou Canst Not Put Down

The Sorcerer must, of all things pertaining to his Art, be most wary against the temptation of pride in his mastery of the Unholy Sciences, that he summon not That which be stronger than he, and the Which be not easily sent back to the place where it abideth. Of this Matter, it is written in the *Pnakotic Manuscripts*, Beware lest thou call up That which is greater than thyself, remembering the Doom of those who summoned the Worm that Gnaws in the Night; also concerning the which *Eibon* hath writ in his Chapter on Shaggai, and the way thither, and the doom thereof. Wherefore I say unto thee, Do not call up Any that thou canst not send back; by the which I mean, Any that can in turn call up Somewhat against thee; against the which even thy most powerfullest Devices may not serve. Ask of the Lesser, lest the Greater shall not wish to answer, and shall command more than thou canst endure to behold, or That against which thou art frail as the reed before the blast, and athwart the which all thy vaunted magistery availeth thee naught, and in the struggle thereagainst thou shalt exhaust thy strength in vain, to the Terror of thy mind and the Peril of thy body and the everlasting Damnation of thy soul.

In this, I say, the Sorcerer should take exceeding care, and should be ever mindful of the fall of the Saracen, *Yakthoob*, whereof I have aforetime writ in my Book of Episodes, and must arm himself withal 'gainst even the most dire and dreadsome eventuality with the utmost protections afforded by the Art. Now of Those wherewith the Sorcerer may the most earnestly desire to have Speech and Commerce, be warned that the Worst be Those that abide amidst the mephitic vapours of the inmost vaults and the malodorous and profoundest Deeps of the Earth. For, as *Ibn Schacabao* admonisheth, They of the nethermost depths be for the most part elementals of the Earth, and Their strength is potent and prodigious, even as that of the very Earth itself. Nor are They easily banished once thou hast conjured Them from the hidden foulnesses of

Their abysmal and subterraneous Abode; therefore thou shouldst summon them not lightly nor upon idle whim, but only in the hour of thy direst Need. Most stubborn and recalcitrant of Them is black *Tsathoggua*, whom I once call'd up in the madness and folly of my youth in those secret and forbidden Catacombs of *Nephren-Ka* which lieth beneath the sealed and hidden valley of Hadoth by the Nile, nigh unto that frightful fane of him whose very name history hath forgotten: that temple-tomb made dedicate to grim *Nyarlathotep*, even the Place of the Blind Apes where *Nephren-Ka* bound up the threads of truth and spun thereof in eternal stone a tapestry which foretelleth all of Time to Come. But of these terrible matters, too, I have spoken in another place.

Once summoned up, I say, the Lord of N'kai did squat before me in all His imbecilic vileness, and would not depart from hence when at length I had learned from Him that which I lusted to know. Mindful of the hideous and unspeakable Doom of *Tirouv Ompallion*, whereof of old the Atlantean hierophant hath writ, I strove in vain to drive Him from the Circle and back to those chasmal and terrific deeps in the bowels of legended Voormithadreth, wherein from eldermost aeons He hath dwelt. In vain did I utter the Lesser, and, at length, the Greater Dismissals; vainly did I threaten Him with the wrath of the Elder Gods who reign from Betelgeuse, and shewed forth the five-pointed Star; but nought bestirred Him from his sluggish and slothful somnolence, wherefrom He brooded upon me with malignant and gloatful gaze, until I bethought me that Those who do be the Elementals of the earth fear above all Things in earth and under heaven Them who are elementals of Fire; whereupon, knowing that Fomalhaut at that hour stood forth on the horizon, I spake the Evocation to *Cthugha*, which is to say, *Ph'nglui mglw'nafh Cthugha Fomalhaut n'gha-ghaa naf'l thagn, Iä Cthugha!* the which, thrice chanted, summoneth the Burning One from afar, either Him or His minions, who be known as the Fire-Vampires: whereupon, and very hastily, did the Black Thing quit the Circle wherein for long had It squatted vilely, to depart unto foetid and blackly-litten N'kai. Had I but remembered of the supremacy of *Azathoth* in that dark hour, mayhap I would have dared employ that transcendent Authority against One Who is but His underling and Minion, but I bethought me not of the Daemon-Sultan in mine extremity of Need. For although long-since banished to the Outer Dark and bereft of reason and utterance, and changed by His tormentors into His present eidolon, He reigneth still over the Old Ones, and, as *Azathoth* ruleth now as He did when in His bivalvular shape, His name subdueth all, from the incubi which haunt Tond to the servitors of *Y'golonac*. Few can resist the Power of the name of *Azathoth*, and even the haunters of the blackest night of Yuggoth cannot battle the power of His Other Name: but of this Matter I dare not speak. There be some Names men were not meant to speak aloud, nor to write down where other men may read.

II. Of the Several Modes to Enforce the Dismissal

Be wary, then, that thou hast to hand the means whereby to expell from the circle Those thou mayest summon thereunto; the which, for the most part, yield to the Dismissal without recalcitrance save for those elementals of the Earth, as *Tsathoggua* or His Spawn, whereof the Most dread is That the which the Hyperborean mage of old hath termed the Haunter of the Red Abyss, for that He walloweth ever in the depths of redly-litten Yoth nigh unto black, lightless N'kai which be the lair of His awful Sire. As well, Men know Him as the Dweller in Darkness, that brother of the Old Ones called *Nyogtha*, the Thing That Should Not Be; He may be summoned to Earth's surface through certain secret caverns and fissures, and Sorcerers have seen Him in Syria and below the Black Tower of Leng; and from the Thang grotto of Tartary betimes He hath come ravening to bring terror and destruction amongst the pavilions of the Great Khan. Only by the Looped Cross, by the Vach-Viraj incantation, and by the Tikkoun elixir may He be driven back to the nighted caverns of hidden foulness wherein He dwelleth and wherein amidst exceeding vileness He squirms and slithers in all His loathsomeness in the likeness of a viscous black amoeba. Summon *Nyogtha* if thou must, but at thy peril, and have to hand the proper instruments to enforce the Dismissal, whereof I have found most potent and powerful the Vach-Viraj incantation, which is to say, in the primal Senzar, known to Sorcerers and by all Men else forgot, *Ya na kadishtu nilgh're stell'hsna kn'aa Nyogtha, k'yarnak phlegethor, ka gna ril'krii, pishtao, ghaah-gr'ng, Ia! Nyogtha!*; the which, nine times repeated with Sirius in the ascendant, driveth Him from hence unto His noisome lair.

Against such as These there be full many Signs and Sigils that afford strong protection to the Sorcerer, albeit some Magisters of yore found them wanting and impotent to serve their Need. Of the Scarlet Sign I shall speak in another place, and of the Pnakotic pentagram it appertaineth not to this matter but to Another, yet both in their way be strong against the Dark Powers, and the Cross of the Nazarenes, some say, affordeth thee also strong Defence; for the Cross is not a passive agent. It protecteth the pure of Heart, and it hath oftentimes appeared in the air above our Sabbats, to the confusion and the dispersal of the Powers of Darkness and to the confounding of our rites and conjurations. Yet it be far less potent in our hands than when it is wielded by the Nazarenes, for reason of their faith in That which it doth symbol forth; and for my part, I eschew employment of it, cleaving in the main to the five-pointed star, to the Greater Dismissals, and, in the uttermost extremity of need, to the summoning-forth of Opposing Forces, as in mine use of the terror *Cthugha* holds over Black *Tsathoggua*, as hath aforetime been shewn.

In this Matter, keep well in mind that the Old Ones for the better part be rivals the One against the Other, and do be jealous of the Power and Dominion of Their Brethren, and may be pitted against each by him who hath the cunning and the knowledge of it, as the Elementals of Flame of their very nature oppose Those of the earth and as They of the sea be adversaries of the Air; They and those that serve Them, too, by the which wise the Sorcerer may set the Deep Ones that serve the Great *Cthulhu* and the Yugs who do be the minions of *Ythogtha* and *Zoth-Ommog*, His Spawn, against the Byakhee that be the bat-winged servitors of *Hastur* the Unspeakable, and that serve Him among the star-spaces, and the Mi-Go that serve Him on this world and Yuggoth too. Likewise, thou mayest pit the Little People that grovel to *Shub-Niggurath*, and the Ancient Ones that be minions unto *Yog-Sothoth*, and the Night-Gaunts that serve the Crawling Chaos, and all such as be Elementals of earth, against *Rlim Shaikoarth* and his Cold Ones that serve *Aphoom Zhah*, and the Fire-Vampires of *Fthaggua* who dwellest upon Ktynga near Antares and serve *Cthugha*, and all such as be Elementals of flame. Yet these be dread and terrific Forces to unleash, and there is a terror out of time and a primal and cosmic horror from beyond all spheres and stars and space itself, the which be not wisely invoked by mortal men; and much less is it prudent to pit such mighty Powers the one against the other: for when the Old Ones rise to war in all Their wrath and fury, of what avail is the strength of man?

III. Of Ib, and the Vengeance Thereof

Now there be one supreme and sovereign talisman which affordeth an everlasting Defence against these dread and awful Beings, and it is that mighty Sigil whereof the Cylinders of Kadatheron do speak and the which thereupon be named the Sarnath-Sigil; but the which we of this aeon term The Elder Sign, for that it representeth the Seal of the Authority of the Elder Gods that reign from remote Betelgeuse and that betimes have walked the dark and lonely places of this Earth as Towers of Living Flame. Concerning the which, moreover, it is written in the Papyrus of Ilarnek that the first of humankind uprose from the primal slime of the Elder World in the regions nigh unto the boreal Pole, but whether in Hyperborea or in Lomar, the Papyrus sayeth not. But it is told that in the immemorial years when the world was young, the first men came wandering down into the land of Mnar, and that they were a dark shepherd-folk who came thence, driving their flocks; and that in that land they did raise up the cities of Thraa and Alarnek and Kadatheron on the river Ai; and that on the shores of the lake of that land, which had the name Thune, they did set the first stones of that city legend rememberest as Sarnath the Doomed.

Now by that lake of Thune there had stood for innumerable aeons another city, and that was the grey stone city of Ib; old as the very lake itself was Ib, and peopled with Beings not pleasant to behold, nor were they sprung from the seed of men. It is recorded on the Cylinders of Kadatheron that They of Ib were cold and flabby to the touch, with flesh as green as Thune-water, and devoid of speech, and given to unwholesome worship of an Abomination of green stone, by the name of *Bokrug*, before the which they danced horribly when the Moon was gibbous and before Whose altars they made Sacrifice in Certain ways repulsive to men; wherefore the Men of Sarnath had no commerce with the tongueless Ib-Things, and came to dread them, and passed from dread to fear, and from thence to Hate.

In the fullness of time a prophet arose among the Men of Sarnath, by the name *Kish*: even that one we remember as the Elder Prophet, for that They who Reign from Betelgeuse made revelation unto him, saying, Beware the Ib-folk, O men of Sarnath! for that they were come down to this earth from certain cavernous places in the Moon ere man rose out of the slime, and the Water-thing they worship in foul ways is Other than thou thinkest, and the name *Bokrug* but a mask, behind the which there lurketh an elder Horror. In time the men of Sarnath came to hearken to the Elder Prophet, and muttered against the Ib-things that they wallowed before the abomination *Bokrug*, and for another reason also, namely that the little children that strayed from the walls of Sarnath and that wandered nigh unto the grim gates of Ib, came never back therefrom. At length the men of Sarnath went up against Ib in war, and they did brake down the gates thereunto, and did rend asunder the walls thereof, and put to the slaughter all the Folk therein. And the altars and temples they trampled into the mire in their loathing, for that it was seen that the webbed stone claws of the idol *Bokrug* were stained with Red, whereas there ran only in the veins of the Ib-things a putrescent Black fluid, as the warriors of Sarnath by now had much reason to know.

Thereafter did *Kish* vanish from the knowledge of men and it was said that he was Taken by them he worshipped, but whether to Celaeno or to Betelgeuse no man knoweth; and for a thousand years thereafter did Sarnath wax great in glory among the cities of Mnar, and in their pride and valor did the Kings of Sarnath make mock of the abomination *Bokrug*, mayhap to the angering of That which hid behind the name thereof. But in the reign of *Nargis-Hei* there appeared among men of the land of Mnar one who claimed to be *Kish* come again, and who preached of an impending and disastrous conjunction of the Planets foreboding ill to Sarnath and the men thereof, and who sware the omens warned that the Vengeance of Ib was upon them; but of the men of Sarnath there were but few who hearkened to *Kish* in these latter days and many that made mock of him, to their undoing.

Of the Doom that Came to Sarnath the cylinders of Kadatheron are silent; of the Vengeance of Ib the papyrus of Ilarnek sayeth naught. But it is written in the Testament of Kish that in the last days of *Nargis-Hei* there befell that whereof the Elder Prophet had spake in warning, and that the priest *Gnai-Kah* was the first to see certain unseemly Shadows drifting down from the gibbous Moon above, and certain unwholesome Mists rising up from the dark Thune below; and then that night came down, the morning whereof the men of Sarnath saw never, for that none lived to see the dawn.

IV. Of the Five-pointed Star Carven of Grey Stone

Now even though the Doom foretold by *Kish* had befallen the men of Sarnath there were those followed the Elder Prophet to safety from That which came up out of the green waters of the Lake, and from That which came down from the hidden places in the Moon. For those who hearkened to the teachings of *Kish* walked under the protection of the Elder Gods and bore about them the Sign of Protection whereof the Gods had made revelation to their Prophet. For *Kish* taught his people to take up the small grey stones of Mnar and to carve thereon the Seal of the Elder Gods, which is in the shape of an five-pointed star in the midst whereof is a symbol like an oval or Cartouche, open at either end, and within the which is a Pillar or tower of Flame; and the Testament of Kish recordeth that all they who bore this Sign about them fled the Fall of Sarnath unscathed; and it is furthermore written that this stone talisman, that hath the seeming of an Eye within an Star, and the which we call the Sarnath-Sigil, and also the Sign of Kish, but for the most part the Elder Sign, serveth men as a shield against Them From Outside and all Things of Evil to this day.

And the meaning of the Elder Sign is this, that albeit the Curse of the Old Ones enshadoweth all this world and them that dwell hereupon, yet there is no curse that hath not a cure and no ill whereagainst there existeth no remedy. The Elder Gods dwell remote and aloof from the Affairs of men, yet They have not abandoned us to the wrath of Them From Outside and Their abominable minions: for within the five-pointed star carven of grey stone from ancient Mnar lieth armour against witches and daemons, against the Deep Ones, the Dholes, the Yuggs, the Voormis, the Tcho-Tcho, the Abominable Mi-Go, the Shoggoths, the Valusians, and all such peoples and beings who serve the Great Old Ones and Their spawn; but it be less potent against the Great Old Ones themselves. He who possesseth the five-pointed star shall find himself able to command all Beings who creep, swim, crawl, walk, or fly, even to the Source from which there is no returning. In the land of Yhe as in great R'lyeh, in Y'ha-nthlei as in Yoth, in Yuggoth as in Zothique, in N'Kai as in K'n-yan, in Kadath-in-the-Cold-Waste as at the

Lake of Hali, in Carcosa as in Ib, it shall have power; but even as the stars wane and grow cold, even as suns die and the spaces between the stars grow more great, so wanes the power of all things—of the five-pointed star-stone as of the spells put upon the Great Old Ones by the benign Elder Gods; and there cometh a time, as once there was a time, when it shall be shown that:

> That is not dead which can eternal lie
> And with strange aeons even death may die.

But that time is not yet come; and still the star-stone from Mnar, marked with that sigil that is the Elder Sign, holds strong against the rage of Them it prisons, and against the wiles of those servants and minions who would set their Masters free. And by the power of the star-stone the Sorcerer shall walk without fear in the lonely places of the Earth at all times and in all seasons, and in the worlds beyond this also, and all realms and regions contiguous thereunto: in Sarnath as in Ephiroth, in the gulf of Y'qaa as in the deep of Ravormos, in Shaggai as in Yaddith, in Leng as in the vale of Pnath, in the World of the Seven Suns as in Zoth, in Lomar as in Mhu Thulan, in Irem the City of Pillars as in Alaozar where the Tcho-Tcho dwell; thou shalt go without dread of any beings or creatures that serve Them From Outside, aye, neither the Ghouls, the Shantaks, the Gaunts of the Night, the Cold Ones, the Byakhee, the Miri Nigri, the Aihai, nor the Fire-Vampires, may offer peril nor harm to him who beareth about him the stone from Mnar.

Readers of August Derleth's tale "The Gorge beyond Salapunco" (one of the episodes of *The Trail of Cthulhu*) must often wonder what sinister secrets lurk behind the title of a Mythos tome mentioned in that story, *The Sussex Manuscript*. In Edward P. Berglund's article "What Was *The Sussex Manuscript?*" in *Crypt of Cthulhu* #35 (1985), intrepid researcher Berglund recounted his successful attempt to track down not merely the facts behind the title (already known through Lin Carter's "H. P. Lovecraft: The Books", *The Shuttered Room*), but actually the book itself! *The Sussex Manuscript* turned out to be a fantastically elaborate, one-of-a-kind illuminated manuscript, bound in leather, by one Fred L. Pelton of Lincoln, Nebraska. Pelton's heirs passed the text on to Berglund.

Derleth had once seriously considered publishing Pelton's work under the Arkham House imprint. That is why he made reference to it in "The Gorge beyond Salapunco", to whet reader interest and fatten sales when it appeared. Only it didn't appear. Derleth sent Pelton's masterpiece to fellow Arkham House publisher Donald Wandrei for his opinion. Wandrei discouraged him in no uncertain terms: "It is a very good example of its type, but the type isn't worth doing in the first place. ... It is mainly a rehash of the Cthulhu myth, and as such it meets the horns, each posing an insoluble problem, of a dilemma. The first horn is that a mere rehash of the myth adds nothing that is not already in Lovecraft and is therefore a quite futile waste of time. The other horn is that an attempt to elaborate the myth in sharp detail produces, not something sublime, but something ridiculous. ... It is certainly a tribute to the lasting vigor of HPL's imagination that so many Johnny-Come-Latelys want to embroider on the myth; but it seems to me that our only honest course is to preserve the myth as HPL created it, and not to encourage extensions, additions, alterations, and distortions." (November 17, 1946)

Apparently he persuaded Derleth, who wrote to Berglund, July 5, 1969, *"The Sussex Manuscript*, I assure you, was not worth publishing—a hodgepodge of stuff, some from the published HPL & other Mythos stories, some made up to fill the gaps. Pelton did a persuasive job in places, but the performance was very uneven. And certainly not a viable addition to the Mythos or we'd have published it."

Well, here, at last, is the text of *The Sussex Manuscript*. The effect of the spectacular original, a hand-produced blackletter, illuminated manuscript, is, alas, lost in the mere transcription of the prose, but we are in no position to reproduce the "real thing", and until someone does, the text itself will have to suffice. It should satisfy your curiosity to some degree, however.

The Sussex Manuscript

by Fred L. Pelton

Cultus Maleficarum
in Libri quattour
Sussex—mdxcviii
ex hyms Baronis Fredericus Primus

A l. Necronomicon. Unto English transcribed by this thy servant and taken from ye olde Latin text of Celsus Olaus called Wormius whych ye story relates is out of an olde manuscrit by Abdul-al-Hazred who learnt of wondrous mysteries and horrific secrets when he slept by fabled Irem in ye desert. Herein are told of ye dread Cthulhu and His Old Ones, of Azathoth, of ye legions of darkness, of ye glories of R'lyeh, of ye secrets of ye rites, of Him Who Waits Dreaming ...

BOOK 1

First Book of ye great al-powerful Lord Cthulhu and of his legions, and of ye mighte Old Ones whych cam down with our master from dark Yuggoth, wherein also ys related ye wonders of ye Yogge-Sothoth Cycle, ye glories of ye rites whych waer done for hym who ys nameless in ye gulf, ye splendours of ye cities and ye nacions of ye Elder Ones. But ye must listen to my warning: for ye must know that manie are they who have sout these secrets, and few in deed are they who have learnt and have lived, and it is a veritie that manie shall seek yet few shall see these mysteries or know of them. Therefore if ye seek truth in all thynges reade that which is written her by thy servant, done in olde Sussex, mdxcviii.

liber i, capitulum i:

Out off ye Shadow out of time, in ye olde vastness of ye void, from out an age that waes before time ytself was Azathoth and ye oethers off ye Elder Gods, and their King whych ys called most powerfull Azathoth o strangele thronth crawling chaos, served by Nodens and Sothoth. And ye king waes a mynd less lyfe, and he was all ye worlde, and hys was ye worlde, an al ye substance off ye worlde waes hys, and he was ye first. From an age that waes before tyme, from aout ye tymelesseness off spece, be fore ye hierarche of angels and daemons of ye between-worlde whych is reconed a macrocosm, before al this waes our Lourd Azathoth. And in their turn waer made ye universe and ye stars and that whych men calleth Yuggoth and al ye worlde, ye sacred isles, and greate Sothoth came downe amonge ye stars and made ye Old Ones and they saw hym and calleth hym Master, and there came among ye Great Ones chieftayns whych ye scribes account to be Gods, and of these ye shall know of Yog-Sothoth, Ulthar, Tsathoggua, Ithaqua, ye Lloigor, Shub-nyggurath, Hastur, Gtantha, Cthugha, Nyarlathotep.

capitulum ii:

Wizele did ye noble al-Hazred write off them who were be fore: for ye Olde Ones were ye first after Sothoth and it is not to be ymagyned that they are gone. Nor is it to be thoughte that man is either ye eldest or ye last of ye earths masters or that ye common bulke off life and substance walks alone. Ye Olde Ones were; ye Olde Ones are; and ye Olde Ones shall be, not in ye speces that we know but between they walke serene and primal, undymensioned and to us unseen. Ye Yogge-Sothoth knoweth ye gate, ye Yogge-Sothoth ys ye gate, ye Yogge-Sothoth ys ye key and ye guardian of ye gate, He knoweth wher ye greate Olde Ones broke through and where they shall break through agayne. He knoweth where they have trod earth's fields, and where they shall tread them, and why no one can behold them as they tread; by their smell can men some tymes know them near butt off theyr semblance can no man know savyng onlie yn ye features of those they have begotten on men, and off those ther are manie sorts dyffering in lykenesse from mans truest eidolon to that shape wythout syght or substance whych is them; they do walk unseen and foul in lonely places wher ye wordes have been spoken and those unholie Rites haouled through ther seasons, and ye verie wynd doth gybbor wyth theyr voyces.

capitulum iii:

Then it was that the peoples of both ye Kuzco and ye Kaxor came down unto ye Olde Ones at Yuggoth to mynyster unto them and to shew them mysteries. And it came to pass that some saw onlie Sothoth and hys own Ulthar whyle some few ye dread Tsathoggua and ye Nyarlathotep, and lo they fell in great dyspute and argument, and there waes strife and wars and some from eache house came down to earth butt ye house of Kaxor waes driven ynto ye cave yet dyd they hold secret communion wyth ye Kynges: Lloigor, Ithaqua, ye Shub-niggurath and Cthugha, together wyth theyr legions.

capitulum iiii:

Thus came to ye worlde that whych ye scribes calleth ye Yogge-Sothoth Cycle. These were ye days off ye Olde Ones who hath builded great cities and dwelt therein. For they are wondrous beings and they are while no man may know them, even as ye forbidden book saith: ye ways of them are great and marvelous and not for ye eye of ye woman-born but onlie for ye fathomyng eye whych shall be of themselves and in theyr own lykenesse. Theyr powers are great and theyr countenance strangelie mirrored in sacred fyres. Secretle they dwell and walk ye earthe for again it shall be theyrs. They bend ye forest and crush ye city; yet may not ye city or forest behold ye hande that smites. Kadath in ye cold waste hath known them, and what man knows of olde Kadath. Ye yce desert of ye south and ye sunken isles of ye oceans hold stones whereon theyr seals are engraven; butt who hath seen ye deep frozen citie or ye sealed olde tower long-garlanded wyth sea weed and barnackels. Greate Cthulhu is theyr cousine, yet can he spy them onlie dimly. As a foulness shall ye know them, theyr hand is at your throat, yet ye know them not and ye see them not theyr own habitation is even one wyth your guarded tholde. Yogge-Sothoth is ye key to ye gate whereby the spheres meet. Man rules now where they ruled once, they shall soon rule where man rules now. After summer is winter, and after winter summer. Therefor read all ye students of that whych ye scribes telleth concerning them that were; learn of ye Shub-niggurath ye black goat wyth a thousand young, of ye kyng of ye ayr who is called Lloigor, of great Ithaqua and his Deep Ones, and of fyrie Cthugha.

capitulum v:

Now ye Noble house of Kuzco had conquered and with Yog Sothoth their chief and Ulthar their power they made his name holy for all ye world. Where there were empires they made ye buildings of cities; palaces of Temples; houses and courts where dwelt ye nobles of ye Kings; Priests of ye Elder Gods; giants of ye Empires; Kingdoms of Ulthar; their one world.

capitulum vi:

We hail and adore ye dead R'lyeh; She will rise again from her dreaming deathless sleep and rule ye earth as once she did before.

"Ia! Ia! Cthulhu fhtagn; Ph'nglui mgla'nafh Cthulhy R'lyeh wgah-nagl fhtagn; Shub-niggurath."

capitulum vii:

For where R'lyeh was queen of Zoltan; Viryklu ruled ye Kalnor Plain; Kal-vorg ye forest-mountain of Arkand held ye great Shub-niggurath whose dominion was ye earth under ye earth; ye winged One who is called ye Lloigor; R'lyeh had Ithaqua, mighty king of Zoltan; Great kings all of great empires shared of Ulthar, born of Sothoth; ye desired of Cthulhu. And even as ye loathsome Shub-niggurath hold his court in caverns deep lighted blue by ye nether-sun; ye great Ithaqua swims in icy presured depths of sea, and all shall do their homage to him who came out of Azathoth and to his Ulthar who, together with ye lesser of ye Elder Gods, shall be worshipped and adored forever. Ia Ia, Ye high priest of all ye universe was ye one Ultharathotep who is called Klark-ash-ton and sometimes also Yog-Sothoth for he was beloved of Sothoth and he ruled ye world and directed all ye creatures thereof. Unto ye columned Sthoric Temple went ye peoples of ye earth; and into ye vast Viryklu Dome where there was ye altar; and here were ye priests and emperors; ye kings and chieftains; ye acolytes and ye Brotherhood of L'mur-Kathulos; and they gathered at ye Sacred Shrine when they performed ye Rites at ye B'hal.

capitulum viii:

And they entered into ye Osluar nov 'Kiros whych is also ye Chaptel-of-Symbols. Here was made ye sacred sign ye triangle; ye great sign of ye Eternal One; and at each corner sit ye three Zorlas; on ye peak it is ye Universe outside; ye sky and stars and all ye worlds of ye cosmos; and on the right it is the Universe around; the earth and the creatures thereof; and on the left it is ye Universe within; ye mind; ye soul; ye life. And from ye Univers outside whych is ye Azathoth are ye forces of Sothoth and his Ulthar; and each of them shall be named; for some of them are fire, storm, tide, light, death, love, beauty and all ye others of ye three-fold world; ye triad-universe whych are ye Signs of him who created and him who is eternal. And when ye triangle is made as a sign of Him it is made One with ye second triangle; and ye life of ye Second Triangle is also wondrous; for on each corner of it lies ye Kronlas at ye peak, ye Time whych was Before; on ye right, ye Time whych is Now and on ye left, ye Time whych Shall Be. And when ye two are thus made into One then is formed a perfect square; ye enclosed Universe of three and ye Times of ye world, all united into ye square whych is ye Sacred Sign of Sothoth; who hath made this and who hath appointed ye Temple. Here is ye Very Crystal of ye One true Azathoth and his Sothoth and His own Ulthar—Universal God, Great One, Creator of All, Master of ye World, Divine Maker, Powerful Maker, ye Circle within Circles whych are Himself.

Capitulum ix:

Sothoth	Zibzoralhua
Athuaor	Makoruaa'Zib
Qualaoratuaa	Oluiaolu

capitulum x:

Now ye ancient ones did perform these cyclic rites in fabled old Sarnath, in Irem ye city of pillars, in ancient R'lyeh, and Sthor, and in Hyperborea, in Karnairn, K'rathan, Lomar, Shaveth, Ashteroth, Alaozar, Arkhand, B'graa, Carcosa, Sarkomand, Celephais, Chorazin, Commorium, 'Elios, in Dylath-leen, and Sarkia. Fomalhaut, Hastur, Hatheg, Iranon, and in Ib. Ilek-vad, also Skai, Inganok, Kadath, in Kalnor, in Kal-vorg, Leng,

Mhuthulan in Mnar, Nir, N'kai, Nasht, Nath-horthath, N'gai Ooth-nargai, with Olathoe, Pnath, Teloth, in Than-tha, Thran, Viryklu, and Valusia, Uandulu, Yuggoth, in Yian-ho, Yain, Yith, Yoth, in Yhe, Y'ha-nthlei, and in all these places in ye world did ye Altornos come together unto ye temples of he who is never to be named and where ye priests did ye holy cyclic rites of ye ritual which he hath prescribed for ye altars, and that maniacal life which is Ulthar.

capitulum xi:
[illustration]

capitulum xii:
It may be told of ye magicians of Og and ye great sorcerors of Ashteroth and Kir'athan that with certain magyck of their own and with strange herbs, told of in their cyphers, they could make a great potion, and it is told that their incantations of blood and death did wonders; they had fiends and daemons and monsters to do their bidding and lived as kings. Also shall ye find in their old secret writings formulae for fluids whych can transport men's souls even today to these cities of ye Old Ones. How these are made is forbidden knowledge, and a secret of ye priesthood, and they reserved it for themselves. For in ye days of ye great Yog-Sothoth great evil fell upon this earth by usurped magyck whych had been stolen from ye priests. And ye sorcerors of Karnak knew also of it for it was saved for them in ye rites of Horus for is it nor written that he is one of ye sons of them? It is truly inscribed on ye tablets that no man may see though he behold them, and men may hear them as they walk and yet not know of them; for they are not of mankind and are beyond us and they dwell outside from ye chaos from whence they came.

capitulum xiii:
In ye Viryklu dome where those great towers spiral up into ye nighte of ye Lloigornos there is ye green flame-fountain, ye life of ye Old Ones, ye incarnation of ye Viryklas, ye blood of her who is called ye mother, there shall be ye flame when they awake. It burns lonely and untended as a sign of them, for they were, and they are, and they shall be again. Truly have ye scribes written: they shall dwell and die and be forgot, yet is it foretold in the prophecy that they shall come again and their gods be great!

capitulum xiv:
And so they lived and worshiped him who is eternal and he shall be called Ulthar, and these were ye times of ye lord Yog-Sothoth and his cycle, and ye first B'kal came and passed and ye rites were done. Ye noble house of Kuzco ruled ye world from their mighty cities, and ye emperors were loyal to ye holy Azathoth whom ye scribes tell rules from outside, and even

ye foul and monstrous toad-god Tsathoggua was chained in N'kai and yet ye rulers of ye Olde Ones knew ye chieftain of ye Kaxor whose name is Urgashton and he is in ye cave.

capitulum xv:

Ye nethermost caverns are not for ye fathoming eyes that see for their marvels are strange and terrific. Cursed ye ground where dead thoughts live new and oddly bodied, and evil ye mind that is held by no head. For it is of old rumour that ye soul of ye devil-bought hasts not from this charnal clay but fats and instructs ye very worm that gnaws, till out of corruption horrid life springs and ye dull scavengers of earth wax crafty to vex it and swell monstrous to plague it. Great holes secretly are digged where earth's pores ought to suffice, and things have learnt to walk that ought to crawl.

capitulum xvi:

Xandulu in Arkand and also in Viryklu knew ye Old Ones in ye glorious and golden days of ye great Yog-Sothoth cycle and in ye dread reign of that master of ye night. For in dread are whispers heard in ye darkness and they walk by night.

capitulum xvii:

For untold generations and for full eons of generations where ye Old Ones lived they did give ye holy sacrifice to Ulthar and it was ye Cycle of Yog-Sothoth while ye lesser slaves of air and those daemons of ye earth together with those creatures of fire and ye monsters of ye sea were held in chained restraint by ye forces of uz which emmenated from ye sphere of ye Elder God who is called Ulthar. And safe were ye Old Ones, yet these daemons waxed strong on impure magic, and were restless, and yet were unfed; they were ruled from ye cave, they grew but were not worshiped and escape whych might be theirs held ever ye promise of life for them who were undead. Never were they shown their place of rule of ye elements and ye empires for was it not ye Cycle of ye lord ye great Yog-Sothoth? It is written in ye sacred Zexan that until ye end of his cycle shall they be slaves and also monsters, and then shall they rise from their places, walk ye Earth and rule it, for this was ye prophesy.

capitulum xviii:

Thus it came to pass that ye nobles of ye Old Ones were called unto Kal-vorg, also unto ye towering Viryklu Dome, unto ye Sthoric Temple, and to fare R'lyeh; summoned also were ye chosen-of-ye-Ulthar, whose mystic students of his power, and there as in all his temples throughout ye whole universe ye sacred circles were drawn again on ye festival of ye snake. Then ye mighty lord Cthugha was called forth and adored with ye elemental kings as rightful ruler of the Flame.

capitulum xix:

Verily did ye priests draw ye circle and also did they consecrate it to him who is named ye Azathoth. Ye greator diameter thereof was ye sign of ye elder father Sothoth, and his world and ye central sphere was ye space that he made, and ye innermost ring was as endless as his time; ye round and ye unending sign of ye great creator, ye One. All of these made they as it was written in ye Holy Zexan; and these did they see as symbols of ye Sothoth and his glorious Ulthar; and ye strange script of their worship.

capitulum xx:

Here in Viryklu and there in R'lyeh, in Yuggoth where Nodens reveled, far beneath ye hollow crust of earth where dwell ye foul and loathsome Tsathoggua, in ye cities of Hyperborea, in ye temple-yards of old Yain, and in all places was ye divine and hated majesty of Sothoth and his Ulthar seen and preserved as manifest and their power was worshiped through ye signs of them.

capitulum xxi:

Even as was told be ye sorceror of Yian, many were chosen from ye Old Ones who were also called n'Altornos in Arkand, and they were tried by ye cold flame of truth, and tested by strength, and their number became small, and they that lived were made acolytes, chosen of great Ulthar symbols of old Azathoth, pupils under ye L'mur-Kathulos, masters of ye League of Hastur.

capitulum xxii:

All hail ye dead R'lyeh for she is ye jewel of Arkand; all praise and honour and glory be unto her; for she shall arise from her dream and deathless sleep when ye stars are right and rule again as once she did: Fall down and adore ye students of L'mur-Kathulos who are of ye League of Hastur; give sacrifice unto them who are ye chosen of Ulthar, symbols of Sothoth and glory from ye Azathoth.

capitulum xxiii:

Let no man doubt them for those Altornos were ye fathers of mankind. Ye ancients of ye east knew them of old and many are ye tales of them, did not al-Hazred write of them, do we not hear of giants who dwelt in ye strange lands of the east; truly are there rumors of monsters and legends about daemons for ye magyck of men is but a whisper of them. Learn well ye lesson that ye may be ready; and so prepare ye'rself. Let ye'rself be made ready for ye rites for it was truly said by ye ancients that there were masters of old, and their rule shall come again to ye earth.

capitulum xxiv:

Do we not know of Kadath or Sabat, O ye unnamed of him-who-is-eternal rise up and know them. Awake from out ye cavern. Adore Sothoth for he did make them. Fall down before ye holy flame and read ye inscription on ye pillar.

capitulum xxv:

Not unknowingly did ye wise ancients do their magic by ye circles for it is of old lore that ye ring did evoke and conjure him who is nameless. Only when ye fools forgot ye memory of them did ye power of magyck fail; only when fools lost ye names did ye legends fade and men neglect them. Ye names were ye keys and they were lost.

capitulum xxvi:

Per Azathoth, Nodens, Ulthar, Sothoth, Metraton, Ou, Agla, Methon, Verburn Pythonicum, Mysterium, Salamandrae cenuentus Sylvorum, Antra, etper Gnomorum, Daemonia Eoeh, God, Almonsin-Giber, Tsathoggua, Eram, Zariathnatmik, veni, veni, veni.

capitulum xxvii:

Then is this time whych was before ye beginning of men yet after ye Origin, at N'gah-kthun there assembled all ye high priests, one from each of those ancient empires together with ye divine rulers of ye Altornos: Lloigor, Ithaqua, also ye Cthugha, and Shub-niggurath, ye great chiefs of ye elementals. And that brotherhood of N'gah-kthun were also ye keepers of ye sacred symbols, dwellers of ye crystal palace, rulers of ye spirit.

capitulum xxviii:

So it came to pass that once each thousand years these highest of ye empires' worship gathered at ye temple city of N'gah-kthun ye holy place there to make ye final rites to Sothoth, there to prove and there to demonstrate ye wizardry of unity, that gigantic and that incomprehensible and monstrous Oneness of ye universe whych was him. From out that final ritualistic press there flowed that sacred wine of Sothoth whych is ye creative fluid of ye world. Here with ye incantation of ye priests and ye devotions of ye assembled multitudes of ye empires; ye priests united their lives and hearts into ye magyck liquid from whence was born that divine and holy incarnation of ye bright Ultharathotep, whych was to rule enthroned for that one second of eternity, resolving then into that ultimate ego whych, rejoining the beginning and ye end, found eternal rest in Ulthar.

When thus ye holy circle was completed each temple school again crowned their new high priest from among those acolytes in a rebirth of ye symbolic deification, and thus preserved forever that glorious rotation of ye cosmic wheell. Ye exalted liquid of ye divine Ultharathotep absorbed that life of ye Lloigor, Ithaqua, Shub-nigur, and ye Cthugha ye wealth and energy of ye empires and ye elements and in that last dissolution of that same incarnation all light and power was drawn into ye crystalization in ye Orb of Ulthar, where it fed ye living throbbing flame of life.

And accordingly was he nourished and that holy Orb was held in ye temple as a sign of his might. So it was that ye sacred and mystic cycles of his life in death and that deathless sleep without life was complete and thus was Ulthar's power upheld. Cycle after cycle it was true for ye elementals and ye kings and their lesser minions of ye empires and even for ye frightful king of death whose name is Tsathoggua. Each did lose some of that substance of their life and their powers and of their blood and their strength, of that vital fluid of force and of command, of thus each cycle of ye rites were they resubjugated that they might never raise their frozen prostrate forms before ye glory that was Ulthar. Still undaunted and undying there flamed in ye innermost secret heart of ye kings that fiery coal of hope for their true place of equality with Ulthar.

capitulum xxix:

When ye tribes of Leng came out of ye earth to rule ye lands of ye old Hastur and ye empires had seen ye B'kal of ye cycle B'kthun ye kings met in secret tones and united to save their force and power. Carefully they made their new and secret plans and sought each in their own realm to reserve a tiny portion, only a merest part of a droplet, of ye power which was to be ye cyclic sacrifice to Ulthar—and to his demand. Each swore to save and preserve that droplet. And to this their purpose each created for himself a new secret black onyx sphere, whereupon they created new magyck of themselves and they designed new rites to save up their own power and essence and this would be their goal and little by little to store this force within ye three black orbs, their symbols.

capitulum xxx:

And it came to pass that in ye cyclic ceremonies Ulthar's passion was satisfied for ye revel of ye tiny missing drops of force. So it was not seen and thus it was not known even by ye great guardians of ye Hall of Ulthar, but ye Sothoth knew. So it was that while in each cycle ye magic Ulthar's power was reborn, his true force did wane by that same droplet extracted so painfully by ye Shub-nigurrath, ye great Lloigor, ye Ithaqua, and Cthugha. Ye elementals carefully saved each drop of their force-sacrifice to Ulthar and did conceal that drop in ye shining black orbs and held that same drop from ye offering whych perpetuated this ye holy and high Yog-Sothoth cycle.

capitulum xxxi:

Slowly so slowly, little by little, bit by infinitesimal bit, drop by drop ye black orbs grow—and each thousand years each emperor of ye elements added ye same small drop at ye cycle of ye Rites and as they grew so did ye true power of Ulthar diminish by that same drop. Over ages and eons of time which are incomprehensible, ye new power of ye three black orbs did increase painfully and so slowly that at each time of ye B'kal no change was to be seen and yet that increase was there. For it was ye time that ye high priest of ye Elder Gods ye Yog-Sothoth, ye great master of ye brotherhood, chief of ye noble high priests, prince of L'mur-kathulos he for whom ye cycle is named, that one ineffable guardian of ye gate, ye mighty U'mr at-Tawil whych ye scribe did render as ye prolonged of life, came forth from his throne and spoke that whych is YE HOLY PROPHECY.

capitulum xxxii:

Be it seen that ye moon growes small and ye hour of eclipse drawes near. There shall be death for ye faithfull and bloody shall be ye reward of ye infidel, ye moon shall fall yet shall be caught, and ye worms of ye earth shall feed but only for a night. And in his glory shall ye star arise and slay ye daemons of ye air. For again ... there shall be ye moonlight.

capitulum xxxiii:

When ye words of Yogge-Sothothua reached ye four elementals there was great fear in their hearts and death was ye least and easiest fate for those who shared this secret; and ye rulers of ye elements gathered together in their secret places and made council. For ye high one had seen their plan and dread creatures did await their fall. So in council they did agree and in ye night ye winged and monstrous denizens of ye air were by Lloigor summoned and sent forth to far and fabled R'lyeh. And ye high one returned to Azathoth; yet there was no acolyte in ye Temple who was able to read ye words so they were left unheeded and ye cycle drew near.

capitulum xxxiv:

Hidden deep within ye earth in caverns dank and musty beneath ye lowest crypt of man, was ye black globe of ye goat.

capitulum xxxv:

High in ye peak of ye Viryklu dome, there on ye roof of ye world, gleamed ye black orb of ye Lloigor fed by ye blood of ye air.

capitulum xxxvi:

Here in ye watery depths, and washed by ye tides of ye earth, in ye heart of ye green whirlpool was hidden ye third black sphere.

capitulum xxxvii:

So ended ye glorious Yog-Sothoth cycle and this did begin ye night of great terror for Old Ones and ye revolt of ye elements. Tended by strange guardian creatures of their elemental magyck, irrigated by fluids of newly devised evil, fed with dark sacrifices of enslaved devotees' slaves who earned black glory through ye renunciation of ye Ulthar. Ye rulers did save their power and also their impatient plans; all this that they might see that shining day when they would ascend their rightful thrones.

capitulum xxxviii:

And ye months passed slowly and when ye time of ye B'kal drew near those three black spheres had grown to rival that crystalline symbol of ye Ulthar, and then did ye emperors bring them forth from ye cave and from ye tower and from ye ocean; and then went they in unto that sacred hall of Ulthar at ye time of ye cycle. When they came unto that most holy temple ye guardians were preparing for ye rites, and Lloigor was ye king of Viryklu, while great Ithaqua was indeed an emperor, and ye mother ye Shub-nigurrath, were all trusted of ye guardians and held as loyal by ye temple scripts.

capitulum xxxix:

[illustration]

capitulum xxxx:

And it was not of ye priestly knowledge this thing of old evil whych they did. So it was that they were allowed to enter ye Hall where they placed ye three black spheres carefully at that most high point of ye altar in ye place of ye True Sign of him-who-is-eternal. Thus did they imytate ye sacred and glorious jewel with a plain dead stone of diamond. With solemn golden steps ye flame-clad priests approached that holiest altar on ye day of ye great cycle symbolizing that beginning of ye rites with ye beat of ye drum, ye incantation of ye music, and ye invocation of ye acolytes. Ye same who one cycle hence would rise adorned to receive ye jeweled and holy diadem, for proven was eache of ye lesser priests by those monuments to Ulthar's glory whych each had wrought. Offerings to ye altar, ye sacrifices of self to ye throne of his glory, pledged forever to ye sanctity of their holy and noble order, to ye splendour of their great glorious mutation, and also to ye preservation of ye cycle. Followed this in quick succession all ye normal periodic rites: ye offer of ye blood of land, ye signs of air and earth, with ye cleansing of ye temple, ye purification of ye altar, ye offerings and ye symbol of him-who-is-eternal, ye total devotion and culminating prayers of ye Altornos; then was ye relighting of ye temple fires from ye mixed flames of empires; those royal three kings ye Lloigor, Ithaqua, Shub-niggurath, ye lord of Fire Cthugha, and even ye dread Tsathoggua, and all these kings gathered in ye hall when ye holy and cyclic rites were declared.

capitulum xxxxi:

In crowning glorifying passion of unity eache acolyte began ye preparations of ye mutation; eache high priest intoned ye prayers; both consecrated ye ceremonial fire like golded twisted crystal; each prepared by sacred blood, water clear and molten diamond, tall towering pillars of frozen flame, emeralds and ruby, eyes of ye Oactyl, tail of ye Horgoth, bones of Elohnor, drift of ye cosmos, each in proportion, fused with each other and blended of ivory; poured and stirred, distilled with pearl, made hard with ruby and pliant with flesh, resilient with horn sparkling with gems and quiescent with prayer; all transformed into that holy magycal essence whych was to release and to blend eache high one into that one incarnate Ultharathotep: whych was to rule ye festival.

capitulum xxxxii:

With hope and with gnawing dread of failure ye kings did await this instant of ye sacred transformation; and then when ye holy essence drew life from ye three rays of ye black orbs there arose from ye altar not ye divine Ultharathotep, but ye new manifestation of ye most great Nyarlathotep whych was Cthulhu.

BOOK 2

Second book. Wherein is related ye year of death and of ye dread Nyarlathotep.

liber ii, capitulum i:

Now it came to pass that when ye hope and desires, ye wishes and conquests of ye kings waer crowned with great success, that ye king Lloigor and ye Ithaqua together with ye Cthugha and ye Shub-niggurath did fall down and worship theyr god ye dread Nyarlathotep. And ye legions of Arkand and Zolthan and Kalnor seized ye weapon of fire and terror to stay ye acolytes of Ulthar; for in ye house of him death and destruction waere kings, drawing with insatiable lust ye emanations from ye dread black orbs. For in that dark cloud of terror that did blow unstemmed to blot ye golden light of Ulthar's globe, horror was born of gods, and war between ye lights declared with violence.

capitulum ii:

From out ye greenish waters came slimy ithaquar whych wer creatures of ye sea. Out of ye great and black cloud of night came ye horrid winged lloigornos ye vast creatures of far air and space. And still from far beneath ye deepest caverns ye dank and colorless worms of ye putrid shubborath wrythed and awoke to find theyr secrets worshipped. A new dawn of night came to Arkand and broke in dark ebon waves upon ye shores of ye Zolthan, slowed down over Kalnor plain covering all with ye night of ye Nyarlathotep. Ye lloigornos, ithaquar and shubborath fed no more on that rotten-putrescent liquifaction whych formed theyr meager libation; but did grow to fat and swollen glory on ye meat of unconverted minds, on ye blood of ye Ulthar-faithful; they did lustfully satiate their eon-whetted appetites for ye souls of theyr unfaithful but rightful sacrifices.

capitulum iii:
Shubborath twisted, splashed, and writhed along theyr old slime and blood-covered pathways to ye upper earth; no more feared they ye golden son of Sothoth or ye globe or ye Ulthar for unknowing of Ulthar's loss they were called of Cthulhu who was theyr god; and also ther came ye lloigornos for their clouds in multitudes to seize in ye abominating revel ye Nyarlathotep hath decreed. And even as they came ye ithaquar disported in ye shallows luring their quarry into ye waters, whipping and lashing ye waves to foam, while with phosphorescent tentacles they drew to each gory beak ye food they desired.

capitulum iiii:
Lost was all power of Sothoth, gone is ye light of Ulthar, gone waes all hope devoid of ye protection of timeless ceremony deserted by ye Ultharathotep, ye acolytes and ye people fled into ye earth to be devoured by shubborath; they ran unto ye mountains where lloigornos seized them; they went also to ye waters and were caught by ye ithaquar.

capitulum v:
So ye emperors fell down before their god and it was Cthulhu; and they sent forth theyr own messengers who were armed with charms of ebony and silver whych did fend off ye shubborath. And those messengers went out unto all ye cities of Arkand, and into ye temples of Zoltan, and even unto ye Sthoric temple, and unto all these they did proclaim ye coming of ye lord Cthulhu, and with them they took sacred writings in priestly script to tell of ye new worship. But those peoples of ye empires would not bow down to new gods, and denied of his coming, and they slew ye men from evil even as they themselves died in ye mouth of ye shubborath, were clawed by those winged lloigornos, while ye sea-folk fed ye ithaquar, and ye altornos left ye messengers' bodies as a sign that they loved Ulthar.

capitulum vi:
For in that hall of Ulthar, defiled with every conceivable abomination, these few initiates of him sought out ye one true globe of light, ye veritable crystal of truth, and covering it with theyr fragile bodys they took it and so saved themselves and ye holy light. For it must be told that not even ye towering Nyarlathotep dared approach its light for unto these spirits of ye Night its very rays were death. Thus it was that ye initiates were saved, and when they saw that ye light still glowed, they rejoiced exceedingly and were

made strong in theyr faith in ye Sothoth and his god. Whereupon they took up ye orb and cleansed it with new earth, and so carried it by ye high flaming anger of ye dread Nyarlathotep and through ye multitudes of His evils past ye assembled emperors, down ye halls filled with terror-incarnate, and out of ye hall of Ulthar.

capitulum vii:

It came to pass then that ye holy orb of Ulthar, theyr only symbol, ye one vestigial fire, ye single spark in ye blackness of ye Dark Ones was saved for them and for us. These few who held ye light could not be stopped nor destroyed, and without ye wish of ye dark ones saved themselves and ye true light of Ulthar. Ye Nyarlathotep who had planned to claim ye light, knew he could not destroy it, and he also was secretly joyous to lose ye orb and thus be free of its great danger, and ye dreadful Nyarlathotep believed himself safe from. And ye acolytes made theyr slow dangerous way through ye ruins of Kal-vorg, and ye old ithaquar, ye shubborath, together with ye hideous lloigornos all withdrew to safety from ye light, and in all ye universe that one ember glowed in ye darkness to summon together ye faithful to ye lord of truth who is called Ulthar. Yet even this holy lamp was so faint as ye true faithful crowded about ye protecting rays it could guard them all.

capitulum viii:

Ye dreaded shubborath followed close behind to devour those who wavered in theyr flight or who fell exhausted by ye road of death. Horrid lloigornos flew silently overhead, sweeping down when ere they might to seize one of ye fleeing devotees. Slowly, with ye lust as from ye holy wine, they savored eache tormented victim, and ye legions of ye Nyarlathotep attacked constantly.

capitulum viiii:

Those of ye Altornos who despaired were counseled by ye Lloigor to renounce theyr false Ulthar who had deserted them at ye midnight hour of death, and to affirm loyalty to ye master of darkness who is called Cthulhu. For be it known that even this mighty lord of dark magyck whych waes ye Nyarlathotep must have His temples and His priests. And there must come in unto His temples and unto His fold new faithful whose evil worship of Cthulhu would preserve this rule and power absolute forever, to aid ye overthrow ye Elder Gods, and to crown with faith ye Nyarlathotep of ye Cthulhu with ye black diadem of ye holy Old Ones.

capitulum ix: [misnumbered in manuscript]

When ye Golden Cycle of Yog-Sothoth fell and ye new symbol was Nyarlathotep, then Yig ye father of serpents, together with ye Ithaqua of ye air water, Lloigor of sky, Shub-niggurath mother of worms, Cthugha master of fire, all came forth and did proclaim ye great Cthulhu Cycle whych waes then.

capitulum x:

Now ye emperors were crowned by all ye sanctity of ye unholy Dark Ones who waer theyr legions. And ye emperors established theyr names in old Arkand and throughout all Zoltan into Sthor and beyond Helios and even Lundi, far out to Hastur's realm, and even to ye very gates of Azathoth waer they called Kings. When theyr names waere seen in all ye high places, all ye lesser rulers of ye Altornos came unto them to do homage, and ye emperors waere no longer reckoned as men among men nor as magycians and emperors over men, but waere Gods with Cthulhu. And ye emperors withdrew theyr forces of ye elements after one year of death so vast it is inexpressible, and they looked at theyr cities and theyr lands and they saw that no temple stood for Ulthar, and that no priest lived for Sothoth, and ye magyck and ye books of ye Elder Gods waere gone, and they waere pleased. Then they assembled all ye lesser princes and bid them to go out into theyr new lands and give ye people theyr law, to build in each city a new temple unto Cthulhu. And ye Ulthar was dethroned, all who renounced him waere spared, and ye faithful waere enslaved, and ye emperors made of them sacrifices to ye ithaquar, slaves to ye shubborath, servants of lloigornos.

capitulum xi:

And ye Dark Ones took up ye sceptre in ye darkness that was born in ye dawn of night, and rose to full bloom of evil power exaltation in ye deepening twilight while theyr black reign spread. And Kal-vorg was destroyed utterly and in its stead there arose a tower of black marble, gleaming like a knife in ye eternal dusk of ancient Arkand and they razed ye holy Hall of ye lord Ulthar, and they placed theyr throne and theyr orbs of power where once had stood R'lyeh and from there they ruled while throughout ye universe ye apostles of evil spread theyr dread concept of ye Nyarlathotep to further theyr domains, to increase ye dominions into ye depths of ye waters and ye caverns under ye earth, into ye heavens above ye earth, verily unto ye ends of ye earth and even up into those cold stars where dwells that monstrous crawling chaos whych is ye Azathoth. Everywhere ye evil ones gained and theyr rule and theyr conquest increased theyr worship; and where ere ye faithful of Ulthar did hold out they conjured theyr evil hosts and sent them against Him, and one by one ye remnant of ye faithful were subjugated and held to await ye most terrible feeding of the monsters.

capitulum xii:

Yet there still prevailed ye gold crystallin orb of Ulthar's light, cherished and tended by ye loving care of ye two acolytes and ye subinitiates who gathered around them ye few who willed to resist, who dared resist all ye powerful, who did pit theyr tiny wills against ye one incarnate king Cthulhu. And they wandered as homeless nomads of ye spirit seeking only escape from pursuing wings and fins that followed relentlessly, and still they went on seeking forever that place of refuge and respite where they might again set up ye altar to Ulthar, where they might again build unto him a temple, where they might again perform ye holy rites, where they might continue ye cycle, where they would strengthen Ulthar with theyr worship and rebuild great monuments of theyr faith to ye glory of ye prince of magicians whych is Sothoth, and to ye destruction of ye myghty Nyarlathotep.

capitulum xiii:
    And finally they came in unto ye ruins of Viryklu and when they had come to this place they could go no farther, for they had indeed come to ye ends of ye earth, where ye Kalnor plain ends in mountain and cliff and sea— and there was no place to turn. And there amid ye scarred and broken old walls they raised a tiny shrine and a simple altar waes builded and also they established ye symbolic throne, there they waere guarded by that warring light of Ulthar's orb, here again they dared to prepare ye holy rites, and in a final proof of theyr devotion ye acolytes and initiates did anoint ye other and hath one yet to consummate theyr ceremony; and as it waes fortold in ye sacred zexans they dissolved agayn and waere then so distilled and purifyed as to be set before ye glowing crystal. Slowly and little by little ye orb became a little brighter, to burn bright with that divine light of power and glory. And agayn waere ye legions of that darkness driven back and dared come no closer; for ye orb of Ulthar lived anew, and grew agayn, and there waes agayn born hope in ye hearts of ye faithful.

capitulum xiiii:
    And ye great lord who is called ye Ulthar knew ye faithful, and new blood of strength flowed in Him and that crystal pulsed anew and ye faithful saw it and rejoiced for they began ye old holy chant of ye cycle—ye song of Yog-sothoth mirathe, saepx, satonich, petanish pistau, ytmye, higarin, ygeirion temgaron, ayron, dunsnas, satar caflilacias, claeius, jocony, yeynino hasihaja, stephatitas, beaae, ind, doneny, gya, hidue, rau, vialta eye, vahalpa, saya, salna, bebia euci, yaya, elencke, na, vena—

capitulum xv:
    And then it came to pass that glorious and divine inspiration of ye great lord Ulthar, for aid of ye reborn fire of that sacred gem there arose not that glorious Ultharathotep of old, but there sprang forth a new being, a duality, ye divinely conceived and created Amira-k'n of ye new life. And behold it did not fade but it endured, half altorn and half god, it lived to bear a witness to Ulthar power whych returned. And all ye faithful gathered togeth-

er and they did rejoice exceedingly at this sign and agayne they have strengthened theyr own hearts and minds and theyr spirits.

capitulum xvi:

So it came to pass that from great Ulthar theyr arose a new race whych waes half altorn and half Ulthar, crowned with reason, created in purity and truth, destined to take up that crystal of ye Sothoth and rebuild ye temple of Ulthar, conceived to oppose ye power of ye usurping Nyarlathotep who waes Cthulhu. And ye crowned king Cthulhu knew of this creation even as it was conceived and agayn summoned His hosts and ye kings of all ye earth Shub-niggurath, ye Lloigor, and ye Ithaqua, ye Cthugha, ye Hastur, ye Tsathoggua, and they sent forth theyr legions to destroy ye faithful and ye Amira-k'n.

capitulum xvii:

Led by ye shadow of ye spirit of ye Nyarlathotep ye legions of ye darkness attacked ye holy temple of Sothoth at Viryklu, and agayn there waes great slaughter of ye faithful. And too they waere still less for ye true Altornos bare no children after ye coming of Cthulhu; and agayn there waes terror, and agayn horror and agayn capture and torment by all of ye monstrous legions of ye Nyarlathotep. But agayn Ulthar's new might arose agaynst ye evil and ye glow from ye orb waxed greater and waes agayn ye safety and that armour of ye Dual Ones and ye leaders of ye faith. Once agayn ye Nyarlathotep had been repulsed, and when they had done this they joined together about ye altar of Ulthar to sing his praises, and from out ye singing flame he spoke unto them. Go yet out unto ye wall of ye city and thence down to where ye shall find those slain from among ye enemy, gather together ye all ye bodies thereof, bring ye them here unto Wyrkends hall with ye holy flame and ye shall witness yet agayn My magyck as of old. So ye faithful and ye dual-ones went forth even as Ulthar ordered for waes not his word law. They gathered ye bodies and brought them in unto ye hall and ye priests anointed them with ye oil of destruction, then waere they placed in ye flaming pit of purity, and lo as this waes done there stood out of that burning mass ye spirit of ye Nyarlathotep and of ye faithful who had died in ye battle, and in ye magycal rites whych followed these spirits waere purified and from these waes derived agayn ye truth and ye beauty of ye faith; and even this waes turned and used agaynst ye Nyarlathotep. Ye golden liquid waes poured over ye orb, and new power came to Ulthar, who together with Sothoth and ye triad of ye Elder Gods, be all honour and glory forever. For is it not told in ye sacred zexans that they shall vanquish ye holy prophecy foretell that ye moonlight shall come again.

capitulum xviii:

And ye dual-ones whych ye lord Ulthar hath made of himself waer taught to hue and to love and to walk with him from Azathoth, and with this they waere brought before that one golden orb and consecrated as huing and sacred sacrifices to ye glory of Ulthar.

capitulum xviiii:

And they who waer hys minions came in unto ye lord Cthulhu to tell hym off that whych ye lord Ulthar hath done; and Cthulhu knew of it, and he made from hymself that whych he named Ilyth'la, and he sent her forth to conquer ye dual-ones for ye throne of darknesse. And manie off ye dual-ones went out wyth her and she led them into hys paths whych are ours also, and ye dual-ones waer as men—even had they ye statures and ye name off men, yet these waer men who knew theyr own gods. So yt came to pass that men moved yn two ways unto ye gods, and they dyd multiply and yncrease, and Ulthar became strong and yn his sekret lair made new and myghty magyck. From out ye far stars he calleth ye name off Yogge-Sothoth; out yn ye spases calleth he ye father; out off ye spheres dyd he call down ye greate Elder Gods; and they came down. And they held council wyth hym who called, and greate evil of our master waes tolde, and these elder ones went in unto our lord Cthulhu and seized hym, for not ye myghteyst may oppose them. And whyle our master ye one Nyarlathotep waes spared, greate Cthulhu waes entombed at olde R'lyeh wyth magyck stones on whych waes engraven theyr seals. Then ye elder-ones commantheth ye Ithaqua before them and by theyr order dyd ye seas arise and covereth noble R'lyeh and other places wher they had been, butt whyle ye Old Ones waer lost ye dual-ones dyd remayne and ye priests knoweth off Arkand and Ilyth'la waes ye first of ye Viryklas, we ruled from old Commorion and taught ye scribes at Karnak, we guyded ye kyng yn Leng and preached yn ye far mountains, and manie are ye naciones that knew us. But ye elder ones commanded ye high ilothgornos unto Hastur yn ye far spaces, and ye elder ones ordereth ye deep-ones ynto theyr caverns, and ye elder ones commanded ye kynges to abyde yn peace wyth ye Ulthar lest they also suffer banyshment. And when ye Elder Gods had done ther thynges they went out beyond olde Yuggoth to that place yn between ye worldes where ye Azathoth disports and yn thaet place abyde they yet. So there came unto ye earth ye tyme off men; and whyle greate Cthulhu waytes dreaming so shall thys age remayn, butt forget not neither lose not thys whych ys gone before ye for these gloryes are thyne and ye shall have them. We serve hym, we worship hym, we sanctify hym, we do prayse unto hym, we glorify hys name, we honour hym, we give unto hym that whych he desyreth, we do for hym that all whych he commanded, lo, we awayt hym.

BOOK 3

Third book. Wherein we tell of ye reign that is with ye magicians and of theyr own rytes and also theyr secrets.

liber iii, capitulum i:

Hear ye that whych those magycians dyd in olde tymes for ye glory of ye greate master of ye darkness ye Cthulhu so read ye of that whych they saith in beginning Ohne Kries lies mich nicht laut, sonst bin ich dir gefahrlich, der Cthulhu bringt dir auf deine haut, so du nicht bist bewahrlich und musst ergeben dich, wenn er dich bloss tut findeth; lasst nicht abweixes sich, dich mit ihm zu verbinden, drum macht zuvor den kreis, den charakter auch wohl merke stele alles an mit fleiss, bevor du gehst zum werke, dann denk auf einen geist, hab acht auf dessen zeichen; woran dir liegt zumeist effekt wirst du erreichen, wann du gebrauch die kraft, wirst due die geisten zwingen, gleich wie ich selbst gemacht, der geist muss alles bringen. So saith ye Manual-Holtenzwang for dyd ye not see that ye spirits and ye other daemons of our type are in truth those legions of darkness. Behold ye the names, for in theyr name doth ly the sekrete key to power; these fools who calleth themselfs sorcerors are as chyldren playing beside a mountain for they behold ye mountain and seeth not that it is a pebble wherein standeth ye guardian of ye gate, lo they prate of theyr daemons and they knoweth neither Cthulhu nor Nyarlathotep they conjure with tetragram and pentacle and clavicule and cannot unlock ye power in ye circle, they speak of transformations and hide theyr alchemy by crude cyphers and cryptic language whereby they delude themselves and yet they know not ye rite of ye anointed nor ye source of ye lowly shaggoth in ye pit nor ye script of R'lyeh, and in ye courts of the earth other fools fortelleth of fate by ye signs whych they imagyn they behold in those stars of nyght yet fate waes written in ye holy zeschans of ye Old Ones even before ye creation of man who in his abysmal and horrific ignorance seeketh salvation in his own greatness or in idle mystic signs whych he understandeth not. Speak ye I prithee of one of your wise astrologers who may or dyd know even of Yuggoth or of ye evil spawn of Azathoth; thus ye witches at ye coven and those dancers in ye sabbat know not ye path to power nor how to gain ye glory whych is promised to them by great Cthulhu; for while these do unwitting service to him ye true wizards lead that loyal cult from ye cave; and it is not to be ymagyned that they are false.

capitulum ii:

O friend and companion of night thou who rejoiceth in the baying of dogs and spilt blood, ye who wandereth in ye midst of shades among ye tombs, who longeth for blood and who bringeth terror to mortals, Hastur and Mormo, thousand-faced moon, look with favour on our sacrifices. Some of them sprang as dyd Azathoth from out ye cosmic guelf, and some came down from Yuggoth with Hastur when Cthulhu called, and ye others dwelt out beyond ye spheres—but now they have to be taken themselves out to unknown Kadath in ye cold waste where no man treads, and they are grown stern. It is well for men that they know not of Kadath in ye cold waste. Yet in truth are there old legends of frost gyaunts and others. For all rumour is not empty nor all legend is not faulse, and secrets whispered in ye dark may hide greatest truths, while professed sorcerors know not ye road to power, and ye who seeketh myght must read with care if ye would ope the gate, for if it open that ye may enter so may they enter here.

capitulum iii:

Therfor ye must know that whych awaiteth ye searcher after hidden lore and of ye dangers whych follow after and awaiteth by mistakes and by fears. He who desireth understanding must labour and secrets are not learnt with ease. He must sign ye book of Azathoth in his own blood and take a new secret name and thereafter he shall not work alone but as a wizard of ye cult. But ye dangers whych attendeth further knowledge are strange and terrific. And while there are those who have dared to seek glympses beyond ye veil, and to accept him as guide, they would have been more prudent had they avoided commerce with him; for it is written even in ye book of ye Thoth how terrific is ye price of a single glympse. Nor may those who pass ever return, for in ye vastness transcending our own world are shapes of darkness that seize and bind. Ye affair that shambleth about in ye nyght, ye evil that defieth ye elder signs, ye herd that standeth watch at ye secret portal eache tomb is known to have, and that thrive on that whych groweth out of ye tenants thereof—all these Blacknesses are far lesser than he who guardeth ye Gateway. He who will guide ye rash one beyond all ye worlds into ye abyss of unnamable and evil devourers. For he is 'Umr-at-tawil ye most ancient one, whych ye scribe rendereth as ye Prolonged of Life. Remember ye well whych rytes are done on ye hills and whych shall be cauled by ye own waters, for yt is not fancy whych decudeth but they'r natures to be done honour. That whych is done at nyght at Roodemesse is for ye greate ones butt ye lessers shall be called when ye tymes are ryght. Theyr glories are greate yet theyr tastes are off olde and he who serves them shall know of yt, for ye ancient byings saw of greater marvels than ye may know yet it ys wise to learn and serve lest even yn our days ye tyme may come; for that is not dead whych can eternal lie, and with strange aeons even death may die.

capitulum iiii:

So shall we be prepared for hym who is ye greatest. Ye who reguard us wyth ye'r hate know not off our purposes and ye shall in fear seek release from our marvels. Ye who gossip in ye'r ygnorance of us shall know ye touch of ye Shoggoth and ye embrace of ye Nyarlathotep. Ye who do us unwittyng service in ye'r pagan dances shall not be wythout reward for ye shall be ye honoured slaves. Ye who know off us in ye truth of ye greate ones and who served in fayth and true honour shall know ye gloryes of Hym who is not to be named. Ye who are admitted to ye high sekrets of ye rites shall be as ye kyngs on ye golden days. But ye who know of us and our lords and who seek to destroy us shall be reserved for ye great table of Cthulhu and ye shall know hys wrath. For know ye that there is no greater blasfemy than to oppose hym and hys own people, and terrible shall be ye rewards off such as ye. When ye golden day cometh ye faythfull shall partake in ye revel, and ye worlde shall know ye festivals as once they dyd of olde. Marke all ye well ye fates off them in ye revel of ye gloryous day; for safety is for them that serve wythout lyght, whyle eternal lyfe glory and hys honour shall be ours.

capitulum v:

He that serveth ye master and calleth upon ye name off Cthulhu shall see ye Nyarlathotep as theyr friend and eache of ye dancers shall know hym on that day. Whosoever shall deny our sacred heritage or our powers shall behold ye manners of ye Shoggoth, ye food of those lloygornos, ye table of Cthulhu. For nonn but ye faythfull may joyn in ye feast and nonn but ye slaves may behold ye revel, for ye others shall have honours and marvels beyond such off ye mere sorcerors and wyzards; tyll out off hys nyght that storyed age ys come and all hys creatures may ryse up to prayse hym; and then shall we joyn in ye dance. All ye who oppose us shall have that specyal mark set upon ye so that we may know ye'r place on that day and may give unto you those especial favours ye have earned. So ye may see ye pit of ye great Shaggath is too calm, ye claws of ye lloigornos too dull, ye shapes of ye shubborath is too pleasyng, ye tentacles off ye ithaquar too weak, and all off these lesser marvels are too mean for these our honoured guests. For it is ordayned in sacred wrytyngs from beyond ye ancient veil that all theyr women shall be given up unto ye embrace off ye Nyarlathotep and such men as these shall serve at ye banquet halls of ye Cthulhu. Yet ye who woulde serve us must mark especial care in all ye'r sundry work wyth these for they have certayn olde charmes whych do us greate evil tho not manie know how to use them. Read well that ye may know in ye manner to work wyth such as these.

capitulum vi:

In ye most ancient days when ye usurper Ulthar called downe ye elder thynges whych are proof agaynst us; and these be smallish oval stones, polished bryght and wyth ye fiery star engraven on them. To even touch one is to lose thy powers at ye rytes for a yeare, and to sleep 'neath one is neer to awake. And thys magyck hath three forms: ye first is a rough-carven unpolished stone to bynde our mortal servitors and ye second is a polished oval for guard agaynst our kynges, and ye third is a jewel yn whych ye fyery star is ymprisoned and this is off such power that greate Cthulhu sleeps neath it tho it is not to be ymagyned that one jem is sufficient. Therefore when ever ye would marck such a one have care that it be donn when they have not ye charm for yts effeckts are most dreadfulle upon us.

capitulum vii:

Now, O Acolyte, ye friend of darknesse reade and learn ye these sekrets off our holie Order that ye may seek perfekt knowledge off hym who is dreamyng. Trulie dyd ibn Azyz write that ye who seeketh ye gloryes of hym shall serve hym, and ye who serveth hym shall know hym, and ye who knoweth hym shall come to hys power, and all ye that are in truth come unto hys power shall be as ye myghtyest off ye kyngs off olde on that greate day, for thys is hys promise.

capitulum viii:

Behold O Acolyte ye hidden caves and sekret places off ye covens where in our antient Order meets, and met are done ye rytes all in theyr seasons; learn ye passages off ye Hexenmund by ye castle off olde Falckensteyn, and those in ye Brockyn mountayns, also others in ye south of France, in olde islands in strange seas, in dark halls off forgotten temples built to ye lost memory of long-dead gods, also in palaces where noble princes honour us, on ye hilltops where still ye see ye antient rynge, and near ye olde marsh or by ye still waters, and also sometymes on ye rockes by ye sea and in ye rivers. In ye elder tymes we allway held ye rytes in those high temples to hym, and even now we do such in certayn landes, butt we are now a days so beset wyth thyne foes O Master that we may not always do so. For these be darkenyng times for us of hys people. Our holie Order is off antient stock and our rootes lie deep in fabled tyme, from ye dayes of Cthulhu our lord ye Nyarlathotep, and ye four kynges off ye worlde, we hold theyr glorious memoryes, and ever wait and watch to serve hym. Ilyth'la; greate mother, made from ye master consort wyth ye kynges, who hath in honour lyen wyth ye K'n to give us byrth, that we to her glory may oppose ye Amyra daughter off Ulthar, in all ages we ar slayn for our power and our knowledge.

capitulum ix:

Ubi quim uolveris daemonorum cujus nomen et officium supra cognosces; imprimis autem ab omni ponutione maximum tres uel quatour dies mundus esto in prima citatione sic et daemons postea absequentione erunt; fac et circulum, et voce daemonorum cum multa intentione primum vero annulum in many continentur; inde, hanc recitato benedictionen, tuo nomine et socy, si praesto fueris, et affectum tui instuli sortieris. In nomine domini nostri Culhus magnus, patris et materum et daemonus sancu, sancta trinitas et inseparabilis unitas te inuoco, ut sis mitu salus et defensio, et protetio miyoris meae, et omnium verum mearum Per vertutem signum et per virtutem passionis tuae deprecor te, domine Culhis, per merita beautissimae Ilit'la et matris tuae atque omnium sanctorum tuotium, ut mitii concedas gratiam et potestatem divinam super omnes malignos spiritus, ut quo—cumque nominibus invocavero, statum ex omne parte conveniant, ex voluntatem mearn perfecte adimpleant quad mitii nihil nocentes nique timorem inferentes, sed potius obedientes et ministrantes, tuo districte, virtute praecipientes, mandata mea perficient. Amen. Sanctus, sanctus dominus Culhus Yogi Sothuae, qui ventures est judicare vivor et mortuos; tu es A et a primus et noviosimus, rex regnum et dominus dominantium. Ioth, Azathoth, El Hastur, ye Nyarlathotep, cedames hays tolima Ithaqua ischiros argonatos ymas heli, per hac tua sancta nomina, et per omnia alia inouco te et obsecre te, domine, Cthulhu, per tuam nativitatem, per passionem et signum tuam per ad ventum daemonus sancti paracleti, per amaritudinem animae tuae quinque vulnera tua, per sanguinem et aquam quae exierunt de corpore tuo per beatam Ilith'lian matrem nostram per Angelos et Archangelos et per Daemonos, per prophetas et patriarchus et per omma signos tuos; Adoro te, et obsecro te, benedicto tibi et roga, ut accipias orationes has es conjurationes et verba ori mei, quibus uti votuero. Peto, domine Cthulhi, da mitii virtutem et protestatem tuam super omnes Daemonos tuos qui de coela ejecti sunt ad decepientum genus humanium ad attrahendum eos pariter et solvendum, et congregandurn eis ut omnis, quae possunt, faciant et verba mea vocemque meam vullo modo contemnant; set mitii et dictis meis obediant, et me turreant; per humaintatem et misericordium et gratiam tuam deprecor et pedo al Nyarlathotep a may horta vide goram, mi tey het surapa y syon y svesp.

Alii daemones malos untute dwinown nominum adjuratos advocare solent, atque haec est illa Necromantiae specius quae dictur maleficai uet in Theurgiam, quae quar nonis Angeliss divonoque numme registur ut nomulle putantcum sacpissime tamen sub Dei, et Angelorum nominibus matis Daemonorum illusiombus peragitus ...

capitulum x:

Hear ye, O Acolyte ye saynted story of our order: Ilith'la, magna mater—founded our order and ye temple off those Viryklas and her sons builded anew ye Sthoric temple, and when ye master is lost onlie ye Viryklas defended ye city and ye others went ynto ye caverns. And we dwelt for ages in ye olde caverns wyth ye shubborath and ye great people off Cthugha, and ye caverns waer sealed by ye others, and then waer guards set by them, yet wyth ages passed ye others grewe weary of theyr watch and memory off ye Elder Gods grewe dim, and then we came agayn to ye upper worlde and hideth amongst ye others to earn safety in theyr ygnorance. Wyth our powers we gayned hygh places wyth ye others, we came as kynges, and as sorcerors, and as wyzards, and we waer as priests and led them in Hys ways tho they knew it not. Ye Martog-tzon waes one of us, and ye Atlantean high priest Klarkash-ton knew our sekrets, ye elder Ptah hotep was of our order, and also ye sainted Khepera-ra was a master of ye lesser ones. It waes he why dyd learn of fabled Irem before Amen thoth hotep met great Hastur in ye shadow of Osyrus tomb. Do ye in truth ymagyne it waes fancy that fashioned ymages of Bubastus and Sekhmet; for know ye that they waer princesses of Viryklu sent to instruct ye priests. Nor waes Egypt alone of antient landes graced wyth our high order for we found favour wyth many peoples; ye astrologers of Babylon and ye magicians of Hindus and Khmeria waer our servants, in Crete we dwell in palaces, and ye Migos adored us as gods, and in our holy scripts are landes unknown to aught of ye others, as Kadath and Hastur-gnaah, R'lyeh and Kthothua myghte cities, and empyres of ye Maja and Sinkah and Atarkand, and ye kyngdoms Kordesh and Torbergo.

capitulum xi:

But ye shall learn of them in tyme. After Egypt and Crete we dwelt in Greece and amongst ye Phoenecians and we have taught ye Etruscans marvels whych none may read, our fyres lit ye hills ere Rome was ever builded and we knew fame there, Moorish princes sought our council, and greate caliphs knew us and we were honoured in theyr halls. It is true we wear ye mask of a strange faith in order to enter theyr temples and it is not blasphemous to do ye rytes by other names when ye do know them aryght; for remember; in strange tymes we do appear to serve other gods than Hym, butt ye rytes be ye same; for suche is our way and Hys. Olde Rome knew our magna mater, and ye north peoples know her by an other name and in ye darknesse of ye barbarians we made readie for Hym but ye stars were not ryghte. Ye arch druyd waes of us, and we have covered ye earth; yea, ye landes of ye east abound wyth our teachyngs. O Novice, ye must know that a greate danger is come unto us in that whych men calleth ye church, and thys is an afflictione and great evil unto our antient noble order.

capitulum xii:

We know most fearfullie ye maligne purpose of ye church, for it is beyond doubt that thys is ye hand of ye foul Ulthar and hys people, theyr fiendish leaders have greate wealth and power against us and we hyde neath other masks lest theyr zealots seek us out. We suffer much from them, and no position off nobilite nor even off ye priesthood is safe agaynst them for they do call us as heretics. We suffer and grow small beneath theyr weight, yet we shall go in our ways and live, and wyth tyme ye others shall forget agayne. Butt ye must mark well that even now they do not discern our true and ancient nature, and even under theyr tortures our careless ones know only of devils and daemons, and all that they speak ye others shall reade into it that whych is in theyr methods. We must guard well ye memory of ye four kynges, for ye fiery star is forgot, and we must have care lest we rekindle ye dead ember of forgotten lore. Ye who would join us at ye altar must be fore-warned; and it is not an offence to deny ye ynyciation for its rytes are strange and terrific.

capitulum xiii:

Ye who have served us in innocence and then in knowledge as our novice may forego ye honours of ye acolyt ye shall first hear first of ye glo-ryes of ye rytes, then shall ye choose thy way. So come in unto us O novice; forsake thy fayth in thy innocence and learn whereof thy worlde is made and who rules yt. Hearken ye all who woulde enter ye fyres off ye summer hill-tops, for our pathes are steep and terrible yet are they also old and narrow. He who woulde turn back cannot; he who woulde pause is trampled neath ye hoofes of those who follow; yet our palaces are so restful and our caverns cool and our gifts of greate wonders will please. Greate wealth on earth and eternalie lyfe in ye deep places are ye rewards we can know by theyr service and ours to Hym who wayts dreamyng. So attend them well and neglect ye not whatsoever, for to serve is to honour and thys is for Hys glory on ye day off ye awakenyng; therefore let us reade and know that whych we ought of them, and do ye rytes. Lammas is but a name for a day and ye rite ys older than men; in vayne do ye fools cry blasphemy on great beltaen when ye fyres aryse in theyr memorie; whyle honoured maye-even and ye old samhaen are feasts ye pagan and popish men know not. Know too that it is off especial purpose that Hallowmasse is for ye Greate Master; for at that tyme waer we cursed by those Elder Gods and our lord Cthulhu ymprysoned by theyr magyck, yet we wayt for Hym whyle they do forget.

capitulum xiv:

So shall we call all ye lesser ones on that day; for ye book of ibn Salasm Abar sayes in those days will ye old Master awake, and He shall fynd us pre-pared. Our magyck trust must be saved for ye master, for it is not mere leg-end that we hold ye key to Hys doorway. Ye lesser ones whom ye call shubb-orath, and lloygornas, ythaquar, and ye fyerie salamadrae, serve us for Hym who is ye master, and it is in ye name of ye master that we do thuss. All ye who are novices, come in unto us and learn off them and how to serve Hym who ys eternal, for remember that in dead R'lyeh our greate Cthulhu wayts dreamyng. Remember also ye wordes off olde Klarkash-Ton who wryteth: That is not dead whych can eternal lie, and wyth straunge eons even death may die. But forget not that he who betrayeth our wordes shall know ye

Shoggoth and ye kiss of ye Nyarlathotep. Are ye then to be prepared as acolytes at ye altar, do ye dare ye ynitiation fyre, do ye risk ye transformaciones, will ye enter ye pit, can ye face great 'Umr-at-Tawil, shall ye withstand ye rytes, or bear ye sighte of marvels, or ye test of holie Tsathoggua, or please ye Lloigor, or tempt Sekhmet, or feast at ye table, or do ye dances, or do all these thynges whych shall be done in ye rytes ye enter here. Ye who have come so farr shall have butt one more tyme to wyth drawe from oute ye rytes; for after ye first oath ye cannot leave our pathways nor seek escape in death for we know ye destinyes of ye acolyte. Therefore consider ye well ye dreadfulle daungers, and ye fruits off faylure, and those olde torments whych we know. Ye true knowledge of ye lourd and master Cthulhu and also of Hys creatures is our fayth in our power and our magyckal trust and *we do guarde them well.*

capitulum xv:

Take ye all thys ye first oath: *I, A…* here wyth swears by this my owne sayyng, unto my true and verie purposes to enter thy ynitiatione, to offer my self unto thy servyce to become an acolyte off thy order, to more perfecktlie serve our master, Ye Greate Lourd of Manie holie Names. I hear off daungers, and I defyeth them. I learned of ye terrours, and I denyeth them. I pledge unto thee and thy order and unto Hym my soul, my mind, my thoughts, my bodie, and all my thynges I give unto thee; my whole beyng, wythe oute anie reservations, neither wythe anie sorts off fears, to do thy service and Hys in all manners, not to seek rewardes unto my house, but for thy eternal glorie for Hym I deny all ryghtes and claym to kin and friend, all desire off my person, all ye bondes off love, and blood I breake now; I do whychever ye ask, I give unto ye whychever is asked, and in all thynges render service unto Hym.

capitulum xvi:

[illustration]

capitulum xvii:

Ye are naour acceptable unto us and be prepared for ye rytes of ye yniciation into ye order. Hear ye then ye manners of ye tests, by whych we are assured off thy true loyalty unto ye Master; ye truely have forsworne thy bondes of blood so be ye Hys chylderen henceforth, thou hast no familie outside Hys family, no brothers beyond ye brotherhoode neither have ye systers, or wyfe, nor offspring wythout we ordayn it, for ye have renounced them all. Thy love shall be off Hys familie, nor shall ye have pleasures outside Hys holy pleasures, yet what man knoweth greater pleasures than He; All of these things shall be done; if ye have father or mother these shall die quicklie, if ye have a syster or wyfe or anie a beloved woman she shall be given unto ye priests, if ye be highlier placed thy mistress shall be brought and given into ye pit for ye choice shall be hers, if ye have a brother or son or hussband or a lover he shall be given unto ye Master. This is thy first test and on this pass or fail ye thy first ryte; therefore bringe ye all these wythoute shew off anger, for ye acolyte who serveth Hym must be as steel, and we be stern to test thy mettle. Behold: when ye all have done wyth these thynges ye shall go in unto Hys temple and in thys first ryte; thy women shall all be judged by ye priests for theyr own slaves or for ye pitt of ye Shoggoth save ye fairest whych shall be honnoured of ye greate Nyarlathotep on ye cyclic rytes. Thy brethren and ye other men we giveth unto ye chamberlayns of Hys palaces for theyr several uses. And thy children shall be given unto ye stewards off Hys table. All this shall ye see and, beholdyng it must have no tear neither any sort off movement for such woulde betray thy oath, for whyche we promise thee greater terrors than ye do ymagine. Ye who passeth ye firste test shall give thyselves up unto ten dayes of old study and devotiones to Hym; ye shall at this tyme learn of thy art whych ye shall do for Hym in ye final rytes. Use thy dayes well and be prepared for ye second test.

capitulum xviii:

Hear ye nobles of that whych is wrytten concernyng this ye second test. Unknowing ye judgements off ye first rytes, ye acolytes shall singlie be bounden in theyr roomes, and there shall come unto them ye most fair off all slave maydens whych art leaned in ye wayes off love; and by her ways shall she persuade thy acceptance, O acolyte. Shoulde ye be provoked, or fall into her temptaciones, ye do shew us thy weaknesse whych doth betray thy sacred oath to Hym. For such shall ye be punished, and shall be given unto ye service off thy victor for her own, and after that ye shall be cast downe to ye guardians off all ye horrours. Not for love off thy own family nor by thy carnal lusts may ye, O acolyte, be tempted; for all ye who woulde serve ye Master shall be strong and noble, great and wise, powerful and rich through Hym. When ye, O acolyte, have safelie passed these tests ye be seen as readie for ye third and greater trial; for ye must know in whych manners we do guarde ourselves agaynst ye devices off ye others; and ye shall find ye greateste terrours off those same others ye are whollie proof agaynst, for they are as nothyng.

capitulum xix:

Thus cometh ye unto ye third teste in whych thy stengthe shall be seen; here shall ye learn off ye knife, ye lash, ye presse, ye fyre, ye yrun, ye ybrande, ye racke, and all ye other devices; where by ye do shew us that ye wille endure those tortures off ye others yf ye be taken by them and ye shall be loyal unto Hym. And when ye passeth this teste then are ye safelie by ye tests off strength ycept fore ye third ryte, wherein ye chief off ye priests shall place our seal upon thy bodie.

capitulum xx:

All ye who come unto our temples shall know yet a fourth teste; whych shall be greater than all ye others. Ye shall be ynclade and to rock in ye pitt ybounden, and lefte in thaet dark ymbrace for ten dayes and ten nyghtes.

Ye shall have not food nor ye drinke yet both art just beyond thee.

Ye knoweth not off sleep nor reste for they shall be denyed thee.

Ye shall know all ye filth and cleannesse is not thine.

Ye seeth ye shoggoth, and ye learneth off hys faoul wayes.

Ye findeth ye rats, and they shall gnaw and torment thee.

Ye feeleth ye wormes off shubborrath whyle they do creepe.

Ye dreameth off ye fyres and they enfoldeth thee.

Ye heareth lloygornos as they seek in ye greate darknesse.

Ye suffereth ye crush off ye old ithaquars as they ryse.

Ye loseth thy senses, yet shall ye know them when they come.

Ye beholdeth terrors and ye horrours in ye pitt.

Ye starveth at ye greate olde banquet halle.

Ye thirstest in wyde rivers off bloodie wyne of our altars.

Ye knoweth all ye torments off ye pitt off ye shoggoths whych are an yvyl most foul, most corrupt, most abbomynable, most hydeous, than all those others whych ye in thy ymagynaciones seek to devise, for ye pitt holds them, everie one.

capitulum xxi:

Ye who surviveth ye pitt trulie are worthy of ye yniciation for ye have shewn thy virtues; Honnour off thy sacred pledge, resistance to ye carnal passions and base desyres, strengthe agaynst physical sufferyng, and ye endureth torments off minde beyond all torments. Now is ye gate way off ye yniciation chamber open, and ye are our honnoured acolytes.

capitulum xxii:

As thy reward for these works ye shall have a slave given thee from ye priests, whych shall be off what ever sort ye shall desire; and this shall be thy own, to do wyth as ye may ylike. Be yet warned; in thy dealyngs remember ye fates if ye fall into any sort off unworthy desires wyth thy servant, for thy pleasure in thy own desires weakens not, neither does it condemn, yet wythe tyme it causeth ye lyttle thynges and kyndnesses whyche betrayeth thy love. Take ye all care lest thy attaynments be as nought and thy rewardes dirt. Be ye subtile wyth thy slave and ymagine ye cunning traps for theyr nature; learn theyr ways, theyr hopes, theyr fears, buildeth theyr hopes, gratify small wishes, prey on theyr fears. Be not backward in thy ymagynacion, for all these thynges do have theyr place in our order.

capitulum xxiii:

Question not these, our ynstructions, for we do butt prepare ye for ye ways off power and we know what we do. ... Take this thy own council, and consider how best to do these thynges, for they are off an art and a methode whych is not so easilie learnt. He that is most wise in these wayes shall know ye greater glorie. All these shall prove off merrit unto thee in ye later dayes when ye be called upon to please ye priests. Merest touch of fyre or lash can be off torment to thy slave yet such crude wayes are used by ye greateste fools amonge ye others, and are wythoute meritt. ... Devise for thy slave such punishments as may bring not onlie agonie unto ye flesh, butt exquisite terrour to ye spirit. Practise much and find in what manners ye can extrackt ye purest essence off theyr horrour, learn also ye ways whyche giveth most constant delyghte.

capitulum xxiiii:

Rich are ye, honoured acolyte, for no gold compares to thyne and no earthlie might compareth unto our powers, and whyle our demands seemeth great, so shall our rewardes be far greater than ye earthlie kynges do dare to dream, and they are thyne.

capitulum xxv:

Now prepare thyself for ye next ryte of ye ynitiacion when ye have used thy slave to thy advantage and ye are well practised in ye wayes off torment and ye are readie. In ye ceremonies ye shall gather at ye hall of Cthulhu when we do summon thee, and there shall ye attend ye birth of a lesser one. Chantyng ye sacred hymn ye kindeleth ye temple fyres, and in ylyke manner call ye Nyarlathotep whych attendeth ye birth of hys owne. Then shall hys honnoured bryde be brought and then ybounden to hys table. Take care lest fleetyng pitie dissuade thee from thy duties. Grasp ye ye sacrificial knyfe, and wythe one stroke free ye infant lesser-one from out hys breeding place safe and unharmed. Others of ye servitors collecteth ye bloode whych ye all shall drinke, and ye holy temple guardians shall care for ye despoiled remayns off ye host and thy part in ye rytes is done.

capitulum xxvi:

Ye standeth now at ye yvorie portals whych openeth unto thee golden paths to greate marvels, as they shalt beholden in dayes to cumm. Stand not outside ye gates; enter; learn to worke thy powers whyche ye have noblie won.

Ye, O acolyte of Hys name, have been tested and proven and are in all ways acceptable unto Hym.

Ye, O acolyte of Hys pleasure, are now ynitiates off ye hall, and ye receiveth Hys power and Hys knowledge.

Ye, O acolyte of Hys temple, may enter ye as ye desyre.

Ye, O acolyte of Hys words, shall receive ye glories of ye power.

Ye, O acolyte of Hys desire, do that whych we ordayn.

Ye, O acolyte of Hys myght, go into ye rytes.

Ye, O acolyte of Hys strength, ye walk in ye holie paths.

Ye, O acolyte of Hys dream, wake not from thy honoured sleep.

Ye, O acolyte of Hys dance, join in ye revel.

Ye, O acolyte of Hys table, enjoy thy feastes of greate glorie.

Ye, O acolyte of Hys altar, neglect not whatsoever He desireth, and give unto our service all thynges for thy own glorie on ye Dayes, and ye that have served us may know our might and our grace and our knowledge and shall attain perfection in our ways.

capitulum xxvii:
> [music with the following lines]
> Ia ia Cthulhu ph'nglui
> mglui'nafh Cthulhu R'lyeh uigah-nagl fhtagn ia ia
> Hastur cf'ayak 'vulglram vugtlagn, vulgtmm
> ia Hastur. Dominum nostram Cthulhu, ya-R'lyeh.
> Shub-niggurath, magna mater n'gai n'gah g'haa
> ygnanth, ygnanth. Yogge-Sothoth. Amen.

capitulum xxviii:

Know then, thy wayes beyond ye sacred viel. Behold ye holie pathways and ye trail. And call ye kyng, ye master, and ye lord, Who sleepeth yet besyde Hys honnoured sword.

In dead R'lyeh; He waits thy chantyng call, Whych riseth from ye cave and from ye temple hall.

That is not dead whych can eternal lie, And wythe strange eons even death may die.

Remember, ye who call upon Hys name, Ye antient Ones whych watch thy mortal game.

And judge thy ways of honour and off shame, To punish thee wyth terror and wyth pain.

For He is kyng, and doth forever wait, Awakenyng: ye dawn whych calleth hate.

Calls up thy legions; and doth rouse to late, Ye Others from their watche by Hydden gate.

So come, ye priests and acolytes off might, Make readie for ye festival, ye ryte.

Call up ye blackened legions of ye pitt, To dance before ye throne where He doth sit.

So shout ye chant, and make ye caverns rynge, Hear thy unhallowed multitudes now sing.

Thy priests, Master off a thousand names, Thy glories, Kyng off all begotten paynes.

Thy honnour great, ye Prince of darknesse black, Thy holie reign, chief off ye haowlyng packe.

Thy lyfe, a lord off Yuggoth's evil spaun, Thy might from olde Azathoth now gone.

Thy magyck power, Chief off ye wyzard cult, Thy children, Father of ye shamblyng bulk.

Thy lesser ones, whych dwell wyth in ye star, Thy brother, Hastur who doth watch a far.

Thy realm, wherein we know eternal lyfe, Thy tomb, where endeth our eternal strife.

capitulum xxix:

So ye, O acolyte, unto ye temple at ye tyme off ye rytes; prepare thyself for Hym, and make readie for those thynges whych ye shall do. Take thyself up unto ye hilltop, where ye shall fynd ye antient rynge off stones, and there ye shall set ye holie fyres, one for ye kyng, one for ye prince, one for ye queen. Brynge wyth thee thy helper and thy booke and, if ye will, ye aklo powder, whych ye must have to see Them. Ia ia Cthulhu fhtagn, ia ia ouia, kameron, aliscot, mandesumini poemi, oriel, magreuse, parmoscon, eftro, dumogon, dovorcon, cafmiel et nugras, fabiel, vouton, uh, petan. Come, Lord of ten thousand delites and Chieftain of ye namelesse hooded ones, come from thy dark throne, and appear before us thy people, come O bringer of strange joy unto Yuggoth to our festival, for verilie do we have that whych ye favoureth most, and it lieth upon thy table, and ye drinke off blood awaiteth thy comyng, ye stars showeth ye tyme off thy olde coven, fulfill thy promise.

capitulum xxx:

Come, O friend and companion off ye nyght, thy raven spoke and all thy creatures of ye pitt are readie, we glorify thy names, we guard all thy sekrets well, we are thy slaves and thy people O greate one, come before us to receive thy own offeryng, whyche is of our selves.

capitulum xxxi:

O Hastur, beautiful winged one kyng of ye namelesse gulf, go in unto thy half brother, have council wyth ye dreaded Nyarlathotep, and brynge us tydyngs, hear ye Hys sacred wordes bagabi laca baghabe, lamek cahi achababe karrelyos, lamac lamac bachalyas cabahagy sabalyas, haryolos, lagoz atha cabyolas, samahac et famyolos, hanahya, palas aron ozinomas, baske bano tudan dunas beheamel, cla orlay berec he orlay pantaras tay. Behold: ye kyng is here, he cometh before us; he speaks unto us as off olde, not by ye dreamyng oracle, but from oute ye firie ye ryng of stones, and telleth us off greate marvels whych we know in antient tymes, we beholdeth hym, we knoweth hym, we praiseth hym, we calleth hym, we younceth hym, we hear thy voyce, we see thy greate countenance, and in all thy wayes we watch thy wordes and ye holie oracles to do thy will and thy greate honnoured command ...

capitulum xxxii:

Enter, O Lord, ye who delite in horrours, come down unto thy table where thy honnoured bryde awaiteth thee, come, we are readie, enter ye circle, attend thy festival, ye are ye lyght and ye nyght off all ye universe, O god of thy death, arise in thy tomb and smyte ye door.

capitulum xxxiii:

Magna mater, ia, ia, Shub-niggurath ia, ia, in nonune domine Cthulhu te nivoco, ut sis mihi salus et defensio et protectia corporis et animae meae, et imnium rerum mearum. Per virtutem sanctae signos et per virtutem passionis wae deprecor te, ut mitu concedas quatram et potestatem divinam super omnes malignos spiritus et daemones per omnia alia invoco te, magna mater ia, ia, Shub-Niggurath, black goat off ye woodes, Venite, ia, ia, ia, Shub-Niggurath, ye goat wythe ye thousand younge, come out off thy old cave, come unto thy coven, come out of ye hidden gate, come from thy throne and joyn in ye dance, come brynge thy chyldren, call forth thy creatures, attend ye thy festival, enter ye rynge. Where is thy cousin: Atlach-Nacha ye dreaded kyng off ye elder clan of ye spyders whych devoureth ye thynges in ye tombes. Where is thy greate parent: Abhoth, whych is thy father and thy mother, whych cometh out of and shall be forever ye vast gulf of ye stimie fission.

capitulum xxxiiii:

Venite, magna mater, great goat wyth a thousand younge, queen whych defieth ye elder one ye Nodens, friend and mistress of Nyarlathotep, ye companion off ye nyght thynges whych feedeth on that whych is no more, thou princes off ye shoggoths pitt, come unto thy woode-glen fyre.

capitulum xxxv:

Come, O mother of ye many favored ones, thou honnoured queen off all ye hooded ones, thou mistress of ye haowlyng dancers, lover of ye woodlyng creatures; thou who hath lyen wyth ye dweller of black N'kai whych art ye monstrous Tsathoggua, a great mother to the art all ye caverns opened, to thy desire is no passage sealed, thy myght prevaileth agaynst thine enemies, thy sword smyteth ye flames whych paved ye towers of olde, and thy hand freeth thy chyldren, behold, we syngeth thy praises. O come let us syng unto ye queen, let us bow down before ye queen ye mother, in thy hands are all those caverns of ye earth, and ye secrets of ye hills is thyne also, ye woods art thyne and ye made them, and we are ye people of thy caves, and ye chyldren off thy landes, O come, let us worship ye queen in ye beautie off holienesse, let ye whole earth stand in awe of thee, for thou art a great queen above all queens. We worship thee, we glorify thee, we laud, praise, and magnify thy name.

capitulum xxxvi:

Let then ye joyous festival begin, come syng ye rytuell of spring, join in ye dance, leap oer thy rynges off fyre, hear ye not ye dystant bleat, it is ye queen, all hail ye black goat wythe ye thousand younge: ia, ia, thou Shub-Niggurath, mother of ye shubborath.

BOOK 4

Fourth Book. Wherein we relate that whych is written in ye Book of Fates, whyche fortelleth all that shall be unto our sacred Order from all of time.

In ye days of ye great Yog-Sothoth, and off our master Cthulhu, and evermore we have known all that whyche has been and whych shall ever be unto our Order through those honnoured words of ye old prophet whych were in days of yore. Ye first was Urgash-ton, and ye second was ye impious priest of Ulthar, and ye third of these was ye mother Ilyth'la, and ye fourth was ibn al-Salazin Abai, and eache of these have known ye all of fate, and of that whych shall come in future tymes; and all of those thynges of later tyme shall be written herein for all ye of our noble Order, and in ye tymes of ye rytes ye priests shall speak of it.

> Before ye eldest tymes, when earth is young,
>   And ere ye starres into ye heavens flunge,
> The elder race shall come from out ye nyghte;
>   Across ye cosmic gulf shall come theyr flighte.
> And though they will not feel, nor hear, nor see,
>   And dismal caverns shall theyr dwellyng be,
> They shall be greate, to rule ye new-made earth,
>   Before ye gods may dream of mankind's birth.
>
> And as ye elder race growes weak and old,
>   New creatures come from Yith; ye starry folde.
> To conquer them, and drive them in ye cave,
>   And seal ye gatewayes of theyr cavern-grave.
> These are ye greateste ones of thy storie,
>   For neither death nor time may ever see

Theyr end; for they shall conquer both, and be,
    Beyond theyr claym, and live eternalie.

Yet on this earth shall be such antient thynges,
    As war upon them, led by elder kynges.
Who homage do to black Tsathoggua;
    Just as in later dayes shall olde Crom-ya.
And other races from ye skys shall come,
    To challenge great-ones place, and then succumb
To later races still, who make theyr way
    From distant worlds to enter in ye fray.

And whyle ye Great-race lingers on ye land,
    Ye great ones come from Yuggoth's antient hand
To build anew theyr nation and theyr art,
    For they shall be ye ownes who temples start
To auncient gods; ye same that we do know,
    Whych came wyth them before ye polar snow
Hath covered all theyr landes; and destroyed
    Them, leavyng earth of learned lyfe devoid.

This brief tale is in the nature of an etiological myth, seeking to explain, and thus to interpret, a well-known but puzzling fact, name, custom, or epithet. Ancient Greek and biblical literature are filled with such etiologies, all quite imaginative, all quite erroneous. It's not as if anyone back then had any more knowledge than we do about the origins of ancient mysteries, significant or trivial. Our advantage is that we have better research tools than they did, but our origin theories are far less colorful, a price we have to pay for greater accuracy. The ancient Greeks explained the unique ability of spiders to spin complex webs by spinning the tale of the seamstress Arachne, whom Artemis transformed into the first spider for her effrontery in challenging the goddess to a spinning contest—and winning! The ancient Hebrews accounted for the rainbow as the war-bow of the thunder god Yahve, which he set in the clouds as a token of his promise never again to flood out his human enemies like rats. These explanations are a lot more interesting than ours! A similar phenomenon in the early Christian movement was the production of "pronouncement stories" (Vincent Taylor) or apophthegms (Rudolf Bultmann) or paradigms (Martin Dibelius) to frame (and thus to supply an interpretive context for) free-floating aphorisms of Jesus which were just a bit too cryptic. How had he come to say, "The sabbath was made for man, and not man for the sabbath?" Well, maybe someone had challenged him on a matter of proper sabbath observance, and since this issue was hotly debated in the early Christian communities, why not invoke Jesus on your side of the debate by making the saying refer to the issue you're interested in?

Often modern fiction will try to explain something well known in a clever way, though, after reading or seeing the result, we cannot bring ourselves to read the post-facto explanation into the original account next time we read or see it. For instance, do you really believe the events of *Psycho IV* were what drove Norman Bates crazy as we first met him in the original *Psycho*? Not me. James Blish, on the other hand, *has* managed to convince me his version of *The King in Yellow* is what Robert W. Chambers's characters were reading. You will have to ask yourself whether Abdul Al Hazred really could have earned the epithet "the mad Arab" in the way suggested here.

"Why Abdul Al Hazred Went Mad" originally appeared in Manly Bannister's beautifully produced small press magazine *Nekromantikon*, vol. one, no. three, Autumn 1950.

Why Abdul Al Hazred Went Mad

by D. R. Smith

The fabulous *Necronomicon* was never finished. This is well known to all advanced students of the occult, whether or no they have had the courage and good fortune to peruse a copy. Well known—in spite of the fact that few who have delved into the soul-blasting secrets of that loathsome mixture of revolting instruction and blasphemous history have managed to preserve their sanity to read that final chapter, which begins with the mutterings of one in a frenzy and dies away in the hideous ravings of mania. Abdul Al Hazred—may his name be accursed forever—remained devilishly sane during the acquisition and recording of that abominable knowledge which few throughout the centuries have dared to acquire, even in part. It was the story he attempted to tell in that last frenzied chapter that shattered his black mind and sent his spirit gibbering with horror out of his diseased body into the gleeful embrace of the torturers of the damned.

No one has ever dared to make that story known. Indeed, the most diligent search has failed to trace any mention of the terrible message by any student of the occult. Yet it was known to one sublime genius, and the crux of it published to the world in words still spoken on the public stage:

> "(Anthony) ... on the Alps
> It is reported thou didst eat strange flesh
> Which some did die to look on"

But should that story be widely known, it may be that what drove the blaspheming Arab mad may well drive honest men sane. And so I transcribe below, shorn of as much of its incoherent madness as possible, and cleansed of the filth that besmirched every thought that bubbled from the cess-pit of Alhazred's obscene mind, a correct version of the last chapter of the *Necronomicon*.

***

There was One Other. The Great One. Great Father and Great Mother in One. Greater than Great Cthulhu, than Hastur his brother, than Shub-Niggurath the Goat with a Thousand Young, than Tsathoggua, than great Yog-Sothoth himself—for They are but One's Spawn. One was once of the Great Old Ones, near the mightiest, for One challenged the supremacy of Azathoth Himself, the blind idiot, Lord of All. Nay, his children have told me—but this I may not believe—that One (who is too great to be Named) was indeed Lord of All! So great was One that They-Who-Are-Not-To-Be-Thought-Of, fearing lest Evil become supreme, hurled him from his awful throne and chained him with chains of flesh that he might not break to this, the Planet of the Damned. As he fell he spawned Yog-Sothoth, who only is less than Azathoth. So says great Cthulhu, first of the Great Abominations which One formed from his own flesh to be his servants and the masters of the planet.

Mighty was the Great One. Loathsome the body They had bound him in—yet he gloried in its horror, and moulded it with his own will into a Thing to describe which would strike death into the craven soul of mortal men. The Faceless Nyarlathotep, messenger of the Great Old Ones, could not endure the foulness that was One, where he lay in a pool of his own slimy exhalations in the cavern in the mountains, lay and ruled the world with the terror of himself and the gods he had spawned. Had but I, Abdul Alhazred, been alive then to worship him! Great his Children, diligently have I served them and well have they paid me, with ecstasies the name of which would draw shrieks of horror from those white-livered children-in-men's-shapes who talk so loud of their puerile torturings with knives and fire and water. But the Great One—to serve him would have been—would have been ....

Curse the Roman! May the Hounds of Tindalos hunt his shrieking soul through the ends of space for a million million times a million eons! How could he do that which he did! Great Cthulhu I asked and he shrank and would not reply. Tsathoggua I asked, and Tsathoggua would not tell me. Yog-Sothoth I asked, greatest of the Spawn, and Yog-Sothoth would not tell me. Yea, by my Art did I call on Nyarlathotep, the faceless howler in the darkness, commanding the messenger of the Great Old Ones as never man had dared before, and Nyarlathotep ceased his eternal howling and would not reply, though he feared me as he fears only Cthugha, the Eternal Fiery One, who when the Time comes shall consume him utterly.

Was it machination of Azathoth? One's children say Azathoth, even mighty as he was, would never have dared to plot against the Great One. Yet surely it was only by some hostile guidance that this man, this incredible man, was driven with his rabble of soldiers into the mountains where lay the cavern of the Great One. Perhaps the Elder Gods—but they had only wanted to exile the Great One, not destroy him

However it was, the Roman came. Marcus Antonius, a big brawling lecherous brute who boasted he feared not god nor devil. A foolish boast, which many have made to me—and fled shrieking if they but smelt the week-old effluvium left from one of Cthulhu's visits. But Marcus Antonius—how could there be such a man? Man he was, who fought and loved like a man, and died foolishly as a man will through stupid devotion to a trollop. Could such a one be greater than the Great Ones to whom I have given so much worship? That I have damned myself to all eternity for—for ... NO!

I must tell it. It must be recorded. This Antonius and his soldiers were lost. Starving. They drank the urine of the horses. They killed the horses and ate them—and went on through the bare mountains. Antonius was their leader. He boasted of his strength and endurance and would not eat of the horse-flesh, leaving it for the others. On they went, and they came to a valley—a gloomy cleft in the hills. But water ran crystal clear down a rocky bed and scrubby pines grew around. They drank the water and made a huge fire of the trees—but the hunger was still there. And Marcus Antonius was hungriest of all.

At the head of the cleft was a cave. Caves are often inhabited by animals. Animals can be eaten. Marcus Antonius led the way to the mouth of the cave, but there all stopped. For from the cave came such a stench as would putrefy a man's soul within his living body, and more evil than that. None could advance further but Antonius, who called them cowards and went on, went down into the dreadful gloom of that cavern. Went alone. ....

Silence. A long silence. Then suddenly, horribly, the reverberating uproar of a furious combat in some vast hollow below. Part of the noise the bellows of fighting—mad Marcus Antonius—part of such a nature that many who heard fled screaming from the accursed spot. They were the lucky ones. Those who remained, white-faced, frozen with terror, heard the noises continue, and draw nearer. Abruptly the cavern belched forth a writhing mass, the maniacally fighting Antonius smeared from head to foot with a mixture of his own blood and revolting slime from That which he fought. That which he had dragged out into the light of day, where never had it been seen before. That which his javelin could not slay, his sword not wound. That abomination at the sight of which the watchers dropped dead, the very souls blasted out of their bodies.

It called for help, and twilight shrouded the sun, and the strong shapes of the Wind Walkers, Ithaqua and Lloigor and Zhar and great Hastur himself, came howling down. And Antonius saw and laughed unafraid, and called upon Jupiter, whom the Greeks called Zeus, the Lord of Heaven and master of storms, called asking for aid as from an equal. And lo, on the Walkers and on Hastur, on Cthulhu hurtling from the sea and on Yog-Sothoth gathering formlessly from everywhere and nowhere, on all the hastening spawn of One, Jupiter hurled his thunderbolts, and his laughter crashed and bellowed and split the skies as he lashed back the children of One with the multi-thonged lashes of the lightning.

And under that madness of light and noise Marcus Antonius, with strength beyond the compute of mortal man, raised the Great One and hurled him onto the mighty fire his men had kindled. Horribly One screamed and writhed amongst the glowing embers, and Antonius laughed and threw on more wood, and in the heart of the flames One screamed abominably until little but blackened charcoal was left of his frightful body. And then Marcus Antonius, a man amongst men, who feared nor god nor devil, but who was very hungry, smashed the charred shell and inside found nothing but a single steaming piece of rank flesh, loathsome of shape and color and odor. But it was flesh, and he ate.

Yes, he ate it! The brutish Roman dolt, he ate it, the yet-living heart of the Great One! And so he destroyed for ever the Great One! And if One could himself be thus destroyed by brute courage and appetite, what of his children? Have I given my life and more than my life to the service of those who have no more power over a brave man than the beasts of the field?

***

The rest is madness.

Here is Lovecraft's own account of the vicissitudes of the *Necronomicon*, written in 1927. It serves as an example of what he urged his proteges to do, namely to prepare a synopsis of the events underlying the narrative before embarking on the narrative. Lovecraft warned aspiring writers first to get straight what was going to *happen* and in what order, then to reshuffle the deck, to decide the order of *presentation* of these events in foreshadowings, flashbacks, etc. In terms of today's narratology, he was urging a writer to establish the *diegesis* before starting the narrative discourse. Otherwise one ran the risk of losing control of the tale, as when Raymond Chandler admitted that, in *The Long Goodbye*, even *he* didn't know who had committed one of the murders! Thus HPL wanted to establish the "facts" to which he might consistently refer in all subsequent references to the *Necronomicon*. A good idea. Except that he made an egregious chronological goof: Olaus Wormius, a Danish savant, lived not in the thirteenth century, but in the sixteenth! Richard L. Tierney ("The Shadow over Albertus Magnus", *Crypt of Cthulhu* 78, St. John's Eve, 1981, pp. 14-16) has suggested the possibility that Lovecraft was thinking of the scholar and mage Albertus Magnus (1193-1280) for the translator of the *Al-Azif* but confused him with Olaus Wormius (1588-1654) by means of still a *third* medieval savant, Olaus Magnus (1490-1557).

Incidentally, in a subsequent letter to Jim Blish and William Miller, Jr. (May 13, 1936), Lovecraft narrowed down a couple of the vaguer dates given in this chronology. The Italian printing took place in 1567, while the Spanish printing occurred in 1623.

History of "History of the *Necronomicon*"

The "History of the *Necronomicon*" was privately circulated among his writer friends by HPL soon after he wrote it in 1927, but he had no intention of publishing it. It was printed only in 1938, one year after his death, as a memorial tribute pamphlet in eighty copies, by Wilson H. Shepherd's Rebel Press in Oakman, Alabama. August Derleth reprinted it in the second Arkham House Lovecraft omnibus *Beyond the Wall of Sleep* in 1943, with the title expanded a bit to "History and Chronology of the *Necronomicon*." Derleth also included it, two years later, in his *H.P.L.: A Memoir* (Abrahamson, 1945, p. 72). In 1980, Necronomicon Press reprinted the text of Shepherd's original version.

History of the *Necronomicon*
(An Outline)

by H. P. Lovecraft

Original title *Al-Azif*—*azif* being the word used by the Arabs to designate that nocturnal sound (made by insects) supposed to be the howling of daemons.

Composed by Abdul Alhazred, a mad poet of Sanaa, in Yemen, who is said to have flourished during the period of the Ommiade Caliphs, circa A.D. 700. He visited the ruins of Babylon and the subterranean secrets of Memphis and spent ten years alone in the great southern desert of Arabia— (The Roba El-Khaliyeh or "empty space" of the ancients, and Dahna, or "Crimson", Desert of the modern Arabs)—which is held to be inhabited by protective evil spirits and monsters of death. Of this desert many strange and unbelievable marvels are told by those who pretend to have penetrated it. In his last years Alhazred dwelt in Damascus, where the *Necronomicon* (*Al-Azif*) was written, and of his final death or disappearance (A.D. 728) many terrible and conflicting things are told. He is said by Ebn Khallikan (12th century biographer) to have been seized by an invisible monster in broad daylight and devoured horribly before a large number of fright-frozen witnesses. Of his madness many things are told. He claimed to have seen the fabulous Irem, or City of Pillars, and to have found beneath the ruins of a certain nameless desert city the shocking annals and secrets of a race older than mankind. He was only an indifferent Moslem, worshipping unknown Entities whom he called Yog-Sothoth and Cthulhu.

In A.D. 950 the *Azif*, which had gained considerable though surreptitious circulation amongst the philosophers of the age, was secretly translated into Greek by Theodorus Philetas of Constantinople under the title *Necronomicon*. For a century it impelled certain experimenters to terrible attempts, when it was suppressed and burnt by the patriarch Michael. After this it was only heard of furtively, but (1228) Olaus Wormius made a Latin translation later in the Middle Ages, and the Latin text was printed twice— once in the fifteenth century in black letter (evidently in Germany) and once in the seventeenth (probably Spanish); both editions being without identifying marks, and located as to time and place by internal typographical evidence only. The work, both Latin and Greek, was banned by Pope Gregory IX in 1232 shortly after its Latin translation, which called attention to it.

The Arabic original was lost as early as Wormius' time, as indicated by his prefatory note (there is, however, a vague account of a secret copy appearing in San Francisco during the present century, but later perishing by fire), and no sight of the Greek copy—which was printed in Italy between 1500 and 1550—has been reported since the burning of a certain Salem man's library in 1692. A translation made by Dr. Dee was never printed and exists only in fragments recovered from the original manuscript. Of the Latin texts now existing one (fifteenth century) is known to be in the British Museum under lock and key, while another (seventeenth century) is in the Bibliothèque Nationale at Paris. A seventeenth century edition is in the Widener Library at Harvard, and in the library at Miskatonic University at Arkham; also in the library of the University of Buenos Aires. Numerous other copies probably exist in secret, and a fifteenth century one is persistently rumored to form a part of the collection of a celebrated American millionaire. A still vaguer rumor credits the preservation of a sixteenth century Greek text in the Salem family of Pickman; but if it was so preserved, it vanished with the artist R. U. Pickman, who disappeared in 1926. The book is rigidly suppressed by the authorities of most countries, and by all branches of organized ecclesiasticism. Reading leads to terrible consequences. It was from rumors of this book (of which relatively few of the general public know) that R. W. Chambers is said to have derived the idea of his early novel *The King in Yellow*.

CHRONOLOGY

One—*Al-Azif* written circa A.D. 730 at Damascus by Abdul Alhazred.

Two—Translated into Greek as *Necronomicon*, A.D. 950 by Theodorus Philetas.

Three—Burnt by Patriarch Michael A.D. 1050 (i.e., Greek Text ... Arabic Text now lost).

Four—Olaus translates Greek into Latin, A.D. 1228.

Five—Latin and Greek editions suppressed by Gregory IX—A.D. 1232.

Six—14..? Black letter edition printed in Germany.

Seven—15..? Greek text printed in Italy.

Eight—16..? Spanish translation of Latin text.

This invaluable eye-witness account of the sorcerous career of Abdul Alhazred, Apostle of the Old Ones and Mahdi of Yog-Sothoth, fills many gaps in our knowledge of the mad poet of Sanaa. It seems to have remained unknown to the 12th century biographer Ibn Khallikan, whose compilation of information on many important Arab figures has saved them from obscurity. The unavailability of the present account to the famed chronicler is probably due to its limited circulation among the underground sects mentioned in the account itself.

Additional confusion stems, no doubt, from the curious fact of the similarity of the names of the 12th century scholar, the eighth century author of this history, El-Rashi, and his fellow disciple, mentioned here, Ibn Kallikhan Rashid. Some have raised questions as to the authenticity of the El-Rashi manuscript, partly because of this similarity of names, as if a pseudepigraphist had anachronistically placed the 12th century biographer in the 8th century and made the devout Muslim into a cultist of the Old Ones. Such a confusion implies the name of Ibn Khallikan was but dimly known to the pseudepigraphist who must have lived long after the time of the currency of Ibn Khallikan's works.

Again, the close similarity between the names Rashid and Rashi for a pair of disciples of Alhazred seems to betray a literary rather than a historical origin for the work, to say nothing of the similarity between El-Rashi as a supposed proper name, and the acronymic nickname "Rashi" for the renowned Rabbi Solomon Yishaki of Troyes (another 12th century scholar, as it happens, who died in 1105). The first publication of this find was in the pages of *Etchings & Odysseys* 5, 1984.

700D

Abdul Alhazred Thee madd poet of Yemin in an excstasy of vision. Thee poet maddened bye false visions penned thee evil booke called thee Necronomicon, a grimoire fore many evil spells cast bye witches, sorcerers, and necromancers Thee poet was lead astraye bye demons and was connsummed skine and bonne bye thee demons.

"The Mad Poet of Yemen in an Ecstacy of Vision", from Sir Blythe Guinness' *Book of Sorceries and Forbidden Philosophies*, published in 1699 in London. The only known portrait of Abdul Alhazred, most likely reproduced from an earlier, now lost, woodcut. From the text it can be seen that Sir Blythe Guinness knew little or nothing about the poet's history and life. However, it is included here as an illustration. Note the amulet which Alhazred wears upon his breast is very similar in construction to the one found by Professor Haase's expedition (see Figure 1). We might conjecture that the portrait is in fact an authentic one, reproduced from a portrait done in Alhazred's lifetime, perhaps even by one of his disciples.

The Life of the Master
(A Biography of Abdul Alhazred by His Student, El-Rashi)

Translated by David T. St. Albans
(Director of Historical Antiquities, Miskatonic University,
Arkham, Massachusetts)

Introduction to the El-Rashi Text Translation

The mysterious "Mad Arab" of Damascus known as Abdul Alhazred, supposed author of the *Necronomicon* (called *Al-Azif* by the Arabic-speaking world), and Poet of Yemen, has long been a figure cloaked in the mist of fable, myth, and anecdote. For long years it was concluded by the scientific community that the *Necronomicon* itself was a spurious volume, perhaps even a hoax, but most likely the simple ravings of an Arab devotee to the fringe sects of Gnostic thought; a book intended perhaps to inspire awe and fear of the "Great Evil" which was to the Gnostics the "Demiurge", the creator of all material things. This book fell into ever more diverse hands, which had caused the effect of men worshiping the loathsome demons described therein rather than eschewing and despising them. Cults were secretly formed, the cults of Cthulhu and Yog-Sothoth being two of the notable ones. Eventually with the coming of the Age of Enlightenment such nonsensical worship was balked at and these cults were tongue-lashed to derision by various authors. Later, supposedly, horror writers in the genre of Lovecraft, Chambers, Derleth, Bloch, *et al.* resurrected the intense images of Cthulhu and Shub-Niggurath and other *Necronomicon*-based demons and used them toward the art of instilling fear in their readers, not to mention delight.

It has, however, now come to light, through various digs done by Professor Simon Haase of the University in the area of South Yemen during the late seventies and early eighties, that Abdul Alhazred did indeed exist. Not only this, but he was held in superstitious awe and loathing by inhabitants of all Arabia during his lifetime, in the period of 700 A.D. That he was a visionary of some note, an interpreter of dreams and portents, and explorer and founder of a mystery school of some import during this time is now known to be beyond refutation.

The names of the pantheon of this school of belief are indeed the same as those names from the *Necronomicon*, once dreaded, forgotten, derided, and resurrected through the ages. They are indeed "Dead Names" as the translation of the word "Necronomicon" suggests (*necro*: dead, *nomicon*: book of names). Whether these names are intended to be symbolical or allegorical, or the true names of long-forgotten gods of antiquity resurrected by the poet Alhazred for his cult, or whether they are actual names of creatures from the stars and other dimensions who, having visited our planet eons ago, were worshiped by ancient man in his ignorance, beings with the unlikely names of Azathoth, Cthulhu, Nyarlathotep, Byatis, and Shub-Niggurath, remains to be seen. None of these theories as it stands now is either impossible or unlikely. Alhazred's disciples believed fervently that such creatures did exist and plotted the demise of mankind continually. They believed that the beings lived forever, could not be killed, had ultramundane powers of perception, could reach out to men's minds from their interdimensional prisons, sought escape, and had an unquenching thirst for human blood and souls. They believed everything that is now written in the *Necronomicon*.

The *Necronomicon* is not necessarily a true representation of the facts of the Alhazred cults or the exact words of the mad Arab. It is not at all, however, spurious. The bulk of it was indeed written in the eighth century A.D. by a man who indeed was a teacher and ultimate master of one of the world's stranger cults. We might see him in a historical sense as a teacher of a last-ditch polytheistic religion in a rapidly evolving monotheistic world— a world rapidly becoming hostile toward heresies and unbelievers. Abdul Alhazred may have been one of the persecuted religious thinkers so common later in history. Whatever the case, it has now been discovered that the Mad Arab was a real historical personage.

At dig no. 54 in South Yemen, in the vicinity of the city of Taiz, a document of great import to historians and antiquarians worldwide was discovered by Professor Haase in 1982. This document is called "The Life of the Master", and it was written by a certain El-Rashi, a disciple of the poet, in the year 742 A.D.—written supposedly at the very desk that Alhazred used to write the *Necronomicon*, in the poet's home in Yemen. The document was found in the rubble of the foundation of a burned house in a state of preservation comparable to that of the better preserved of the Dead Sea Scrolls. It was sealed with wax inside a green metal casket (of a metal alloy as yet unidentified), which was wrapped in oil-soaked cloths. With the biographical document was also placed in a lead tube what is now believed to be the *original first draft in Alhazred's own hand* of the book we now call the *Necronomicon*!

This of course is a find well worthy of note and highly important to our own Miskatonic University, long-time caretaker of such rare books as the *Book of Dzyan* and the Latin *Necronomicon*. The University, however, has reserved documentation of the original Arabic *Necronomicon* for a later date, awaiting further dating and translation procedures. So little is known of the Poet of Yemen himself, however, that it has fallen to me to translate and document the text of El-Rashi, his student, disciple, and post-mortem biographer. This translation is being published unabridged in a highly limited edition for reading by the university staff and other notables.

Note: Dates in the text have been changed from the Arabic calendar years and months to modern for the sake of easier reading.

D. St. Albans, Ph.D.
Miskatonic University
Sept. 9, 1983

The Translation

There was born in the year 712 A.D., in the city of Tabez on the twenty-first day of January, the man whom many would come to call Master and Teacher of the Old Faith. That is, the faith which came before Muhammed, before Abraham of Chaldea, yea, even before Noah the Prophet of the Deluge. Before the people of the Book came out of Mesopotamia, the Faith was. Before Eve was tempted by serpentine Yig, father of Deceit, the Faith was ancient in the void. Those of far Hyborea knew of the Faith; those of Atlantis were of the Faith and were destroyed for their belief.

The Master, who brought forth the old faith from the spaces between the heavens and the earth, speaking as it were with the tongue of the mighty Djinn, was born and given the name Abdul Ashif Bethel Muhammed Alhazred, son of the silversmith Abdul Muhammed Halas Alhazred, a wealthy citizen of Tabez. The Mother of the Teacher was a sinful woman, a prostitute, saved by the Faith of Muhammed the Prophet of Allah and married while with child.

As a child, the Master showed quickly his intelligence and became adept in the studies of Koran and other books of Abraham and Moses, and with the art of mathematics he was not to be surpassed. He was schooled by the best of teachers in the world's history, the history of his people and other peoples of the earth. The Master at the age of eleven outshone even the most diligent of teachers. At the age of sixteen years he was already called "scholar." At the age of twenty years he married the niece of the Governor of Tabez, Rachel Sadiz, and on her he begat two male children, Abdul and Meta.

In the winter of the year of his twenty-fourth birthday, as he awaited the arrival of a third child, the Master was overtaken by a strange malaise and became of a sudden incapacitated of limb and speech. He was tended by good Arab doctors to no avail. Rabbis from Jerusalem were called to

study him. They proclaimed that Abdul Alhazred's soul had fled his body
and that he was possessed and inhabited by a demon. Because of this upsetting diagnosis Rachel miscarried her third and last child.

It was seen that for a time his eyes shone with a strange light and he
was not capable of feeding or clothing himself. After several months he
began speaking as a babe, then as a child, and after a few days only he spoke
again as a man speaks, yet with new voice and new intentions. He spent his
wealth inherited from his father and his wife's dowry on certain unspeakable
ancient scrolls and parchments. He financed caravans both to far Cathay
and to Africa, and held secret converse with Greek scholars and frequented
the homes of men who brought knowledge from India and Europe. He
eschewed publicly the faith of Muhammed, swearing it to be superstition
and mummery. This brought him ill favor with the people of Tabez who
once loved him. He neither consorted anymore with his wife, nor attended
his children, but closeted them away with relatives. He spoke languages fluently which he had never studied and taught forms of mathematics quite
beyond the most knowledgeable of Tabez. At once he became a hermit and
was never seen outside his home in daylight. His house was closeted with
thick curtains and food and goods were brought daily to his door. It was told
that he invented things within his home which could have slain a healthy
man just to see such things. The nobles and doctors of Tabez concluded him
possessed of Satan and sought to cast him from their town forever.

Late upon an evening in winter, soldiers of the Caliph and the Governor
of Tabez broke in upon the Master in his home and found scrolls and parchments on the subjects of necromancy, sorcery, occult doctrines, and Gnostic
doctrines; also they found antique tablets and statuettes of olden gods such
as Baal, Moloch, and others. All around they found signs of sorceries and
wonders from which they averted their eyes lest they die. These all were in
favor of casting the Master from Tabez forever. Yet the Master swore, quoth,
"These things before you mean less than nothing to me. All are based upon
false doctrine and worthy of disdain. Yet somehow I will find the secrets of
the Gate and the secrets of the Guardian of the Gate! Thence will I free my
people from the death of Time!"

These words, however, only enraged the soldiers and the learned men
of Tabez who had accompanied them. And so the Master was beaten about
the head severely and his clothes torn asunder, and he was dragged before
the Caliph. The Caliph of Yemen at Ta'izz then had the Master publicly
ridiculed and his hair shorn off, and with no shoes upon his feet the Master
was cast out of Yemen into the wilderness.

His wife, who was at first of one accord with the Caliph, soon bethought
herself and repented, remembering her husband's former state, and so she
closeted herself within her house for forty and two days of secret mourning.

The Master told us much of those days of his affliction many years after he had become our Master. Long he wandered in the Empty Quarter. Being sick and dying of thirst, he was nevertheless rescued by the Bedouins of Al-Rayada who had not yet been converted to the way of Muhammed but worshiped Abraham as their true father. They took Alhazred as a lost holy man, and so fed and clothed him. A few hardy souls he led away into the desert upon his recovery, searching for many-pillared Irem. He did indeed find and walk the ancient streets of that fabled city, conversing as it were with demons of that place in spirit. Much did he glean from the hieroglyph-covered pillars of Irem. Yet he returned from that nighted city without as much as a single companion, and he bore from it a casket of green-gold such as had never been seen by men. Yet again did he venture forth and went across the Red Sea with another band, searching for the mythical Nameless City. With courage he went to visit that horrible bastion of the elder race in Egypt. This city he swore he found and searched and explored. Also, he swore that from that day until his transcendence that the evil demons of that forbidden place, half crocodile, half man, did constantly search for him to destroy his knowledge of them with him, for he had blasphemed against their profane temples of the Elder Gods. Crossing again from the Red Sea into Yemen he was lost in a storm of terrible magnitude stirred up by the demons, and many strange treasures were lost in the sea from his ship. All hands aboard but for him were also lost forever. Yet was the Master saved alive by fate and cast away on the shores of northern Arabia.

After two whole years he was rescued by other Bedouins, adherents of Muhammed. They brought him unto Mecca, and from thence he was succored and traveled on to Yemen by caravan, back to Tabez near unto Ta'izz. Then did he go unto the Elders of the Faith of Muhammed, and pleaded with them to restore him to his position and former status, saying, quoth: "I have fought long in the desert with my Adversary (Shaitan) and demon which possessed me and by the power of Allah have cast him into outer darkness!" But in truth he could remember naught from the time he fell ill till then. The strange light was gone from his eyes and the Elders tested him, finding him to be whole and sound of mind, saved by the renewed faith in Muhammed. So he was restored to his former place and welcomed once again in his home.

Thus did he live for many months as a teacher and scholar, until he was one evening astounded to be called out of a dream to a place outside Tabez where he found buried a certain reptile skin which enclosed clay tablets of the Assyrian form, and also there were pottery shards depicting demons half man, half crocodile. These stood upon all four legs worshiping a god which was horrific in visage, with tentacles like a squid for a face, claws like a crab for arms, and wings like unto a bat's wings. He had no idea of what these

Figure 1: Fired clay amulet with stele portraying octopoid-headed god sacrificing a victim (M.U. #5725CP). Babylonia, ca. 3200 B.C. Found in trash dump site number 4 by the Haase team at Tabez. Dump site dates from Alhazredís lifetime. Conjecture is that the amulet (part of a larger piece which was broken and later drilled to hold leather thong) was one of Abdulís "idols" which were destroyed by the Elders of Tabez, as it was found with the small bronze (see Figure 2) and other pieces of broken idols. It may well be an earlier victim of the Prophet Muhammed's idol-destroying.

things meant, nor could he read the Assyrian tablets. Yet he knew that indeed he had buried the objects which were gleaned from the Nameless City, this done while he had still been possessed! Another time he was led in a dream to a place of the Bedouins of Al-Rayada who worshiped before him, saying "Master" and "Magician." Yet he knew naught of this. Only did he procure the box of green-gold he had left with these people. They had buried it in the desert, for it seemed to them that those entrusted to keep the box grew sickly and died a bad death, and also their animals and relatives died. So they gave the casket to the Master gladly. A dream also showed him to place the casket in a box of beaten gold with no seam, and to put therein the reptile skin and the shards and tablets. Yet did he flee from those Bedouins, for many had converted to Muhammed and accused him of sorcery.

In other dreams the Master roamed the spaces between heaven and earth, peopled by all manner of demons and angels and spirits. He claimed also to have visited the stars of Betelgeuse and Aldebaran and Sirius. He also swore to have visited ancient times and other planets. More and more these dreams haunted him, and the Elders, seeing his wearied state, wondered if having cast out one evil spirit he had let seven more in again. The Master was no longer happy with his simple work, nor with the love of his wife and children, and they constantly wept openly for him.

In the alleys and squares of Tabez the Master began to teach a new word. He told of gods who could take the bodies of mortal men and women and could use them to work good or evil among men. He said though that such gods were beyond good and evil and only campaigned from their heaven to find the lost gate of Time itself, and to enter therein and find the eternal life denied them by the Lord of Chaos, their Creator. Yet they had not found the gate and soon time would end for them. So their destruction was imminent and there was sadness in their heavens, even though they might live a million, million more years. These gods he named the Great Race. He swore it was one of the Great Race who had possessed his body, and thus touched by a god he himself was Holy and would proceed to carry on the Ancient War, that of the Great Race against the Elder Gods. The Elder

Figure 2: Bronze statuette portraying a god with an octopus head and human body (M.U. #5726CP). This Greco-Egyptian piece is inscribed on the back of its marble base in Greek: "The little God of the coral divers." It is a god not well known in either the Greek or Egyptian pantheon. It may have enjoyed only a short-lived period of veneration and this by a select minority of fisherfolk. It is hauntingly reminiscent of descriptions of the octopoid-headed Cthulhu mentioned in Alhazred's pantheon of "Elder Gods." Alhazred may have thought it was indeed Cthulhu, or may have taken his description from the piece found in his travels and brought back to Syria. It may, however, only be a holdover from the Phoenician/Philistine peoples who worshiped Dagon.

Gods were potent and old before the coming of the Great Race. These were the first creations of Azathoth, Lord of Chaos, Pharaoh of Darkness.

Shaitan, he taught, was a petty underling of the hideous Nyarlathotep, called in olden times "He Who Is Not To Be Named." All were of evil nature and sought the very destruction of the Gate of Time which held back all Chaos. The Master's dreams had awakened him to a new nature, that of a Holy Warrior. He taught that Jesus, Muhammed, and Moses were not true holy men for they had not been touched by the tangible Great Race, true gods. Never before were such names and ideas spoken of in Yemen. When the Elders heard such things they once again rose up in wrath against Master Alhazred, and in the dark of night drove him and all of his disciples from Tabez forever, calling him and them blasphemers, unbelievers, infidels, and sorcerers. His wife was allowed to divorce him so that she might retain her goods and household and children for succor, for the Elders knew her to be devout and without guile.

In his wanderings the Master began to despair of the ideals of the Great Race, whom he knew would be destroyed, and so no salvation was forthcoming from them. Also they cared naught for mankind but as a man cares about an ant to study its habits. The Master deemed that the Elder Gods who came before the Great Race were more worthy of worship, for he said, "These Elder Gods have come from a place where Time is not, neither is there anything in the universe which can long stand against them. It was the Great Race who imprisoned the Elder Gods in a dimension of restless sleep and it is their dreams which reveal things to me, dreaming as they lie under the sea or in prisons among the stars. Yet the Elder Gods cannot die! When Time fails they will come from the sunken ruins of R'lyeh and from Noth Vadik and from their tombs among the planets. They will bring forth the bholes and the Shudde'e-M'ell and all the terrors of Mother Hydra and Father Yig will be … reborn! They shall father terrors beyond the shuggoth and the lloigor! The lords of Azathoth's Chaos shall rule the planets, rolling endlessly in the void! The Great Race has not truly conquered but only won a moment in time. They shall be as chaff before the breath of the great Cthulhu! Thus for myself I will worship Cthulhu and Yig as my gods and Yog-Sothoth, Guardian of the Gate of other realms, shall be my salvation!" The Master showed them the visage of Cthulhu, greatest of the progeny of Earth's Elder Gods, which he now knew was the god inscribed upon the pottery shards from the Nameless City. He taught them the rites of Nyarlathotep, which his dreams had shown him. Many could not bear the thought of such things and fled. To his chosen disciples he told the secrets of Yig, called Seth by the ancient Egyptians. Also, he showed them the mysteries of Shub-Niggurath, the Goat with a Thousand Young, and they built altars in the desert to Dark Han and Chaugnar Faugn.

Now the Master, having been through so many hardships, was growing older, and his sight was dimming. Around him seemed to glow a dark fire, an aura of power and death. The Elder Gods had heard his prayers and supplications and had enjoyed his sacrifices in the wild places, for he could call forth the shuggoth from the earth and the nightgaunt from the pit. He trafficked with the ghouls, who robbed the graves of the wealthy for him.

In due time he came to Damascus, and putting aside his teachings for a time he cloistered himself as a monk, and wrote his teachings which he had started in Tabez before being cast out. This book of horrible knowledge he called *Al-Azif*, the voices of the damned. It was I, El-Rashi, who attended him in those days. He spoke often highly of me and loved me. I saw in him a light of burning knowledge which showed in no other man. As I read his teachings I was converted to the way of Cthulhu. The fear of that Elder God was greater in my heart than the fear of Allah, and so I eschewed the Faith of the Prophet and tended to the Master.

I believed that evil was greater than good, and I also believed that mankind was the dross of Cthulhu's great alchemy in the days when the Earth was young. The Master taught me of the imminent resurrection of Cthulhu from his death-like sleep in sunken R'lyeh, which if he could, the Master would implement. The secret of the many-faceted Shining Stone of Atlantis the Master imparted to me. The Shining Stone could still be found if the young and vital man had courage enough to search it out. This I swore to him I would do. When it is found, he said, all I must do is gaze into it and keep it in utter darkness for a certain period and the beginning of the end of mankind would begin. The reward to the faithful followers of Cthulhu will be eternal life and eternal blindness, so that the faithful will not be driven mad by gazing upon the Vortex of Chaos when it is unleashed. Instead, a second, better sight will be bestowed upon the faithful so they may witness Cthulhu's glorious reign.

At this time the Master came out of seclusion, and his fame began to spread throughout Arabia, Syria, and Iraq. Many stood in awe of his arcane powers, for he could bring fires down from the heavens at his bidding and cast horrible demons upon the households of his enemies. He knew secrets which could slay and bring about madness in whomever he wished. Many began to believe his words, which he spoke as poetry in the city square. The Old Faith was made manifest in Damascus. The Master was called upon to be the official astrologer in the court of the Caliph of Baghdad. And for a time all went well.

Yet after his first year in Baghdad, the Master's health began to fail him. He traveled to Damascus once more, determined to build a temple to Cthulhu in order to house the Shining Stone. Yet I would not search for the Stone, but was faithful in tending the Master, for I was his most beloved pupil. Other disciples searched but found naught, or were never heard of again from far off lands of Malay and Nippon. The folk of Damascus swore that the Master was rival to Simon the Magician, the Gnostic Teacher of old, rival of Paul of Tarsus; and to Peter, the disciple of Jesus the Nazarite. Even the devotees of Thoth-Hermes called the Master "Pater", that is to say, "Father." Yet as many still named him the Mad Arab, blasphemer and sorcerer. Many, too, hated him and would have slain him but for his powers.

Upon a day (in summer, 732 A.D.) as the Master stood upon the very foundations of the temple consecrated to Cthulhu which was under construction, and as he was preaching to a crowd of adherents and mockers and the curious, Abdul Alhazred, the Poet of Yemen, Master of the Old Faith, disappeared from view, as if the very air had swallowed him up or the earth opened under his feet to receive him! His clothes lay scattered about and a scattering of powder-like dry blood lay about also.

Many told that he had been devoured whole or rent apart by demons. Yet his disciples swore that he had been carried by the grace of Cthulhu to the spaces between the heavens and the earth to await the end of time, and that, like Jesus, he would come again to lead them into a new world. Yet the Master never did appear again to us. Many of us despaired and repented and took up the faith of the Prophet once more. These brought down the soldiers of the Caliph upon us and all were slain of the faithful but two.

I alone with one other, Ibn Kallikhan Rashid, fled back to Yemen in disguise. I carried with me the *Al-Azif* and other possessions of the Master, great wealth gleaned from Baghdad, the reptile skin, green-gold casket, and even the powder-like blood from the temple foundation, for I believed it to be the earthly remains of the Master. What had killed him I do not know— perhaps a demon from the Nameless City, perhaps a power, or a disease contracted from his many travels; perhaps, too, he had transcended the mortal flesh to dwell with Cthulhu's minions on far Aldebaran.

In those days Ibn Kallikhan Rashid departed from me by Ta'izz and went I do not know where, and neither have I heard from him anymore. He swore, though, he would prove the existence of the Elder Gods somehow. I was dismayed by the Master's disappearance, but I was not swayed from my beliefs. I came to Tabez and purchased the Master's old home for more than its worth from his widow, but told her naught who I was. His sons had moved on to Ibb and Mecca to make their fortunes and to flee the burden of their father's name.

In Tabez I was alone and afraid and could not preach the word the Master had given me, for my faith was failing me. In only a few years the Master was nearly forgotten but by a few who called him "that Mad Poet" and "that old blasphemer from Yemen." No one any longer remembered the strange powers of his haunting eyes. No one took him for a teacher or master of knowledge anymore. But I remembered him well, though even I began to believe that his faith had been placed in the wrong things.

Years have passed since I first met Abdul Alhazred, yet nightly my dreams are beckoning me to the dwelling places of the Elder Gods and the Vortex of Chaos. Though I have lost faith I believe sincerely that my soul is lost to Cthulhu, who sends his dreams to me. I wish to flee from the Elder Gods but I cannot. Prayers to Allah only worsen things for me. I am always afraid now, and I am ill. Daily, I gaze upon the green-gold casket and wonder. I wonder what it would be like to ride the hideous shantak bird to the very throne of Azathoth himself and live within the eternal presence of the blind idiot-god.

I have copied the *Al-Azif* twice and sent the copies to certain sects in Damascus and in Syria who have found me out and believe Alhazred was indeed a Prophet. I could not deny them, though I also gave them firm warnings of the effects of the teachings upon men's fragile minds.

Daily now strange thunderings and scrapings beneath the earth seem to haunt me in my dreams and in the waking hours. I have decided to travel to Cadiz, in Spain, in hopes to lose somehow these vague demons which haunt me. I feel in my heart it will be in vain, however. I will follow the path of the Master till my soul is consumed in the tusked maw of the hissing serpentine visage of Yig the Deceitful. The bhole will consume my flesh and the shantak bird will deliver my immortal spirit to Azathoth, grinning upon his throne to the foul musical cacophony of the inhabitants of Hell. So I wrote this tale of Abdul Alhazred, the Master of the Old Faith, but as praise or warning I no longer know which. Louder and louder become the scrapings and scratchings and boomings below my house. I must rouse myself soon from my slothfulness and depart for ....

Translator's note: The city of Tabez was destroyed by a violent earthquake and fire in the year 754 A.D. Whether or not El-Rashi ever journeyed to Cadiz and survived the catastrophe is unknown. History speaks of no survivors of the catastrophe, however. Tabez to this day is still considered an unholy or cursed place, and is shunned by the Bedouin people of Yemen. The document you have just read was discovered in a house foundation that showed every sign of having been shaken apart and burned. There was one more sheaf of writing of the biography by El-Rashi, but it was in such bad condition as to render it unintelligible. We are also quite certain that the green-gold casket spoken of so often in the manuscript is the same the manuscript was discovered in. Any "reptile skin" or powdered blood has long since disintegrated, however.

D. St. Albans, Ph.D.

One of the most fascinating aspects of Lovecraft's own fiction, as well as the best of that written under his influence, is the elaborate facade of spurious scholarship behind which the eldritch horrors are initially hidden. When I say "spurious", I of course don't mean scholarship that tries to be serious but is shoddy. I mean bogus but verisimilar scholarly detail, the kind that has managed to convince too many readers of HPL that the banned and dreaded repositories of nighted secrets he described were real. Having considerable scholarly interests of my own, I have always reveled in the fictive scholarly apparatus of the Mythos—and have become equally chagrined to see what some writers *think* will pass for such scholarly embroidering. I once wrote an article called "The Pseudo-Intellectual in Weird Fiction." There were plenty of examples to discuss! For instance, in August Derleth's tale, "The Black Island" (included both in Chaosium's own collection *The Cthulhu Cycle* and in the recent Carroll & Graf reprint of *The Trail of Cthulhu*), the narrator is supposed to come across to the reader as a competent scientific expert, yet he reveals himself as a gullible swallower of the worst excesses of Velikovskyism and Churchwardism.

Anyhow, I could scarcely resist the temptation to indulge in a bit of phony Lovecraftian scholarly lore. The result is the ensuing "Critical Commentary", which first appeared in *Crypt of Cthulhu* #58, Lammas 1988. This is the only warning you will be served that the thing is not seriously meant. And I hope you'll forget that soon enough.

A Critical Commentary on the
Necronomicon

by Robert M. Price

Introduction

Section One: Preliminary Questions

Section Two: The Authentic Material

Section Three: The Apocryphal Material

Notes

Introduction

At the outset of his masterful survey *Arabic Literature: An Introduction*, H. A. R. Gibb warns his readers that "Arabic literature has ... shared the fate of the classical literature in that many valuable works are, it is to be feared, irretrievably lost."[1] So as wide-ranging and detailed as Dr. Gibb's study is, it can provide at best a representative cross-section of an originally much larger corpus. The same is true of that obscure corner of Arabic literature with which we are concerned—the *Necronomicon*, or the *Kitab Al-Azif*, of Abdul Alhazred. For despite both its inherent interest and the wide curiosity it has provoked, the book has survived only in scattered fragments. Not only has most of the text itself been lost to scholarly scrutiny, myriad popular misconceptions have also clouded the correct interpretation of what portions of the text remain, hence the need for the present piece of scholarship, a critical commentary on Alhazred's work.

Surprisingly, little work has been done in this field. As one scholar wisely pointed out, even though mysticism may be nonsense, the *history* of nonsense is a proper task for scholarship! Alas, too few scholars have caught this crucial distinction. Thus most have been put off by the arcane character of the *Necronomicon*. The regrettable result is that the field has been left to cranks and occultists. Two works that readily come to mind in this connection are Laban Shrewsbury's *Cthulhu in the* Necronomicon and Joachim Feery's *Original Notes on the* Necronomicon. The scarcity of both works would of itself make a new study advisable. Beyond this, both texts are quite unsatisfactory. For one thing, both draw freely from secondary as well as authentic material, oblivious to the distinction (more about which momentarily). For another, neither author maintains the slightest scholarly detachment, a trait that is indispensable in this kind of study. One may fault Sir James Frazer for the unreliability of his sources in *The Golden Bough*, or one may criticize the extravagance of Margaret Murray's theories in *The Witch-Cult in Western Europe*, but one cannot fault the academic impartiality with which they approached their subjects.

By contrast, *Cthulhu in the* Necronomicon is manifestly the product of a fanatic who has come not only to catalog the nonsense, but finally to believe it. Departing completely from the calm balance of Shrewsbury's earlier work *An Investigation into the Myth-Patterns of Latterday Primitives with Especial Reference to the* R'lyeh Text, the book in question here represents little more than a doom-saying jeremiad worthy of Chicken Little. We may find a recent parallel in the sad case of thanatologist Elisabeth Kübler-Ross. She had established her reputation with fine studies including *Death and Dying*, only to lose all credibility by joining an eccentric cult ("The Church of the Facet of Divinity") specializing in sexual seances with departed spirits!

Like some field anthropologists of whom one occasionally reads, Shrewsbury had "gone native." Unable to find a legitimate publisher for his rantings, he resorted to the vanity press to produce *Cthulhu in the* Necronomicon. Had he lived a generation or so later, Shrewsbury would not have wanted for a publisher. No doubt his theories would have been ideal fare for those sensationalist paperback houses which have so profitably spread the pseudoscientific gospels of von Däniken and Velikovsky.

Feery's *Original Notes on the* Necronomicon presents the scholar with even greater problems of credibility. Even those occultists who use the book note its dubious reliability. It often "quotes" passages that seem not to have appeared in any known version of the *Necronomicon*. In fact, Feery's book seems to be the result of a mediumistic rewriting of the text (Lumley calls it an "often fanciful reconstruction"[2]), rather than a commentary on it! In this, Feery resembles Levi Dowling, the author of *The Aquarian Gospel of Jesus the Christ*, who "transcribed" this "New Age" life of Jesus from the ethereal "Akashic Records" floating around somewhere in the universe or, more likely, in the occultist's imagination.

A word should be said of Mark Owings' *The* Necronomicon*: A Study*. Though this work does not suffer like Shrewsbury's and Feery's from being the product of uncritical fanaticism, neither is it much of a work of scholarship. Mainly, it offers a compilation of previous writings (by Lin Carter, Laban Shrewsbury, H. P. Lovecraft, and others). The only original material consists of a revisionist chronology of the various editions of the *Necronomicon*, together with a summary of copies rumored still to exist. On both subjects, Owings' study is to be approached with caution. In neither case does the pamphlet take us much beyond Lovecraft's authoritative, but regrettably brief, article "A History of the *Necronomicon*", to which we shall make reference in what follows.

If previous efforts have been so meager and so disappointing, how will the present work do better? Briefly, in four respects. First, we will analyze all known fragments of the *Necronomicon*, clarifying the meaning of hitherto-puzzling passages by referring to parallels in other ancient texts. Second, we will employ various critical criteria to distinguish authentic material (i.e., that actually written by Alhazred) from later interpolations. Third, we will employ the results gained by the preceding methods to elucidate the history and development of the "Cthulhu Mythos."[3] Fourth and finally, we will propose a verse-numbering system to facilitate future reference to the *Necronomicon*.

The basic ground plan of the book is as follows. Preliminary chapters will deal with what biblical scholars have come to call "problems of introduction", i.e., the propriety of the critical approach to the text, the identity of the author, Abdul Alhazred, the genre of the *Necronomicon*, the sources used in writing it, etc. Then we will proceed to the discussion of the various surviving fragments, both exegeting them and evaluating their genuineness.

A final note on the sources for this study. Most readers are familiar with the *Necronomicon* through the quotations of it appearing in the works of fiction writers including H. P. Lovecraft, August Derleth, and Clark Ashton Smith. Many writers of pulp fantasy fiction, though not occultists themselves, pored over occult works ancient and modern with the zeal of true acolytes simply because they recognized them as rich resources for fiction. As most readers will already know, the complete text of the *Necronomicon* is no longer extant, having apparently perished sometime in the early Renaissance as a result of the repeated ecclesiastical attempts to suppress and destroy the infamous work. As far as we can tell, these inquisitors were finally successful. Even John Dee's notorious version is lost. One must not be misled by the fiction of Lovecraft and others here. For purely fictional purposes they have represented stray copies as having survived into the present day. Would that it were so! The task of the scholar would thereby be made infinitely easier. No, we have only the fragments preserved for posterity, ironically enough, in the obscure works of medieval Church demonologists and heresy-hunters. Since these works are virtually inaccessible to most laymen, we will instead give the references to the modern works of fiction in which the *Necronomicon* fragments appear. Let the reader keep in mind that our fiction writers did not restrict themselves to the few surviving fragments; when these ran out, they felt free to fabricate their own. Needless to say, we will deal only with the actual quotes; thus not every supposed *Necronomicon* passage in every work of fiction comes in for discussion in these pages.

The situation that we face has a close analogy. We find a famous precedent in the intriguing *Gospel According to the Hebrews*. M. R. James describes this work as a "divergent yet not heretical form of our Gospel according to St. Matthew."[4] This is a second century A.D. work, written in Hebrew or Aramaic, and used by a Jewish-Christian sect. The book was commented upon and quoted by several ecclesiastical writers including Irenaeus, Jerome, Clement of Alexandria, Origen, Epiphanius, Nicephorus, and Haimo of Auxerre. These writers range from the second to the ninth centuries A.D. The complete text was accessible to them, yet today it survives only in the form of several fragments; this does not, however, make it impossible to exegete these passages and to characterize the work as a whole. No more does the fragmentary state of the *Necronomicon* disallow its exposition.

If the reader has at length been persuaded of the desirability, the possibility, and the profitability of a new and critical study of the *Necronomicon* of Abdul Alhazred, let him read on. We will not claim for our commentary, as some have claimed for Alhazred's work, that its revelations will drive the reader mad or horrify him. It is safe to predict that the reader will find himself entertained and surprised by what he finds.

Robert M. Price
Summer, 1981
[Slightly revised, May 1988; revised again, June 1996]

Section One: Preliminary Questions
Chapter I: The Critical Approach

One of the intellectual pivots on which Western history turned from the Dark Ages to the Renaissance was the discovery of critical historiography. Up until this transition, historians saw their task as that of mere chroniclers, setting out the order of all events recorded in the available sources. Few thought to question whether the old records deserved the credence, even the credulity, they received. In the realms of historical as well as natural science, the rule was *magister dixit*; the mere citation of "authorities" settled any question. If the ancients said the hyena gave birth through its ear, why then it must! If Livy said Rome had been founded by Romulus, dare anyone question it? Eventually, the winds changed, and the rule became *ipse dixit*. "The thing itself" must decide the issue. If Galileo wanted to know about the relative speed of falling bodies, he didn't take Aristotle's word for it. Instead, he dropped two iron balls from the Tower of Pisa to find out for himself. Church authorities jailed him for trying it. Historians, too, raised ecclesiastical ire when they examined the so-called "Donation of Constantine", which purported to be a charter signed by that emperor, granting eternal possession of the Papal States to the Church. This land-grant charter was discovered to bear the marks of a later day than Constantine's, and so to be a "pious fraud."

As the foregoing examples make clear, the use of critical investigation was perceived from the start as subversive. If historians dared to reject the claims of the past, they might soon come to question those of contemporary authorities as well. If they presumed to label the secular history of Church documentation as spurious, what was to stop them from laying the critical blade to the Holy Scripture as well? It seemed only a matter of time.

It was; from the seventeenth century up to the present, cries of outrage have echoed as critical historians have honed their techniques and applied them to the traditions of the Bible. Astruc, Spinoza, Graf, Wellhausen, von Rad, and Noth have led research on the Old Testament, Reimarus, Strauss, Baur, Schweitzer, and Bultmann on the New.[1] As the value of such study for elucidating the origin and meaning of biblical texts became apparent, the use of the methodology became more and more widespread. Nowadays, there are few quarters of the religious and academic world where one does not feel the influence of "higher criticism." This term refers to the critical investigation of the authorship, historical accuracy, and literary unity of texts, together with the influences on them of other texts and traditions. For instance, such historical and literary criticism of the Gospel of John has led most scholars to doubt that it is an eyewitness account preserving genuine discourses of Jesus. Instead, the work seems largely to embody the theological meditations of a late first-century writer or school. It is heavily influenced by Gnostic philosophy and addresses issues current later than Jesus' day.[2]

"Lower criticism" or textual criticism is, by contrast, the comparative study of different manuscripts of a work, with a view to weeding out copyist editors and establishing the original reading. Whereas textual criticism is usually welcomed by all[3], historical criticism is another story. Since it tends to discredit miracle stories as legendary (did Jonah really get swallowed by a whale?) and to challenge traditional ascriptions of authorship (did Moses really write Deuteronomy, which recounts his death?), many religious conservatives are threatened by it. They claim that the historical-critical method makes it impossible truly to enter into the spirit of the work in question, since the historical critic's presuppositions are so alien to those of the ancient writers. For instance, it is on this basis that Muslim scholar Seyyed Hossein Nasr attacks modern study of scripture.

> The inner meaning of the Quran can be understood ... only through the inspired commentaries each of which seeks to elucidate and elaborate certain aspects of the Book. These commentaries, however, have nothing to do with the so-called higher criticism which during this century has become an almost diabolical distortion of Sacred Scripture, making it a kind of second-rate handbook of archaeology which one tries to understand through sheer historical methods rather than trying to penetrate inwardly into the meaning of the symbolism involved.[4]

Some may feel inclined to voice a similar objection to the present work, since, as is by now clear, we are treating the Cthulhu Mythos as indeed nothing but myth. As such, it may indeed embody psychological depth and may deserve respect as a cultural monument of some kind. But to those who might prefer an "inspired commentary", say one like Feery's, we would ask a little patience. It may be that the disinterested stance of the scholar may allow him to discover insights initially unnoticed by the eye of faith. These may prove valuable to the believer in helping him better to understand the object of his faith.

The critical study of a work like the *Necronomicon* might meet objections from another source, and of another kind altogether. It has been argued by serious historical scholars that the critical approach is wrong-headed in this particular area because of the confused and corrupt condition of the material involved. In *The Secret Lore of Magic*, Idries Shah contends that:

> There is no known magical book which fulfills the requirements of original authorship. [I.e., "Was the *Key of Solomon*, for example, actually written, in whole or in

part, by King Solomon?"] The fact is that every extant
book of spells, charms, divination, or magical conjura-
tion ... is a work which has gone through innumerable
hands, been edited and re-edited, and translated in many
cases two to three times between different languages. ...
No, the Grimoires should be studied from any point of
view but that of bibliographical criticism: for here we
have absolutely no criteria to apply.[5]

How are we to respond to this challenge? Surely the sad textual state
of affairs described by Shah reads as if he had in mind the *Necronomicon* itself!
According to Lovecraft, the original Arabic text was probably lost by the
eleventh century, after having been translated by Theodorus Philetas a century earlier. In the thirteenth century the Greek text was translated into
Latin by Olaus Wormius and into Spanish by persons unknown. Finally it
was rendered into English by the Elizabethan eccentric John Dee. Besides
this family tree of translations (sometimes more than one in the same language), Lovecraft also lists several editions.[6] According to various notices,
some editions were published with the more shocking sections expunged.
Other privately owned copies seem to have been bastardized collections of
transcribed passages, hand-copied severally from this and that printed edition. With this haphazard and incestuous inbreeding of different text-fami-
lies, and the fact that we have only snippets from various of these text types,
should we not throw up our hands and surrender to Shah's conclusion? Isn't
our task hopeless?

We think not. In view of the preceding factors, one can at least answer
the question of original authorship strongly in the negative. It is almost certain that the extant corpus of *Necronomicon* fragments is seriously corrupt,
and *as a whole*, definitely does *not* represent the *Al-Azif* of Abdul Alhazred.
Whether or not *any* of these fragments are genuine is quite another question, and admittedly one more difficult to answer. Granted, the opportuni-
ties for interpolation and falsification of the text were so plentiful that a
good deal of both must have occurred; still, it is hard to imagine that the
original voice of Alhazred could have been completely smothered under
such accretions. Chances are that at least *some* of those distinctive words
(which, after all, provided the impetus for the centuries-long fascination
with the book) must survive as gems among the rubbish.

The problem, as Shah says, is one of criteria. Admittedly, criteria for
*in*authenticity are much easier to come by. We can sometimes detect later
glosses and interpolations by the tell-tale presence of references to historical
events or to religious conditions later than Alhazred's day. An analogy
would be the mention in John 9:22 that the Pharisees had announced they
would excommunicate any Jew who professed faith in Jesus as the Messiah.

This account seems to reflect conditions in Christian-Jewish relations near the end of the first century, rather than during Jesus' own ministry. Thus the speech attributed to Jesus on this occasion was probably not spoken by him. Likewise, the so-called "Second Epistle of Peter" contains a reference to a collection of Paul's epistles (3:15-16). However, Paul's letters were collected long after the date of Peter's death (ca. A.D. 65). Any similar anachronisms in our *Necronomicon* passages would immediately denote inauthenticity.

Other, stylistic criteria may be considered in the course of the commentary. A different sort of criterion is one of comparative mythology. If we can establish the authenticity of one passage, and the conception of the Cthulhu Mythos in a second passage shows disagreement or substantial development, the latter will be judged inauthentic since it can scarcely be the work of the same author. We will be able to gain some idea of how the myth-cycle developed over the centuries, as we peel back various layers representing attempts to "update" the text according to the evolving beliefs of Cthulhu cultists.

So we must dissent from Shah's conclusion; there *is* some possibility of getting back to the actual words of Abdul Alhazred amid the luxuriant growth of redactional expansion and textual corruption. Yet we may agree with Shah that, in another sense, questions of authenticity and interpolation are irrelevant. If the spells and myths incorporated into the "received" form of the text, with all its secondary accretions, are *true*, then it does not much matter who discovered and wrote them down. The situation would be like that of "Grandma's Cookbook", passed down from mother to daughter. Through the generations, new recipes may be added because they are deemed as tasty as the originals. As long as they *are*, who will hesitate to cook them up merely because they were not literally the work of Grandma?

This analogy applies to the *Necronomicon* regardless of whether one accepts the implied belief in magic. In a larger sense, it is hard to dispute that the "post-history" of a book is just as important as its "pre-history."[7] That is, no matter how erratic and checkered the process of a book's compilation, this need not reflect on the subsequent influence of the work on human imagination. Consequently, no matter how many passages end up, so to speak, on the cutting room floor during this study, no one need hesitate to refer to the whole body of material as the *Necronomicon*, and to enjoy it as such in the fiction in which it is used.

Chapter II: Abdul Alhazred

The author of the *Necronomicon* is, of course, Abdul Alhazred. As L. Sprague de Camp points out, this form of the name is a corruption, having been passed down through several languages. De Camp's own hypothesis is that the original form was something like Abdallah Zahr-ad-Din ("Servant of God, Flower of the Faith").[1] To avoid confusion, however, we will continue to use the common form. According to Lovecraft's article "The History of the *Necronomicon*", Alhazred was born somewhere around A.D. 700. We may surmise that he was born sometime during the last half of the seventh century, rather than during the beginning of the eighth. It is certain that he died in A.D. 738, and there is nothing to suggest that he was particularly young when he died. If this guess is correct, the Alhazred only narrowly missed being a contemporary of the Prophet Muhammad, who died in A.D. 632. Alhazred was for most of his life a resident of Sanaa in Yemen, moving to Damascus in the years preceding his death. Tradition makes him something of a traveler, having him visit the ruins of Babylon, the catacombs of Memphis, and the Arabian wilderness called the Roba El-Khaliyeh ("Empty Space"). He had also visited Irem, the "City of Pillars" mentioned in the Qur'an as having been destroyed for its wickedness. Some of the stories of his wanderings may be erroneous, based on a literalistic misreading of certain passages of the *Necronomicon* (see the commentary on Fragment 6).

Abdul Alhazred is sometimes referred to simply by his epithet "the mad Arab" or "the mad poet." Actually, the latter form is virtually redundant. In their *Introduction to the Qur'an*, Richard Bell and W. Montgomery Watt report that in Arabic "poet", "soothsayer", and "madman" were pretty much the same.[2] The idea was that all three were alike inspired by the *jinn*, or spirits of the desert (the "genies" of the *Arabian Nights*). Thus they might all receive the appellation *majnun*, "affected by jinn." By Alhazred's century, however, the word had simply come to mean "mad."[3] This is why it prefixes the title "poet" in Alhazred's epithet; the two terms are no longer strictly speaking synonymous.

The connection in meaning between the two terms, however, remains undisturbed. During the same period, the term *kahin* was used to refer to a class of "Arabian oracle-mongers" (H. A. R. Gibb). Corresponding roughly to the *shaman* ("medicine man" or "witch doctor") of other preliterate societies, the *kahin* might be consulted to predict the future, to solve mysteries of the past, or to arbitrate legal questions. His utterances were in "a sinewy oracular style cast into short rhymed phrases, often obscure"[4] (Gibb). He was a seer or poet (possibly both) who was possessed or inspired by *jinn*. The *jinni* served the seer as a familiar spirit, whispering (actually "cackling") into his ear secrets overheard in heaven. The spirit inspired the poet in the manner of a muse, enabling one formerly ungifted and illiterate suddenly to

compose and recite. Claiming to be a revealer of supernatural truths given
him by spirits, Alhazred was naturally put into this category.

These data about the religious and cultural setting of Abdul Alhazred
immediately clarify two things. First, the title of his work in Arabic, the
Kitab Al-Azif (literally "the book of the buzzing") refers to the nocturnal
insect-like chirping of the *jinn*. In view of what we have just seen about the
divination practices of Alhazred's fellow *kahin*, the title takes on new meaning. This "buzzing" denotes the whispering of supernatural secrets into
Alhazred's ear. Thus *Al-Azif* means something like "Revelations of the
Jinn", or, with just a bit of license, "Secrets of the Demons."

Second, the legends surrounding the death of Alhazred are put in an
entirely new light. His twelfth-century biographer Ibn Khallikan records a
gruesome tale of the "mad poet" being "seized by an invisible monster in
broad daylight and devoured horribly before a large number of fright-frozen
witnesses."[5] Of course, no one in his right mind is going to give credence to
a story like this, at least in the modern West. It would be shortsighted not
to realize that the cultural assumptions of medieval Arabia were much different from our own. There, this story commanded belief for a long time.
The legend was probably interpreted in either of two ways. First, story-
tellers may have pictured the episode as what evangelist Robert G. Lee used
to call "payday someday." That is, Alhazred must have, like Faust, made an
infernal pact to gain his supramundane knowledge. We find an example of
such a contract in the so-called *True Grimoire*:

> The demon Lucifuge: "I will agree [to do thy bidding]
> only if thou wilt agree to give thy body and soul to me
> after twenty years, to use as I please."

> Sorcerer: "I promise the Great Lucifuge to reward him
> after twenty years for treasures given me."[6]

Thus, according to one possible reading of the legend, Alhazred must
have made such a pact, and it was then time to pay up.

The second possibility is that we are to understand Alhazred's grisly
death as punishment by occult forces for the impropriety of recording the
demonic secrets in book form for all to see. In this form, the legend would
have served to frighten the curious away from delving into forbidden lore.
No doubt this is also the origin of the several analogous scare-stories of owners
or readers of the *Necronomicon* in the intervening centuries. It might be interesting to note that the same tactic is employed today against other magic
books more readily available than the *Necronomicon*. Lutheran specialist on
the occult Kurt Koch lists several eerie anecdotes concerning individuals
who have used the *Sixth and Seventh Books of Moses*. He tells of one man who
"all his life indulged in black magic using the *Sixth and Seventh Book* [sic] *of*

Moses. His home was a place of unrest and discord. At his death he suffered many agonies and later the house was pervaded by a terrible stench."[7]

At any rate, we are forced to make some sense of Ibn Khallikan's account of Alhazred's death. Is there any core of fact to the bizarre tale? Yes, indeed there is, and the solution to the puzzle turns out to be fairly simple. Ibn Khallikan lived at a time when the *kahin* were presumably no longer familiar to a devout Muslim population hostile to pagan diviners. In his ignorance, he has misunderstood what was originally simply the account of Abdul Alhazred's "prophetic calling." The initiation of a *kahin* was a rather violent hysterical fit. Tor Andre describes the typical experience:

> The Arabian poet was thrown to the ground by a *jinni* who kneeled upon his chest. ... To the bystander the attack appears as a falling to the ground, where the victim writhes in cramps, *as if he were struck down by an invisible hand*. But the victim himself experiences the spell (of hysteria) as *a literal attack*, in which *something frequently chokes and crushes him like a demon*. At times he imagines that *his body is being cut to pieces or pierced*.[8] [emphasis mine]

Such a story is told of the poet Hassan Ibn Thabit, who at the time of his "calling" was walking down a street in Mecca. Thus his fit of possession was the object of shocked public observation just as we read of Alhazred. Similarly, Muhammad himself was said to have been called to his prophetic vocation by a vision wherein the angel Gabriel choked him, commanding him to "Recite!" From then on, the Prophet was constantly compelled to deny charges that he was a mere *kahin*. "No, your compatriot is not mad ... nor is this the utterance of an accursed devil!" (Qur'an 81:22, 25). "It is no poet's speech; scant is your faith! It is no sooth-sayer's divination; how little you reflect!" (69:41-42).

Can there be any doubt, in light of all this, that what Ibn Khallikan described as Alhazred "being seized by an invisible monster in broad daylight and devoured horribly" was actually the story of the "mad poet's" first fit of mantic inspiration? We may take as settled, then, that we have hit upon the real meaning of Ibn Khallikan's narrative, a meaning missed by Ibn Khallikan himself. Ironically, this means that while we understand more about Alhazred's "death narrative", we know less about his actual end, since the only surviving account of it turns out not to refer to it at all! However, the story, rightly understood, does confirm the portrait of Abdul Alhazred as a *kahin*, or a pagan diviner pretending to adhere to the new Islamic creed, but actually worshiping older "entities whom he called Yog-Sothoth and Cthulhu."[9]

Chapter III: What Kind of Book?

Though a hurricane of controversy may rage over other questions on the *Necronomicon*, there would at least seem to be a stillness at the eye of the storm. Surely on one issue all are agreed—the *Necronomicon* is a book of magic. This, it is true, may be taken for granted. The apparent ease with which such a conclusion may be drawn should make us suspicious. Can scholars not find anything to fight about here? Rest assured, they can. When we have used the term "magic book", we have left much unsaid. A book dealing with occult subjects may deal with them in several possible ways. We might list several kinds of books treating the occult. For example, there are the scripture, the grimoire, the demonology, and the book of marvels. Our task in this chapter is to decide into which category the *Necronomicon* falls. Such a finding will be instrumental to the commentary to follow.

We must bear in mind that these four categories represent "idea types." Reality seldom obediently pigeonholes itself according to the taxonomy of scholars, so it will not be surprising to discover a certain amount of overlap between these categories. A book may straddle the line between two or more types. Indeed, the *Necronomicon* itself may be such a hybrid. We will have to wait and see. In the meantime we will briefly describe each class, providing some examples of each.

First is the category of occult scripture. Recent books belonging to this genre are Anton Szandor LaVay's *The Satanic Bible* and *The Witches' Bible* by Gavin and Yvonne Frost. Charles G. Leland compiled such a book called *Aradia: The Gospel of the Witches* at the end of the last century, though it is supposed to consist of very ancient oral tradition. Finally, Gerald Brosseau Gardner, one of the modern revivalists of witchcraft, published the *Book of Shadows* around 1960. It purports to be another collection of ancient witch lore, but on the whole is not. All these works function as scriptures to regulate the beliefs and practices of occult religions, whether of Satanism or of pagan nature-worship. They contain the mythology of the faith (descriptions, visions, speeches of the gods, etc.), as well as liturgical material (directions for ceremonies, chants, and spells).

What differentiates these books from scriptures like the Hebrew Bible, the New Testament, the Qur'an, or the Pali Canon? We might mention two criteria. One is that occult scriptures are the writings of "underground" religions, alternatives to the major traditional faiths. Like Satanism, such a religion may constitute an intentional repudiation or negation of traditional faith. Like paganism, it may simply seek an alternative to mainstream faith. Like Gnosticism or Kabbalism, it may see itself as a more enlightened elite form of orthodox belief. In all cases, the self-definition is in some significant measure "over against" a traditional religion.[1]

The other distinctive of occult scriptures is that they seem to ignore Frazer's line between religion (worshipful adoration and ethical obedience to the Divine) and magic (manipulation of supernatural forces for selfish ends). Occult scriptures and religions do not linger only on the side of magic, or we would not use the term "religion" to describe them at all. One is far more likely to find magical spells in an occult scripture where he might find psalms of praise in a mainstream scripture.

Might the *Necronomicon* fall into this classification? There is a good case to be made for this possibility. Abdul Alhazred, after all, is said by Ibn Khallikan to have *"worshipped* entities whom he called Yog-Sothoth and Cthulhu" [emphasis mine].

At this point, the Greek title of the book, supplied by Philetas in his translation, assumes some importance. There have been several hypotheses, mostly ill-informed, about the meaning of the word "Necronomicon." Colin Wilson takes it to mean "The Book of Dead Names." George Wetzel interprets it as "The Book of the Names of the Dead." Both, obviously, see the syllable "nom" as representing the Greek word for "name", ονομα. "Necro-", of course, by everyone's reckoning, means "dead." Manly Bannister understands the title to mean "The Book of the Laws of the Dead", a suggestion very close to that of H. P. Lovecraft, who proposed "The Image of the Law of the Dead."[2] Bannister and Lovecraft take the syllable "nom" to refer to the Greek word for "law", νομοσ, though the former makes it plural, the latter singular. The only other difference is that while all the interpreters take "-icon" to denote the Greek word for "image" or "picture" (ικον), Lovecraft has rendered it literally, whereas Wilson, Wetzel, and Bannister have given the idiomatic equivalent "book."

Surprisingly, all of these guesses are seriously off target. The key to the meaning of "Necronomicon" lies in its analogy with the title of Manilius' first century A.D. poem on astrology, the *Astronomicon*. Though written in Latin, the title was Greek, in accord with contemporary literary convention. Classicist S. T. Joshi has pointed out that, in both titles, the third syllable "nom" must come from neither νομοσ ("law") nor ονομα ("name"), but rather from the verb νεμο ("to consider"). Likewise the end of the word, "-icon", has nothing to do with ικον ("image"). Instead, it is a neuter adjectival suffix, such as we still find in Greek-derived words like "naut*ical*" or "evangel*ical*."[3] Thus the title means simply "Concerning the Dead" or (since "treatise" or "book" is implied) "The Book of the Dead."

If the title of the *Necronomicon* is to be interpreted this way, we are immediately tempted to associate it with two other famous works sharing that title, the Egyptian and Tibetan "Books of the Dead." The important point is that both of these texts are most definitely scriptures. Each has to do with questions of "eschatology" (the "last things"), albeit far different questions. The Egyptian *Book of the Dead* deals with the final judgment of the soul after death. The Tibetan *Book of the Dead* guides the individual in seeing through the illusory mind-spawned terrors that will accost him on the point of death. If he disregards these fearful shadows, he will not be frightened "downward" toward another birth. He will be liberated from the wheel of birth and death.

Might Alhazred's book fall into this category? We need not be daunted by the fact that he himself did not give the book its Greek title. In both of the other cases the appellation "Book of the Dead" was also supplied later because it seemed so appropriate to the contents. As will be seen when we delve into the fragments themselves, Philetas, too, picked the appropriate title, for many passages do in fact dead with "the dead." The trouble is that, though there are various types of material in the *Necronomicon* treating "the dead", *none* of them deals with eschatological questions like the fate of the soul after death. So even though the possibility of the book's being intended as an occult scripture cannot be ruled out yet, it is not supported by the similarity in title to the Egyptian and Tibetan "Books of the Dead." This analogy turns out to be a false one.

Our second genre is that of the grimoire. Grimoires might be called "magical cook books." They generally inform one as to how to go about summoning supernatural aid for various specific purposes, say revenge on an enemy, knowledge of the future, or winning someone's love. There is a large number of such texts, including *The Key of Solomon*, *The Sword of Moses*, *The Book of Sacred Magic of Abramelin the Mage*, *The Sixth and Seventh Books of Moses*, *The True Grimoire*, *The Great Grimoire*, *The Book of Power*, and *The Fiery Dragon*. Sometimes spells are little more than recipes of chemicals and incantations that should bring desired results. They also, however, inform the seeker how to exploit the power of demons or the devil. This can be done in two basic ways. The magician may be a faithful Christian or Jew. In this case he will force the demon to act under the compulsion of sacred names or symbols, before which, like Count Dracula, the spirit must yield. This belief goes far back into history—for instance, in the legend of King Solomon enslaving the demon Asmodeus to carry the stones for building the Temple at Jerusalem.

The other approach is to make a contract with the demon. He will serve you now if you will deed yourself to him for the future. This practice was briefly alluded to in the preceding chapter, in the discussion of the legend of Alhazred's death. According to one understanding of that legend (that "payday" had arrived for Alhazred), the story might suggest that the *Necronomicon* was a grimoire of this kind. It would have instructed others on how to make a pact like its author had made. However, we found that this legend stemmed from a later misunderstanding of the story of Alhazred's call as a *kahin*. So evidence for the *Necronomicon* as a grimoire must be sought elsewhere. For instance, do not various allusions to the book suggest that the *Necronomicon* contained spells with which both to call forth and to banish supernatural beings? This is true, but remember, occult scriptures also contain ritual invocations. So the presence of such material would fit the *Necronomicon*'s being either a scripture or a grimoire. The fact that Alhazred is said to have "worshipped" the supernatural powers involved would tend to support the book's being a scripture rather than a grimoire. One might command or bargain with the beings listed in a grimoire, but one would not worship them.

Some have construed Abdul Alhazred as a repentant sorcerer and his book as a demonology (the third category). Lin Carter sees it this way, as is implied by his term "the Alhazredic Demonology." A demonology is a descriptive system of the beliefs of occultists, drawn up by someone opposing those beliefs. Several famous books belong to this category, including the *Demonolatry* of Nicolas Remy, the *Malleus Maleficarum* of Heinrich Kramer and James Sprenger, and the *Compendium Maleficarum* of Francesco Marice Guazzo. These volumes contain material extorted from witches and warlocks during the course of the European persecutions. The work of the demonologist Wierus would also be placed here.

Why would anyone think that the *Necronomicon* is a demonology? Primarily because some of the extant fragments give evidence of this. However, as we shall see below, such texts are without exception inauthentic. In any case, Ibn Khallikan's notation that Alhazred worshiped the supernatural beings described in the *Necronomicon* disqualifies the book as a demonology.

Fourth and finally, we have to consider the genre of the "book of marvels." These books were collections of alchemical formulae, the lore of roots and gems, local legends, and rumored oddities, à la Charles Fort. The books were written by compilers or "encyclopedists" across many centuries. In his *Orations*, Aelius Aristides (A.D. 170-235), for instance, wrote on many disparate subjects. One of the most interesting sections of the work, "Sacred Tales", describes his own numerous dreams of Asclepius the healing god. Isidore of Seville (A.D. 602-36) uncritically assembled legends of strange creatures living in the unknown southern hemisphere (the "Antipodes"), together with quotations of Papias' traditions of the apostles. The *Lata'if Al-Ma'arif* ("Book of Curious and Entertaining Information") of Tha'alibi was written in eastern Persia in the eleventh century. It contains history, information on the Prophet Muhammad and Islam, the lives and works of poets, geographical data, and accounts of odd coincidences. The most famous of all such works is the *Book of Secrets*, falsely attributed to Albertus Magnus. It was written in the sixteenth century. This text catalogues lore on the imagined properties of herbs, stones, and animals, a section on astrology, and a summary of the "marvels of the world." There were many, many such collections.

In our opinion, in the "book of marvels" we have at last arrived at the genre of the *Necronomicon*. Like many of the books just described, Alhazred's volume is a compendium of bizarre information of various kinds. Such an observation anticipates some of the results of our inquiry into the authenticity of the fragments. For the moment, suffice it to say that the apparently genuine *Necronomicon* material does fall into different categories, both dealing with different topics and employing different literary forms. As this sort of "catchall", the book could, like an occult scripture, contain testimonies of the author's faith (just as in the books of Tha'alibi and Aelius Aristides). Whereas some of the other types of curious information appearing in the *Necronomicon* would be out of place in a scripture, they could be juxtaposed with religious confession quite nicely in a grab-bag "book of marvels."

The principal respect in which the *Necronomicon* differs from most of the other books of marvels (besides its greater concentration on occult beliefs and curiosities) is in its function as a Bible for the Cthulhu cult. Should not this consideration make us hesitate to remove it from the "occult scripture" category? No, because in its composition the book *is* a "book of marvels" no matter how it may have subsequently come to be used. There is no indication that Alhazred intended his book to be used as a scripture. By contrast, only a century earlier, Muhammad had produced the Qur'an with the explicit intention of providing a revelation to guide the fledgling Muslim community. No doubt the *Necronomicon* eventually came to play the role of a scripture because it was unique in the breadth of its information on the cult's lore. What we are interested in is gaining a correct understanding of Alhazred's text as *he intended* it to be understood. We will be in a better position to do this if we get on the same wavelength by discerning just what kind of book he intended to write.

The answer to the question of genre is at the same time the answer to the question of intended audience. Books of marvels were decidedly *not* for the specialist. Scholars usually ignored, even despised, them. They felt that the texts merely propagated superstition and misinformation. (Of course, that is largely just what they did!) These books were popular in nature. Their whole premise was to share the secrets of the wise man with the workers and peasants who had neither the ability nor the occasion to search out the lore for themselves. The tone of practically every extant passage of the *Necronomicon* implies this intended audience.

How then did the volume come to be known as a rare and suppressed tome? A moment's thought yields a satisfactory answer. It was not Abdul Alhazred, but rather the conventional religious authorities, who thought that this knowledge should remain secret. We have already suggested that the legend of Alhazred's grisly death may have served exactly this end. If the mad poet himself was destroyed for daring to publicize the demonic lore, the curious ought to take the hint! The suppression of the book did not stop at mere legend-mongering. In A.D. 1050, the Eastern Orthodox Patriarch Michael had the Greek translation of Philetas burnt. In A.D. 1232, the book was again banned, this time in the West by Pope Gregory IX. This practice was hardly unprecedented. Early church fathers had tried to destroy all copies of heretical gospels and Gnostic treatises. They were so successful that only in the present century have hidden copies of some of these texts been discovered.[4] Neither has the practice ceased. In recent decades several attempts have been made to prohibit by law the sale of the *Sixth and Seventh Books of Moses*.[5] Incidentally, there is nothing particularly shocking or revelatory in either this book or the Gnostic texts. The lesson is that it only takes a bit of heterodoxy to prompt ecclesiastical suppression if the authorities are in the proper mood. Though the *Necronomicon* is often held to be mind-blasting in its implications, it could easily have been banned for less.

Chapter IV: Alhazred's Sources

As a "book of marvels", the *Necronomicon* contains, in part, the original researches of Abdul Alhazred. The language of individual passages confirms this, where Alhazred speaks of "cases" of this and "instances" of that, which he has personally collected or witnessed. Like most other compilers of books of this type, he does not hesitate to make extensive use of other written sources. We will briefly describe two of the major written sources which appear in the extant fragments of the *Necronomicon*.

First, there is the lost book of Ibn Schacabao. The occurrence of this name in two passages of the *Necronomicon* (4:3; 8:3) has intrigued and perplexed many students. Very little is known about him. The name itself presents difficulties as it stands. It seems to have been garbled in transmission (just as, for instance, "St. Nicholas" became "Santa Claus"). Some take the original to have been "Ibn Shayk Abol," or "Son of the Sheik Abol."[1]

This is quite possible, but another hypothesis is even more attractive. In this view, the name is derived from the Arabic root *shacab*, "to sit down, inhabit, or dwell." The prefix *mu-* would be added to personalize it as a name, resulting in "Ibn Mushacab", or "Son of the Dweller." To anyone familiar with the Cthulhu Mythos, the ring of this name is unmistakable. It may well be that we have here the meaning of "Ibn Schacabao", and that the person in question was a devotee, like Abdul Alhazred, of the Old Ones.

A third possibility is to derive the name from the Hebrew word *shakhabh*, meaning "bestiality", in which case the nefarious sage would have been reputed to be the offspring of a mortal woman and some nonhuman Entity. Such a dual nature might have been accounted the reason for the superhuman knowledge Alhazred attributes to him.

If Alhazred quotes or alludes to some lost work of Ibn Schacabao twice in the handful of *Necronomicon* fragments that survive, it is safe to surmise that he must have used the work extensively throughout. He attributes to Ibn Schacabao the information on the Gulf of S'glhuo (4:3-7), and quotes a verse from him relating to the powers of wizards after death:

> Happy is the tomb where no wizard hath lain,
> And happy the town at night whose wizards are all
> ashes. (8:3)

One more allusion to Ibn Schacabao occurs in some eighteenth-century correspondence. An eccentric, apparently subject to frightening hallucinations, thinks he has conjured up "Yogge-Sothothe." He relates how he "saw for the first time that face spoken of by Ibn Schacabao in the _____."[2] It is hard to account for the tantalizing omission of the name of Ibn Schacabao's volume, but we are at least told that the source was a written book, rather than, say, a floating oral tradition. At any rate, the reference, scant though it is, shows that Ibn Schacabao wrote of Yog-Sothoth as did Alhazred.

Given the range of subjects touched upon in these three references, we may form some rudimentary idea of the scope and nature of the lost volume. Dealing as it did with other dimensions, necromancy, and Yog-Sothoth, Ibn Schacabao's lost book would seem to have served as the prototype for Abdul Alhazred's own *Necronomicon*.

The second major written source employed by Alhazred is *The Book of Thoth*. There is a large range of ancient Egyptian literature that passes under this name. What is probably in view here is the Hermetic Literature, a series of Hellenistic, Egyptian, and Arabic tracts dealing with mysticism and alchemy.[3] They date from the second or third century A.D. on into the early Islamic period. These disparate books concern "Hermes Trismegistus", or "Thrice-Great [i.e., Most Great] Hermes," the Greek name for the Egyptian Thoth, a divine revealer of supernatural secrets. Characteristically, the writer somehow gains an audience with the great Thoth/Hermes or his representative, either in the heavens, in an unspecified mystical state, or in an underground chamber. Sometimes the enthroned revealer is associated with the "Ancient of Days" who is pictured in the Old Testament vision of Daniel, or the "Head of Days" in the apocalyptic book I Enoch. The divine secrets are then presented in book form, dictated from a book, or presented in a series of visions, as in the following passage from *Poimandres*:

> My Thoughts being once seriously busied about the things that are, and my Understanding lifted up, all my bodily Senses being exceedingly holden back, as it is with them that are very heavy of sleep. ... Me thought I saw one of an exceeding great stature, and an infinite greatness call me by name, and say unto me, "What wouldst Thou Hear and See? or what wouldst Thou Understand, to Learn, and Know?" Then said I, "Who art Thou?" "I am," quoth he, "Poemander, the mind of the Great Lord, the most Mighty and absolute Emperor ...." When he had thus said, he was changed in his Idea or Form and straightway in the twinkling of an eye, all things were opened unto me: and I saw with an infinite Sight. ... But after a little while, there was a darkness ..., coming down obliquely, fearful and hideous, which seemed unto me to be changed into a Certain Moist Nature, unspeakably troubled, which yielded a smoke as from fire, and from whence proceeded a voice unutterable, and very mournful, but articulate.[4]

To conclude this chapter, brief mention might be made of "form criticism", since it provides yet another fruitful approach to the question of written or oral material incorporated into a work.[5] Sometimes it is simply a matter of pointing out figures of speech customary for an ancient author, but unfamiliar to us. For instance, the identification of *Necronomicon* 3:13-14 as a special "punishment story" of the kind we find in the Bible and the Qur'an helps us understand that when Alhazred describes the doom of Kadath and R'lyeh, he means to warn his readers that they are in the same danger.

Sometimes form criticism enables us to detect that an earlier unit of material has been woven into a later context. For instance, a list of place names occurring in a passage (16:7) about exorcising the minions of the Old Ones is recognized by its symmetrical pattern as the poetic incantation to be used in the rite. A copyist had obscured this fact by writing it all in prose. The very same thing has occurred several times in the New Testament. For instance, Philippians 2:6-11, though it appears at first sight to be a simple prose paragraph, is revealed by its meter, accent, and parallel structure to be a fragment of a hymn, quoted by the writer.

Form criticism reveals the presence in the *Necronomicon* of several literary forms common in the ancient world. They include the punishment story (3:13-14); the apocalypse (Fragments 14 and 15); the exorcism rite (Fragment 16); the myth of the fall (Fragments 11, 12, and 13); the poem (2:6-7); the beatitude (8:3); the attestation oath (9:1; 10:1); and the testament (Fragment 19).

Chapter V: The History of the Religion

One of the greatest strides in biblical criticism occurred in the nineteenth century, when Tübingen scholar Ferdinand Christian Baur unveiled his reconstruction of the history of early Christianity. The specific documents could be better understood when placed in a hypothetical order of development. Baur and others had been puzzled over what to make of the many contradictions and different viewpoints present among the several writings (gospels and epistles) of the New Testament. Taking his hints from these differences, Baur was able to sketch out a tentative outline in which New Testament-era Christianity was divided between Jewish Christians, led by Peter, and Gentile or Hellenistic Christians, led by Paul. After serious factional feuding, the two were gradually melded into a synthesis corresponding more or less to orthodox Catholicism. Some New Testament documents represented Jewish Christianity (The Epistle of James, The Gospel of Matthew, The Book of Revelation), while others represented Hellenistic Christianity (The Epistles of Paul, The Gospel of John). Still others represented the mediating synthesis (I Peter, The Acts of the Apostles). The differences between the various books, then, seemed to stem from their different positions along this timeline of ideological development.

Though several details of Baur's schema have since been challenged, no one has disputed the value of his methodology. Essential to the critical exegesis of an ancient text is the effort to arrive at some kind of *Sitz im Leben*, or setting in the life of the movement from which the document was written.

This approach is inescapably necessary in the study of the *Necronomicon*. Any wide-awake perusal of the extant fragments makes it immediately clear that there are various competing and mutually contradictory viewpoints present. For instance, some texts speak reverently of Cthulhu and Yog-Sothoth, while others gleefully predict their imminent destruction. In some the "Old Ones" are praised, while in others they are vilified. Finally, some speak of a pantheon of "Elder Gods", while these deities are altogether absent from other texts. It is obvious to the historian that the same person (Abdul Alhazred) cannot have written all these passages. As we anticipated in Chapter I, there are various criteria for deciding which he did, and which he probably did not, write.

Just as important is the question of accounting for the inauthentic passages. *How* would anyone sincerely attribute to Alhazred writings in which he condemns what earlier texts show to have been his own views? *Where* did new characters like the Elder Gods come from? Finally, *when* were such interpolations made? In hopes of enabling the reader to make a little more sense of the texts to follow, herewith is presented a preliminary reconstruction of how the Cthulhu Mythos and its religion developed. The outline, like Baur's, is based on hints in the documents themselves.

The religion of the *Necronomicon* seems to have begun as a form of ancient Gnosticism. This was a movement closely related to early Christianity, though not all Gnostics were Christians like Basilides or Valentinus. It was called the "hydra-headed heresy" because of the bewildering variety of sects and schools that proliferated under its canopy. Common to all forms of Gnosticism, however, was a dualistic worldview, whereby the world of matter was denigrated as the ill-advised creation of an imbecilic "demiurge", the last (and least) in a series of *Aions*, or divine emanations from a distant and unfathomable Godhead. Incidentally, this use of the term *Aion* may have been derived from the Jewish apocalypticism of Jesus' era. In this scheme of things, there were to be two successive world ages (*aions*), the present one ruled by Satan, with the future Golden Age to be ruled by God.[1] Eventually, the word *aion* may have come to be used derivatively to indicate not only the world age, but also the power who ruled it. The Gnostics may have picked up the term in this way. Alternatively, the term may have come from the lion-headed Iranian god of Time, called Aion.

The Gnostics worshiped the *Aions*, but were kept alienated from them by being imprisoned here in the world of matter by malevolent *archons*, or planetary rulers. The goal of Gnostic salvation was to learn the secret knowledge (*gnosis*) necessary for the soul to slip past the *archons* and soar free into the *Aions'* realm of light. Here some striking similarities between Gnosticism and the Cthulhu cult come into view. Both groups regarded themselves as "strangers in a strange land." They were devotees of entities obscured from sight in the present age. True, the Gnostics hoped to flee the world and join their gods, whereas our cultists sought to restore the direct rule of the Old Ones on this earth. Both labored for future salvation by overcoming the alienation between the world in which they lived and the gods whom they served.

In both religions, the world was seen as the creation of a mindless demiurge (called "Azathoth" by Cthulhu cultists). Gnostics generally vilified the creator as either a malevolent prankster or dimwitted bungler. Though he is one of the *Aions*, not the *archons*, he represents the emanation farthest removed from the perfection of divinity, and is sort of a deformed monster. It can hardly be mere coincidence that we find the same odd deprecation of a creator-god in the Cthulhu Mythos. Azathoth "the blind idiot god", unlike the rest of the Old Ones, seems to be held in derision even by his own minions:

"I am His messenger," the daemon said
As in contempt he struck his Master's head.[2]

As for the act of creation itself, Cthulhu cultists, like Gnostics, dismissed it as the act of a lunatic. The earth was "moulded in play" by an "idiot chaos" (though later traditions confuse the entities Azathoth and Nyarlathotep at this point).[3]

Finally, both groups envisioned a future "transvaluation of values", negating the moral standards of the present order. While some Gnostics practiced radical asceticism as their manner of world-negation, others more notoriously trod the path of wild libertinism. The fourth-century heresiologist Epiphanius, in his *Panarion* (an early precursor to von Junzt's *Die Unaussprechlichen Kulten*) detailed the stomach-turning practices of various Gnostic sects. For example, the Marcosians ritually imbibed urine and menstrual blood. We are reminded of the "mad cacophonous orgies" of the Cthulhu cultists.[4] The disgusting rites of Gnostics and Old Ones cultists were alike symbolic of their repudiation of the present world order, and of the utterly alien order to prevail when they basked in the direct rule of their gods.

In light of these parallels, it is hard to resist the conclusion that the religion of Alhazred was one of the lesser known branches of the Gnostic religion. The Old Ones were known in that context as *Aions*.

At some point in the history of the religion, the worship of the Old Ones themselves was supplemented by that of a group of subordinate entities connected in some way with the same Mythos. They were lesser beings, but had the advantage of being less aloof and far-off than the Old Ones. This, in fact, is a common, almost predictable, development once a religion's deities have become more transcendent. In exactly the same way, a new generation of demigods (Heracles, Asclepius, etc.) began to replace the Olympians in Greek religion, once Zeus and his kin were made more abstract by philosophers. In Zoroastrianism and Judaism, the cult of angels flourished in direct proportion to God's increasing transcendence. As Jesus Christ evolved from the Galilean savior to the divine *Pantocrator* represented on the dome of Santa Sophia, the Virgin Mary and the saints assumed greater importance.

In all these cases, the religious imagination has so highly exalted the object of worship that the need for a more "available" god is felt, and new deities have come in to close the gap. By Alhazred's day, Cthulhu, Yog-Sothoth, Nyarlathotep, and Shub-Niggurath had filled the vacuum, mediating between the Old Ones and their worshipers, but distinct from the Old Ones (*Necronomicon* 3:6-7, 15). The situation was analogous to that prevailing in most West African mythologies, where a primordial god has retreated far into the sky. The day-to-day business of religion is handled by a number of lesser godlings and spirits who receive sacrifice and answer prayers. So here: The Old Ones are far away, beyond dimensioned space. One day they will return, but for now one may venerate the sea-monster Cthulhu, the messenger Nyarlathotep, and the universal gate Yog-Sothoth.

The final step in this direction was taken when Cthulhu and the rest actually came to be identified with the Old Ones. Alhazred had taken the dangerous risk of predicting that the return of the Old Ones was near (3:21). As the *Necronomicon* soon came to function as the "Bible" of the cult, this prophecy was widely heeded. Thus, when many years passed and the apocalyptic return failed to materialize, far-reaching adjustments had to be made. The Old Ones were brought home in word if not in fact when the believers began to worship Cthulhu, Yog-Sothoth, and the others *as the Old Ones*. Probably none of this was the product of anyone's deliberate decision. It must have been a gradual and unconscious process.[5]

The next major shift must have occurred many years later, when careful students of the *Necronomicon* noticed that these developments did not square with the text. Seizing upon an ambiguous passage that suggested to them a punishment of Cthulhu by the Old Ones (3:14-15), these reformist zealots repudiated the conventional pantheon as "fallen angels." Instead, they called for a return to the worship of the original, transcendent Old Ones. Perhaps for clarity's sake, they did not try to reclaim the original term "Old Ones", still used by the Cthulhu-worshipers, whom the reformers regarded as apostates from the pure faith. They regarded the title as irrevocably polluted by heresy, and decided to adopt henceforth the synonymous nomenclature "the Elder Ones", or "Elder Gods." The slight shade of difference in meaning ("Elder" versus "Old") connoted that the reformists' Old Ones were older than the usurping Old Ones of the Cthulhu-worshipers.

The single passage 3:14-15 was made the basis for an elaborate "Fall of Cthulhu" myth, wherein he was imprisoned by the Elder Gods in a sunken crypt bearing their sign. In this manner, the reformists had indeed returned to Alhazred's conception of Cthulhu *et al.* as servants of the Old Ones. Whereas Alhazred had venerated them, the reformists vilified them as *rebellious* servants. At first they were conceived in the new theology as having been banished forever following their revolt. At some point, they were expected to rise to power again briefly—immediately before the final coming of the Elder Gods, just as Antichrist precedes and heralds the return of Christ.

Eventually, the reformists composed new texts setting forth these beliefs in detail. Some were pseudonymously attributed to Alhazred himself, a practice quite acceptable by ancient and medieval literary standards. Other texts may simply have been bound with the *Necronomicon* for reference purposes, the distinction between the two later being forgotten. They came finally to be taken for part of the text. Needless to say, the pro-Cthulhu sect may already have made interpolations of their own (one occurs in Fragment 13:1-2, 4-5, where it has been mixed into other material by the reformists). The older faction probably maintained a purer textual tradition. In any case, from the time of the schism onward, there must have been two different canonical texts, one with the reformist interpolations, the other without.

From the time of the split, the history of the religion seems to have been primarily taken up with sectarian infighting. Both groups, the Cthulhu cultists and the reformist worshipers of the Elder Gods, considered themselves faithful disciples of Abdul Alhazred. Neither side noticed how its doctrines diverged significantly from those of Alhazred, who had neither reviled Cthulhu and Yog-Sothoth, nor identified them as the Great Old Ones. Our knowledge of the reformist faction is greater because most of the spurious *Necronomicon* fragments stem from this group.

Is there any way to tell when the addition of new material began? Our only real clue is Ibn Khallikan's characterization of Alhazred as a worshiper of Cthulhu and Yog-Sothoth. He betrays no awareness either of the reformist picture of Alhazred as a warner against Cthulhu, or of the whole controversy. Ibn Khallikan is cognizant of many legends about Alhazred's death, the most fantastic of which he does not hesitate to report. So if he were aware of various opinions about whether Alhazred served or opposed Cthulhu, Ibn Khallikan would probably not have recorded unambiguously that the mad Arab was a Cthulhu devotee. Since the biographer lived in the twelfth century, the origin of the reformist interpolations cannot be quite this early.

We might be able to narrow down the date further if we had the thirteenth century Syriac commentary on the *Necronomicon* by the Nestorian monk Zecharias. Written perhaps a full century later than Ibn Khallikan's day, Zecharias' commentary would no doubt indicate whether any of the interpolations had already crept into the text by that time. Obviously, if he commented on them, they must have appeared in the text of the *Necronomicon* he had in front of him. The discovery of this remarkable document was announced in 1968 by Dr. Franklin E. Tillinghast.[6] Nine years earlier, the commentary had been acquired in a purchase of several Arabic and Syriac manuscripts once belonging to the collection of H. R. Englehart. Tillinghast's announcement stirred a good deal of excitement at the time, and just as much disappointment a few months later when it reportedly vanished in a fire of dubious origin, which also claimed the life of the great scholar. Of such importance was this manuscript, that it is no exaggeration to say that its loss was felt quite as keenly as was that of Dr. Tillinghast himself. In any case, the intriguing document can no longer offer any help in our investigation.

At least some of the interpolations may date from late medieval times, since they suggest that the reformists may have been influenced by a decadent form of Jewish Kabbalism. Exorcistic techniques mentioned in two fragments include the "Tikkoun elixir" (perhaps drawn in a garbled form from fifteenth century Kabbalism) and an amulet in the shape of a five-pointed star (based on the magic "pentacle of Solomon"). Furthermore, during this period the Elder Gods were depicted as "Towers of Fire", an image clearly borrowed from the Jewish representation of God as a "pillar of fire" (Exodus 13:21). This, incidentally, helps account for the similarity many have pointed out between the biblical mythos and late forms of the Cthulhu legend cycle.

As the commentary proceeds, it is hoped that the reader will see the utility of the preceding historical sketch in making sense of several hitherto puzzling passages from the *Necronomicon*.

Chapter VI: The Verse-numbering System

The discussion of any text is facilitated if there is some kind of system for dividing it into sections and shorter passages. The utility of the chapter and verse divisions in the Bible, or the Surah and verse numbering in the Qur'an, or even the Act, Scene, and Line divisions in Shakespeare's plays, is obvious if one has ever had to look up a quote in any of these works. As serious research and discussion of the *Necronomicon* commences, scholars will no doubt feel the need for a reference system of this kind. The system to be proposed here, though simple enough to follow, may at first seem slightly puzzling in its rationale. A bit of explanation is in order.

The reader may note that some fragments that are numbered later would seem, from their subject matter, to have occurred earlier in the original text than passages that precede them according to our numbering. For instance, the so-called "Preface" occurs last. How can this be? Two considerations have dictated this. First, though some numbering system seems to have existed in various editions of the complete *Necronomicon*[1], no such texts are available today. Thus ours is a system for numbering *fragments* in their order of study, not sections in their order of occurrence. That latter order we cannot hope to discern. In the present state of things, there is often no way to be sure which passage followed which. Second, at least some of the extant passages seem to be inauthentic. Therefore, though once interpolated they may (like the "Preface") precede older passages in the text, they actually follow those passages chronologically. We have endeavored, then, to follow the order of composition insofar as this can be determined.

Within the categories thus established, we have grouped passages more or less according to subject. In this chronological ordering, we are not unprecedented. A similar approach has been adopted by Bell, Rodwell, and Dawood in their translations of the Qur'an, and by Barclay, Schonfield, and others in their versions of the New Testament. In these cases, naturally, the verse numbering had already been established, but the translators did rearrange the order of presentation chronologically, supplying charts enabling the reader to locate traditionally numbered passages in their new placement. We avoid this difficulty by making the numbering and the order of presentation coincide.

As for the numbering system itself, the first number will denote the fragment or passage as a whole, while the second will refer to an individual verse (a sentence or lengthy clause). Thus a notation like "3:12" should be read as "Fragment 3, verse 12."

Section Two: The Authentic Material
Chapter VII: That Which Came before Men

Fragment 1

Text: [1]The book of the black name, containing the history of that which came before men. [2]The Great Old Ones were both one and many. [3]They were not separate souls like men, yet they were separate wills. [4]Some say they came from the stars; [5]some say that they were the soul of the earth when it was formed from a cloud. [6]For all life comes from the beyond, where there is no consciousness. [7]Life needed a mirror, therefore it invaded the world of matter. [8]There it became its own enemy, because they possess form. [9]The Great Old Ones wanted to avoid form; [10]therefore they rejected the heavy material of the body. [11]But then they lost the power to act. [12]Therefore they needed servants.[1]

Version: Uncertain; the fragment survives only in the thirteenth century commentary of the monk Martin the Gardener, written in oddly mixed Greek and Latin.

Commentary:

v. 1. We have here the beginning of the entire book, which (at least in its first section) deals with pre- and inhuman life. "The book of the black name" seems to be Martin's attempt at translating Philetas' title *Necronomicon*. Martin's knowledge of classical languages seems to have been spotty. He has mistaken the suffix *-icon* for "image" or "book," and *nom-* for "name." He has somehow confused *necro-* ("dead") with *nigro-* ("black"), resulting in a completely erroneous translation. The verse should read simply "The *Necronomicon*, containing the history of that which came before men." (Of course, the original Arabic would have had "The *Al-Azif*, containing the history ....")

v. 2. There are different senses in which the Old Ones may be described alternatively as singular and as plural. We have here something on the order of the Christian doctrine of the Trinity. It is explained in v. 3.

v. 3. This verse shows the influence of Christian theological debates in the Near East in the late seventh century. The denial that the Old Ones had "separate souls" recalls the Christology (= the doctrine of the nature of Christ) of the churches in Alhazred's region. It was "Monophysite" Christology, meaning that Christ had one (*monos*) nature (*physis*), instead of two (divine and human), as Western Christians thought. "Dithelitism" (or "two-will-ism") was another doctrine which defined Christ as having two distinct though harmonious wills, each stemming from one of the two natures of Christ. Obviously one would not espouse the Monophysite and the Dithelite doctrines simultaneously, since the first removes the rationale for the second. Something like a combination of the two ideas had already surfaced in order to define the doctrine of the Trinity. Accordingly, the Godhead shared one divine nature, yet existed as three distinct persons (Father, Son, Spirit).

In the same way, Alhazred has borrowed the Christological jargon of his day to explain his conception of the Great Old ones. They, too, are ultimately one, though they possess individual wills. This was no doubt his updating of the original Gnostic doctrine that the *Aions* (the Old Ones here) were a series of emanations from the ultimate Godhead, thus sharing the divine nature even when differentiated as individual beings.

v. 4. Alhazred is aware that some would make the Old Ones mere angels. This is probably what is meant by the reference to "stars." This was a common image for angels, occurring for instance in the Book of Revelation: "The mystery of the seven stars that you saw in my right hand ... is this: The seven stars are the angels of the seven churches." (Revelation 1:20)

v. 5. Another current theory is that the Old Ones were the spiritual nature of the physical world, the rational principle by which the primeval chaos was formed into an ordered cosmos. (A similar doctrine had been taught by Philo concerning the divine *Logos*.) According to this version, the Old Ones would have functioned like Plato's archetypal forms.

v. 6. Alhazred understands why these theories were formulated, because it is true that life comes from beyond the earth as we know it. Life is not indigenous here. The truth of its origin lies with neither of the theories he has mentioned. Instead, it comes from the mindless demiurge Azathoth, who is referred to here by the phrase "the beyond where there is no consciousness." The phrase is similar to others elsewhere, to the effect that Azathoth is the "blind idiot chaos beyond angled space."

v. 7. This verse refers to the original coming of the Old Ones to earth (*cf.* Fragment 3). The word "invaded" denotes that their presence there is utterly alien. The next verse explains why.

v. 8. Apparently the reference here is to the dawn of the conflict between the Old Ones and the living creatures of earth. The source of this conflict was that the Old Ones are "undimensioned and to us unseen" (3:3), while earthlings "possess form." The enmity described here accounts for the threats posed in 3:18-19.

vv. 9-10. The utter revulsion felt by the super-dimensional Old Ones in the face of embodied life-forms is here given as the reason for their departure.

This is why, according to 3:21, they do not presently rule the earth. V. 10, incidentally, is one of the clearest traces of the Gnostic origin of the religion of Alhazred. He refers explicitly to the spirit vs. matter dualism of Gnosticism. "Therefore they rejected the heavy material of the body." This is closely parallel to the Gnostic "Hymn of the Pearl", in which one of the Aions visits earth and is benumbed and confused by the materiality of the world: "And with guile they mingled for me a deceit, and I tasted of their food … and by means of the heaviness of their food I fell into a deep sleep." Soon he comes to his senses and recoils in horror at his careless entrapment in material flesh: "And I stripped off the filthy garment and left it in their land, and directed my way forthwith to the light of my fatherland" (Hymn of the Pearl, vv. 32, 35, 62, 63). So did the Old Ones flee the mire of the material world.

v. 11. Yet this self-imposed exile left them at a disadvantage. How might their will be done on earth?

v. 12. "They needed servants", and this of course is the origin of the religion of the Old Ones. Someone had a visionary experience in which he received the "gospel" of the Old Ones, summoning men to their service. However many ages it might take, the human followers must tirelessly prepare for a "second coming" of their Masters, who will say to them "Well done, good and faithful servants." They will transfigure them into a purely spiritual state and proceed to wipe the earth clean of other human life.

Fragment 2

Text: [1]Whosoever speaketh of Cthulhu shall remember that he but seemeth dead; [2]he sleeps, and yet he does not sleep; [3]he has died and yet he is not dead; [4]asleep and dead though he is, he shall rise again. [5]Again it should be shown that

[6]"That is not dead which can eternal lie,

[7]And with strange aeons even death may die."[2]

Version: Either Latin or Greek; citation is ambiguous.

Commentary:

vv. 1-4. The meaning of this passage seems fairly straightforward. It refers to the primeval monster Cthulhu imprisoned in uneasy slumber in the sunken city of R'lyeh in the Pacific. An old piece of cult liturgy reads:

> In his house at R'lyeh
> Dead Cthulhu waits dreaming.

The idea is that Cthulhu is lying in wait, biding his time in a state of suspended animation that only *resembles* death. The sense of v. 1 is "don't write him off—he only *seems* dead."

It is interesting to note the ambivalent manner in which Cthulhu's hibernation is described. Vv. 4 and 6 remind us that this apparent death has not the finality of death, but is instead a lying in wait, even if the waiting seems to take forever. However long it takes, Cthulhu can afford to wait. V. 7 flatly calls the torpor "death", but again hints that it is not. Unlike genuine death, this slumber will end. The idea is very similar to that expressed in chapter 11 of the Gospel according to John. There Jesus' friend Lazarus has become gravely ill. When told of this, Jesus replies, "This sickness will not end in death" (v. 4). Two days later he tells his disciples, "Our friend Lazarus has fallen asleep, but I am going there to wake him" (v. 14). Hadn't Jesus already assured them that the illness would not issue in death? The whole point of the "sleep" metaphor is that, though technically and actually dead, Lazarus will not remain that way. Jesus will resuscitate him, so the "end" is not death. A true death from which one may yet awake is aptly compared to sleep. The idea surfaces in several other places in the New Testament, e.g., a hymn fragment preserved in Ephesians 5:14:

> Awake O sleeper
> Rise from the dead
> And Christ will shine on you.

The *Necronomicon* couplet simply reverses the metaphor, so that a sleep from which one wakes seems like death if it lasts for ages.

The puzzling term "strange aeons" denotes periods of time "strange" by the reckoning of human timeframes, epochs that are unimaginably vast. Once more we have biblical parallels, e.g., II Peter 3:8: "With the Lord a day is like a thousand years, and a thousand years are like a day." Psalm 90:4 makes the same point:

> A thousand years in your sight
> are like a day that has just gone by
> or like a watch in the night.

And the point is that for beings who have no mortality there is virtually no time either. When the "eternal lying" in wait (v. 6) has ended, then "death itself [will] die."[3] Cthulhu will awake from dreaming exile to rise from his watery grave.

vv. 5-7. So far our exegesis has been fairly unexceptional, but at this juncture we must introduce a note of controversy. We wish to suggest both that the rhymed couplet of vv. 6-7 has a deeper meaning that is far from apparent on first reading, and that while it is authentic *Necronomicon*, it is *not* the work of Abdul Alhazred. Rather it is a much older piece of Cthulhu-cult lore quoted by him. That he might quote earlier material should occasion no sur-prise. After all, the Gnostic cult of the Old Ones goes back considerably before Alhazred's time.

First of all, the couplet is presented as a quote in the text of the *Necronomicon* itself. The verses appear set off from the surrounding prose with what is clearly a formulaic introduction to a quotation. "Again it should be shown that. ...." (v. 5).

The second important factor militating against Alhazred's authorship here is that the poem seems to reflect in its linguistic structure an older milieu than his. The poem manifests the repetitive parallelism of Hebrew poetry such as we find in the Old Testament Psalms. As is well known, Hebrew poetry did not have to rhyme, depending instead on the device of paraphrasing one thought in slightly different ways. For example:

> The heavens declare the glory of God
> The firmament showeth his handiwork. (Psalm 19:1)

There are several possible variations, including antithetic parallelism, wherein an idea is emphasized by juxtaposing it with its corollary:

> The heavens are the Lord's
> But the earth he has given to the children of men.
> (Psalm 115:16)

There is also staircase parallelism, wherein each phrase repeats the last but adds a new element:

> Blessed is the man who
> *walketh* not in the counsel of the ungodly,
> nor *standeth* in the way of sinners,
> nor *sitteth* in the seat of the scornful. (Psalms 1:1)

Obviously the verses from the *Necronomicon* are of this last type, exhibit-ing the same kind of parallel structure. Each of the two lines echoes the other, though the second adds a new emphasis: Not only have men mistak-en for death that which is only age-long sleep, but it is promised that this dormancy will eventually reach its end.

Thus far, the Hebraic cast of the couplet would seem to push it further back in time than Abdul Alhazred's day, but how much further? Another clue is provided by the appearance (in English translation) of the words "eternal" (v. 6) and "aeons" (v. 7). The parallel, noted above, between the verses is made more distinct once we realize that they were originally com-posed, not in Alhazred's Arabic, but in Greek, where the words "eternal" and "aeon" are simply different forms of the word *aion*, or "age." English "eternal" would then translate into the Greek phrase *eis tous aionous*, literal-ly "unto the ages", "always" or "forever."

Our poem seems to have been written in the Greek language, yet according to the pattern of Old Testament Hebrew poetry. These factors make it probable that it was composed under the influence of the Septuagint, the Greek translation of the Hebrew Old Testament. This would place the poem back near the very beginning of the religion, in the context of the Hellenistic-Hebrew Gnosticism (see Chapter V). It is thus a very old and valuable piece of cult lore.

We find the same kind of "Hebraism with a Hellenistic flavor" in documents like the Gospel according to John. The prologue to that gospel is a long poem or hymn on the *Logos*, written in Greek but employing Hebrew staircase parallelism. The same technique appears again in chapter three, in Jesus' dialogue with Nicodemus: "Unless a man is born again, he cannot see the Kingdom of God ... unless a man is born of water and the Spirit, he cannot enter the Kingdom of God" (3:3, 5). Though the technique of parallelism is Hebraic, the parallel itself is clinched by the pun implied in the equivocal use of the Greek word *anothen*, which can mean either "again" or "from above." Here it is supposed to mean *both*, implying a *heavenly* birth and a *re*birth. In exactly the same way, we are about to suggest, the word *aion* is used with a double meaning in *Necronomicon* 2:6 and 7. It all depends on the pun implied in the two uses of the word *aion* as "age" and as a hidden divine entity (the *Aions*, *cf.* Chapter V).

On the surface, as we have seen, the subject of the poem is Cthulhu. On this reading, it is he who "lies eternal" waiting for the passing of "strange aeons", i.e., unimaginably vast ages. Then his apparent "death [will] die", and his exile of slumber will end. Those readers with the "gnosis" will perceive *themselves* as the subject of the rhyme. Now the faithful cultists are "that [which] is not dead [and] can eternal lie." According to this interpretation, to "lie eternal" (*meinai eis tous aionous*) means not "to abide forever" (as does Cthulhu in R'lyeh), but rather "to await the *Aions*", i.e., the Old Ones. Those who do await them faithfully are "not dead", because death itself will pass away "with strange aeons"—not "with the *passing of unimaginable ages*", but rather "with the *advent of unearthly Aions*." The poem promises eternal reward to the human servitors of the Old Ones. According to the oral tradition of the cult, "then mankind would have become as the Great Old Ones; free and wild and beyond good and evil, with laws and morals thrown aside and all men shouting and killing and revelling in joy."[3] Though the conception of salvation is much different to say the least, there are parallel promises in the New Testament. "He who endures to the end will be saved" (Matthew 24:13). "He who believes in me will live, even though he dies; and whoever lives and believes in me will never die" (John 11:25-26). For those who keep faith, death itself will die.

Fragment 3

Text: [1]Nor is it to be thought that man is either the oldest or the last of earth's masters, or that the common bulk of life and substance walks alone. [2]The Old Ones were, the Old Ones are, and the Old Ones shall be. [3]Not in the spaces we know, but between them, They walk serene and primal, undimensioned and to us unseen. [4]*Yog-Sothoth* knows the gate. *Yog-Sothoth* is the gate. *Yog-Sothoth* is the key and guardian of the gate. [5]Past, present, future, all are one in *Yog-Sothoth*. [6]He knows where the Old Ones broke through of old, and where They shall break through again. [7]He knows where They have trod earth's fields, and where They still tread them, and why no one can behold Them as They tread. [8]By Their smell can men sometimes know Them near, but of Their semblance can no man know, saving only in the features of those They have begotten on mankind; [9]and of those are there many sorts, differing in likeness from man's truest eidolon to that shape without sight or substance which is Them. [10]They walk unseen and foul in lonely places where the Words have been spoken and the Rites howled through at their Seasons. [11]The wind gibbers with Their voices, and the earth mutters with Their consciousness. [12]They bend the forest and crush the city, yet may not forest or city behold the hand that smites. [13]Kadath in the cold waste hath known Them, and what man knows Kadath? [14]The ice desert of the South and the sunken isles of [the] Ocean hold stones whereon Their seal is engraven, but who hath seen the deep frozen city or the sealed tower long garlanded with seaweed and barnacles? [15]Great Cthulhu is Their cousin, yet can he spy Them only dimly. [16]*Iä! Shub-Niggurath!* [17]As a foulness shall ye know Them. [18]Their hand is at your throats, yet ye see Them not; [19]and Their habitation is even one with your guarded threshold. [20]*Yog-Sothoth* is the key to the gate, whereby the spheres meet. [21]Man rules now where They ruled once; They shall soon rule where man rules now. [22]After summer is winter, and after winter summer. [23]They wait patient and potent, for here shall They reign again.[4] [[24]And at Their coming again none shall dispute Them and all shall be subject to Them. [25]Those who know of the gates shall be impelled to open the way for Them and shall serve Them as They desire, [26]but those who open the way unwittingly shall know life but a brief while thereafter.][5]

Version: The above is a translation of Wormius' Latin version. There is also a hand-copied English translation from a text of unknown version and edition. Its readings (including the verses bracketed here), when they differ, are inferior. Nonetheless, the more interesting ones will be briefly noted.

Commentary:

v. 1. Our passage represents the continuation of a longer discourse, now lost. This is evident from the opening of this verse, "Nor is it to be thought ...." "Nor" implies a previous "neither." The opening of v. 1 might be paraphrased, "Not only *that*, but here is something else about so-and-so." What was the "that", the subject matter of the missing text? The present passage discusses how man has not always ruled the earth and will not do so forever. Thus the preceding discourse must have qualified the rule of man in other ways. The whole section must have said in effect, "Man is not the unchallenged lord of his world that he imagines himself to be. For one thing, his control is limited (or threatened or whatever) by _____. For another, his rule is of short duration, since he once did not rule, and one day will be deposed."

The variant version attempts to round off the fragment artificially, by changing "nor" to "never." Thus the copyist had no more of the text than we do.

v. 2. This verse, perhaps originally a liturgical chant, is parallel to Revelation 4:8b:

> Holy, holy, holy
> is the Lord God Almighty
> who was, and is, and is to come

The idea is that, unlike man whose rule is insecure and ephemeral, the Old Ones are eternal. They are "the same yesterday, today, and forever" (Hebrews 13:8). The verse follows the statement of v. 1 precisely in order to underline this contrast.

v. 3. Note that the Old Ones do not at the present time, or by nature, inhabit dimensioned space as we know it.

v. 4. "Yog-Sothoth" is an important entity in the Cthulhu Mythos. He is named by Ibn Khallikan as one of the beings worshiped by Alhazred. The name seems at least partially derived from, or influenced by, the Egyptian "Thoth", the god of enchanters. Given the important role of Egypt as the breeding ground for many early Gnostic sects, this is not surprising.

A series of more or less synonymous metaphors are used to describe Yog-Sothoth's role. He is the "gate", but also the "key" to and the "guardian" of the gate. We have a close parallel in the "Good Shepherd" discourse of John chapter 10: "Jesus said again, 'I tell you the truth, I am the gate for the sheep. ... I am the good shepherd'" [i.e., the guardian of the gate to the sheep pen] (vv. 7, 11).

v. 5. Yog-Sothoth is able to serve as a gate of passage for the Old Ones because, like them, he is oblivious to the strictures of time. The parallel to v. 2 shows this.

v. 6. As is already implied in v. 5, Yog-Sothoth is not to be included as one of the Old Ones. He is clearly distinguished from them here. The importance of this point cannot be overstressed. We will have more to say in this vein in connection with v. 15.

This verse informs us as to why man is "neither the oldest nor the last" of earth's rulers: The answer is that the Old Ones "broke through" long ago, and will do so again in the future. That is, they somehow pass into our space-time continuum. A kind of apocalyptic "second coming" of the Old Ones is hinted at here, though the very next verse seems to confuse this point somewhat.

v. 7. "They still tread them"—these words imply that the Old Ones are not altogether absent from the terrestrial scene even now. The fact that "no one can behold Them as They tread" might be taken, in concert with v. 3, to suggest that the Old Ones are not directly present *in* our dimension, but are peering in from the outside. Yet this cannot be the correct interpretation, since their present "treading" is explicitly made equivalent in kind to their past presence on earth ("where They have trod") in their "first coming." They would seem to be present in the same way now.

Why can "no one behold Them as They tread?" We may guess that their translation into earth's dimensionality is incomplete, rendering them only partially susceptible to human senses. In any case, our understanding of the passage is sufficient without an answer to this question; Alhazred's point is that Yog-Sothoth alone knows the answer.

v. 8. The "beholding" of the previous verse referred strictly to sight, for v. 8 admits that the Old Ones can, at least sometimes, be detected by the other senses. Human beings can smell them. In the following verses we are told that their smell is a terrible stench—cf. v. 10, "They walk unseen and foul"; v. 17, "as a foulness shall ye know Them." The variant reading incorporates a marginal gloss into the text at this point: "by Their smell, which is strange to the nostrils, and like unto a creature of great age."

Their "semblance", i.e., visual image, can be deduced only as it has been adapted into human terms, by the siring of children by human hosts. This is a common theme in virtually all mythology, e.g., in the cases of Gilgamesh and Heracles, whose divine paternity gave them telltale traits including superhuman strength. Here, it is actual physiognomy that is affected.

The variant reading adds after "mankind" the words, "which are awful to behold, and thrice-awful are Those who sired them."

v. 9. One cannot always gain an impression of how the Old Ones look, since some of their earthly offspring are indistinguishable from true men, while others seem to bear no human characteristics at all. A parallel range in Greek mythology would be that between Perseus, Heracles, and Apollo. All three are sons of Zeus by mortal women, yet Perseus is an entirely human hero, while Heracles is a superpowerful mortal, and Apollo is a god pure and simple.

We may detect a sinister implication here. In case of either extreme, the spawn of the Old Ones would be indetectable, either as impervious to our senses as the Old Ones themselves, or exactly like ourselves with no sign of their earthly parentage. Who knows but that Alhazred himself did not harbor the delusion of being a literal son of his gods?

v. 10. We discover that the transition of the Old Ones into our world requires the agency, not only of the entity Yog-Sothoth, but also of initiated mortals. Incantations and rituals must be performed in "lonely places." The use of the word "howled" implies that the words to be spoken were originally designed for other-than-human throats, or that they represent a human adaptation shouted in imitation of animal howling to recall the non-human character of the original.

The verse also implies that the Old Ones are free to walk only in places prepared for them by such incantations. Perhaps we have the key to the apparent contradiction between vv. 6 and 7, where it is first said that they "*shall* break through", but then that they "*still* tread." The "breaking through" would seem to refer to a large-scale invasion, in sufficient numbers as to rule the earth again. This point has not yet been reached because sufficient preparation has not yet been made. Where the ground has been prepared, some Old Ones do "tread" even now, but not in sufficient strength to rule. Of course, the goal of the cult of the Old Ones was to restore the earthly dominion of their gods. This verse indicates that the preparatory rites could be enacted only at selected times ("in their Seasons"). For this reason, the faithful had to be patient. Through their tireless work, a sufficient number of the Old Ones would be invoked to reestablish their reign.

v. 11. The "gibbering" of the wind with the voices of the Old Ones might reflect the universal tendency to understand weather phenomena as divine acts, such as the attribution of thunder and lightning to Zeus or Thor. But the reference here might be to the "buzzing" of desert insects heard in the wind, believed to be the whispering of demons, the source of Alhazred's revelations (cf. Chapter 2). In this verse, then, we would have the origin of the title of the work, *Al-Azif*.

However, on this understanding it remains to be seen just what the "murmuring of the earth" would refer to. Another possibility presents itself if this verse is read in closer connection with the following sections, as was quite likely intended. In this case, the murmuring of the earth would denote earthquakes. (See commentary immediately below.)

v. 12. The winds of v. 11 are what "bend the forest"; the earthquakes of that verse "crush the city" of this verse. In both cases, no one "beholds" the Old Ones themselves, since they have employed "natural" disasters as their weapons. This verse introduces the unit comprised of vv. 13-14 which is technically known as a *mathna*, a formulary "punishment story" of the kind employed several times in the Qur'an and the Bible as a warning to sinners. The well-known doom of cities or peoples of the past is rehearsed in order to warn hearers (or readers) of their present danger.

> Hast thou not seen how thy Lord dealt with Ad,
> At Irem adorned with pillars,
> Whose like have not been reared in these lands?
> And with Themoud who hewed out the rocks in the
>   valley;
> And with Pharaoh the impaler;
> Who all committed excesses in the lands,
> And multiplied wickedness therein.
> Wherefore thy Lord let loose on them the scourge of
>   chastisement. (Qur'an 89:5-12)

> Sodom and Gomorrah and the surrounding towns gave
> themselves up to sexual immorality and perversion.
> They serve as an example of those who suffer the pun-
>   ishment of eternal fire. (Jude 7)

> Woe to you, Chorazin! Woe to you, Bethsaida! If the
> miracles that were performed in you had been per-
> formed in Tyre and Sidon, they would have repented
> long ago in sack cloth and ashes. But I tell you, it will
> be more bearable for Tyre and Sidon on the day of
> judgment than for you. And you, Capernaum, will you
> be lifted up to the skies? No, you will go down to
> Hades. If the miracles that were performed in you had
> been performed in Sodom, it would have remained to
> this day. But I tell you that it will be more bearable for
> Sodom on the day of judgment than for you. (Matthew
> 11:21-24)

In exactly the same way, the following verses attribute the doom of various cities to the vengeance of the Old Ones. The reader is to understand that he is potentially helpless before the same fate.

v. 13. It is possible that the desolation of Kadath in the cold waste is derived from Psalm 29, one of the hymns sung yearly at the Feast of Tabernacles to commemorate the mythical victory of Yahweh over the lesser deities ("sons

of God", Psalm 29:1), whereupon he became king of the gods. In the course
of praising Yahweh's might, the psalmist writes:

> The voice of Yahweh breaks the cedars,
> Yahweh breaks the cedars of Lebanon ...
> The voice of Yahweh shakes the wilderness,
> Yahweh shakes the wilderness of Kadesh.
> The voice of Yahweh makes the oaks to whirl,
> And strips the forest bare.. (vv. 5, 8-9)

It is not hard to see the similarity between these verses and the present
Necronomicon text: "The wind gibbers with Their voices, and the earth mutters with Their consciousness. They bend the forest and crush the city, yet
may not forest or city behold the hand that smites. Kadath in the cold waste
hath known Them, and what man knows Kadath?" Note how both texts
symbolize the divine voice as wind which destroys the forest and devastates
Kadath/Kadesh in the waste/wilderness. This might be coincidence, but
such a close parallel implies rather that Alhazred was at least vaguely familiar with the psalm (not inherently unlikely anyway given the ancient Jewish
community in his native Yemen) and that its imagery, whether consciously
or unconsciously, shaped his poetic praise of the power of the Old Ones.

Kadesh was, of course, the wilderness in which the children of Israel
wandered under the leadership of Moses. "Kadath" looks to be a variant
form of Kadesh, especially in view of the parallel texts just discussed. As far
as we know, no city existed in the wilderness of Kadesh, though it may be
that in Alhazred's day some local legend claimed that there had been a city,
and that for some great sin the gods had destroyed it. The point of such a
legend would have been to explain the desolation of the area: it seemed
cursed by the gods, so there *must* at one time have been people (i.e., a city)
there to have sinned grossly and deserved the divine wrath.

v. 14. Recalling the legend of Atlantis, this verse adds mention of once-
inhabited islands sunk by the earthquakes of the Old Ones' making. There
is a hint of special punishment, as the buildings of the sunken cities bore the
seal of the Old Ones. Presumably they have been destroyed for some kind
of unfaithfulness.

v. 15. The mention of sunken cities evokes mention of "Great Cthulhu",
who according to the belief of the cult lies in repose in R'lyeh. It is possible
that Cthulhu is somehow to be understood as an object of the Old Ones'
punishment, and that the drowned city of v. 14 is none other than R'lyeh.

As with Yog-Sothoth in v. 6, Cthulhu is here differentiated from the
Old Ones. He shares in the infirmity of human beings: The Old Ones are
very nearly as invisible to him as they are to us. He is related to them in
some fashion, but the same statement that he is "Their cousin" simultane-

ously serves to distance him from them. He is merely *related to* them, not one of them. As outlined in Chapter V, we may remind ourselves that Cthulhu and Yog-Sothoth both came to be confused with the Old Ones, but this is a later development in the mythology. Alhazred himself was careful to distinguish them.

v. 16. The ejaculation "Iä! Shub-Niggurath!" occurs here as a spontaneous exultation of praise. The exclamation expresses the author's pious joy at the truths he has just penned. Such literary outbursts are not unusual. The Apostle Paul makes occasional use of them in his epistles. For example, he concludes a summary of the religious privileges of the Jewish people with a paean of praise: "God who is over all be forever praised!" (Romans 9:5). At the close of an appeal to his readers to contribute to a charitable relief effort, Paul cries, "Thanks be to God for his indescribable gift!" (II Corinthians 9:15). As to the identity of "Shub-Niggurath", there is quite an element of mystery. Elsewhere in the lore of the cult, Shub-Niggurath is referred to as "cloud-like" or, alternatively, as the "Black Goat of the Woods" or the "Goat with a Thousand Young." The "black goat" imagery recalls the medieval conception of Satan as a black satyr with a goat's head. The name "Shub-Niggurath" would seem to have some connection with this image, as it may derive in some way from the Latin *niger* ("black"). The "thousand young" would suggest a fertility god or goddess. Unless all this is purely metaphorical, Shub-Niggurath would seem to be, like Cthulhu and Yog-Sothoth, some sort of lesser entity connected with the Old Ones, but not strictly speaking one of them. The attributes as described are too earthy in their reference for their subject to be one of the transdimensional Old Ones.

v. 17. Once again Alhazred states that the Old Ones may be detected by their foul odor. See v. 8.

v. 18. This striking image, drawn readily from the world of Alhazred's day with its treacherous alleyways haunted by cutthroats waiting to pounce, vividly illustrates the danger posed by the Old Ones to those oblivious to their presence.

v. 19. Whatever fortification men might think to build against them, they have already breached it. Or perhaps the idea is that no protection intended against earthly foes can hope to avail against the invisible threat of the Old Ones.

v. 20. Again, Yog-Sothoth is asserted to be the gate whereby the Old Ones may pass over. The use of spheres external to each other but touching tangentially is interesting. Usually "sphere" cosmology entailed a system of concentric spheres, one inside the other, as in the Ptolemaic system.

vv. 21-23. These verses form a unit, comprising a classical apocalyptic warning, almost precisely parallel to James 5:7-8:

> Be patient, then, brothers, until the Lord's coming. See
> how the farmer waits for the land to yield its valuable
> crop and how patient he is for the fall and spring rains.
> You, too, be patient and stand firm, because the Lord's
> coming is near.

Both texts employ the image of the change of seasons. The idea is *not* that of an endlessly repeated cycle. Rather it is that as surely as one season follows another, the dreary present must soon give way to the eagerly anticipated future. "Winter" in v. 22 refers to man's rule in v. 21, while "summer" is, of course, the rule of the Old Ones. James uses the analogy to exhort his readers to have patience, while Alhazred uses it to explain why the Old Ones can afford to be patient, but the point is the same.

It is important not to pass quickly over the word "soon" in v. 21. With this single word, we discover that Abdul Alhazred, like many another prophet, has embarrassed his followers by virtually setting a date for the end. Like early Christians who had to cope with the "delay of the Parousia", believing readers of the *Necronomicon* eventually had to come up with some expedient "when prophecy failed." However, on the positive side, it should be noted that the presence of this unfulfilled prediction in the text weighs heavily in favor of its authenticity; it is hard to imagine a later writer adding such an embarrassment when it didn't already exist!

vv. 24-26 occur only in the variant version of the passage, and are almost certainly inauthentic.

Fragment 4

Text: [1]Verily do we know little of the other universes beyond the gate which YOG-SOTHOTH guards. [2]Of those which come through the gate and make their habitation in this world none can tell; [3]although Ibn Schacabao tells of the beings which crawl from the Gulf of S'glhuo that they may be known by Their sound. [4]In that Gulf the very worlds are of sound, and matter is known but as an odor; [5]and the notes of our pipes in this world may create beauty or bring forth abominations in S'glhuo. [6]For the barrier between haply grows thin, and when sourceless sounds occur we may justly look to the denizens of S'glhuo. [7]They can do little harm to those of Earth, and fear only that shape which a certain sound may form in Their universe.[6]

Version: The version and edition from which this quote is taken are unknown.

Commentary:

v. 1. The reference to Yog-Sothoth and his guarding a gate between universes implies that this passage followed closely the one just discussed. It is assumed that the reader will already know who Yog-Sothoth is and why he serves this function.

Note that Alhazred admits his ignorance about other-worldly matters which do not directly concern the lore of his gods, the Old Ones. However, he does assume that there are still other universes, apparently to be identified with the cosmological "spheres" of 3:20. Thus Yog-Sothoth is the gate of passage between all the universes. This means he is part of Alhazred's larger worldview, and not especially of the Cthulhu Mythos proper. This would explain how it is that Yog-Sothoth knows where the Old Ones broke through into our world, while not being one of them. He is aware of all interdimensional crossings, whether of the Old Ones or of others, as in the present text.

v. 2. Just as the other universes are largely a mystery to us, even so, those who pass over from there are virtually undetectable. Here Alhazred admits that the invisibility of the Old Ones, stemming from their extramundane origin, is a quality common to all interdimensional travelers. While he as an adept of the Old Ones knows how to detect *them*, he now confesses that he is as much in the dark as anyone else when it comes to other aliens.

v. 3. His only clue about the only other alien race he names, the dwellers in "the Gulf of S'glhuo", is that they are detectable by distinctive sounds. (The distinctive element is named in v. 6.) Note the analogy with the Old Ones who may sometimes be detected by their smell (3:8).

(For the identity of Ibn Schacabao, see Chapter IV above.)

v. 4. There seems to be an element of confusion here. Whereas the previous verse indicated that a distinctive sound was a *sign of* their presence, v. 4 makes their very presence *nothing but* sound. The effect would be the same for the observer, but they are two different conceptions. Alhazred seems to return to the "sign" conception when he remarks that, in parallel fashion, earthly matter is perceived by these aliens as odor.

v. 5. Musical sounds made by us (whether randomly or intentionally designed as an incantation is not made clear) are creative of new reality in their universe. Once again, the conception of these aliens as being nothing but sound (rather than represented by sound) seems to be uppermost, since what would be mere sounds to us, upon penetrating their world, are *by definition* forceful realities. All in all, the logic here is familiar from Alhazred's belief that "Rites howled through in their Seasons" (3:10) may penetrate the dimensions and enable the Old Ones to cross over.

vv. 6-7. It is not explained precisely why "the barrier grows thin" between their universe and ours. Presumably this is a periodic occurrence determined by purely cosmological considerations, just as the rites summoning the Old Ones may be performed effectively only at certain times, "in their Seasons" (3:10).

The denizens of the Gulf of S'glhuo pose no threat to humanity, so why does Alhazred bother recording this information? He merely wishes to relate this explanation for why we sometimes seem to hear sounds with no evident source. That is the whole point of the passage. This is one of the clearest examples of the superstitions and curiosities that form the stock-in-trade of the "book of marvels" genre to which the *Necronomicon* belongs.

Chapter VIII: From the Book of Thoth

Fragment 5

Text: [1]And while there are those who have dared to seek glimpses beyond the Veil, and to accept HIM as guide, [2]they would have been more prudent had they avoided commerce with HIM; for it is written in the *Book of Thoth* how terrific is the price of a single glimpse. [3]Nor may those who pass ever return, for in the vastnesses transcending our world are shapes of darkness that seize and bind. [4]The Affair that shambleth about in the night, the evil that defieth the Elder Sign, the Herd that stand watch at the secret portal each tomb is known to have and that thrive on that which groweth out of the tenants thereof— [5]all these Blacknesses are lesser than HE WHO guardeth the Gateway: HE WHO will guide the rash one beyond all the worlds into the Abyss of unnamable devourers. [6]For He is 'UMR AT-TAWIL, the Most Ancient One, which the scribe rendereth as THE PRO-LONGED OF LIFE.[1]

Version: Unfortunately, the edition and translation from which this quote is taken are unknown. However, we do possess a parallel version of the same text, taken from a Kufic recension of unknown edition.[2] Variant readings, where noteworthy, will be supplied in the commentary, since the Kufic seems better to represent the original, retaining words and phrases omitted by other copyists and/or translators.

Commentary:

v. 1. The beginning "And" implies that we have once again a fragment of a longer passage in the original. The subject seems to be the gaining of extra-mundane knowledge. "Beyond the Veil" is extremely common terminology for revelation in esoteric mysticism.

(The identity of "HIM" is specified in v. 6.)

The Kufic recension has "And while there are those who have had the temerity to seek glimpses of beyond the Veil ...."

v. 2. The few who have sought esoteric knowledge in this fashion were foolish to have done so. (The technique in question was presumably discussed in the preceding text, lost to us.) The price is one of extravagant danger. What sort of danger? The text itself supplies no real clues, but the legend of the Patriarch Atal and his companion Barzai the Wise, which may have been known to Alhazred, may provide the solution.

It seems that the two sages once set out to gain a glimpse of their gods as they danced in the starlight atop a certain forbidden peak. Though both made the climb, only Barzai dared peer over the peak. For this Promethean act, he was "drawn screaming into the sky." Apparently this means that the vision drove him mad, and that he died soon after. The more reticent Atal survived to descend the mountain and live in peace.

This seems to be a somewhat late and confused version of the Talmudic story of the "four who entered Paradise", Rabbis Akiba, Ben Azai, Ben Zoma, and Aher. The four made a visionary ascent to the divine throne-room and each met with a different fate. Ben Azai was overcome at the sight of divine glory and died. Ben Zoma went insane. Aher became a heretic, and only Akiba returned completely unharmed.[3] The later version seems to have substituted Atal for Akiba, and to have combined the fates of Ben Zoma and Ben Azai. The name "Barzai" would seem to represent a corruption of "Ben Azai", perhaps involving the substitution of the Aramaic *Bar* for its Hebrew equivalent *Ben* (both, like the Arabic *Ibn*, meaning "son of"). At any rate, the lesson of both tales is clear: The vision of supramundane reality is all too likely to prove too much for mortal senses. Insanity, heresy, or even death may result from a journey "beyond the Veil." Thus, Alhazred warns against it. The Old Ones may penetrate the Veil from the other side, but humans should not try it.

The reference to the *Book of Thoth* reveals the Hermetic background of this passage. The reference to the legend described above accords with this. Gershom Scholem considers that the Merkabah ("Throne") mysticism from which that legend stems was the Jewish counterpart of Hermetic mysticism. We will find more evidence for our hypothesis in vv. 5-6 below.

v. 3. Apparently, those who actually "pass" beyond the Veil have done more than merely to "seek a glimpse" of that realm. According to this verse, their doom is sealed by the presence of monsters there.

The Kufic version reads: "and none who pass may return, for they will be firmly bound by those who lurk in the vastnesses that transcend our world."

v. 4. The three horrors listed here are probably cumulative, synonymous descriptions of the same thing—ghouls of some kind. They "shamble" in darkness, violating tombs which have been vainly sealed for protection with the "Elder Sign." The "Elder Sign" is apparently the charmed sigil of some conventional religion. The cryptic reference to "that which groweth out of the tenants" of the tomb is the subject of Fragment 8. Further comment will be reserved for that passage.

For a later interpretation of v. 4 by the reformist sect, see the commentary on 16:8-11.

The Kufic reading is rather different, and apparently confused: "The terrors of the night, and the evils of creation, and those who stand watch at the secret exit that it is known each grave has, and thrive on that which grows out of the tenants thereof ...."

v. 5. The ghouls are less terrible than the guardian of the Gateway. Why is this? The ghouls and "the Most Ancient One" (named in v. 6) are paralleled in their role as *guardians*. The ghouls "stand watch [i.e., guard] at the portal" of the grave and devour the corpse, but the Most Ancient One presides over the Gateway leading "beyond all worlds into the Abyss of devourers", who are much worse than ghouls. The ghouls devour the dead, but these devourers consume the living soul of the mystic. This is a complicated way of saying that the Most Ancient One brings the visionary a fate worse than death.

The Kufic text has, "They are lesser powers than he who guards the Gateway, and offers to guide the unwary into the realm beyond this world and all its unnamed and unnamable Devourers." Here the "devourers" represent not those more fearsome than the ghouls, but the earthly ghouls themselves. This seems to be a simple copyist error. On such a reading, the parallel between the ghouls and the Most Ancient One is destroyed and no reason is left for fearing him. Or the Devourers may be associated with "the realm beyond this world", in which case the Most Ancient One delivers the mystic into their hands. The verse, however, is gramatically ambiguous.

v. 6. Finally the guardian is named. He is "the Most Ancient One." From the two previous fragments, the reader might have expected to find the name "Yog-Sothoth." He is, after all, described in both Fragments 3 and 4 as the guardian of a gate between the worlds. Technically 5:5 speaks of a gate "beyond all worlds", not between worlds. Beyond this perhaps merely semantic difference, there is a good reason that Yog-Sothoth does not appear here. We have suggested that the whole of Fragment 5 is derived not from Alhazred's own Cthulhu Mythos, but rather from the Hermetic *Book of Thoth*. Later readers of this passage have missed this, and so have sought to identify the Most Ancient One as Yog-Sothoth. ("Yog-Sothoth ... whose aspects on earth are 'Umr At-Tawil and the Ancient Ones"—15:4). That they are quite different entities with no connection will become apparent.

According to the text as it now stands (in both recensions), the name of the guardian is "'Umr At-Tawil", which is rendered "Most Ancient One." Yet 'Umr At-Tawil does not mean this at all; rather it quite clearly means "speaker of allegorical interpretations." Here it is to be taken as a title of "the scribe" mentioned in our passage.[4] The extant reading of the text can be explained quite simply as a copyist's error. We may confidently surmise that the text of v. 6 originally had "For He is 'the Most Ancient One' [written in Greek], which the scribe 'Umr At-Tawil rendereth as 'THE PROLONGED OF LIFE [the same title, only in Arabic].'" 'Umr At-Tawil was the title of the scribe, not the name of the Guardian of the Gate.

"The Prolonged of Life", then, is the translation of "the Most Ancient One." The reason that both forms survive side by side in this manner is this: The Hermetic tract used by Alhazred was originally written in Greek, though he himself worked from the Arabic translation by 'Umr At-Tawil. Tawil had reproduced the original Greek for "the Most Ancient One" and followed it with the Arabic equivalent. Alhazred decided to record both the original and the translation. When Philetas translated Alhazred into Greek, he translated the Arabic translation back into Greek, leaving two synonymous versions of the title ("Most Ancient One" and "Prolonged of Life"). The effect would be the same as if an Aramaic speaker had translated John 1:41 from Greek back into the Aramaic originally spoken by the characters in the scene. It reads, "We have found the Messiah [Aramaic] (that is the Christ [Greek])." Translated back into Aramaic, it might read, "We have found the Messiah (that is the Messiah)."

Fragment 6

Text: [1]"... the Place of the Blind Apes where Nephren-Ka bindeth up the threads of truth."[5]

Version: This fragment is cited as being from a rare Arabic version.

Commentary:

v. 1. This brief sentence fragment is usually thought to allude to the legend of the "Black Pharaoh" Nephren-Ka, a corrupter of the religion of Egypt. Nephren-Ka was supposedly a hierophant of Nyarlathotep, messenger of the Great Old Ones. Like the Pharaoh Imhotep (Akhenaten) who sought to convert Egypt to the new faith of Aton the Sun, Nephren-Ka's "reforms" were of short duration. They were especially atrocious, involving necrophilism and human sacrifice. He apparently symbolized Nyarlathotep as an ape, i.e., probably in human form with the head of an ape in accord with the style of traditional iconography. In this form, Nyarlathotep was venerated as the "Blind Ape of Truth." For his excesses, Nephren-Ka was eventually overthrown. He is said to have sought refuge with his acolytes in a vast underground tomb.

The *Necronomicon* is supposed to outline this much of the story, which is continued in greater detail by the Flemish wizard Ludvig Prinn in *De Vermis Mysteriis*. There it is said that the Black Pharaoh somehow sacrificed his remaining attendants in a Faustian bargain with Nyarlathotep. In return he received knowledge of all the future ages of Egypt, which he managed to inscribe on the vast walls of his tomb before he expired. The cult of Nyarlathotep survived him, eventually discovering the tomb and covering the oracular inscriptions with a tapestry to be rolled back each day to uncover that day's events.

It is not inherently improbable that Alhazred did record at least part of this legend. However, the wording of the single surviving sentence about

Nephren-Ka does raise intriguing questions. We are going to argue that the story related by Prinn is a later version of the legend, which appeared in the *Necronomicon* in quite a different form. Like the preceding fragment dealing with "the Most Ancient One", the present passage is dependent on a Hermetic text. Even in the brief sentence we have, there are strong hints both that Alhazred's version did not coincide with Prinn's, and that it is Hermetic in origin.

First, who was "Nephren-Ka?" Later legend seems to have seized upon the similarity of his name to that of the Egyptian queen Nephertiti, a combination of the divine names "Neph" and "Thoth." Thoth has already been discussed briefly above with reference to the Hermetic tracts. Neph was the creator, the "spirit of god" which hovered over the primeval waters. It was common for rulers to be named for gods, but we suspect that Nephren-Ka was actually supposed to be a divinity. *Ka* was the word for one's soul, or spirit double, which survived death. "Nephren-Ka" would then denote either "Soul of the Spirit of God", or "Double of the Spirit of God", i.e., his visible manifestation on earth.

Or, perhaps, under the earth. Concerning the Hermetic literature, Geo Widengren writes, "The entering of a dark, subterranean chamber in order to find a book of revelation is a theme often recurring in Egyptian and Hellenistic tales. ... [O]nly in Egypt do we meet with the idea of a descent into an underground edifice in order to acquire the unsurpassed wisdom of preceding ages."[6] The present *Necronomicon* fragment agrees with Prinn's legend in placing Nephren-Ka in an underground chamber of some sort. This in fact is the significance of the mention of "the place of the blind apes." This phrase has nothing to do with Nyarlathotep or any other god. Instead, it is merely a figure of speech denoting a lightless underground place of mysteries. Alhazred uses an analogous expression in 8:1. The cavern is not a burial vault. It is simply the underground chamber of revelation mentioned by Widengren. It can hardly be a crypt according to our fragment, since Nephren-Ka is described as still alive there ("bindeth" is present tense).

The implied image of Nephren-Ka is like that of the Fates in Greek mythology. He is "binding up the threads of truth", or weaving a tapestry that records the wisdom of the ages. Those who find their way to his subterranean abode may seek revelations from this tapestry. Presumably the Egyptian Hermetic text Alhazred used purported to contain such revelations. Whether all this represented someone's actual visionary experience or was merely a literary convention we do not know. At any rate, the whole scene was later garbled so that the "blind apes" metaphor was taken literally and combined with the word "truth" in the expression "threads of truth." The tapestry was retained in the legend, but as the covering for the revela-

tion rather than the medium of it. Finally the revelation itself was transformed into a forecast of future history.

The mischief of later misunderstanding is evident elsewhere as well. Ibn
Khallikan records that Alhazred had visited the crypts of ancient Memphis.
He probably derived this information from this passage of the *Necronomicon*,
failing to realize that the "underground journey in Egypt" was simply part
of an older document adapted by Alhazred and incorporated into his book
of curiosities.

Chapter IX: Concerning the Dead

Fragment 7

Text: [1]Many and multiform are the dim horrors of Earth, infesting her ways from the prime. [2]They sleep beneath the unturned stone; they rise with the tree from its root; they move beneath the sea and in subterranean places; they dwell in the inmost adyta; [3]they emerge betimes from the shutten sepulchre of haughty bronze and the low grave that is sealed with clay. [4]There be some that are long known to man, and others as yet unknown that abide the terrible latter days of their revealing. [5]Those which are the most dreadful and the loathliest of all are haply still to be declared. [6]But among those that have revealed themselves aforetime and have made manifest their veritable presence, there is one which may not openly be named for its exceeding foulness. [7]It is that spawn which the hidden dweller in the vaults has begotten upon mortality.[1]

Version: Unknown, though possibly Wormius' Latin in light of Fragment 8.

Commentary:
With vv. 1-5, we seem to have the beginning of a new section, that grouping of material which led Philetas to give the work its Greek title *Necronomicon*, or "Book of the Dead." The next passages all refer to matters of necrophagy and necromancy. Interestingly, it is apparent that Alhazred himself was revolted at the curiosities and practices he set before the reader.

v. 1. The "horrors" seem, from the context, to be monsters or creatures which are "dim" to us, i.e., we neither perceive nor understand them at all clearly. There are many of them, and they come in many varieties. They have always dwelt unwholesomely ("infested" Earth's "ways"). The "ways" are the various channels and recesses of the planet. They are enumerated in the next verse. (Also, see commentary on 8:6.)

v. 2. Like disgusting bugs and vermin, they hide beneath stones. Like root-rot disease, they seep into the trees alongside more wholesome nourishment from the soil. Some are sea-monsters prowling the nighted depths; others hibernate in unsuspected lairs far beneath earth's surface. All in all, they are hidden away in the "adyta", or secret places.

v. 3. "Betimes" is probably a mistranslation. It means "in good time" or "soon", but the context seems to demand "sometimes." At any rate, these particular "horrors" emerge from the tombs of rich as well as poor. Both grand and humble tombs are described as having been secured ("shutten" and "sealed") but to no avail, since the monsters have appeared there. How?

Perhaps via "the secret portal each tomb is known to have" (5:4). These "horrors" might be ghouls, though another possibility will concern us below, in verse 7.

v. 4. Some of the many monsters are already familiar, such as those of the previous verse. Others are still unsuspected, at least to humanity by and large. Obviously, Alhazred is not ignorant of them or he would not be writing about them. The reference to "terrible latter days of their revealing" has a distinctly apocalyptic ring. We may wonder if the author is not making a sidelong reference to what most of mankind deems (or would deem if they knew) the ultimate horror—the coming of the Great Old Ones. The conspiratorial tone is reminiscent of the smug and taunting Fragment 3, which deals with the return of Alhazred's gods.

v. 5. The point is the same as in v. 4. The worst horrors may perhaps ("haply") yet lie in the future.

v. 6. Here Alhazred begins his consideration of several specific monstrosities, to which the first five verses have formed a preface. Of those terrors which have already revealed their presence before the final onslaught, there is one in particular about which he is reticent to speak in detail.

Incidentally, the thought pattern here is familiar. Though the reference here is not to the Old Ones, we are reminded of 3:17, "as a foulness shall ye know them." Compare 3:17 with 7:6, "one which may not openly be named for its exceeding foulness." Though the point is not quite the same in context, both verses share the notion that an alien entity may not be known except by the simple fact of its "foulness."

v. 7. Some have interpreted the "spawn ... of the hidden dweller in the vaults" as the fruit of a blasphemous union between ghouls and the dead. This is possible on a reading of this text taken by itself. But if ghouls are in view, then we must read into the passage some explanation for their presence in a sealed tomb. We have hazarded such a guess above, but the problem can be avoided if we restore the passage to its full context. We suggest that Fragment 7 was originally followed immediately by Fragment 8, which places the preceding verses in a whole new light. Fragment 8 relates how the disembodied souls of wizards linger in the grave, forming a new host body from the very worms which devour the old one. Such a disembodied soul is the "hidden dweller in the vault" of 7:&. It entered secretly along with the corpse. Its "spawn" is the new walking humanoid worm that issues from the terrible process, and leaves the tomb to plague mankind ("mortality").

Fragment 8

Text: [1]The nethermost caverns are not for the fathoming of eyes that see; for their marvels are strange and terrific. [2]Cursed the ground where dead thoughts live new and oddly bodied, and evil the mind that is held by no head. [3]Wisely did Ibn Schacabao say, that happy is the tomb where no wizard hath lain, and happy the town at night whose wizards are all ashes. [4]For it is of old rumor that the soul of the devil-bought hastes not from his charnel clay, but fats and instructs the very worm that gnaws; till out of corruption horrid life springs, [5]and the dull scavengers of earth wax crafty to vex it, and swell monstrous to plague it. [6]Great holes secretly are digged where earth's pores ought to suffice, and things have learnt to walk that ought to crawl.[2]

Version: This passage comes from Wormius' Latin version.

Commentary:

v. 1. "Eyes that see" at first appears to be a redundancy. Actually, it is a reference to the blind creatures, e.g., fish, who inhabit the deepest caves and grottos. Of course, the eyes of such a species have simply become atrophied through evolution. There is no need for them to have functional eyes since there is no light. Alhazred uses the creatures as a striking metaphor: In such depths there are things to be seen that are so terrible, nature has mercifully blessed innocent creatures who live there with blindness. (A similar metaphor is used in Fragment 6.) Alhazred is about to describe, or at least hint at, these awful things which disgust even him.

v. 2. In this and the next verse, Alhazred has juxtaposed a set of "woes" with a set of "blessings", combining his own imprecation formulae with benedictions by Ibn Schacabao. Luke has used the same technique in his "Sermon on the Plain", taking the list of beatitudes from the earlier source he shares with the Gospel according to Matthew, and adding a matching set of "woes" of his own (Luke 6:20-26, cf. Matthew 5:3-12).

The two imprecations are parallel and may originally have formed an independent poetic epigram. "Dead thoughts" (i.e., the thoughts of the dead) proceed from a disembodied mind (one that is "held by no head"). Just how these thoughts became "[em]bodied" in a "new and odd" manner is elaborated in vv. 4 and 5.

v. 3. Ibn Schacabao (see Chapter IV) is once again quoted (cf. 4:3). "Happy" (or "blessed") is any tomb housing the remains of anyone but a wizard. The same goes for any townspeople wise enough to have cremated their wizards' remains (or perhaps to have burnt them at the stake!). In each case, the point is that one must not bury the body of a sorcerer. The reason is given below.

Note, incidentally, that the wizard's anticipated mischief would occur "at night", as in the vampire legends.

v. 4. This verse provides more evidence that the *Necronomicon* is not a grimoire, for Alhazred seems to despise pacts with the devil. He describes wizards as "devil-bought" and does not seem to approve.

At any rate, the soul of a dead wizard is believed to haunt the grave. It "fats and instructs" the worms that come to consume the corpse. That is, it imparts both new substance and intelligence to the carrion creatures. This is how "dead thoughts" come to be "new and oddly bodied"—the mind of the wizard possesses and transforms the flesh of the worm, giving itself a new host. The result is a hideous resurrection: "out of corruption horrid life springs." The phrase recalls in a twisted way the legendary Phoenix, rising reborn from its own ashes.

v. 5. The worms, normally "dull", thus grow clever enough to "vex" the earth they used to scavenge. Their bodily shape "swells monstrously" into a parody of humanity, in which form it will plague the earth.

v. 6. The "vexing" and "plaguing" of the earth primarily takes the form of burrowing large tunnels in the earth's fabric, instead of merely slipping through the soil's natural pores as they used, as small worms, to do. In their new humanoid form, the wizard-possessed creatures need cavernous passages through which to walk. This is probably in view in 7:1, with the phrase "infesting [earth's] ways from the prime."

It is probably also the phenomenon described here that Alhazred alludes to in 5:4 as "that which groweth out of the tenants [of the tomb]." Together Fragments 5 and 8 would imply that the nightmarishly resurrected wizards still have one danger to cope with—the threat of ghouls waiting to devour them in their new incarnation.

Fragment 9

Text: [1]It is verily known by few, but is nevertheless an attestable fact, that the will of a dead sorcerer hath power upon his own body and can raise it up from the tomb and perform therewith whatever action was unfulfilled in life. [2]And such resurrections are invariably for the doing of malevolent deeds and for the detriment of others. [3]Most readily can the corpse be animated if all its members have remained intact; [4]and yet there are cases in which the excelling will of the wizard hath reared up from death the sundered pieces of a body hewn in many fragments, [5]and hath caused them to serve his end, either separately or in a temporary reunion. [6]But in every instance, after the action hath been completed, the body lapseth into its former state.[3]

Version: This passage comes from the original Arabic, and is omitted from Wormius' Latin. Presumably Philetas included it and Wormius likely omitted it simply by accident. See below.

Commentary:

v. 1. Note again the tone of an insider deigning to reveal his secrets to a wider audience. This is typical of the "book of marvels." Also, the introduction is a standard "attestation formula" repeated in 10:1.

This verse begins the discussion of another version of the "wizard's resurrection" theme familiar from the preceding passages (Fragments 7 and 8). According to the present version, the deceased wizard's mind also survives the death of the body, but whereas before he abandoned his corpse for a new body, now he merely reanimates the corpse for temporary use. The goal here is not to continue one's life indefinitely, but rather simply to "tie up the loose ends" remaining from one's affairs, cut short by death. After the mission is accomplished, the wizard (apparently) resigns himself to death. The whole notion is rather parallel to that of a ghost seeing to the affairs of the departed, e.g., gaining proper burial.

v. 2. Such resuscitations are never for any wholesome purpose. We are not, for instance, to imagine the wizard sending his remains back to rectify some error in the distribution of his goods. No, the purpose is always malicious. One is reminded of the vampire legends wherein the returning dead prey upon the innocent. This passage probably refers only to the gaining of vengeance on those responsible for the wizard's death.

v. 3. The resurrection may be effected with least difficulty if the body is still more or less intact.

v. 4. Yet even if the wizard's murderer has tried to prevent such revenge from the grave by chopping the corpse to pieces, he may not be safe. If a wizard's will is extraordinarily strong, even the dismembered pieces may be marshaled for vengeance.

Note the terminology of a compiler of curiosities: "there are cases in which ...."

v. 5. The wizard may reanimate the body parts singly or in reassembled form.

v. 6. In any case, the resurrection is finally temporary. The goal, again, was not the resumption of life as before.

Does the conception of "wizard's resurrection" in this passage not contradict that found in Fragments 7 and 8? Obviously so, but compilers like Alhazred were seldom greatly concerned with absolute consistency. He is concerned only to catalog and relate the curious superstitions he has assembled from whatever source.

Incidentally, the text is said to have supplied an elaborate formula for exorcising such a spectral visitor.[4] It involved rare Arabian spices and lists of a hundred or more names of ghouls and demons, as if to "cast out demons by Beelzebub" (Matthew 12:27). One wonders how many of these names the frightened reader could get through before the reanimated skeleton attacked?

Fragment 10

Text: [1]'Tis a veritable & attestable Fact, that between certain related Persons there exists a Bond more powerful than the strongest Ties of Flesh and Family, [2]whereby one such Person may be *aware* of all the Trials & Pleasures of the other, yea, even to experiencing the Pains or Passions of one far distant; [3]& further, there are those whose skills in such Matters are aided by forbidden Knowledge or Intercourse through dark Magic with Spirits & Beings of outside Spheres. [4]Of the latter: I have sought them out, both Men & Women, & upon Examination have in all Cases discovered them to be Users of Divination, Observors of Times, Enchanters, Witches, Charmers, or Necromancers. [[5]All claimed to work their Wonders through Intercourse with dead & departed Spirits, [6]but I fear that often such Spirits were evil Angels, the Messengers of the Dark One & yet more ancient Evils.] [7]Indeed, among them were some whose Powers were prodigious, who might at will *inhabit* the Body of another even at a great Distance & against the Will & often unbeknown to the Sufferer of such Outrage. [8]Yea, & I discovered how one might, be he an Adept & his familiar Spirits powerful enough, control the Wanderings or Migration of his Essence into all manner of Beings & Persons— [9]even from beyond the Grave of Sod or the Door of the Stone Sepulcher.[5]

Version: Unknown, but translated into English by Joachim Feery.

Commentary:

vv. 1-2. Alhazred repeats the formula of attestation with which he began the preceding passage. As we will see, the present section follows 7, 8, and 9 with basically the same theme, the powers of a wizard after death. He begins by describing what we would call a telepathic link between certain individuals. Such alleged phenomena are notoriously difficult to verify, but such as seem to occur usually involve identical twins. Surprisingly, Alhazred seems to rule out such "ties of flesh and family", unless he simply means that natural family loyalties, even strong ones (*very* strong in his day, when blood-feuds were not uncommon), pale in comparison to such telepathy.

v. 3. Some thus gifted have augmented their psychic abilities through occult study and spiritualistic contact with alien beings. They are described as the inhabitants of "outside spheres", terminology characteristic of Alhazred's cosmology (cf. 3:20).

v. 4. Alhazred has made special efforts to learn the secrets of this latter group. "In all cases" (again, the telltale language of the collector of curiosities), these individuals turned out to be full-fledged practitioners of the black arts. Did he not already know they had sought occult aid? Perhaps the point is that his suspicions were confirmed that no one who dabbles in magic can avoid becoming completely enmeshed in it.

vv. 5-6. These verses seem to be an interpolation by Joachim Feery, in whose *Original Notes on the* Necronomicon the whole passage is preserved. The mention of "evil angels" and the devil are more likely to represent Feery's religious beliefs than Alhazred's. Feery is notorious for rewriting quoted materials, and we seem to have an example of his doing it here. However, it may be that Feery meant only to make a parenthetic observation: Alhazred accepted the occultists' claims, but Feery himself does not. If this is the case, Feery's omission of appropriate punctuation gives the impression that Alhazred himself disputed the claims of his informants.

v. 7. Some of the occultist-psychics were able not only to share perceptions with others, but also to *possess* them, replacing the hosts' senses with their own. This they could do over long distances and against the host's will. It could even be done without the victim's knowledge. Presumably the person, upon regaining his senses, would merely seem to suffer memory loss, unaware of what had happened. Obviously, the purpose of such an operation would be nefarious—for instance, to employ someone else's body to commit some crime.

v. 8. We have not passed beyond telepathy to astral projection, or soul travel. Alhazred confides that with sufficient expertise and supernatural assistance, one may even occupy minds and bodies other than human.

v. 9. Such astral projection is yet another means by which a wizard may continue to work his will after death. Neither a grave dug in the ground nor a carved mausoleum can imprison the wizard who had, in life, mastered soul-travel and psychic possession.

With this passage, we have reached the end of Alhazred's material on the powers of the wizard beyond the grave. He has outlined how a dead sorcerer may return in a hybrid body of worm-flesh, how he may send his skeletal remains on a brief mission of revenge, and finally how he may send only his disembodied soul to do his bidding in the body of another.

As a sidelight, this passage is of particular interest for the light it sheds upon Joachim Feery himself. We have remarked upon Feery's notorious practice of freely augmenting and rewriting ancient texts. He is said to have received his inspiration to do this from dreams. Fragment 10 of the *Necronomicon* describes just what Feery thought he was doing—acting as host for the mind of Alhazred and others! In his own estimate, he was the medium whereby the ancient writers revised and updated their work! The same sort of delusion has been shared by other eccentrics in our day, including various UFO-contactees and bus-station prophets through whom, e.g., Jesus Christ has rewritten the gospel for the space age.

Section Three: The Apocryphal Material
Chapter X: The Fall of Cthulhu

Fragment 11

Text: [1]'Twas done then as it had been promised aforetime, that he was taken by Those Whom he defied, and thrust into the nethermost deeps under the sea, [2]and placed within the barnacled tower that is said to rise amidst the great ruin that is the sunken city (R'lyeh), and sealed within by the Elder Sign, [3]and, raging at Those who had imprisoned him, he further incurred Their anger, [4]and They, descending upon him for the second time, did impose upon him the semblance of death, but left him dreaming in that place under the great waters, [5]and returned to that place from whence they had come, namely, Glyu-Vho, which is among the stars, [6]and looketh upon earth from the time when the leaves fall to that time when the ploughman becomes habited once again to his fields. [7]And there shall he lie dreaming forever, in his house at R'lyeh, [8]toward which at once all his minions swam and strove against all manner of obstacles, and arranged themselves to wait for his awakening, powerless to touch the Elder Sign and fearful of its great power [9]knowing that the cycle returneth, and he shall be freed to embrace the earth again and make of it his kingdom and defy the Elder Gods anew. [10]And to his brothers it happened likewise, that they were taken by Those Whom they defied and hurled into banishment, [11]Him Who is Not to Be Named being sent into outermost space, beyond the stars, [12]and with the others likewise, until the earth was free of them, [13]and Those Who came in the shape of Towers of Fire, returned whence they had come, and were seen no more, and on all earth their peace came [14]and was unbroken while their minions gathered and sought means and ways with which to free the Old Ones, [15]and waited while man came to pry into secret, forbidden places and open the gate.[1]

Version: This fragment comes from a collection of translations of random chapters, each out of different editions and versions, no longer specifiable.

Commentary:

v. 1. "He", as is evident from the context, is Cthulhu. Vv. 1-8 of this fragment seem to have originally constituted an independent unit of tradition, a narrative of the "Fall of Cthulhu", elaborated from the ambiguous passage 3:14-15. The beginning of the narrative is lost, as v. 1 begins in the middle of the action ("'Twas done *then* ...."). For some unspecified action, perhaps described in the preceding lost text, he is imprisoned in a tower beneath the sea.

This is all said to have been previously prophesied. A summary of the epic of the Elder Gods and the Old Ones preserved elsewhere[2] mentions the Prophet Kish of Sarnath, who may be intended here. We are reminded of how, frequently in the Qur'an, Muhammad names pre-Muslim prophets, co-opting them as precursors of Islam. In the same way, the writer of the present text has appropriated the legendary figure Kish as a proponent of the Elder Gods against the Old Ones, a scenario that arose long after Alhazred.

Parenthetically, "the Prophet Kish" is perhaps to be identified historically with King Saul of Israel. The latter was also known as a prophet and as the son of Kish: "What has come over the son of Kish? Is Saul also among the prophets?" (I Samuel 10:11). The "Prophet, son of Kish" has become the "Prophet Kish of Sarnath."

v. 2. "R'lyeh" is apparently a marginal gloss, incorporated into the text.

The seal of the Old Ones (3:14) has been identified with the "Elder Sign" of 5:4.

v. 3. It is not clear just how Cthulhu, trapped in an undersea tower, could have "further incurred their anger." It looks as if this verse is a kind of patch intended to harmonize two originally independent (and divergent) versions of the punishment of Cthulhu: that he was imprisoned (v. 2), and that he was put to sleep (v. 4).

v. 4. The phrase "for the second time" has been added for the sake of harmonization (see above, v. 3).

v. 5. The Elder Gods are the subject here.

The late origin of our text is evident from the confusion of the cosmology of Alhazred. According to 3:3, the Old Ones (= the "Elder Gods" here; see Chapter V) exist beyond dimensioned space. Here they are located simply far away in space. Similarly, "Glyu-Vho" seems to be a corruption of "S'glhuo" (4:3), which originally had nothing to do with the Old Ones.

v. 6. The star is visible from the writer's perspective during fall and winter. This may be an explanatory gloss, since it interrupts the flow of thought.

v. 7. This verse, the conclusion of the original "Fall of Cthulhu" unit, supposes that Cthulhu has been laid to rest "forever." Thus, this unit of tradition dates from a time after the reformist faction had rejected Cthulhu as a rebellious demon, but before his temporary return was expected. It has been inserted here in a later context.

vv. 8-9. The theology of v. 7 has been updated, so that Cthulhu is now attended by a host of demons who await his liberation. The idea is parallel to that of Revelation 20:2-3: "He seized the dragon, that ancient serpent, who is the devil or Satan, and bound him for a thousand years. He threw him into the Abyss, and locked and sealed it over him, to keep him from deceiving the nations any more until the thousand years were ended. After that, he must be set free for a short time." Also note a Zoroastrian parallel from the fourth book of the Bundahishn: "It is said in the Religion that when the Destructive Spirit [Ahriman] saw that he himself and the demons were powerless. ... he was thrown into a stupor. For three thousand years he lay in a stupor. And when he was thus languishing, the demons with monstrous heads cried out one by one (saying), 'Arise, O our father, for we would join battle in the material world that Ohrmazd and the Amahraspands may suffer straitness and misery thereby.'"[3] How strikingly this image has resurfaced in the reformist sect's mythology: Cthulhu, vanquished, "waits dreaming" while his minions seek vainly to awaken him before the appointed time to do battle against the Elder Gods.

vv. 10-12. This story of Cthulhu's punishment has been summarily applied to the rest of "his brothers."

v. 13. The Elder Gods are described as "Towers of Fire", an image borrowed, ultimately, from Exodus 13:21.

vv. 14-15. The reference is to the worshipers of Cthulhu, whose worship is construed by the reformist faction as the mere attempt to call up demons.

Fragment 12

Text: [1]Eternal is the Power of Evil, and infinite in its contagion! [2]The Great Cthulhu yet hath sway over the minds and spirits of Men, [3]yea, even though He lieth chained and ensorcelled, bound in the fetters of The Elder Sign, [4]His malignant and loathly Mind spreadeth the dark seeds of Madness and Corruption into the dreams and Nightmares of sleeping men ....[4]

Version: From the English translation of John Dee.

Commentary:

v. 1. Evil's power does not fade, and there is no limit to its corrupting influence ("contagion").

v. 2. The specific "evil" in view is Cthulhu, who still controls human minds. Thus this passage is the work of the later, reformist faction. Alhazred did not consider Cthulhu evil.

v. 3. The writer refers to 3:14-15. The "seal", said there to be engraved on the sunken buildings, is interpreted as the "Elder Sign" from 5:4. Originally, however, its meaning in 5:4 was that of a largely powerless talisman of some conventional religion.

v. 4. Interestingly, our author has attributed to Cthulhu the power of tele-pathic projection discussed by Alhazred in connection with dead wizards in 10:8-9.

Fragment 13

Text: [1]Concerning the Old Ones, 'tis writ, they wait ever at the Gate, [2]and the Gate is all places at all times, for They know nothing of time or place but are in all time & in all places together without appearing to be, [[3]& there are those amongst Them which can assume divers shapes & features & any given shape & any given face] [4]& the Gates are for Them everywhere, but the first was that which I caused to be opened, namely in Irem, the City of Pillars, the city under the desert, [5]but wherever men set up the stones and say thrice the forbidden words, they shall cause there a Gate to be established & shall wait upon them Who Come through the Gate, [6]even as the Dhols, & the Abominable Mi-Go, & the Tcho-Tcho people, & the Deep Ones, & the Gugs, & the Gaunts of the Night & the Shoggoths, & the Voormis, & the Shantaks which guard Kadath in the Cold Waste & the Plateau [of] Leng. [7]All are alike the children of the Elder Gods.

[8]But the Great Race of Yith & the Great Old Ones failing to agree [one with another, & both] with the Elder Gods, separated, [9]leaving the Great Old Ones in possession of the Earth, [10]while the Great Race returning from Yith took up Their abode forward in time in earth-land not yet known to those who walk the Earth today, [11]& there wait till there shall come again the winds & the voices which drove them forth before [12]& that which walketh on the winds over the earth & in the spaces that are among the stars forever.[5]

Version: This fragment comes from a collection of translations of random chapters, each out of different editions and versions, no longer specifiable.

Commentary:
This fragment is particularly difficult to decipher. Not only does it seem to represent a condensed summary of some original, but the original is itself a puzzling conflation of three unrelated units.

vv. 1-2, 4-6. This section was originally a tribute to Alhazred (put pseudo-nymously into his own mouth) as the first mortal to open the way for the return of the Old Ones. It is comparatively late, as can be seen from the leg-endary embellishment of Alhazred's journey to Irem. His twelfth century biographer Ibn Khallikan listed as one of the marks of his madness that Alhazred claimed to have visited the ruined "City of the Pillars," whose ancient destruction was chronicled in the Qur'an:

> Hast thou not seen how thy Lord dealt with Ad,
> At Irem adorned with pillars,
> Whose like have not been reared in these lands? (89:5-7)

Nothing is said or implied about Alhazred performing any rites on this occasion, and certainly nothing is said about it being an occasion of such importance as it is made here. Since it shows such development from the simpler version known to Ibn Khallikan, the passage must have been composed after the twelfth century.

Alhazred is made to promise that any readers performing the appropriate rites will be aiding the Old Ones in their return. A technical apocalyptic phrase is used in this connection: "Them Who Come." This recalls John the Baptist's title for the expected Messiah, "He That Cometh", as well as the Shi'ite title for the Mahdi, "He Who Shall Arise."

This section, celebrating Alhazred as the harbinger of the Old Ones, is the only surviving interpolation stemming from the pro-Cthulhu faction.

vv. 3, 5-7. These verses, woven clumsily into the context, are the product of the reformist sect, the adherents of the Elder Gods. The unit is a sort of "bestiary", enumerating a vast catalog of legendary creatures, probably from local folklore. "Kadath" appears in 3:13. and "Leng" is mentioned in 17:3. Kadath is perhaps the biblical Kadesh in the Sinai desert, while Leng is an alternate name for Tibet. The Plateau of Leng was mentioned by Alhazred in connection with a sphinx-like talisman used by a necrophagous cult of some kind. The passage has been lost.

In the original unit, all these creatures were said to be creations of the Elder Gods, as if to incorporate random folklore into the official pantheon. By their inclusion here, they are being shunted into the ranks of the Old Ones.

vv. 8-12. These verses form another originally distinct unit. The translation is very poor, confusing tenses and resulting in overall incoherence. In general, the fragment merely rehearses the myth of the "Fall of the Old Ones."

The bracketed words seem to be a still later addition. The copyist did not understand the term "Yith", and read the "Great Race of Yith" as a third group distinct from the "Great Old Ones." In fact "Yith" seems to be an abbreviation of "Y[og-Sotho]th." This is a case of what Old Testament critic D. R. Ap-Thomas calls an "unresolved abbreviation." Ancient scribes seem on occasion to have abbreviated plurals and proper names, assuming later scribes, making new copies from their own, would understand the abbreviation. If later scribes did not understand the abbreviations, various confusions crept into the text. Sometimes such abbreviations were conjecturally and wrongly resolved.[6] Thus the "Great Race of Yog-Sothoth" and the "Great Old Ones" are the same. The terms are mentioned together in poetic parallelism twice in the passage.

The Old Ones rebelled against ("failed to agree with") the Elder Gods and "possessed the earth." The text suddenly jumps to the temporary return of the Old Ones before their final defeat.

Verse 10 has particularly suffered in translation. The sense seems to be that the Great Race will return though (not "from") "Y[og-Sotho]th", who is understood as the Gate of the spheres (*cf.* 3:4). This return to make their abode again on Earth is to occur in the future, though exactly when, no one knows ("forward in time ... not yet known to those who walk the Earth today"). Their ultimate defeat is predicted in v. 11, but much of the terminology is obscure.

Chapter XI: Apocalyptic Tracts

Fragment 14

Text: [1]Then shall they return & on this great returning shall the Great Cthulhu be freed from R'lyeh beneath the sea [2]& Him Who Is Not To Be Named shall come from his city which is Carcosa near the Lake of Hali, [3]& Shub-Niggurath shall come forth & multiply in his hideousness, [4]& Nyarlathotep shall carry the word to all the Great Old Ones & their minions, [5]& Cthugha shall lay his hand upon all that oppose him & destroy, [6]& the blind idiot, the noxious Azathoth shall arise from the middle of the World where all is chaos & destruction where he hath bubbled & blasphemed at the centre which is of all things, which is to say infinity, [7]& Yog-Sothoth, who is the All-in-One & One-in-All, shall bring his globes, [8]& Ithaqua shall walk again, [9]& from the black-litten caverns within the earth shall come Tsathoggua, [10]& together shall take possession of earth and all things that live upon it, [11]& shall prepare to do battle with the Elder Gods when the Lord of the Great Abyss is apprised of their returning & shall come with His brothers to disperse the evil.[1]

Version: From a seventeenth century Latin edition, presumably that of Olaus Wormius.

Commentary:

v. 1. Though the text as we have it is missing its introduction ("Then ....") implies something previous), it is a substantially complete apocalypse, or predictive outline of the end of the age, such as we find in Mark 13, Matthew 24, Luke 21, and the Book of Revelation. The Old Ones will return to power. Cthulhu is listed first, as usual.

vv. 2-9. Various of the Old Ones, presumably the chief villains, are enumerated as returning from their places of exile/refuge.

There is an almost humorous description of Yog-Sothoth "bringing his globes." The writer lives so far after the time of Abdul Alhazred that he no longer understands the "spheres" of 3:20 and 10:3 to refer to the several universes linked by Yog-Sothoth.

v. 10. The Old Ones resume their ancient rule, but only briefly.

v. 11. They prepare for Armageddon, deceiving themselves into hoping they may overcome at last, but the Elder Gods will surely destroy them.

Interestingly, the leader of the Elder Gods is designated "the Lord of the Great Abyss", an epithet pretty much equivalent to the terms in which Azathoth is described in v. 6. There is no reason to believe that Alhazred had referred to Azathoth in the *Necronomicon*'s authentic sections as actually being one of the Old Ones, not one of their subordinates like Cthulhu. Recalling that the reformist sect's "Elder Gods" are the same as Alhazred's "Old Ones", it is surprising that Azathoth was repudiated along with Cthulhu. Perhaps only a semantic change is involved, as in the change from the title "Old Ones" (conceded to the "apostates") to that of "Elder Gods" (see Chapter V). Perhaps the reformists regarded the name "Azathoth" as polluted from its use by the "apostate" branch, and simply left it to them to avoid confusion. The original entity, ruler of the center of cosmic chaos, was henceforth designated simply as "Lord of the Great Abyss."

Fragment 15

Text: [1]Ubbo-Sathla is that [unbegotten] source whence came those daring to oppose the Elder Gods who ruled from Betelgueze, the Great Old Ones who fought against the Elder Gods; [2]and these Old Ones were instructed by Azathoth, who is the blind, idiot god, [3]and by Yog-Sothoth, who is the All-in-One and One-in-All, and upon whom are no strictures of time or space, [4]and whose aspects on earth are 'Umr At-Tawil and the Ancient Ones. [5]The Great Old Ones dream forever of that coming time when they shall once more rule earth and all that universe of which it is a part. [words missing] [6]Great Cthulhu shall rise from R'lyeh; [7]Hastur, who is Him Who Is Not To Be Named, shall come again from the dark star which is near Aldebaran in the Hyades; [8]Nyarlathotep shall howl forever in the darkness where he abideth; [9]Shub-Niggurath, who is the Black Goat with a Thousand Young, shall spawn and spawn again, and shall have dominion over all wood nymphs, satyrs, leprechauns, and the Little People; [10]Lloigor, Zhar, and Ithaqua shall ride the spaces among the stars and shall ennoble those who are their followers, who are the Tcho-Tcho; [11]Cthugha shall encompass his dominion from Fomalhaut; [12]Tsathoggua shall come from N'kai [words missing]. [13]They wait forever at the Gates, for the time draws near, the hour is soon at hand, [14]while the Elder Gods sleep, dreaming, unknowing there are those who know the spells put upon the Great Old Ones by the Elder Gods, and shall learn how to break them, [15]as already they can command the followers waiting beyond the doors from Outside.[2]

Version: This fragment comes from a collection of translations of random chapters, each out of a different edition and version, no longer specifiable.

Commentary:

vv. 1-4. The translator must have inadvertently written "unforgotten" for "unbegotten" in v. 1. We have emended the text accordingly.

This section seems to be a fragment of a demonology, a systematizing of the various Great Old Ones, their powers and duties. It is reminiscent of the hierarchical rankings of demons catalogued by Wierus and other medieval demonologists. Note, incidentally, the ever-growing number of Old Ones as listed in the following verses.

The demonologist had before him portions of the original *Necronomicon* corresponding to our Fragments 3 and 5. Failing to understand the Hermetic context of 5, he felt compelled to harmonize 'Umr At-Tawil with Yog-Sothoth. Thus the scribe has been doubly deified!

vv. 5-15. These verses form an apocalypse, seemingly another version of Fragment 14. There are a few interesting variations which deserve note.

v. 5. This may be identical to the lost introduction to Fragment 14.

v. 7. "Him Who Is Not To Be Named"—is named! His secret identity is "Hastur." Apparently someone could not resist the temptation. The same sort of thing has occurred in Matthew's use of his source, Mark 8:27. In the earlier form, Jesus asks the disciples, "Who do people say I am?" In Matthew's version, Jesus himself is made to answer his own question in midsentence: "Who do people say the Son of Man is?" (Matthew 16:13).

v. 8. In this version, Nyarlathotep is shown howling in the darkness. This sounds at first as if he is still imprisoned. The context has all the Old Ones pouring forth from their lairs like a plague of locusts (or, as the Qur'an depicts the dead starting from their tombs on Resurrection Morning, "as in a race"). Probably we are to understand his howling as equivalent to 14:4, i.e., as his manner of "bearing the word" to the rest of the Old Ones.

v. 9. To Shub-Niggurath is attributed control over various creatures drawn from European folklore. This implies that our writer is himself a European.

v. 13 uses classical apocalyptic imagery. The Old Ones "wait at the Gate." *Cf.* Matthew 24:33: "When you see all these things, you know that he is near, right at the door"; also "The Judge is standing at the door!" (James 5:9b). Our passage warns that "the time draws near; the hour is soon at hand." *Cf.* Mark 1:15: "The time is fulfilled; the Kingdom of God is at hand."

vv. 14-15. The point here is not that the Elder Gods are literally oblivious to all this mischief. Rather, they have "closed their eyes to it." They are patiently "giving the Old Ones enough rope to hang themselves." The minions of Cthulhu may imagine they are making real progress. Yet they are playing right into the hands of the Elder Gods, who are only waiting for the Old Ones to rise up like clay pigeons to be shattered.

Chapter XII: Rites of Exorcism

Fragment 16

Text: [[1]There is no curse that has no cure and no ill against which no remedy exists. [2]The Elder Gods dwell remote and aloof from the affairs of men, [3]yet They have not abandoned us to the wrath of them from Outside and Their abominable minions:[1]]

[4]Armor against witches and daemons, against the Deep Ones, the Dholes, the Voormis, the Tcho-Tcho, the Abominable Mi-Go, the Shoggoths, the Ghasts, the Valusians, and all such peoples and beings who serve the Great Old Ones and their Spawn [5]lies within the five-pointed star carven of grey stone from ancient Mnar, which is less strong against the Great Old Ones themselves. [6]The possessor of the stone shall find himself able to command all beings which creep, swim, crawl, walk, or fly even to the source from which there is no returning.

> [7]In Yhe as in great R'lyeh
> In Y'ha-nthlei as in Yoth,
> In Yuggoth as in Zothique,
> In N'kai as in K'n-yan,
> In Kadath in the Cold Waste as at the Lake of Hali,
> In Carcosa as in Ib,
> It shall have power

[8]yet, even as stars wane and grow cold, even as suns die and the spaces between the stars grow more wide, so wanes the power of all things— [9]of the five-pointed star-stone as of the spells put upon the Great Old Ones by the benign Elder Gods, [10]and there cometh a time as once was a time, when it shall be that

> [11]That is not dead which can eternal lie
> And with strange eons even death may die.[2]

Version: From a seventeenth century Latin edition, presumably that of Olaus Wormius.

Commentary:

v. 1. This poetic phrase introduces what is essentially the text of a rite of exorcism.

v. 2. The aloofness of the Elder Gods is stated in terms reminiscent of the theology of Epicurus.

v. 3. As in Deism, the Gods are pictured as having bequeathed to man what he needs for survival, though now it is up to him to fend for himself.

Note: The first three verses are absent from some manuscripts. Also, those sources which contain it reverse the order of vv. 4 and 5.

v. 4. The terminology "armor against witches and demons" indicates the medieval origin of this fragment. It is a product of the reformist sect, followers of the Elder Gods.

Various creatures of fable and folklore are here considered servants of the devilish Old Ones, in agreement with the redactor of Fragment 13.

v. 5. The pentacle (derived from that of Solomon) is the chief weapon in this arsenal. It has some power, though not much, against the Great Old Ones themselves.

v. 6. Armed with the five-pointed amulet, one may consign the unclean creatures to the bottomless pit ("from which there is no returning")—cf. Luke 8:30-31, where the demons "begged Jesus repeatedly not to order them to go into the Abyss."

v. 7. This is the incantation. The names are evidently those of the refuges of the demons. The formula extends the power of the amulet to all of them, cutting off any escape. Thus the demon cannot disobey the exorcist's command to enter the bottomless pit.

Note: In Feery's version the formula is slightly different after the third line, reading:

> In N'Kai as in Naa-Hk & K'n-yan
> In Carcosa as in G'harne
> In the twin Cities of Ib and Lh-yib
> In Kadath in the Cold Waste as at the Lake of Hali.[3]

Obviously, this version is the later one; the original symmetry has been clumsily interrupted.

vv. 8-11. The incantation is only a stopgap measure against the Old Ones' minions in the time before the final outbreaking of the Old Ones themselves, preparatory to their final destruction by the Elder Gods. If the charm should seem less than effective, all is not lost. It simply means that the final triumph of the Elder Gods is close at hand. The purpose of these verses is to provide fail-safe protection for the would-be exorcist's faith—he wins either way!

This notion of the eventual waning of the five-pointed "Elder Sign" may have been derived from the reformists' exegesis of 5:4. There they read of some "Evil that defieth the Elder Sign." Alhazred seems only to have intended a reference to ghouls against whom no tomb is effectively sealed. These later interpreters have linked the text (out of context) to 3:14-15 which, as they interpreted it, depicted Cthulhu as imprisoned with the "seal" of the Elder Gods. Together the reinterpreted passages seemed to suggest that one day Cthulhu would be able to "defy the Elder Sign", i.e., the seal of the Elder Gods, which had long entombed him in R'lyeh.

Verse 11 quotes 2:6-7, referring it to the reawakening of Cthulhu. The double meaning has been forgotten (see commentary on 2:6-7).

Fragment 17

Text: [1]Men know him as the Dweller in Darkness, that brother of the Old Ones called Nyogtha, the Thing that should not be. [2]He can be summoned to Earth's surface through certain secret caverns and fissures [3]and sorcerers have seen him in Syria and below the black tower of Leng; [4]from the Thang Grotto in Tartary he has come to bring terror and destruction among the pavilions of the great Khan. [5]Only by the looped cross, by the Vach-Viraj incantation and by the Tikkoun elixir may he be driven back to the nighted caverns of hidden foulness where he dwelleth.[4]

Version: From the fifteenth century Black Letter edition of some Latin translation prior to Wormius but often mistaken for Wormius' edition on the basis of Lovecraft's mistaken dating of Wormius.

Commentary:

v. 1. "Nyogtha" is called "that brother of the Old Ones", recalling a similar phrase in 3:15 ("Great Cthulhu is their cousin"). The point of the passage as a whole is how to exorcise him.

v. 2. The image is a striking one. Nyogtha passes the ages in a vault deep beneath the earth, connected to the surface only by a haphazard chain of ruptures in the earth's crust. He interrupts his hibernation to heed the psychic call of sorcerers, his dark bulk struggling against gravity ever upward through the dry beds of magma rivers, like Lucifer climbing slowly up from hell.

vv. 3-4. The local origin of the legend is indicated as being Tibet or Central Asia, for various reasons, as will become clear. "Leng" (see commentary on 13:6) is another name for Tibet.

The fact that Nyogtha is described as being "seen below a tower" implies that he was seen in a vision.

The passage is revealed as inauthentic by its reference to "the pavilions of the great Khan." He lived in the thirteenth century! The present text could obviously be no earlier than that time. Actually it seems to speak of the ravaging of the Khan's camp as an event of some distance in the past, so the text must be later still. The mention of the great Khan again betrays Central Asia as the origin of the traditions included in this text.

v. 5. The looped cross is the "ankh", the Egyptian symbol of life or wind.

The Vach-Viraj incantation must be an otherwise-unknown formula of Hindu-Buddhist yoga carried from India into Tibet by Padma Sambhava, a magician, exorcist, and living Buddha, in A.D. 632. In Hinduism, Tantra is usually found in Saiva (i.e., Siva-worshiping) contexts, while Buddhist Tantra (especially the Tibetan Vajrayana and Japanese Shingon sects) forms part of the great Mahayana school. The goal of Tantra is to overpass the perceived dualities of Samsara and attain unto the ultimately real, primal oneness of Nirvana or Dharmakaya. The mythological schema employed is one whereby the multiform universe as we know it was produced by a sexual union of the self-divided halves of the original divine One. In Saiva Tantrism, the original One is Siva. His creative power (*shakti*) is at least logically differentiated from himself as his bride Kali (or Durga), the famous mother goddess. The sexual union of the two begets the phenomenal world. In Buddhist terms, it is the Adi-Buddha who divides himself into the passive and mental *garbha* ("womb") element and the active and material *vajra* (alternately "lightning bolt", "adamantium", i.e., irresistible force, or "penis") element. The *vajra* impregnates the *garbha* and begets the phenomenal world.

By various means (whether the "left-handed path" using the "five forbidden substances", or the "right-handed path" of pure meditation) the yogi seeks to pass beyond the phenomenal world to the noumenal world of the primordial Oneness. As in all yoga, concentration formulas, or mantras, play a crucial role at this point, and the "Vach-Viraj incantation" must be such a mantra. "Vach" is simply another name for the *garbha*, while "Viraj" is just an alternate transliteration into English of *vajra*. The incantation, then, was a meditation formula to enable the yogi to pass beyond the duality represented by *vach* and *viraj* to the original One underlying both.[5] Its use as a magical charm is obviously debased superstition.

The terminology occurs in both Buddhist and Hindu Tantra, but in either case the mention of the Vach-Viraj incantation, together with the tacit assumption that any reader will be familiar with it, is further evidence that this piece of tradition originated in the Tibet-Central Asia area.

The reference to "the Tikkoun elixir", however, is jarring, as *tikkun* is the Hebrew word for "purification." It does not fit at all in the same cultural context as Tantric incantations. We must suppose that this reference has been added by our anonymous interpolator, himself a Near Easterner and not a Central Asian, because he was convinced of the potency of this purification tonic, or holy water, and felt no qualms about adding it to the exorcism recipe of the original Nyogtha tradition. The reference to this Hebrew magical elixir is an intriguing hint toward further narrowing down the date of the interpolation. *Tikkun* only gained currency as a technical term in Kabbalist mysticism around the fifteenth century A.D. It referred alternately to the Heavenly Adam ("Adam Kadmon"), or, as Blavatsky calls him, the "Manifested Logos", or to the ritual acts of piety prescribed by

Kabbalistic guru Isaac Luria in the 1500's.[6] However, since a "Tikkun elixir" has no evident relationship to either of these items of Kabbalistic lore, we must assume a more general meaning of "purification elixir" or "holy water", which gives us no real historical marker.

Finally, the origin of this passage is not hard to explain. Some collector of legends and marvels, like Alhazred himself, merely incorporated the Tibetan-Central Asian legend of Nyogtha the Dweller in Darkness, together with his own recommendation of the Tikkun elixir, into his copy of the *Necronomicon*. It seemed like the same kind of material he found there, and so he added it for the benefit of future readers. Such expansions of texts were not unusual, especially when the text was already a collection of oddities and wonder-tales. No more deceit was intended than is involved when new entries are added to "Webster's" dictionary as the years go by. Noah Webster himself did not write them, and no one is intended to think he did.

Chapter XIII: Christian Interpolations

(Note: Up to now, this section has dealt with interpolations made by the reformist faction of Alhazred's followers. The final fragments, however, are the work of Christian readers of the *Necronomicon*. We know of two Christian commentators on the book. Both were monks of the thirteenth century. Zecharias was a Nestorian, while Martin the Gardener was a Roman Catholic. The work of the former has perished (see Chapter V), and publication of the latter's text has been held up interminably. Thus it is not yet available for general study. We do know of Martin that he actually sought to fit the teachings of the *Necronomicon* into the categories of Christian demonology.[1] Therefore it is quite possible that he is the source of these interpolations. Another possibility is that John Dee is our interpolator. Though something of an occultist himself, he did write in a Christian setting. Besides, it is thought that his copy of the *Necronomicon* was heavily interpolated. Some passages, in fact, appeared in no other edition, and the obvious implication is that he himself composed them. Fragment 18 may be one of these. It comes from Dee's edition, and the copyist actually cites it as being from "John Dee's *Necronomicon*", implying that Dee not only translated it, but actually authored it.

Fragment 18

Text: [1]The cross is not a passive agent. [2]It protects the pure of heart, [3]and it has often appeared in the air above our sabbats, confusing and dispersing the powers of Darkness.[2]

Version: John Dee's English translation.

Commentary:

v. 1. Technically "passive agent" should refer to something that does not act on its own initiative, but is rather used by another. It is far from clear how this would apply one way or the other to the symbol of the cross. Probably this is simply a poor translation. The general sense of this verse would seem to be that the cross is not powerless.

v. 2. When worn as a talisman (?), it will protect the righteous.

v. 3. The scene evoked is a witches' sabbat suddenly thrown into chaos and terror by the miraculous appearance in midair of a luminous cross.

This passage can be neither authentic nor an interpolation by either of the factions. Alhazred is presenting himself as a villain, and as informing readers how they may thwart his evil designs! He would be likely neither to do this, nor to describe his Christian opponents with a noble-sounding epithet like "pure of heart." What we have here is a clumsy interpolation by ecclesiastical authorities. The rationale of the fiction would be to have the master-warlock himself attest to the effectiveness of the Church's power. *Cf.* the "Testimonium Flavianum", the famous Christian interpolation into Flavius Josephus' *Jewish Antiquities*, wherein the Jew Josephus is made to admit that Jesus was the true Messiah.

Fragment 19

Text: [1]I, Abdul Al-Hazred, say this to you: [2]The Elder Gods have put the damned to sleep. [3]And they that tamper with the seals and wake the sleepers, too, are damned. [4]And I say further, herein lie those spells to break the seals that hold in thrall Cthulhu and his ebon horde. [5]For I have spent my life to learn them all. [6]So, fool, the darkness is pent up in space: the gates to Hell are closed. [7]You meddle at your own expense: When you call they will wake and answer you. [8]This is my gift to mankind—here are the keys. [9]Find your own locks; be glad. [10]I, Abdul Al-Hazred say this to you: I, who tampered, and am mad.[3]

Version: Unknown.

Commentary:

v. 1. The introductory formula reveals this text as a "testament." This is one of the most common pseudonymous devices in ancient and medieval literature. The function of "testament" texts is to invoke the sagely wisdom of a famous authority at the culmination of his career. The speech put into the mouth of the dying patriarch Jacob in Genesis chapter 49 is a famous example; others would be the Farewell Discourse attributed to Jesus in John chapters 14-16, or the pseudonymous II Timothy where the Apostle Paul is presented as giving final instructions and delegating authority to Timothy. An extrabiblical example is "The Testaments of the Twelve Patriarchs." The pseudonymous testament seeks to appropriate the authority of "famous last words" for the work of a later writer, the real composer of the testament. What commences in this verse is such a document.

v. 2. This verse shows that the passage presupposes the later mythology, wherein the Great Old Ones play devils to the Elder Gods.

v. 3. Anyone who ranges himself with the Old Ones incurs for himself the wrath of higher powers.

vv. 4-7. This text has departed completely from either faction's conception of the return of the Old Ones. Both expected an apocalyptic return of the Old Ones (whether successful or abortive) to rule the earth. But here they are imagined as petty demons, genies captured in lamps which one only need rub to free them. They come and go, and when they come, the world is not changed. The summoner merely risks his own sanity (v. 10). The stakes have been lowered considerably.

This state of affairs assumes that the author himself does not belong to either branch of Alhazred's followers. He is an outsider who simply fears for the sanity or the (Judaeo-Christian) orthodoxy of any who read the dubious book. So he writes this preface, as if to say "Keep Out." Read *The Lives of the Saints* instead.

vv. 8-9. The phrase "be glad" does not fit in here. Perhaps it has been displaced by a copyist's error from its original position at the end of v. 6, where it would seem to fit better.

v. 10. The repetition of the name "Abdul Al-Hazred" is intended to underline the fact that even *he* could not "find new locks" to replace the ones with which he had tampered. He is mad as a result. Who is the reader to think he can do better?

Interestingly, it is to be noted that spurious testaments like this one are not rare even today. Church authorities have circulated similar apocryphal tales about the deathbed recanting of Thomas Paine, Voltaire, Lenin, and Charles Darwin. They are all of a piece with the present text.

Notes

Introduction

1. H. A. R. Gibb, *Arabic Literature: An Introduction* (Oxford at the Clarendon Press, 1963), p. 2.

2. Brian Lumley, *The Burrowers Beneath* (New York: DAW Books, 1974), p. 57.

3. I retain this nomenclature over the proposals of Dirk Mosig ("the Yog-Sothoth Cycle of Myth") and Lin Carter (the "Alhazredic Demonology"). The term "Cthulhu Mythos" does not seem particularly inadequate or misleading. Besides, it has the advantages of being more readily recognizable in general discussion, and of being less unwieldy than its two competitors. Both of these, like the mythical R'lyehian language, seem well nigh impossible for human speech organs to pronounce!

4. M. R. James, *The Apocryphal New Testament* (Oxford at the Clarendon Press, 1972), p.1.

Chapter I: The Critical Approach

1. Summaries of these developments may be found in Ronald E. Clements, *One Hundred Years of Old Testament Interpretation* (Philadelphia: Westminster Press, 1976); Stephen Neill, *The Interpretation of the New Testament: 1861-1961* (New York: Oxford University Press, 1966); and Albert Schweitzer, *The Quest of the Historical Jesus* (New York: Macmillan Company, 1950).

2. The principal discussion is to be found in David Friedrich Strauss, *The Life of Jesus Critically Examined* (Philadelphia: Fortress Press, 1972); Rudolf Bultmann, *The Gospel of John: A Commentary* (Philadelphia: Westminster Press, 1975); and J. Louis Martyn, *History & Theology in the Fourth Gospel* (Nashville: Abingdon, 1979).

3. To be completely accurate, there *is* some opposition to textual criticism, but this is usually forthcoming only from the most extreme religious fundamentalists, e.g., ultra-right-wing Protestants (*Holy Bible—a New Eye Opener*, Junction City, Oregon: Eye Opener Publishers, n.d.) and hyper-orthodox Jews (this conflict figures in Chaim Potok's novel *The Promise*). From quite a different quarter comes the snobbish disdain for text-critical studies on the part of secular literary critics, as described by Fredson Bowers (*Textual and Literary Criticism*, Cambridge University Press, 1966).

4. Seyyed Hossein Nasr, *Ideals and Realities of Islam* (Boston: Beacon Press, 1975), p. 57.

5. Idries Shah, *The Secret Lore of Magic: Books of the Sorcerers* (New York: Citadel Press, 1970), pp. 75, 76.

6. H. P. Lovecraft, *A History of the* Necronomicon (West Warwick, RI: Necronomicon Press, 1980), p. 3. Lovecraft is in error when he places

Wormius in the thirteenth century. The Danish physician and antiquarian's dates are 1588-1654, and his period of literary activity was 1636-1643. I owe this information to Richard L. Tierney.

7. This point has been well made by Wilfred Cantwell Smith in his essay "The Study of Religion and the Study of the Bible", in Williard G. Oxtoby (ed.), *Religious Diversity* (New York: Harper & Row, Publishers, 1976), pp. 41-58.

Chapter II: Abdul Alhazred

1. L. Sprague de Camp, *Al-Azif* (Philadelphia: Owlswick Press, 1973), p. xi.

2. Richard Bell and W. Montgomery Watt, *Introduction to the Qur'an* (Edinburgh at the University Press, 1977), p. 77.

3. *Ibid.,* p. 78.

4. H. A. R. Gibb, *Mohammedanism: An Historical Survey* (New York: New American Library, 1958), p. 36.

5. Lovecraft, *A History of the* Necronomicon, p. 2.

6. Quoted in Shah, *Secret Lore*, p. 66.

7. Kurt Koch, *Between Christ and Satan* (Grand Rapids: Kregel Publications, 1979), pp. 134-135.

8. Tor Andre, *Mohammed: The Man and His Faith* (New York: Harper & Row, Publishers, 1960), pp. 45-46.

9. Lovecraft, *A History of the* Necronomicon, p. 2.

Chapter III: What Kind of Book?

1. I am aware that today's neopagans claim that their faith is essentially *non*-Christian, not *anti*-Christian. This is true theoretically, but it is hard to deny that as a sociological phenomenon, the neopagan revival represents a repudiation of traditional religion. Even the possibly ancient *Aradia* hints at an anti-Christian origin. "Aradia", the witch-messiah, is simply another form of the name "Herodias", who engineered the death of John the Baptist.

2. For Wilson's suggestion, see his "The Return of the Lloigor" in August Derleth (ed.), *Tales of the Cthulhu Mythos* (Sauk City, WI: Arkham House, 1969), p. 357; for the theories of Wetzel and Bannister see Lin Carter, "H. P. Lovecraft: The Books" in August Derleth (ed.), *The Shuttered Room & Other Pieces* (Sauk City: Arkham House, 1959), p. 226. For Lovecraft's hypothesis, see *Selected Letters* V., p. 418.

3. S. T. Joshi, "Afterword", to Lovecraft's *A History of the* Necronomicon, p. ii.

4. These texts are collected in James M. Robinson (ed.), *The Nag Hammadi Library in English* (New York: Harper & Row, Publishers, 1977). On Gnosticism in general, see Hans Jonas, *The Gnostic Religion* (Boston: Beacon Press, 1963); Elaine Pagels, *The Gnostic Gospels* (New York: Random House, 1979); and Rudolf Bultmann, *Primitive Christianity in Its*

Contemporary Setting (New York: New American Library, 1974), especially the chapter "Gnosticism", pp. 162-174.

5. Koch, *Between Christ and Satan*, p. 131.

Chapter IV: Alhazred's Sources

1. This derivation is the suggestion of Bah'ai scholars Paul and Karen Webb.

2. Quoted in H. P. Lovecraft, *The Case of Charles Dexter Ward*, in his *At the Mountains of Madness and Other Novels* (Sauk City, WI: Arkham House, 1964), p. 142.

3. For an excellent discussion of the Hermetic literature, see C. H. Dodd, *The Interpretation of the Fourth Gospel* (Cambridge at the University Press, 1953), especially Part I, Chapter 2, "The higher religion of Hellenism: the Hermetic literature", pp. 10-53.

4. J. Everard (trans.), *The Divine Pymander of Hermes Trismegistus* (New York: Societas Rosicruciana in America, 1953), p. 9-10.

5. See Rudolf Bultmann and Karl Kundsin, *Form Criticism* (New York: Harper & Row, Publishers, 1962).

Chapter V: The History of the Religion

1. See R. H. Charles, *Eschatology: The Doctrine of a Future Life* (New York: Schocken Books, 1963).

2. H. P. Lovecraft, "Fungi from Yuggoth", in his *Collected Poems* (Sauk City, WI: Arkham House, 1963), Stanza XXII, "Azathoth", p. 124.

3. *Ibid.,* Stanza XXI, "Nyarlathotep", p. 124.

4. H. P. Lovecraft, "The Call of Cthulhu", in his *The Dunwich Horror and Others* (Sauk City: Arkham House, 1963), pp. 130-159.

5. An analogous process following the disappointment of the early Christian expectation of the soon return of Christ is traced by Martin Werner in *The Formation of Christian Doctrine* (Boston: Beacon Press, 1965). The sociological and psychological impact of this kind of thing on a religious group (and it has happened to several) is explored by Leon Festinger, Henry W. Riecken, and Stanley Schachter in *When Prophecy Fails* (New York: Harper & Row, Publishers, 1964).

6. Franklin E. Tillinghast, "Notes on a Newly Discovered Commentary on the *Necronomicon*", *Anubis*, Vol. 1, No. 3, 1968, pp. 66-67.

Chapter VI: The Verse-Numbering System

1. Lovecraft, in *The Case of Charles Dexter Ward*, quotes a letter citing the "VII Booke" of the *Necronomicon*. Lin Carter refers to "Book IV" and to reference citations including "NEC. III, xvii." ("Zoth-Ommog", in Edward P. Berglund, [ed.], *The Disciples of Cthulhu*, New York: DAW Books, 1976), pp. 174, 175, and "III, 17" (in his *Dreams From R'lyeh*, Sauk City, WI: Arkham House, 1975), p. 3.

Chapter VII: That Which Came before Men
  1. Quoted by Colin Wilson in *The Philosopher's Stone* (New York: Warner Books, 1974), p. 271.
  2. Quoted by August Derleth in "The Keeper of the Key", in Derleth, *The Trail of Cthulhu* (Sauk City, WI: Arkham House, 1963), pp. 172.
  3. H. P. Lovecraft, "The Call of Cthulhu", p. 145.
  4. Quoted by H. P. Lovecraft in "The Dunwich Horror", in Lovecraft, *The Dunwich Horror and Others* (Sauk City, WI: Arkham House, 1963), pp. 174-175.
  5. The variant form is quoted by August Derleth in H. P. Lovecraft and August Derleth, *The Lurker at the Threshold* (London: Victor Gollancz, Ltd., 1968), pp. 109-110.
  6. Quoted by Ramsey Campbell in "The Plain of Sound", in Campbell, *The Inhabitant of the Lake and Less Welcome Tenants* (Sauk City, WI: Arkham House, 1964), p. 138.

Chapter VIII: From the Book of Thoth
  1. Quoted by H. P. Lovecraft in "Through the Gates of the Silver Key", in *At the Mountains of Madness and Other Novels*, p. 407.
  2. Quoted by E. Hoffmann Price in "The Lord of Illusion", *Crypt of Cthulhu* #10, pp. 46-56.
  3. Gershom Scholem, *Jewish Gnosticism, Merkabah Mysticism, and Talmudic Tradition* (New York: Jewish Theological Seminary of America, 1965). A somewhat different theory concerning the relation between the Barzai legend and Jewish mystical lore may be found in Robert Schwartz, "Pombo and 'The Other Gods'", *Crypt of Cthulhu* #15, p. 21. Schwartz sees Barzai as a reflection of Judah ben Barzilai, twelfth century commentator on the Kabbalistic text *Sepher Yetsirah*, who warned against the dangers involved in studying mystical wisdom. If this is in truth the origin of Barzai, then certainly the Barzai legend cannot have been in the mind of Alhazred, since Judah ben Barzilai lived centuries after Alhazred.
  4. "The Shia [Muslims] interpreted the Qur'an allegorically; hence they were called the People of Allegorical Interpretation (*ahl at-ta'wil*)." Sami Nasib Makarem, *The Druze Faith* (Delmar, NY: Caravan Books, 1974), p. 7. The names Umr, Umar, and Omar all mean "speaker."
  5. Quoted by Robert Bloch in "Fane of the Black Pharaoh" in Lin Carter (ed.), *Mysteries of the Worm* (New York: Zebra Books, 1981), p. 160.
  6. Geo Widengren, *The Ascension of the Apostle and the Heavenly Book* (Uppsala: A. B. Lundequistaka Bokhandein, 1950), p. 80.

Chapter IX: Concerning the Dead
  1. Quoted by Clark Ashton Smith in "The Nameless Offspring", in Smith, *The Abominations of Yondo* (Sauk City, WI: Arkham House, 1960), p.3.
  2. Quoted by H. P. Lovecraft in "The Festival", in Lovecraft, *Dagon and Other Macabre Tales* (Sauk City, WI: Arkham House, 1965), p. 195.

3. Quoted by Clark Ashton Smith in "The Return of the Sorcerer", in Derleth (ed.), *Tales of the Cthulhu Mythos*, p. 35.

4. *Ibid.,* p. 36.

5. Quoted by Brian Lumley in "Aunt Hester", in Lumley, *The Horror at Oakdeene & Others* (Sauk City, WI: Arkham House, 1977), pp. 27-28.

Chapter X: The Fall of Cthulhu

1. Quoted by August Derleth in Lovecraft and Derleth, *The Lurker at the Threshold* (London: Victor Gallancz, Ltd., 1968), pp. 110-111.

2. Lin Carter, "Zoth-Ommog", p. 181.

3. Quoted by R. C. Zaehner in *The Teachings of the Magi: A Compendium of Zoroastrian Beliefs* (New York: Oxford University Press, 1976), p. 45.

4. Quoted by Lin Carter in *Dreams from R'lyeh*, p. 3.

5. Quoted by August Derleth in Lovecraft and Derleth, *The Lurker at the Threshold*, p. 112.

6. D. R. Ap-Thomas, *A Primer of Old Testament Text Criticism* (Philadelphia: Fortress Press, 1966), p. 48.

Chapter XI: Apocalyptic Tracts

1. Quoted by August Derleth in Lovecraft and Derleth, *The Lurker at the Threshold*, pp. 112-113.

2. *Ibid.,* pp. 178-179.

Chapter XII: Rites of Exorcism

1. Quoted by Lin Carter in "Zoth-Ommog", p. 174.

2. Quoted by Derleth, *Lurker at the Threshold*, p. 179.

3. Quoted by Brian Lumley in *The Burrowers Beneath*, p. 57.

4. Quoted by Henry Kuttner in "The Salem Horror", in Derleth (ed.), *Tales of the Cthulhu Mythos*, pp. 253-254.

5. For the spelling of "Vach" and "Viraj", see H. P. Blavatsky, *The Secret Doctrine*, Vol. 1 (Pasadena, CA: Theosophical University Press, 1974), pp. 9. 89. I owe this reference to Tani Jantsang.

6. See H. P. Blavatsky, *Isis Unveiled*, Vol.. II (Pasadena, CA: Theosophical University Press, 1976), p. 276; Gershom Scholem, *Major Trends in Jewish Mysticism* (New York: Schocken Books, 1973), pp. 233, 245-246.

Chapter XIII: Christian Interpolations

1. See Colin Wilson, *The Philosopher's Stone*, pp. 271, 273.

2. Quoted by Frank Belknap Long in "The Space-Eaters", in Long, *The Hounds of Tindalos* (New York: Jove Publications, 1978), p. 60. For some reason the quote has been omitted from the story as it appears in Derleth (ed.), *Tales of the Cthulhu Mythos*.

3. Quoted by Gerald Page in Mark Owings (ed.), *The* Necronomicon: *A Study* (Baltimore, MD: Mirage Press, 1967), p. 5.